Praise for *Hotel*

"Talia Carner has a sharp eye for de... telling eloquence. *Hotel Moscow* is a finely drawn tale of a country emerging from its dark Soviet past into a present over-shadowed by a new kind of terror and lawless corruption. Told from the point of view of an American woman, Brooke Field-ing, who is in Moscow on business, this is a frightening journey into a world of violence and power struggles that will keep the reader mesmerized. A wonderful evocation of time and place and an insightful post–Cold War thriller that reminds us that in Russia the more that changes, the more that stays the same."

—Nelson DeMille, author of *Radiant Angel*

"*Hotel Moscow* is a tantalizing book full of corruption, extortion, and shocking treatment of women—and that is just the tip of the Russian iceberg. Talia Carner's engaging style draws you in with its powerful description of life in Russia twenty months after the fall of communism. I was mesmerized from beginning to end."

—Deborah Rodriguez, author of *The Kabul Beauty School*

"With the urgency of a thriller and the sharp, atmospheric lens of a great documentary, *Hotel Moscow* hurls you into the vortex of the corrupt, outlaw world of the Soviet Union morphing into modern Russia. A fascinating and ultimately gripping read!"

—Andrew Gross, *New York Times* bestselling author of *One Mile Under*

"*Hotel Moscow* is bold and breathless. A smart story about a fearless New York woman who arrives in Russia with more baggage than she knows, it explores both the personal and the political with compelling prose, heartfelt insights and gripping action. An impressive achievement!"

—Ellen Meister, author of *Farewell, Dorothy Parker*

"Rich with insight and detail, as well as drama and emotion. . . . A heartening story about the possibilities for change and empowerment that follow when brave women work creatively together to forge a better future."

—Rodney Barker, author of *Dancing with the Devil: Sex, Espionage and the U.S. Marines*

"Carner deftly mixes in the changing landscape of Russia with an emotional story about a woman coming to terms with her heritage."

—*Sun Sentinel* (South Florida)

"Action-packed, steamy and suspenseful."

—*Jerusalem Post*

"An eye-opening exposé of life following the collapse of the Iron Curtain. . . . Vividly drawn characters and taut suspense add up to a real-life dystopian page-turner of the un-put-downable variety."

—*Library Journal*

"Talia Carner sweeps us away along with her brave and determined heroine to an exotic and complex time and place, and keeps us riveted with the tension and dangers of international intrigue. A real page-turner!"

—Tami Hoag, *New York Times* bestselling author
of *Cold Cold Heart*

Praise for *Jerusalem Maiden*

"A fascinating look at a little-known culture and time. . . . Tuck *Jerusalem Maiden* in your beach bag."

—*Star Tribune* (Minneapolis)

"Talia Carner uses beautiful language, exquisite storytelling, and detailed research to transport the reader into the world of old Jerusalem. . . . This is a book to savor and discuss."

—*Jewish Book World*

"A welcome glimpse into a little-understood world."

—*Kirkus Reviews*

"Engaging. . . . Carner renders Esther's world with great authority and detail, revealing intimate familial rituals within the larger political and socioeconomic context."

—*Publishers Weekly*

"Esther Kaminsky is a true heroine—talented, passionate, opinionated—and I wanted her to succeed on every page of this novel. But for me the truly marvellous thing about *Jerusalem Maiden* is how deeply Talia Carner is able to evoke Esther's faith and the complexity of the choices she faces. A beautiful and timely novel."

—Margot Livesey, author of *The House on Fortune Street* and *Eva Moves the Furniture*

"*Jerusalem Maiden* is at heart a story of revolution. . . . Talia Carner's story captivates at every level, heart and mind."

—Jacquelyn Mitchard, author of *The Deep End of the Ocean* and *Second Nature*

"*Jerusalem Maiden* is a page-turning and thought-provoking novel. Extraordinary sensory detail vividly conjures another time and place; heroine Esther Kaminsky's poignant struggle transcends time and place. The ultimate revelation here: for many women, if not most, 2011 is no different than 1911, but triumph is nonetheless possible."

—Binnie Kirshenbaum, author of *The Scenic Route*

"Exquisitely told, with details so vivid you can almost taste the food and hear the voices, *Jerusalem Maiden* is a coming-of-age story set in a time and place that few of us know. Talia Carner has written a moving and utterly captivating novel that I will be thinking about for a long, long time."

—Tess Gerritsen, *New York Times* bestselling author of *The Silent Girl*

"*Jerusalem Maiden* is a fascinating story of how a talented, artistic woman from a conservative faith must balance the responsibilities of her heritage against her passions for love and art. . . . This is a story that brings an elusive time and place to life and makes you question the strengths of your own beliefs."

—Vanitha Sankaran, author of *Watermark*

"Talia Carner is a skillful and heartfelt storyteller who takes the reader on a journey of the senses, into a world long forgotten. Her story of a woman who struggles and seeks the light is universal and inspiring. Read this book and savor."

—Jennifer Lauck, author of the *New York Times* bestseller *Blackbird* and the newly released *Found: A Memoir*

"*Jerusalem Maiden* won me over from the first moment I began reading it. . . . It is meticulously researched, and steeped in thorough knowledge, no less than deep understanding, of both this community and of the world of art in Paris at the beginning of the twentieth century. . . . I could not put it down."

—Eva Etzioni-Halevy, author of *The Triumph of Deborah, The Song of Hannah,* and *The Garden of Ruth*

"Talia Carner's *Jerusalem Maiden* is an exquisitely explosive journey back to the final days of the Ottoman Empire in Jerusalem. . . . It immerses us in a provocative and astonishingly realized world filled with evil spirits, arranged marriages, prayer, poverty, and the pain of breaking free."

—Michelle Cameron, author of *The Fruit of Her Hands*

The
Third Daughter

Also by Talia Carner

Hotel Moscow
Jerusalem Maiden
China Doll
Puppet Child

The
Third Daughter

A Novel

Talia Carner

WILLIAM MORROW

An Imprint of HarperCollins*Publishers*

P.S.™ is a trademark of HarperCollins Publishers.

HarperCollins books may be purchased for educational, business, or sales promotional use. For information please email the Special Markets Department at SPsales@harpercollins.com.

FIRST EDITION

Designed by Diahann Sturge

Library of Congress Cataloging-in-Publication Data has been applied for.

ISBN 978-0-06-289688-9

21 22 23   10 9 8 7 6

To the millions of girls and women ensnared
into sexual slavery—then and now—
let this story be your cry for help.

To my daughters—Tomm Yariv Miller, Eden Yariv
Goldberg, Melissa Carner Simon, and Cheryl
Hoffman Carner—may you use your ample talents
to make this world a better place for women.

I am a procurer. I provide the public with merchandise, merchandise that everyone knows but no one speaks of. My business, if you want to know, is everywhere, in the entire world: Paris, London, Budapest, Boston. My main office, though, is in Buenos Aires. . . . I have an eye for the goods. One glance and I can tell you how much it's worth and how far it should move. In my business, though, a sharp eye alone is not enough. One also needs a keen nose, a sniff that will tell you from a mile away what kind of a dog is buried there. . . . What do I deal in? Ha, ha! Not in Hanukkah candles, my friend, not in Hanukkah candles!

—Sholem Aleichem, "The Man from Buenos Aires," 1909

Author's Note

This novel is inspired by real events, a buried shameful chapter in history that has rarely been explored in English-language fiction. It is the tragic story of over 150,000 women who in the late nineteenth and early twentieth centuries were deceived and lured from Eastern Europe into prostitution in South America.

The Yiddish storyteller Sholem Aleichem hinted about this outrage in his short story "The Man from Buenos Aires" (which appeared in the same *Railroad Stories* collection that features the memorable character of Tevye the Dairyman).

This novel is the fictional story of a young Jewish woman who meets that mysterious, shady *man from Buenos Aires*. It is a tribute to the few women who found the strength and courage to rise above the tragedy of their fate and fought back.

The historical events in the novel actually took place between 1892 and 1910; however, the pimps' union, Zwi Migdal, operated with impunity for seventy years. All the characters in this novel are fictional except for the Jewish German baron Maurice de Hirsch, whose ambitious vision for world Jewry and his unprecedented generosity have been largely forgotten.

—New York, 2019

The
Third Daughter

Prologue

Russia, 1889

*B*lood pounded in Batya's temples with the effort of pushing the cart. On the rutted road, the mud-crusted wooden wheels clanked with each turn, and the axles screeched in protest of the heavy load. The late autumn world was silent, indifferent, the fields drained of color. Batya breathed in rhythm with the axles: Turn, clank, screech—gasp in. Turn, clank, screech—sigh out.

At her side, her mother struggled to push, and her groans reverberated in Batya's fourteen-year-old heart. Up front, her father labored to pull the cart, and although the heap of their salvaged belongings blocked Batya's view of him, she could hear him pant. She was worried that her parents' exhaustion might doom them to the fate that the bloody pogrom had left unfinished.

At least the barking of the dogs that accompanied their exile from Komarinoe had faded. Batya dared not glance back to see the flames of their burning hut rising like a cry to heaven. She dared not turn her head, as if from this distance she could glimpse her friend Miriam lying in a red pool, defiled.

Yesterday's rain had turned the ground soft, and a wheel sank in the mud. Batya's father pulled harder, grunting with the effort. If only they had their horse. As old and emaciated as Isadore was, he had served Batya's father, Koppel, on his daily rounds, delivering cheese and butter to his customers. But the horse had been commandeered—led away from their yard by the constable—while their Russian neighbors, friends Batya had known all her life, looted their home. They didn't wait until her family had departed, nor did they offer money to buy the stove, cot, and chicken the family couldn't take along. They had just carried them out.

The stuck wheel wouldn't budge. Batya and her mother tucked the hems of their long dresses away from the mud and, leaning forward, pushed with all their might. Twelve-year-old Surale dropped the rope with which she led Aggie the cow to lend the little strength in her thin arms.

The cart wouldn't budge.

"Remove the heaviest things," Batya's mother told her. "The table." She pointed, and Batya's heart skipped a beat. *No!* This was their sturdiest piece of furniture, her mother's dowry—inherited from her own grandmother—and her source of pride.

Couldn't they just lower the table until the cart dislodged, then put it back on top? Before asking the question, Batya understood that her mother wished to ease the effort of pushing the cart. The loss pulsating in her heart, Batya climbed up and pushed the table off. It tumbled down and crashed, two of its legs flying into a ditch. Batya's mother bent to stroke the tabletop, now splintered, a top she had wiped and waxed thousands of times until it shone with her love.

Batya readjusted the large tin pot her mother used to churn butter, tied together with the tools for cheese making. These were her family's livelihood. She resecured them over the bedding, but tossed down the bench, now useless without the table.

"That will do," her father called out to her. He crouched to slide the broken bench seat under the wheel to create a ramp. With the next push, the cart lurched forward, freed.

As they continued on the road, pulling and pushing the cart, Batya's head became light from the exertion. Perspiration cooled her face, but left it itchy, attracting flies. Her knitted socks chafed. Blisters burned. Hours from now, when she would finally take off her wooden clogs, she would find gaping holes in the bottom of the socks.

At last, they stopped to rest at the side of the road. The chill of the day confirmed the approaching winter. How long could her family continue like this, Batya wondered, and where were they to go if the entire region was being cleared of its Jews? If only her two older sisters hadn't dispersed to their lives—each joining a man with whom she had fallen in love, flouting their father's traditional role in finding them a match. They had broken his heart, and now, with Surale still so young, Batya was left to worry about their parents alone.

Her father turned his head upward to God. "When a man becomes his own horse, does a horse turn into his own master?"

"Where are we going?" Surale asked the question Batya dared not bring up.

"To America, of course," he responded with exuberance in his voice.

"Isn't it too far to walk from Russia?" Batya asked. In her mind's eye she tried to visualize the world map Fishke had shown her before he ran off with her sister Keyla. Fishke, a wandering scholar her father had picked up on his travels to tutor his daughters, had planned to start the revolution but ended up in a Siberian gulag as a guest of the czar. Keyla had written that she hired herself as a farm laborer near her husband's prison, hoping to visit him once a month. "America is even farther away than Siberia," Batya added.

"Just a locomotive ride to Odessa, then a ship across God's vast ocean," her father replied.

A locomotive! Batya had heard of this steam-spouting dragon that roared over metal tracks. Railroads dug through mountains and soared high on bridges, never to be swallowed whole in the belly of the rock nor to fall into the abyss of deep valleys. She rose on her toes and looked over the field into a distant, blurred line of a white birch forest, searching for tracks. Once they happened on them, would she just wave to the locomotive the way one would to a passing wagon? Would the iron beast stop in its rush and let them all climb in?

The idea of being carried away from here lifted Batya's spirits, but her mother grumbled to her husband her usual practical considerations.

"You tell me who has the money for that locomotive, let alone for a ship's passage?" she asked. "A passport alone costs fifteen rubles for each person. When was the last time you saw sixty rubles in one pile?"

"The Master of the Universe—not you—decides who gets to go to America."

"So the Master of the Universe buys you tickets with no rubles?"

Batya looked around her at the wilderness, at the cart heaped with whatever had been left of their lives. She wanted so much to believe in her father's dream, or she'd fall into despair.

Part I

"No one leaves home unless home is the mouth of a shark."

"I do not know where I am going, where I have come from is disappearing. . . .
I am unwelcome, and my body is burning with the shame of not belonging."

—Warsan Shire

Chapter One

*B*atya's family had been on the road for two days when a kind innkeeper who had been Koppel's customer allowed them to settle on the hay in his barn. He brought over a pot of steaming soup rich with vegetables and three-day-old bread.

Hunger and fatigue had knitted into Batya's body. Her feet throbbed from the days-long flight. Her blisters oozed, and she couldn't wait to release her feet from the clogs. Her stomach rumbled.

"Wait," her father said, as the four of them sat down around the bowl set on the ground. He dipped his fingers into a bucket of water and mumbled the blessing for the food so fast that his words jumbled.

The soup smelled delicious, and Batya had already torn a piece of bread and dipped it, when her mother, her hungry eyes on the food, said, "It's not kosher."

Not kosher. Batya's hand hung in midair, the aroma filling her mouth with saliva.

Her father winked at her. "It is said in the Good Book, 'All that are hungry should come and feast.'"

"It's in the Passover Haggadah's tradition about inviting strangers into our home for the meal," Batya replied. It had nothing to do with breaking the kashrut prohibition that required adherence to strict Jewish ritual in the slaughtering of animals and food preparation. Still, smiling at her father's permission, she put the bread in her mouth, then dipped a spoon in the bowl. Surale followed.

Straightening, Batya noticed that her parents still sat back on their haunches. She took in her mother's pale face, and a wave of protectiveness washed over her. "*Pikuach nefesh,*" she said, referring to the principle that the preservation of human life overrode any other commandments, even the laws of kashrut.

"Another Talmudic maven in the family," her mother replied. Nevertheless, to Batya's satisfaction, she dipped her spoon in the bowl.

As the flavor filled Batya's mouth, her relief was instantly dampened by the vision of Miriam lying spread-eagle, covered in blood. The screams Batya had heard coming from her friend's house while hiding with Surale in a nearby tree resounded in her ears. She shook her head to make them disappear. She mustn't weaken her spirit with the horrific sights and sounds of the past.

Her father was unloading the bundle of beddings. Batya rose to help, and as soon as she stretched their one featherbed on the hay, her mother lowered herself to lie down. A cry of pain escaped her lips.

Surale dropped down next to her. "Mama! Mama, what's the matter?"

"She needs to rest," Batya said. The fear and worry that had accompanied her for days returned to fill her lungs. *Make Mama healthy and strong,* she prayed. She found a pail inside the barn door and rushed to the well by the trough. Hanging with all her weight on the handle of the pump, she managed to bring up water, then carried the heavy pail to the barn. She ladled water with their tin cup and, propping her mother's shoulders, brought it to her mother's lips.

"Sleep now," Batya told her after a few sips, gently lowering her mother's head.

"Hear, O Israel, Adonai, our God, Adonai, is one," her mother recited the Shema prayer before bed, then opened her eyes. "Remember, Batya. No matter where you are, say your prayer. It will protect you from demons that come during the night searching for innocent souls."

Hadn't the demons arrived in the form of the uniformed Russian soldiers and the *muzhiks,* the wild peasants, who came looting, burning, and killing? Batya silenced the memory of the constable's mocking voice when he had darkened their door and told Koppel that because he was "a good Jew" his family would be spared death if they left.

She soaked the family's single towel in water, then wiped her mother's face, examining the wrinkles that framed her eyes and mouth. Her mother had married young. At thirty-eight now, she was already a grandmother to Hedi's baby, although she would never meet that child. Two years earlier, scandalizing the family, Hedi had eloped with a goy. With his love stretched past the breaking point, their father had declared Hedi dead and forbidden the rest of the family ever to see or speak of her. But how could Batya erase that sight, when, on the dawn of their escape, she saw her beloved Hedi—very much alive—standing behind the fence of their burning hut? Through the haze of smoke and trembling hot air, her sister's silhouette seemed ethereal as expected from a betraying daughter-declared-ghost. Their mother reached out her arms from the distance, as if to hug her supposedly dead child.

"Ignore the ghost," Batya's father ordered, then raised the shafts of their cart and began marching. Only Batya saw the tears streaming down his cheeks and disappearing in his beard, which, overnight, had turned gray. Batya had wanted to wave back to her sister, but had been afraid of the calamitous consequences of returning a gesture from a ghost.

Batya was exhausted. In the only light of dusk streaming from the cracks in the barn walls, she collapsed on the bedding next to her mother.

"You're a good daughter," her mother murmured. "The light of my days."

Batya's eyelids were just closing when the innkeeper returned.

Batya's father rose to meet him. "God will reward you for your kindness."

The man collected his pot. "Until He does, maybe your wife can come to the kitchen to clean up? The inn is full of guests, and my wife is complaining—"

Although they spoke Russian, Batya understood enough. "I'll go," she said quickly to her father in Yiddish. "Let Mama rest."

"Maybe my two daughters help instead? As the Good Book says, 'Two are better than one.'"

The innkeeper's glance hovered over Surale's small frame, curled into a ball. "Maybe she can scrub the floors later, when we close for the night."

The evening stretched long in the hot kitchen. Batya helped the cook chop onion, boil sausages, and fill up bowls of food that were almost too heavy for her to carry, but whose aroma made her mouth water all over again. She had never known fatigue like this; it settled in every joint and muscle in her body and made her eyelids drop even as she forced them open. When she was sent to the cellar to bring up coal, she sat down and fell asleep for what seemed like a few seconds, until she was jolted awake by the cook's angry cry: "Where is that Jewess girl?"

Hoisting the sack of coal on her back, Batya lumbered upstairs. She unloaded it by the oven and saw that the coal had added to the sorry state of her filthy blouse and faded pinafore.

"What a lazy girl you've sent me," the cook complained to the innkeeper's wife.

Batya vowed not to sit down again even if she fell right into the fire of the open oven. She must continue to work hard so the innkeeper would allow her family to stay in the barn one more day, then maybe another, until her mother regained her strength and they could continue walking to the train that would take them away from this misery.

The moon had traveled to the other end of the canopied sky when Batya finally stumbled back to the barn, ready to fall onto the hay. She didn't stop to let her eyes adjust to the dark and collided with a horse at the spot where her family had previously been. She stood still for a moment until she could make out a second horse and a large unhitched covered carriage that had been rolled in front of her family's two-wheeled cart.

"Up here," her father called to her in a loud whisper. "The ladder is to your right."

Her eyes adjusting to the darkness, Batya climbed up to the hayloft. "Wake up Surale to go wash the floors," she murmured as she fell asleep at her father's feet.

No time must have passed before she felt a small tug on her foot. "The cook is calling you to help with breakfast," Surale said.

Batya swam up from the depth of her sleep, groaned, and glanced at her sleeping parents. Her mother's breathing was calm, and her father was snoring. "Will you milk Aggie?" she asked her sister.

She had no idea what to do with all the milk. Her mother was too weak to put in the hours of whipping milk into cream or churning it into butter, and they couldn't hang their gauze cloths for the days it took soured milk to turn into cheese. Nevertheless, Aggie must be milked or the pressure would build up, she'd get sick, and her milk would stop.

Batya lit a candle and fixed it on a tin plate so she could see when ladling out some of yesterday's milk, its freshness preserved by the cold weather. She scooped the cream that had formed on top, placed it on a piece of leftover bread, peeled off a layer of onion, and gobbled it all down.

As she hurried back to the kitchen in the dark, she prayed, *"Thank you, God, for watching after my family—"* She stopped. God wasn't here, where His Jews were being tortured and exiled, if not murdered. Maybe He was in the Holy Land—but more likely He was in America, where everyone prospered and ate chicken every day.

Only after the midday meal did the innkeeper's wife let Batya rest. She gave her a bowl of potatoes and sauerkraut with tiny pieces of sausage peeking out to take to her family, and then draped a dress set over Batya's arm.

"Here. Tidy up so you can help serve dinner in the tavern."

Batya's heart sang as she rushed back to the barn. Serving dinner would be cleaner and less exhausting than hauling coal. She was being elevated! She halted outside the barn and fished out with her fingers the pieces of sausage, surely made of pork and horsemeat, and hurled them toward the dogs tied near the shed. In her head, she asked God for forgiveness. The unkosher meat, *tref*, had contaminated the entire dish, but even He would have agreed that it was more important that her parents ate.

With a moan, her mother rose on one elbow from the hay. She reported that Koppel was out, trying to sell whatever milk and dairy products he could carry on his back. Earlier he had split wood for the innkeeper and tended to the guests' horses.

"I'm sorry to be a burden when we need all our strength," her mother added, then whispered, her voice breaking, "If only Hedi had married the postman instead of her *goy*, she'd be alive and we would all be riding to America in his fancy coach with bells."

"Just rest, Mama."

"Why did Keyla have to run off to Siberia? When will I ever see her again?"

You have me. I'll make up for all the disappointments.

Batya fell into a deep sleep, but a dream of Komarinoe and Miriam's murder woke her up with a start, horror contracting her heart. She missed her dark-eyed, laughing, inventive friend. Just last month, the two families had shared the festive Rosh Hashanah dinner, after which their fathers sang joyous wordless *nigunim,* "bim-bim-bam," and "ai-ai-ai."

She must forget Miriam and Komarinoe. She mustn't think of her two willful sisters. It fell upon her to be the rock for her parents, work hard, and hope that the innkeeper would allow them to stay until she somehow found a way to help her father get them to America.

Batya filled the pail of water at the well and then hid behind a heap of hay at the back of the barn while she washed herself with a rag as best as she could. Feeling clean made up for the freezing water that prickled her skin. Right after the full moon, she would have to take care of her monthly flow. It had started five months before, and she'd learned to wash and hang the rags to dry. How could she do that when her family was out on the open road again, pushing their cart? She shoved away the apprehension. Tonight she had work to do, honest work that would guarantee her family's safety here from road bandits and from the snow flurries that now swirled in the air before early sunset.

Surale combed the hay out of Batya's hair and plaited it into twin braids, then wrapped them around Batya's head like a crown, using a dab of butter to flatten the stubborn tendrils into submission. There was nothing they could do to stop the itching of lice or remove the white eggs visible down the strands of Batya's blond hair. The lice would continue to multiply along with the fleas in their bedding.

Batya hadn't worn a good dress since she'd outgrown her Shabbat *sarafan,* the long, printed pinafore worn over a blouse, an outfit that had first served her two older sisters. When passed to Surale, the shirt had been patched too often, and the dress's printed flowers had faded and looked no better than the tattered ensemble passed down to Batya from her mother. It felt so good now to put on the fresh white blouse and slip on the new brown pinafore.

Tying the strings of the high-waisted, striped apron behind Batya's back, Surale gushed over its hem and collar trimmed in red and green. Batya whirled to feel the ample fabric of the skirt rise and fall against her ankles. She laughed, grabbed both of Surale's hands, and pulled her into a spin, round and round. It seemed so long ago when they had last romped in joy, when only poverty was their steady companion, not fear and loss and the uncertainty of the coming days.

"How will we find a good *shidach* if there's no matchmaker around?" Surale asked.

"You're crazy to think of such a thing at your age!" Laughing, Batya hid her embarrassment that this past year some new longing had awoken in her, too.

"I hope my groom will be handsome and interesting and well-off," Surale said. "Like Hedi's—"

"Hedi?" Batya stopped dancing. "She betrayed us—and all our people. She permitted the Jew-hating priest to marry her!" Batya squeezed Surale's hands until her sister winced. "The most important mitzvah you and I can ever do is honoring our parents. Be loyal and obedient. Two daughters have already disobeyed them. We're never to do that, too. Do you understand?"

"Sorry," Surale mumbled.

Batya softened. "We're too poor and have no remarkable lineage to appeal to a good match. But even without *yichus,* when the time comes, Papa will find each of us a good man."

"Mama says that Papa is a dreamer."

"He's survived many pogroms. He speaks directly to God and can read the Bible. Didn't the neighbors come to him to read their letters for them? Papa knows what's good for us." Batya looked at her feet. "For now, all I want is a new pair of socks." Buried in the cart was a stained child's sweater her mother had bought from a peddler with the intention of unraveling the wool to reuse. Batya had no time now to dig under the heap of the family's possessions for the yarn and the knitting needles.

Ten minutes later, she stopped at the tavern door and examined her reflection in the window. The uneven pane of glass distorted it, but not enough to hide the green of her large eyes and the pink of her too-full lips.

"I'll be worthy of Your name," she whispered. Her name, Batya, meant God's daughter, and as such she was destined for great things. Her first mission was to help her family survive.

Her hand on the door handle, a new understanding washed over her of an internal shift: since their escape, her parents could no longer protect and provide for her. She had grown up.

Chapter Two

*W*ork in the tavern's dining hall proved more grueling than the labor in the hot kitchen. Batya had to rush among tables squeezed together, forced to brush against male guests no matter how much she tried to minimize herself. At their urgent calls for food and drink, she struggled to carry heavy trays, refill tin cups without spilling, haul pitchers of beer and vodka, collect dirty dishes and run them to the kitchen, only to bring more plates, bowls, and cups, all without dropping anything. Her muscles burned, and the blisters on her feet from the rough wooden clogs reopened. But her family was safe. Tonight they had a roof over their heads. They had been fed. If she focused on the tasks, performed them to perfection, then tomorrow her mother would be able to rest again.

Once Batya caught the crinkle of a smile on the face of the innkeeper when he handed her a tray of filled vodka glasses. She lowered her eyes in shyness, encouraged that he was pleased with her work.

At a small table against the wall, one man sat alone, apart from most of the guests seated on the benches that flanked the two long tables. His brown hair was combed and parted neatly on the left side, then slicked down; in the light of the hanging lantern, its top shone golden. Unlike the peasants and peddlers around him, he was dressed in the most elegant clothes Batya had ever seen—a dark blue suit of good wool, a sparkling white shirt with a clean collar, and a wide, short tie with a gold pin that matched the buttons on his shirt. A large diamond glittered on his middle finger. He drew from his pocket a gold watch that was secured to his jacket button by a gold chain, glanced at it, tucked it back in, and then motioned with his finger for Batya to refill his mug. He tilted his chair back, chewed a cigar under his thin, waxed moustache, and examined the gaiety in the room without joining the laughter that seemed contagious among the others.

When Batya served this man of great importance his plate of fatty meat and boiled cabbage, he thanked her softly in Yiddish, which surprised her. In all her father's stories about his customers, the rich Jews of Bobruevo, whose *dachas* had a separate back door for peddlers like him, he'd never described a man who dressed this well. Even the landowners and officials Batya had seen, all Russians, wore worn and mended clothes.

The man's presence in the inn created a great excitement in the kitchen. The cook and the innkeeper's wife gossiped that he had traveled all the way from America to find himself a virtuous Jewish wife. He was on his way to his home village, where several potential brides had been lined up for him to choose from.

The evening stretched on, and the raucous merriment in the

room grew louder. When Batya came through with a pitcher of beer to refill glasses, one man grabbed her waist, and his big arm closed around her narrow frame. She tried to pull away, her heart pounding, recalling the thugs who had violated Miriam. The man's arm tightened.

"Let go of her," the elegant stranger called out in Russian. "Don't you see she's just a girl?"

The man hesitated, then released his hold and, still leering, returned to his beer.

For the rest of the evening, Batya was careful to serve that table from its other side. This kind stranger's future bride would be a lucky woman to have a husband who was both rich and good-hearted. That bride, Batya imagined later, when she finally lay down beside her parents, would be beautiful and come with a sizable dowry, her trousseau packed in two, maybe three, huge trunks: bed linens made of soft cotton and embroidered in silk with her initials; furs, each with its own hand muff and hat—a short white fox cape and a chestnut-colored sable coat reaching down to her ankles; at least four dresses. And then there would be leather boots and gloves, silk shoes, lace-trimmed handkerchiefs, and silk underthings. That lucky bride would most likely be the daughter of the village's rabbi or the butcher.

Batya's hopes to stay in the barn one more day were dashed when the innkeeper showed up the next morning. His grim, knotted brows showed none of his earlier kindness.

"Koppel, my priest says that it is unchristian to shelter you," he told Batya's father.

"It's Friday." Her father held both hands in supplication. "May God be with you, but could we at least stay till the end of the day tomorrow?"

The innkeeper shook his head. "Speaking of God, the priest says you people deserve His just punishment. Who am I to defy His will?"

Batya's father lowered his head. "We thank you for the kindness you have shown us until now. May blessings fall on your head like stardust."

As they gathered their belongings, Batya's mother cried into Batya's shoulder. "How can we prepare for Shabbat, let alone welcome it with dignity?"

Batya wished they could have stayed in the home they'd been forced to flee. A thatched-roof hut of only one small room with a ceiling so low she could reach up to grab a dangling spider, it had a stove with a wide loft built over it where the family slept together to keep warm during the long winter nights. Next to the stove had sat their table, two chairs, and the backless bench— now abandoned broken on the roadside. On the opposite wall, her father had fixed shelves to hold her mother's few cooking pots and utensils, and the pair of candlesticks—brass, not silver—that waited all week to be taken down on Friday, polished with sand until they shone, then placed on a white tablecloth. Theirs had been the most humble of houses, yet when her father returned from the prayers at the makeshift synagogue—a *shtiebel* lacking a rabbi or a cantor, and where the floor was porous clay—their home became richer with his warmth and cheer.

With a heavy heart, Batya returned the pretty brown dress

with its white blouse and striped apron to the innkeeper's wife and put on her frayed, dirty *sarafan* and stained canvas apron.

She had failed her family. Had she been a couple of years older, not a small-framed, thin adolescent, perhaps she would have been more valuable to the tavern owner. Perhaps he would have kept her working at least until after Shabbat.

As they trudged again on the furrowed road, Batya pushed the cart doubly hard, while her mother leaned on it as she struggled to walk. But her father sang.

> *My father buys a little horse that neighs*
> *Whose name is Mutzik,*
> *Buys a puppy that barks*
> *Whose name is Tsutsik.*

Batya tried to draw strength from her father's spirits, but rather than buoying her mother's mood, the singing only distressed her further. "Do you hear him, Batya? A poet I married. The only train to America is the train of his singing."

"What's the first thing you'll do when you reach America?" Batya asked her mother in an attempt to distract her.

Raising her head heavenward, her mother said, "Get myself a gold front tooth from all the gold that's paving the streets."

"I'll be so rich that I will have a candy every day," called Surale from behind, where she was leading Aggie. "Or maybe a slice of orange?"

"In America everyone gets a *whole* orange every day. It showers down like manna from heaven," Batya's mother said. "And there's so much sunshine that people must wear special dark glasses or their eyes can't sleep at night."

"I'll have a hot bath in a real tub." Batya's tone was dreamy. "I'll wash my hair in rosewater until it shines." When combed with fragrant oil, the blond streaks would emerge. Her curls would fall on the back of a lovely new sky-blue dress she'd wear, its full satin skirt like Queen Esther's.

"First get rid of the lice," her mother said. "In America they have a special concoction for it."

"I'll go dancing at a ball." Twirling Aggie's rope, Surale swiveled in a jig.

"How can you dance on an empty stomach?" Their mother smiled. "First we'll eat the feast Americans will prepare for us upon our arrival: *kneidlach* soup brimming with fat, a whole goose cooked on a spit, and kreplach filled with mushrooms."

The long sentences seemed to dissipate her energy. She breathed hard as she and Batya resumed pushing the cart. Batya gave it a heroic shove to also help her father in front. It was still early morning. How could they go on the whole day—and where to?

From behind, the pounding of hooves signaled an approaching carriage. Batya's father pulled the cart to the side, and Batya navigated its wheels to make room on the narrow road.

As the carriage passed, the coachman, perched outside the enclosed cabin, called his horses to a halt. A head leaned out the cabin's window, and Batya recognized the rich patron from the tavern.

"Where are you heading?" he asked Batya's father.

"Wherever my horse will take me."

The man looked around, puzzled, then laughed as he caught the joke. "A Jew can't get very far like this," he said. "May I invite the ladies to ride with me?"

Batya couldn't believe their good fortune. She helped her father hitch the cart to the back of the carriage and tied Aggie behind, and after her father conferred with the coachman about the pace Aggie could keep, Batya climbed with her mother and Surale into the cabin. While her mother fingered the red tassels framing the windows, Batya turned to check on her father as he settled on top of their belongings.

"I'm the king presiding over my kingdom," he called out, grinning.

Batya could hear in her head her mother's reaction, unuttered in front of the thoughtful stranger: *When God decides to punish a man, He starts by removing his brains.*

Inside the carriage, Batya leaned back into the smooth leather of the seat. Beneath her, sturdy springs absorbed bumps on the uneven road, and the rubber-covered wheels did not squeak.

"I am Yitzik Moskowitz from Buenos Aires," the stranger said, smiling.

"God should shower blessings on your head for your generosity, Reb Moskowitz." Batya's mother bowed her head in respect as she addressed him with "reb," the title of veneration for a man of distinction.

"Aren't we Jews commanded to stand for one another? Who else would help us, the goyim?" He chuckled. "God, blessed be He, has been generous with me. Some would say too generous with Yitzik the Pitzik, who came from humble beginnings just like yours. I was beaten and punched. I starved until my stomach became glued to my spine. Now I am ordered by Him to do mitz-vahs wherever I go, wherever I can, with whatever means He's made available to me."

"Reb Moskowitz, I've never heard of your shtetl. Is it beyond the Mountains of Darkness?"

"It's far away in America." He shook his head with vehemence. "There, I drink fruit nectar every day. But I return to visit my birth country here, and what do I discover? The czar is still at it: heavy taxes on anything Jewish—from the ritual slaughtering of cows to burial. Now he wants us out. Out!"

"Or dead," Batya's mother said.

He leaned forward without removing the cigarette dangling from the side of his mouth. "You tell me how I can help."

Batya's mother shrugged. "Speak to the czar?"

"I may do that." He laughed.

Batya sucked in a quick breath. It was common knowledge that some men of substance—Jewish or not—helped the czar fill his coffers. How amazing that she should meet one such man in the flesh just when her family needed help the most. Her father had been right to throw in their lot with God.

"Where, may I ask, are you all heading?" Reb Moskowitz asked.

"The Pale of Settlement," Batya's mother said, mentioning the only area of Russia where Jews were permitted to live. "Unless the czar, may he be afflicted with a blister on top of a boil, has moved the borders again. Some shtetls that were within the Pale's boundaries last year are now suddenly outside it."

"I'll drive you there. That's the least I can do for my fellow Jews."

"May God bless you with good health and long life."

Reb Moskowitz relaxed back in his seat. His lemon-and-cinnamon fragrance filled the cabin. "What are your names?"

"I'm Zelda, and these are my daughters, may the evil eye keep away from them, Batyale and Surale."

"Batya," Batya mumbled. Her sister might not mind the diminutive of her name, Sarah, but Batya hated it.

Reb Moskowitz tossed her a sympathetic glance, and Batya shrank into the seat. Even occupying the same space as this man was above her place in society. Here was a man who drank fruit nectar every day. Who was she, who wore filthy clothes and whose uncombed hair was lice-infested, to have his attention bestowed upon her?

"And what does a gentleman of your high standing do in that place where you say you live?" Her mother's voice was tinged with respect even though her brazen questions made Batya wince.

"Buenos Aires. It's in America. But I have business interests all over the world." Reb Moskowitz's hand brushed one of his lacquered, pointed shoes to remove a speck of dust that didn't seem to be there.

Business interests. Both words so foreign, they silenced even Batya's mother.

During the many hours of the ride, Batya mulled over the words "business interests." She knew what a butcher, a tailor, a blacksmith, a shopkeeper, a peddler, a water carrier, a cantor, a money changer, an undertaker, a scribe, a winemaker, and a dairyman did. She even knew what a tax collector and a *ganef,* a thief, did. But what did a man with "business interests" do?

Chapter Three

*B*efore sunset, they reached the Pale of Settlement. With luck, the first village would give them a place to stay at least until tomorrow, when the three stars announcing Shabbat's departure would appear in the sky.

The carriage entered a shtetl that at first looked as dilapidated as Komarinoe, although larger. The smell of woodsmoke, excrement, and mold welcomed Batya with the sense of the familiar, but Reb Moskowitz pulled out a white handkerchief, doused it with rosewater from a vial he retrieved from his leather case, and brought the handkerchief to his nose. *As any nobleman would do,* Batya thought.

Soon, the muddy thoroughfare became a cobblestoned street, and low wooden huts were replaced by two-story buildings. The right side of the street even had a paved sidewalk. People were rushing about for Shabbat—to home or, as the rolled towels under their arms attested, to the *mikveh,* the communal ritual bath.

Batya's eyes took in the many small stores with goods displayed in their windows or still outside their doors. Merchants lugged in barrels of merchandise; some were already boarding up their doors. Everyone, except her family, had a home to go to.

The carriage stopped in front of the synagogue, a square wooden structure with a pitched roof, under which a Jewish star had been nailed. Men wearing black felt hats and yarmulkes came out to greet Reb Moskowitz, who opened the window, leaned out, and waved to them like a king to his subjects below. Then he retrieved an umbrella from under his seat, climbed down from the carriage, and accepted the well-wishers' extended arms.

He had such a dignified air with that umbrella hooked on to his arm! The congregants surrounded him, clapping and bowing their heads. One man, probably a tailor, fingered the edge of Reb Moskowitz's suit and nodded in awed approval. Another bent down and wiped the fresh mud off Reb Moskowitz's lacquered shoes, while another rolled out a rug so the distinguished guest wouldn't dirty those shoes in the two steps to the door. The congregants babbled profuse words of welcome as they swept him through the narrow doorway.

"They've been waiting for him," Surale said. "Why?"

"This is his home village, where he'll be introduced to his future bride." Batya scanned the street to glimpse the line of beautiful girls, but only two mature women were in sight, hurrying along, surely to prepare exquisite tables at their homes for Shabbat. Batya imagined that after the prayers, when the men returned to their families, Reb Moskowitz would be led to the home of the wealthiest man in the village, whose house would have two rooms, maybe even three. The dining table would be covered in white lace, fine china, and polished silver, and a sparkling crystal chandelier would shine down from overhead on the loveliest lucky daughter of the rich man.

Reb Moskowitz's horses were led away to be brushed and fed. Batya helped her father unhitch the cart from the carriage and tow it onto a dry mound on the windowless side of the synagogue. She hugged Aggie's neck and wondered where to turn.

Her father raised his head toward heaven. "Master of the Universe, can You explain to me, why does one Jew get to eat a buttered roll and another gets to eat dirt?" Still looking up, he shook his head. "If You want my advice, You can give me a buttered roll once in a while. Metaphorically speaking, of course."

"He got your meaning," Batya's mother said. "He doesn't need your advice. If He'd meant things to be different, they would be different."

"I should write again to my brother in America to get us the tickets," Batya's father said.

"What brother?" his wife countered. "He hasn't replied in years!"

"That's a good sign that he's doing well."

All her uncle needed to do, Batya thought, was scoop up the gold in the street and exchange it for passages for them.

A tall man with a talis, a fringed prayer shawl, draped around his shoulders came out of the synagogue and approached. "Might you give us the honor of joining us for a minyan?" he asked Batya's father, referring to the Talmudic requirement of a ten-man quorum for public prayer.

"As the Good Book says, 'Completing a minyan is the greatest mitzvah a Jew can perform,'" Batya's father replied, and went in.

The man turned to Batya's mother. "Someone from the Benevolent Society will come to see to your needs."

"It's almost Shabbat," Batya's mother replied, her tone demanding. "She'd better hurry."

Batya sat down on the cart to wait with her mother, while Surale milked Aggie into the bucket, then transferred the fresh milk into their large tin canister. Batya rose to pour a cup of milk for each of them in turn before buckling the canister's lid.

Dusk was descending, and the air became colder. Batya pulled on her only warm garment, a long wool cardigan with holes she had patched with whatever color yarn she could find. She had hoped for a new coat, but now there would be no money for one, and she had outgrown the one Surale was now buttoning up. Soon, when Batya ventured outside, she would have to borrow her mother's shawl.

"Do you know the story about Rabbi Chanina and his wife?" Batya's mother began. The daylong carriage ride had tired her, but it had not exhausted her the way walking and pushing the cart had done. "They were so poor that often they had nothing to cook for Shabbat. Every Friday, before Shabbat, Rabbi Chanina's wife would throw a burning coal into the oven, so that smoke would drift out of her chimney and the neighbors would assume that she cooked.

"A nasty neighbor said, 'I know that they don't have anything. Let me go and see what all that smoke is about.'

"When Rabbi Chanina's wife heard the knock on the door, she was mortified and went to hide in the inner room. The nosy neighbor entered anyway and opened the oven. But a miracle occurred, and she found it full of loaves of challah.

"She called, 'Come! Come! Bring the spatula. Your challah is starting to burn, and you need to get it out quick!'

"Rabbi Chanina's wife returned, saying, 'That's what I went in to get.'" Batya's mother smiled broadly. "You see, she was telling the truth. Trusting God, she was so accustomed to miracles that she wasn't surprised that the coals had turned into challahs." She paused. "We, too, should trust God and welcome Shabbat right here. Batya, find the Shabbat candles and candlesticks."

Batya's stomach rumbled. They might not have a miracle challah, but they did have a wheel of yellow cheese wrapped in hay, an unopened jar of pickles, and the remainder of the loaf of bread the innkeeper had handed them that morning. Nevertheless, giving the miracle one more chance, she scanned the street for their expected salvation.

"Why are you standing there like a tree? Let's light the candles," her mother said.

Batya dug her arms deep into the pile of belongings, but couldn't find the candlesticks. Her search turned frantic. She couldn't unpack the cart and drop their belongings on the dirt, then repack it all when it was already Shabbat. Yet it was inconceivable not to light Shabbat candles. She felt like crying; God would know that her family had transgressed. "What shall we do without them?"

Her mother tightened her shawl around her head and shoulders. "Let's go inside and do another mitzvah." Her tone was brave, yet Batya knew she was hiding her sorrow. No Friday evening had ever gone without her performing the decreed lighting of the candles. Her mother added, "God cares more about us remembering His Shabbat than about the poverty of our attire."

Formal praying in the synagogue was meant for men; women prayed there only in times of great distress. In their daily lives, they uttered the many prayers and blessings at home. Batya said nothing as she and Surale filed into the synagogue behind their mother and headed to the back. The women's section was tucked behind a lattice partition, protecting the men from the temptation to turn their heads, glimpse the women, and become inflicted with impure thoughts.

Only half a dozen women sat there, peasants like Batya's family, but clean, their hair freshly wrapped in kerchiefs, their shoes brushed. Two women buried their faces in their hands, mumbling prayers and weeping.

Batya's mother drew her book of *tkhines* from her skirt pocket. Batya noticed that none of the women had this special book of women's prayers, written in Yiddish instead of the holy Hebrew, which, although using the same alphabet from right to left, most women didn't understand. She felt a flicker of pride. In spite of her mother's sorry state—not even washed from the dust of travel—she alone among these women knew how to read.

With Surale on her other side, Batya's eyes followed the text of the book while her mother murmured the words so as not to disturb the others or, God forbid, allow her voice to reach the men and distract them.

"He who blessed Sarah, Rebekah, Rachel, and Leah, may He bless every daughter of Israel," her mother whispered, then went on to embellish a prayer. *"We wish to celebrate Your holy day, but we are unable to. We wish to adorn ourselves for You, but we*

cannot. May You accept our memories of our past celebrations of Your holy Shabbat instead of our failure to light the candles tonight. Please forgive me and my daughters at my side and my husband out there, and cast upon us Your protection and lead us to a safe haven. Amen."

When the men's service concluded, Batya grasped her mother's elbow to usher her out first, before the more respectable women could look down upon them.

Batya's father emerged from the synagogue a few moments later, his face beaming. "God is with us. We are honored to have been invited to the Shabbat table of a generous cobbler." He nodded his head toward the synagogue. "We can sleep in there tonight."

"Since when is it an honor to dine at a cobbler's table?" Batya's mother waved her hand in dismissal, and Batya understood that her mother was hanging on to her last thread of dignity. They were the poorest among the poor, yet the status of a dairyman like her father, who filled people's stomachs with healthful delicacies, was higher than that of a cobbler who dealt with people's dirty feet and repaired foul-smelling shoes.

"Who are we to complain?" Batya's father told his wife. "On the other hand, Zelda, He's God, so He can take a lot more than your complaints."

"You hear this, Batya? A philosopher I married."

Batya sensed the tenderness in their bickering. But she couldn't help feeling shame. In just a few days, her family had turned into beggars who now waited in vain for the charity of the Benevolent Society and who must be grateful for any crumb of kindness they were shown.

From the corner of her eye, she saw Reb Moskowitz being guided toward the street by a man wearing a good hat. Before she had dared address him directly and thank him for his generosity, he was gone. "May God give you ten times your fortune and a hundred times your happiness," she mumbled a blessing for him, hoping her gratefulness somehow reached its destination.

Chapter Four

*T*he wife of the cobbler clapped her hands at Batya's family's arrival. "*Oy vey iz mir,*" woe is me, she chanted her ambivalent welcome. Her face sour, she moved from the narrow door to allow her husband to enter. "What do we have here?"

Batya wished her parents would turn and leave.

The cobbler pulled a whole orange out of his coat pocket. "To decorate the table," he said, his tone appeasing.

His wife's eyes rounded in delight. "Who lent it to you?"

"The treasurer of the synagogue." The cobbler held the orange to the light, and his children, crowding around him, jumped up to try to touch it. "Be careful," he told them, depositing the precious fruit in his wife's palm. "We must return it in the morning."

In spite of her grumbling, the cobbler's wife seemed pleased to be the recipient of this loan and basked in her newly elevated status, one notch above the unexpected guests. "It's a mitzvah to share Shabbat with poor people," she said, her tone haughty, and pointed to the bench at one end of the table. A moment later, by the nearby stove, she whispered to her husband, "So you've got yourself a bit of honor in the synagogue by volunteering to take food out of your children's mouths?"

The words echoed in the tiny hovel, suffused with smells of leather, glue, and dye from the cobbler's work area in the corner. Batya's mother's sunken cheeks blushed in humiliation.

Six children with running noses assembled along two sides of the table, which was covered with a cloth that had seen too many washes, but none in recent months. After the kiddush prayer, for which the host passed one small wineglass around to all present, the hostess explained that the few chicken parts she had received from the butcher were too paltry to share with unanticipated company. "Had I known, I would have cooked a whole goose for you," she added.

Batya cringed and looked at her mother for a reaction to the insult. Her mother's head was bent; only her palms, pressing hard together, told Batya of her anger. The orange sat in the middle of the table, round and indifferent.

The cobbler's wife doled out boiled potatoes to her family, then passed the bowl to Batya's father. There were only two small potatoes left. He halved them, giving each member of his family a portion.

"That was supposed to be my second helping," the cobbler's teenage son whined.

"Maybe the guests are not hungry," the cobbler's wife said pointedly.

Koppel, taking a hint, raised his half potato to the boy.

"No," she interrupted as the boy reached for it. "Let his father, who wants to act rich, who thinks that food grows on trees, give his portion to his children."

The cobbler's tin plate was already empty. He sat silently, gazing down, as his wife grumbled about his inadequacies.

Batya's father passed his half potato to the boy. "As the Good Book says, if a poor man has a coat, he should give it to the poorer man who doesn't." Then, glancing at his own hungry family, he said, "Since we aren't partaking in the chicken, the law of kashrut doesn't apply to us." Before Batya could protest that the law forbidding mixing meat and dairy still applied to them, he asked the hostess, "May I use your dairy dishes?"

She tossed on the table two chipped enamel plates. As if he didn't notice her derision, Batya's father went out to their cart and brought butter and cream to mash into their potatoes, drawing envious stares from the children.

The rest of the meal passed in strained silence. Charity recipients deserved no better, Batya thought. She shouldn't feel the resentment that was bubbling in her.

Before parting amidst words of thanks, Koppel filled the hostess's milk jug and gave her a piece of cheese for the next day.

"Who fed whom?" Batya's mother asked once they were outside. "This woman invited the evil eye upon herself."

"As the Good Book says, 'Each according to his abilities,'" Batya's father responded.

Batya smiled, recalling Fishke's lessons. That was a Marxist saying, not the Good Book's.

Clouds moved to block the stars and the moon. From behind, Surale clutched the hem of Batya's dress, while Batya held both her parents' elbows as they felt their way in the dark to the unlit synagogue.

Because of Shabbat, they couldn't light a candle. When their eyes adjusted to the darkness in the synagogue, they settled on the straw mat that covered the packed-dirt floor.

Batya's mother pulled out the leftover bread and broke a piece for each member of her family. "Pretend this is our challah," she said.

"Baruch ata Adonai Eloheinu Melech Ha'olam hamotzi lechem min ha'aretz," her father intoned the prayer for the bread.

Batya had been sleeping when she was awakened by her father's voice conversing outside the synagogue door. The moon had broken through the clouds, and in its faint light entering from the high window she saw her mother sitting with her back against a column, Surale's head in her lap. At first Batya thought that her father was chatting with God, although even God would be sleeping at this late hour. But then she heard a second man's voice.

Her heart skipped a beat, and she curled into herself. Was another pogrom following them? In the first pogrom Batya had survived, the constable had shown up in the middle of Shabbat dinner—not to drink with her father, as had been his habit, but to inform him of the order from above. He then stood watching as the town's thugs dragged Koppel by his beard, beating and kicking. Batya and Miriam ran with their mothers and sisters to the woods, where they all huddled, listening to the attack on the village's Jews, praying for Batya's father's life. When they returned the next day, they found him injured but alive. All they could do was bandage his rib cage and place warm compresses on his open wounds before turning to the mitzvah of preparing the dead for burial. Short-handed in performing the sacred act of purification of the deceased, Batya's and Miriam's mothers hadn't been able to prevent the girls from seeing the pregnant woman whose belly had been slashed, nor the little boy whose head had been smashed against a wall.

After that, theirs were the only two Jewish families remaining in the village. Now, none.

In this latest pogrom, the constable's warning had helped Batya escape with Surale by climbing the oak tree from which their rope swing hung. They had shivered there together throughout the long night, while Miriam was defiled and murdered.

"What's going on?" Batya now whispered to her mother, who was stroking Surale's hair.

"Shhhhhhh."

Batya tiptoed to the door and put her ear to it.

"What would you want with her? She's not ready to reproduce," she heard her father say.

The other man replied, "She's quiet and obedient."

Batya crept back to the beddings. "Is Papa selling Aggie?"

"Shhhhhhh," her mother repeated, and Batya returned to her spot at the door.

"As the Haggadah says," her father quoted, "'She comes naked': that means with nothing."

"What would I want with your money?" the man replied, and the hair on Batya's arm stood as she recognized Reb Moskowitz's voice. "I've just given the treasurer a thousand rubles to build a grand new synagogue—with a tin roof, mind you—and to hire a rabbi."

"Come back here," her mother whispered, and when Batya crawled onto the bedding, her mother pulled her head toward her shoulder. "Let me tell you a story that was told to my father by the great Rabbi Nachman: A group of sages wanted to dig deep into the kabbalah to find the Truth. The one Truth above all others. They retreated to the desert to contemplate the puzzle. After months of ponderous discussions, they discovered that each animal—a bird, a reptile, or a mammal—had its own shadow. Uniquely its own. But you know what else they found?"

"What?"

"That each fowl had its own branch, the one where it preferred to dwell. God had not assigned a place for each of His creatures, but rather let each creature choose its own."

Batya was too sleepy to contemplate the fable. "What does it mean?"

"Some decisions we make are not predestined, but we are placed in a position to make the right one," her mother whispered. "Go back to sleep now. It will be clear when the sun shines bright on all of us."

Relieved by her mother's mood change, Batya fell asleep in the warmth of her arms, for the first time in days being comforted rather than giving comfort.

In the morning, she rose up to milk Aggie, letting Surale sleep. She hugged the cow's rump, love filling her in her anticipation of loss. When she returned to the cart to pour the milk into their tin canister, her father was there, drinking milk from the previous day.

"Are you selling Aggie to Reb Moskowitz?" she asked.

"Why would I do that?"

"I heard you talk during the night."

"No, Batyale. Reb Moskowitz wants *you*. For his bride."

"What? That's not possible . . ." Batya's words trailed off as shock spread through her. "I'm only fourteen!"

"That's what I told him. That you must wait until you are at least sixteen, as your sisters were when they got married." He chuckled. "Not that they asked my permission."

Batya's mouth felt dry. "Why would he want me?" she asked. And he was so old, perhaps thirty.

"A pretty face is half a dowry, as the saying goes. As for the other half, Reb Moskowitz saw how hard you worked at the tavern. As the Good Book says, 'A good Jewish wife is her husband's helpmate.'"

Batya's head swam in confusion. She had worked hard at the tavern so the innkeeper would let them stay in the barn, not for this. Maybe that was the sages' conclusion about each creature having its own shadow. It followed her whether she wanted it to or not.

The sound of her mother's voice summoned Batya inside. "We must pack the bedding before the congregants arrive for the morning service."

"Is that true, that Reb Moskowitz wants me for a bride?" Batya asked as she shook a blanket to air it.

Her mother waved dismissal. "Whoever heard of a man who is both the groom and his own matchmaker? It's never done."

"Fishke, he didn't bother because Keyla already had done the asking," Surale piped in. Batya hoped she wouldn't mention Hedi's goy; he had sought his priest's approval, not his bride's father's.

Batya's mother shook her head sadly. "In these tough times, we must still believe that good things can happen, too."

"What is a good thing?" Surale asked.

"If a kosher matchmaker should bring the right groom for each of you, that's a good thing."

"Reb Moskowitz is an excellent groom," Surale said. "He's so rich!"

Their mother shook her head. "A matchmaker is a must." Her tone softened. "Batya, remember the daughter of Pesha, my second cousin three times removed? She married a visiting scholar from Germany. Even though there was no rabbi, it was the matchmaker who brought two witnesses, and the wedding took place in a *shtiebel*."

"What happened to her?" Batya asked.

"She moved to Germany, where every year she vacationed in hot springs. She sent money to her mother and promised a train ticket to a city called Frank-something, but then Pesha, the poor soul, one day caught a cold and died."

"Where is she now?"

"Pesha? I'm telling you she's dead."

"No. Her daughter. Where is she now?"

"How would I know? Probably getting pampered in a hot spring."

Some girls, even poor ones like Pesha's daughter, were lucky, Batya thought. Maybe Surale was right to dream of a match so high above their low social station. But certainly her mother was right about a matchmaker; her father must have misunderstood Reb Moskowitz's interest.

Congregants began to file into the synagogue, and Batya's father was recruited again for the decreed minyan.

The day was cold, so the three women found refuge again in the women's section. Even chilled to the bone, at least they were dry and could sit down, albeit on hard backless benches. Batya was hungry for warm food that wasn't cheese or un-cooked onion—a cup of hot, sweetened tea maybe, or even her onion, but fried in chicken fat.

While the men were praying, a woman dressed in a wool suit approached Batya's mother. "I'm the representative of the Benevolent Society," she said, not bothering to give her name. "Come with me."

Wearing leather boots that withstood the mud, she led Batya's mother up the street, with Batya and Surale trailing behind. She made a left turn into a narrow alley and stopped in front of a hut. It had been abandoned, the woman explained, and now could be rented from the Society for a pittance. "It has a table, a bench, and a sturdy loft for sleeping." She paused, then added, "We'll lend you a working stove."

Batya eyed the pack of mangy dogs that roamed the street. Their thinness reflected the poverty of the village, where even the shopkeepers couldn't spare scraps of food. "We can't rent a hut if we're on our way to America," she told her mother, but her mother gestured to her to hold her tongue.

"What about pogroms?" Batya's mother asked.

The woman shrugged. "We're always a target. But where can

we go?" She glanced at Batya and Surale. "If I were you, I'd dig a hiding space for them."

A shiver went down Batya's spine. Where could they be safe?

The negotiation concluded when the woman agreed to give the family a loan to pay the rent. At that, Batya understood. They would never have the huge sum required for the train, passports, and ship's passages. America was nothing but a dream.

She examined their new home. Rain had cratered holes in the dirt floor. The cracks between the slats of wood needed to be filled with tar, the window shutters fixed, and the thatched roof repaired. Batya sighed. Never mind the stench of moldy hay and dog feces. Never mind that until they built an outhouse, they would relieve themselves in the woods. At least their trek in the muddy road was over.

Batya's mother pulled the bench against the wall, leaned back as she sat down, and let out an audible breath. She could now rest for a few hours until Shabbat exited.

Batya sat next to her and took her hand. "Tell me a story."

Her mother smiled. "A man was traveling through the desert, hungry, thirsty, and tired, when he came upon a tree bearing luscious fruit and affording plenty of shade, underneath which ran a spring of water. He ate the fruit, drank the water, and rested in the shade.

"When he was about to leave, he turned to the tree and said: 'Tree, o tree, with what should I bless you? Should I bless you that your fruit be sweet? Your fruit is sweet. Should I bless you that your shade be plentiful? Your shade is plentiful. That a spring of water should run beneath you? A spring of water runs beneath you.'

"The man thought for a moment. 'There is one thing with which I can bless you: May it be God's will that all the trees planted from your seeds should be like you!'"

"Like our oak tree at home," Batya exclaimed, "the one your father's father planted." Their beloved tree in whose thick foliage she and Surale had hidden. She pointed toward the window. "We'll plant an oak tree right here." It would grow big and strong, and would serve their family for generations to come.

Chapter Five

*B*atya tightened her cardigan. In spite of the cold, her heart felt light. Her family had a hut with a door to close. Although it was very late in the season, she and her mother could begin cultivating a vegetable garden behind the house. They could still plant cabbage and even parsnips. For now, she'd search for mushrooms and berries in the forest. It wasn't labor, she reminded God, just a Shabbat pastime.

Holding a stick in case a pack of hungry dogs might chase her, Batya circled the outskirts of the village and eyed the edge of the forest for fallen trees. Her father could saw them into boards to fix the hut, and she'd help him split smaller pieces to burn in the stove. They could bury some wood in a covered pit, where a low-burning flame would produce charcoal. Before the earth froze, perhaps they could dig potatoes from deserted fields. At least this coming winter they would be warm and have some food.

If only the threat of another pogrom didn't hang over them.

Stepping into the forest, she let her eyes search for ripened berries that might still cling to the shrubs, mushrooms peeking from under rocks and tree roots—and for a spot to dig out a shelter where she could hide with Surale. She spotted a small mound that wouldn't be flooded. A memory from just a few weeks ago resurfaced, of giggling with Miriam about their possible future matches. Miriam had her eye on the handsome son of the rich man from Bobruevo, who had sent his spoiled boy to Koppel to instill good values in him. Batya had envied her friend for having met someone she could dream about. Now Miriam was dead.

Batya forced herself to push away the memories. She picked a handful of berries and sucked their sweet-sour juice. Tomorrow, after Shabbat, she would bring a basket to collect the succulent mushrooms.

She walked on, circling the village, imprinting in her memory its dirt-packed alleys and the paved streets with two-story houses where merchants lived above their now-closed stores. In the coming weeks she would meet the baker and the fishmonger, the butcher and the roaming peddlers. Maybe she'd meet a girl her age and she'd have a friend in this new home.

At the end of her second round, outside the cemetery fence behind the synagogue, she came across her father and Reb Moskowitz speaking again. She turned away, but her father spotted her. "Come here, my Batyale." He crooked his finger for emphasis.

Batya froze, staring at her own clogs. Somewhere, frogs broke into a concert of croaking. She had wanted to thank Reb Moskowitz for his kindness in giving them a ride here, but now the idea of speaking directly to this important stranger overwhelmed her with the same sense of insignificance she had felt in the carriage.

"Come here, Batyale," her father repeated.

Her mother would be furious if her husband had embarrassed them again with his misinterpretation of Reb Moskowitz's intentions. Batya approached with small, hesitant steps; she'd have to mitigate her father's big-dream talk.

"Batyale, Reb Moskowitz here is intent on having you as his bride—when you grow up, of course." Her father stroked his beard, a glint in his eyes. "What do you say?"

How could it possibly be true? Reb Moskowitz's gaze was upon her, scrutinizing her face. He smiled. "I came all the way from across the ocean to find a bride here. Do you know why?" Without waiting for her reply, he answered, "American women are spoiled. You are virtuous."

Feeling her cheeks burn, Batya lowered her eyes. She couldn't begin to imagine what American women were like, spoiled or not. The heat spread down into her collar, doubling her discomfort. With the tip of her clog she drew circles in the mud.

Her father wiped his brow. "Where will she live? There are some cultured Jews in Moscow and St. Petersburg, but who wants to be so close to the czar?"

"Who's talking about Russia?" Reb Moskowitz laughed. "Remember. I'm from Buenos Aires."

"You want I should send my little girl to America alone?"

Batya raised her eyes to see Moskowitz's arm sweeping the village. "Where else will she have any future? Here?"

"On the other hand," her father said, "we're all going to America, to my brother in Pittsburgh—"

"When will that be?"

"With Hashem's help, before the Messiah arrives."

Reb Moskowitz drew his billfold out of his trouser pocket and opened it, exposing a thick wad of pinkish rubles. Batya had never seen paper money. Her father was always paid in coins, mostly kopeks, rarely even a single ruble, and not ever a gold one. "We're forbidden to handle money today, so I won't touch it." Reb Moskowitz fanned the open billfold. "But to look? To look we're permitted. See this? There's a lot more where it comes from. This evening, I'll be at your home with a generous gift that will help your family manage until Batya is of age."

Her father gulped. "Money is the most perishable substance, more than cheese and cream." His eyes glued to the billfold belied his dismissive words.

Batya didn't know whether to stare at Moskowitz's money or examine his face. Could this respectable man really be her husband one day? She closed her eyes, wanting to curl up in a corner and was unsure why. Matchmaking talk was supposed to be good news; girls were happy at getting betrothed. With this man for a husband, she would be eating an orange every day.

"It's a great surprise," she heard her father's soft voice say and was uncertain whether he spoke to her or was explaining her shyness to Reb Moskowitz. "On the other hand, a Jew is never ready for what God plans for him."

God's plans. Batya wasn't ready to entertain thoughts of marriage. Yet she also hadn't been ready for the pogrom, or for Miriam's death, or for exile.

"Batyale, what do you say?" her father asked her.

In all these catastrophes, she hadn't been asked. Now she

was. How could she have an opinion about such a fortunate *shidach,* one she'd just told Surale was impossible for poor girls like them? Her finger found a loose thread in the cardigan. She glanced at Reb Moskowitz. He was more than twice her age. His features were pleasing, not handsome—his cheeks rounded, his pale eyes small. But their corners crinkled when he smiled, which he did often. His gaze didn't burn with the dark intensity Keyla had found in the anarchist Fishke's. He certainly didn't have the tall, broad stature that made Hedi feel secure under the protection of her goy. What Reb Moskowitz had was his importance, as every rich man had. He was probably the richest man in America.

He was also kind, she reminded herself. If her parents found him suitable, she must trust their choice. Dreamer though her father was, he sought the best for her.

Both men's eyes were upon her, waiting for her to speak.

No nuptials will take place until I grow up, she told herself, and placed her hand on her heart to still it. And when she was ready, she would have a decent man for a husband, one who would share his riches with her parents.

Her tongue stuck, she managed to nod her assent.

"Wonderful." Reb Moskowitz hugged Batya's father. "Koppel, my future father-in-law, I'll come over after Shabbat."

Disbelieving what had just transpired, Batya didn't turn to look at the back of the man to whom she'd just promised herself.

They walked to the new hut, where her father broke the news to her mother. "It's done! He proposed and she agreed!"

"Are you talking about Reb Moskowitz?" Her mother's eyes

searched both their faces. She took Batya's hand. Hers was cold and clammy. "Batya, did you hear it with your own ears?"

Batya nodded. Her eyes brimmed with tears, although she was unsure why.

"What did Reb Moskowitz actually say?"

"That I'm virtuous, not like American women."

"What happened to the brides lined up for him?" Surale asked.

Batya brought her shoulders up.

Her father spoke. "You see, Zelda? God doesn't inflict pain without sending the right medicine for it. Reb Moskowitz is the medicine for all our afflictions."

Batya's mother looked into Batya's eyes. "Are you sure? He proposed without a matchmaker. What else did he say?"

"That when I'm sixteen I'd live with him in America."

"He did say it?" Batya's mother's face brightened, and she clapped her hands. "Oh, Batya, even without a matchmaker, such a fine man as a match is what I hadn't dared dream for any of my daughters." She gathered Batya in her arms and kissed her cheek.

"He also talked about 'a generous gift,'" Batya's father said. "If it's fifty rubles, God willing, we'll buy a second milk cow and a new horse—a bit old because I'll forever miss my dopey horse—"

"Koppel." Batya's mother snapped her fingers in front of his face as if to wake him up. "We're talking about our daughter now, not your horse. What if Reb Moskowitz finds a more suitable bride and returns two years from now, not to marry Batya but to demand we return the money?"

"I know an honorable man when I see one. He would never do such a thing. On the other hand, Zelda, we will follow our daughter to America."

"If there's anything left after you buy yourself a horse and a cow, we need to get Batya a trousseau, and maybe there will be some left for a samovar."

Chapter Six

*T*hree stars shone bright in the sky, indicating that Shabbat was over. The three women were busy unloading their belongings off the cart and setting up the household. Batya located Surale's old rag doll and gave it a quick hug before turning to lift her mother's butter-churning bowl. Just then Reb Moskowitz knocked on the open door and walked in.

A whiff of his lemony cologne entered with him, momentarily masking the hut's stench of mildew. His shirt under the brushed suit gleamed white, which meant that he owned more than one good shirt.

"I apologize for not having cooked borscht to welcome you into our humble abode," Batya's mother mumbled, bowing her head, and Batya's heart ached at her mother's face-saving pretense that she had beetroots and just hadn't had the time to cook the soup.

"But I have something for you," he told Batya's mother, and handed her a small package wrapped in red cloth.

She unwrapped the cloth to reveal a beautifully painted wooden box. She set it on the table, and the family gathered around it.

"Take a good look at this miracle—and it's not even Chanukah yet." Reb Moskowitz wound a small key on the side of the box, then lifted the lid.

A collective gasp escaped everyone's lips. Batya stared as a delicate ballerina twirled to music as clear and dainty as bells. The mirror set on the inside of the lid twinned her into a harmonized pair.

"This is the most beautiful thing I've ever seen," whispered Batya's mother.

"It's yours. Now try winding it yourself."

"I wouldn't dare." Her eyes were riveted to the music box.

Batya's father bent to peek at the back of the box to decipher the miracle.

"Zelda, it will give me great pleasure if you do," Reb Moskowitz told her. "Please don't be afraid."

She relented, and soon the girls took turns winding the marvel and squealing with delight as the music repeated, and the ballerina in her pink tulle tutu never tired of dancing.

Reb Moskowitz turned to Batya's father. "Koppel, my father-in-law-to-be, my future *shver*, are you ready to celebrate the engagement?"

"Let's go to the tavern to drink to it." Batya's father slapped Reb Moskowitz's back. "As the Good Book says, 'If not now, when?'"

"I got it right here." Reb Moskowitz withdrew a flask from his inside pocket, uncorked it, and took a gulp, then handed it to Batya's father. "Lechayim."

"Lechayim." Batya's father tipped the flask into his throat, then wiped his mouth with the back of his hand. "This is how things are meant to be, and the proof, as the saying goes, is that it is happening."

"I'll drink to that." Reb Moskowitz took another swig.

It was Batya's third turn at the music box, but instead she was watching the men. Their celebration of her nuptials sealed her future. All afternoon she had been unsure whether to dread or look forward to the mystery that would be her adult life, telling herself that her future husband was wealthy and generous. Why didn't she feel elated as a bride should?

Her mother put her arms around her. "I'm so happy," she whispered, her chest heaving. "Some people have money, but we are rich with daughters. You'll be our salvation, long before the Day of Judgment."

Surale joined their hug, and Batya breathed in her sister's still childish smell and her mother's warmer musk. Her mother was right. Not only would they all be saved by this marriage, but Batya would also be rescued from the soul-crushing poverty of life in the shtetl—and fear of pogroms.

Reb Moskowitz opened his billfold again, and this time withdrew a pinkish bill sporting the number 100 in two corners. When he placed it on the table, the whole family gaped at the sight, none daring to touch it.

"No dowry is one thing," Koppel said. "But as the Bible tells us, Jacob worked seven years for Rachel, and then seven more years to pay for her after marrying her sister."

Reb Moskowitz laughed. "You want I should labor for fourteen years—or may I pay in kind?" He opened his arms as if for a hug. "Now that we'll be family, it behooves us to share my bounty."

Batya's mother elbowed her husband. "Whoever here can change such a large bill?"

"Don't you have coins?" Batya's father asked Reb Moskowitz.

"Coins? If I carried all this money in gold and silver, its weight would make a hole in the ground and I'd be buried in it." He tapped Batya's father on the shoulder. "Koppel, my friend, my new family, you've made me a very happy man." He turned to Batya. "Say your goodbyes."

She felt her brow furrow, and her parents exchanged a look, but the confusion was settled when Surale chirped, "Goodbye, Reb Moskowitz."

Batya's mother raised the corner of her apron and dabbed her nose. "Blessings upon you, Reb Moskowitz, in your long travels."

"As the Good Book says, 'Go in health, and return in health.'" Batya's father waved. "We'll see you in two years' time."

Reb Moskowitz's surprised gaze moved from one to the other. "I must not have explained properly. I'm not coming back. Batya will come with me." He turned to Batya and smiled. "You will live with my sister until you are of age. She'll teach you how to run a house, how to use your china and silver, how to supervise the servants that polish the mahogany furniture and care for the brocade upholstery. She'll have French seamstresses outfit you in beautiful silk dresses. You do want to learn how to be a lady of means, right?"

Batya's father raised his hand as if to stop him. "The river won't catch fire if Batya waits here until you send for her."

"Don't you trust your future son-in-law?" asked Reb Moskowitz.

"Oh, yes. Of course, of course," Batya's mother said quickly. "But it's too fast."

A sad expression passed Reb Moskowitz's face. "Unfortunately, I must leave tonight. My business interests require my immediate attention."

Something boiled inside Batya like a teakettle on the stove. She was supposed to be happy at seeing all those rubles changing hands, all because of her. It was a blessing, yes, but also a huge misunderstanding. She wasn't ready to leave her family.

Batya's mother shook her head. "I must consult my grandmother Tzipporah in the next world." She lowered her voice to a whisper. "For such a weighty decision, I'm sure that tonight she'll visit me in my dream."

Reb Moskowitz turned to Batya's father. "You know how business goes. You turn your eyes for a moment, and your competitor steals your deals."

"Of course. Of course. That's the way of business." Batya's father tapped his belly like a landowner. "Where in America will our daughter live?"

"In Buenos Aires. My beautiful city."

Batya's father's beard twitched. "Is that near Pittsburgh?"

"South of it."

Batya's mother glanced at the music box. "We need to reflect on it," she said to Reb Moskowitz. She motioned to her husband to step outside.

"Those things are a mother's department," Batya's father said to Reb Moskowitz, his tone apologetic, and gestured to the girls to follow. It would not have been appropriate to ask the distinguished guest to wait outside, nor was it appropriate to leave girls alone with a man.

Once outside, Batya's mother said, "It's not right to let Batya go with a groom who has no matchmaker to vouch for him." She turned her face heavenward, as if her grandmother could see her.

"Did you see how much respect he received at the synagogue?" her husband replied. "They know him. Rather than just a single matchmaker, the whole congregation is vouching for him. Besides, doesn't the Talmud teach us that forty days *before* a child is born, a voice from heaven announces, 'The daughter of this person is destined for so-and-so?'" He pointed his finger over his head. "The Master of the Universe has led Reb Moskowitz to our humble abode. All along, our unexpected luck has been in God's planning."

Batya's hand wrung the edge of her apron. Yes, her life had been preordained. She could lavish her loved ones with luxury and rescue them from Russia, but she couldn't bring herself to acquiesce.

She felt herself tremble.

It was dark now, and they were standing outside in the cold air. The moon rose on the horizon, full and yellow, so close that Batya could reach out and touch it. "I don't want to leave you." She hugged her mother, then moved to hug her father. "Please. Not yet."

"If we don't let Batya go with him, he might find another bride on his travels," Batya's mother said, as if thinking aloud. "My mother always said that if it's supposed to, a miracle will find you."

Her father touched Batya's hair. "Maybe God has answered our prayers? Finally, we got our *bissele mazel*."

Batya felt numb with the enormity of what was required of her now, not in two years' time. What if she refused to leave? What if she threw a fit, screaming and crying, proving to Reb Moskowitz that, rather than virtuous, she was a shrew he wouldn't want for a bride?

Her father grabbed both his wife's hands. "Zelda, here is our *mazel*, and it's not even little."

Disengaging his hold, she turned to Batya. "Did I want to leave my mama to get married? Every bride-to-be is scared, and every mother bird is unhappy when she must push her chicks out of the nest so they can fly."

She turned to enter the hut. Her husband followed her, half hopping in glee. Batya and Surale trailed behind him. Surale was quiet, but her chin quivered with suppressed tears.

Batya looked at her mother's back, straight with determination, and registered her father's joviality in the lightness of his steps. After her sisters' disappointments, how could she put them through this anguish again, dashing their hopes?

Once inside, her father broke down crying. He hugged the waiting Reb Moskowitz. "My heart is so full of happiness and sadness that it runs over into my eyes."

Batya's thumb fingered a hangnail, its sharpness telling her this was real. She sneaked a look at her groom, this distinguished man standing in the middle of her sorry home. He had nothing in common with her or her world, even if he'd come from a shtetl. *No!* she wanted to shout. *This is all one big mistake.* Yet, like the inevitable shadow, the Divine had assigned her a groom. She had felt destined for great things as God's daughter, and now her parents' assent proved it. One thing was certain: life in America would be as wonderful as it was promised to be.

Her father turned to her. "While you are living in gravy, make sure you visit your uncle. Give him our blessings and ask him to write." He rummaged among the pile of belongings still on the floor and fished out a yellowed envelope showing foreign words and stamps. "Here. Sew it into your dress."

"Take my candlesticks," her mother said, pushing the brass set into Batya's hands.

"Keep them. She'll get herself a gold set as soon as we reach Buenos Aires." Reb Moskowitz's fingers twirled the end of his moustache, and his diamond ring sparkled. "Gold there is like snow here."

Surale hugged Batya, then handed her the rag doll. "Keep this so you'll remember to find me a good husband, too."

"You're too young to think about that," Batya murmured, and took the doll.

"Where I come from there are a hundred men to one woman," Reb Moskowitz told Surale. "Your groom is already waiting for you."

Batya's mother wrapped a piece of cheese in gauze cloth. "For the road," she said, and Batya, feeling dizzy, didn't have the heart to refuse, even though she knew her mother needed the gauze to make more cheese.

Her father didn't bother to wipe his face as he hugged Batya. "These are tears of joy. It's your bright future that I see."

She breathed in the sour dairy scent of his beard. A sob broke through her chest. She forced herself to suppress it; she was doing it for them all.

"Take care of my child," her mother whispered to Reb Moskowitz.

"I will care for her as if she's my daughter," he replied. "Until she's ready to marry me."

"May God be with both of you."

Chapter Seven

*B*atya's head reeled in confusion. So much had happened in the last few days that none of it made sense. How was it possible that merely days after Miriam's murder, Batya was being carried away in a fancy carriage harnessed to two magnificent horses, like a princess in a fairy tale? The man seated across from her could very well have been a prince who'd awakened her from a nightmarish dream.

Darkness had fallen upon the earth. Through the small front window, Batya saw the coachman's silhouette against the full moon. Inside the cabin, Reb Moskowitz pulled on his cigarette, the flare from its tip casting a reddish glow on the lower part of his face. Batya breathed in the fragrant aroma of his tobacco, so different from the raw cigarettes that her goyim neighbors smoked, made of weeds and smelling of field dust.

She was supposed to feel bliss, but her brain felt numb. Only the jolts of the road, cushioned by the soft seat, made the moments real. Mist filled Batya's eyes. Was it only two hours ago that she had exchanged hasty goodbyes with her family? How could she wait two years, till she turned sixteen and married this man, before seeing her family again?

The image of the paper money her father had received made it worthwhile. It was twice as much as he had hoped for—and she was the one daughter who'd finally brought him happiness and hope.

The horses accelerated the rhythm of their trotting hoofs. Batya took out the piece of cheese, and, taking small bites, the taste of home brought her mother closer.

"Are you hungry, my dear?" Reb Moskowitz asked her.

She nodded, although she wasn't sure that this was what made her insides rumble.

"You'll have a queen's meal as soon as we reach our inn," he said. "Try to sleep now."

She rewrapped the cheese in its gauze and curled up on her seat, her head resting on Surale's rag doll.

She woke when the carriage came to a stop. Sitting up, Batya found that she was covered in a soft wool blanket. She fingered its silk trim. Her father, too, would have covered her, although not with a blanket as fine as this one. Reb Moskowitz was indeed showing his care, just as he had promised.

Looking out the window, she saw a manor house, three floors high, with twin columns flanking its entrance. Its many windows were lit as they would be only in homes of the rich.

Reb Moskowitz was standing outside the carriage and offered his hand when she climbed down, but she blushed and reached for the side handle to help herself. Her skin felt clammy and cold. With one hand she tightened her wool cardigan around herself, and with the other she gripped the small cloth bundle with all she'd brought from home: the rags she would use for her menstrual cycle, the leftover cheese, Surale's doll, and her uncle's letter.

"I'll be right back, my dear." Reb Moskowitz disappeared behind the front door. A stable hand came to lead the coachman and the horses away, leaving Batya alone in the chilled air. She checked her surroundings and, seeing no one, crouched behind a bush to relieve herself. Straightening up, she was about to follow the stable hand so she could enter through the back door, when Reb Moskowitz reappeared and signaled to her.

Touching the small of her back, he guided her up the few steps to the front double doors made of heavy, dark wood. Inside, a warm fire danced in a huge stone fireplace, flanked by chairs upholstered in brocade and sofas covered in deep green velvet with gold tassels. The wood of the floor, visible between exquisite rugs, was polished so bright that it reflected the crystal chandelier above.

Batya examined the chandelier. It shone more brilliantly than a dozen candles—yet with no candles. Reb Moskowitz remarked, "Gas lighting," and before Batya could ask what that was, he relinquished her to the care of a maid.

The woman tramped up many stairs lit by more fixtures without candles until they reached a small room with only a large tub in the center. Speaking Russian, the maid gestured for Batya to strip down and submerge herself in the water.

Batya couldn't believe her good fortune. She hadn't even arrived in America yet, and her first wish was fulfilled. She lay in the warm water, stared up at the light fixture so close to the ceiling, and wondered how it didn't start a fire. The maid didn't seem concerned, though, as she massaged foul-smelling liquid into Batya's hair. It burned Batya's scalp. This must be the concoction her mother had mentioned that people in America used against lice; they didn't need to always pick them out of each other's hair. Batya closed her eyes and wiggled her toes in the warm water. The wonders of America were already here.

It took the maid so long to comb Batya's hair thoroughly and pick the lice eggs that Batya dozed off in the warm tub. She woke up when the water had cooled, and the woman rinsed her hair in rosewater. She brushed Batya's hair several times and dabbed lavender-scented oil into it before wrapping a towel around it.

Batya raised her hand to touch the towel, amazed at its thickness. Her family had used one piece of cotton cloth as a towel; it had none of the soft, absorbent texture of this fabric.

When she finally emerged from the bath, her skin pink, Batya stood still, shy at the ministering of the maid, who dried her as if she were a baby, then pulled a good cotton night frock over Batya's head and placed soft wool slippers on the floor. Eager to fall into bed, Batya followed the woman to a room down the corridor. The bed by the wall was covered with what looked like a puffed-up down comforter, but Batya's fatigue evaporated at the sight of a table set by the fireplace, laden with fine dishes and food.

Reb Moskowitz was seated on one side. "Feeling refreshed, my dear?" He had changed his wool suit into a loose burgundy jacket with rope piping along its collar and cuffs.

"Yes, thank you very much." She blushed and glanced down to ensure that even her ankles were covered.

"I hope you don't mind the late hour," he said.

She lowered her eyes. At home, without a clock, they kept the time according to the sunrise and sunset.

The aroma of the food was delicious. At Reb Moskowitz's gesture, Batya sat down and lifted the bowl of root-vegetable soup. She drank it in a few swallows.

"Slow down, my dear, or you'll be sick," he said.

She blushed, then dug her fingers into the plate of boiled chicken with cabbage and carrots.

"Use your utensils."

Chastened, she picked up her fork, and was relieved that his smile had the hint of a parent indulging a child.

The honey cake at the end, served with tea sweetened by three spoonfuls of sugar, capped off the best meal she'd ever had. Reb Moskowitz lit a cigarette and sipped some red liquid out of a tiny glass cup. Batya's eyes kept closing of their own volition.

"Go to sleep now." He pointed to the bed, and after she crawled under the cover, which was as airy and full as a cloud, he dimmed the gas light of the bedside lamp, then stepped up to the door. "You've had a long day, my dear."

She sank into the softness of the bed. One day, her entire family would be making this trip in luxury. As unexpected and painful as her departure from them had been, it was worth it: she was on her way to America to save them all. No more dread of the pogroms. No more hunger. Goodbye, poverty.

Happy, she recited the Shema prayer and fell asleep.

She was startled when, in the dark, something heavy dropped

upon her. Still in a dream, Batya thought that the thatched roof of her parents' home must have fallen in, and the hands wrestling at her were trying to rescue her—but no, they were pulling up her gown. Fully awake now, she tried to sit up, but a face buried itself in her neck, pinning her down, and lips leeched onto her skin. Her scream came out muffled against a hand that clamped her mouth. Suddenly fingers probed her private parts, and a moment later the heavy body pushed hard into her, tearing her inside.

Batya shrieked into the hand at the searing pain.

The pumping was over fast, but the burning and fright lingered. When the weight moved off her, she broke into a shocked sob.

She was crying so hard, hugging the pillow to her center, that she didn't look to see who crossed the room until she heard his voice.

"You are mine now," said Reb Moskowitz. "Forever."

Stunned, Batya looked up to see the door open and Reb Moskowitz's silhouette against the corridor's backlight, before he gently closed the door behind himself.

Weeping, she forced herself from the bed and followed the faint outline of the window to pull the curtain open. In the moonlight she located the dresser upon which she had seen a washbowl. Sobs convulsed her body as she sponged the blood and stickiness from the insides of her thighs.

A night bird screeched—or was it a bat that hit the window? The house creaked. More evil winds were searching to harm her further, like Miriam's assailants. Trembling in fear, Batya crawled under the bed. The pain had dulled, but not the shame. She curled into herself, her back against the cold wall.

How could an honorable man do such a thing?

Then a greater horror struck her. Not only had he betrayed her, but he had invalidated the agreement he'd made with her parents. Having traveled all the way from across the ocean to find a virtuous wife, he would surely send her back now that she was no longer pure.

A fresh fit of tears caused a wave of hiccups. All her parents' hopes for her bright future—and her plan to bring them to America—were destroyed.

Chapter Eight

*B*atya's hiding spot failed to protect her from the morning sunrays. She woke from a fitful sleep when she heard the door open. Her eyes registered the maid's feet in felt slippers. She froze, unable to face the woman who had bathed her last night, who had tended to her virgin body, now defiled. She had been spared a gang of Russian brutes, only to suffer the same fate the first night she had left home—at the hands of the man who was supposed to be her protector.

She heard the maid place something on the table, then watched her feet approach the bed. The woman kneeled down and touched Batya's shoulder. Her hand traveled down Batya's arm, and she tugged at her, speaking softly in Russian. When Batya wouldn't budge, she crawled under the bed too and snaked a hand around Batya to massage away the hiccups racking her body.

A few minutes passed, then the woman retreated, returning

with a cup of hot tea that she placed on the floor, where the fragrant steam wafted to Batya's nostrils. When the maid once again tried to pull Batya from under the bed, Batya let her. The maid sat her at the table and nudged the tray toward her.

A fresh boiled egg nestled upright in a cup, and a bowl of warm porridge glistened with a dollop of melted butter in its center. Next to them, on its own plate, she spotted what must have been a section of an orange. An orange.

The bounty only made Batya's stomach tighten.

The maid gestured at Batya to open her mouth and, as if Batya were a child, placed the orange in her mouth. Batya sucked the sweet, tangy juice, then retched.

Undeterred, the maid kept trying to feed her until embarrassment made Batya take over the task. The few spoons of porridge she took tasted like wet straw. She hung her head.

The maid brought a fresh washing bowl and a clean towel. She draped on the chair a long gray pinafore adorned with a wide red, green, and yellow trim and a white blouse with puffed sleeves. Curious in spite of herself, Batya noticed that the garments were new and the *sarafan* large and shapeless enough for her to grow into. Next to them, the maid laid a folded set of what looked like new underthings made of white muslin. She set a pair of leather shoes with new socks on the floor.

The maid slipped out, and at the sound of the key turning, Batya walked to the door and pressed the handle. It was indeed locked. She jiggled it up and down, then banged on the door. The maid did not respond.

She was a prisoner. Batya covered her face with her hands,

weeping again as her skin and mind recalled her shame. Her tears deepened into sobs. She pounded on her chest, and its echo was as hollow as her heart felt.

She must get dressed and run away to find her parents in their new shtetl. No matter how many versts the carriage had traveled yesterday—and how many days it might take her to run or walk back—she must let them know what a mistake they'd made in trusting Yitzik Moskowitz, who no longer deserved to be called "reb" like an honorable man. Her parents would take her back in spite of what she'd done, in spite of the disgrace that must now be imprinted on her forehead like the mark of Cain.

She peeked out the window. Outside, the tall buildings were stone and brick, not wood, and the street was the busiest she'd ever seen. It wasn't a market day, with carts lining the road with produce, livestock, and household goods, yet there was a crowd on the paved sidewalks moving not with the air of humble peasants but with that of self-assured masters. Covered coaches, open carts, and even one horseless carriage—she'd only heard about them—traveled on the cobblestoned street. This was what a city looked like.

But which city was this?

She unlatched the window and looked down. It was much too high to jump, far higher than the roof of her parents' hut in Komarinoe. She stood still, pondering her options.

Behind her she heard a key turn in the lock, and the door opened. She recoiled and pressed her back to the corner, trapped.

"Did you sleep well, my dear?" asked Yitzik Moskowitz.

She dared not speak of her dishonor, of his assault of her body. "Why was the door locked?" she asked, her tone meek.

"For your protection, my dear. You never know who prowls around an inn." He raised his arm and held up a blue coat. From across the room, she could see that its fabric and style were that of a rich lady's garment. "Hurry now. We have a train to catch," he said.

She glared at him, refusing to be appeased. "I want to go home."

"No, my dear. You don't."

Years later she'd recall the moment when she'd stepped down to the street and was almost alone. Yitzik Moskowitz was speaking to the coachman on the other side of the waiting carriage before he stepped back to Batya, before he gripped her arm and guided her in. She had stood in the midst of the scene she had watched from above, and up close it was terrifying: dizzying commotion, chaotic noises, the air reeking of horse manure, soot, and perfume. She was a small mouse, a guilty one.

Batya wrapped her arms around herself. The passersby must all be able to read her shame. They were all so much taller than she, so imposing in their elegant garb. She pressed herself against the wall, her heart pounding, and watched men in top hats with big important bellies walk purposefully, graceful women in elegant costumes hanging on their arms. Across the street, two nurses wearing gleaming white caps pushed baby prams. Everyone was busy, yet no one seemed to be working—no peddler announcing his wares, no knife sharpener offering his service, no sound of a blacksmith hammering his iron.

That was the only moment Batya was unsupervised. She should have escaped, she'd realize later with regret. She was wearing good leather shoes that would have taken her as far as her legs could run. Yet, still a peasant child, disoriented and confused, she dared not even cross the street for fear of being trampled. Whatever courage she'd had had seeped out of her during the night, like milk from a bucket full of holes.

Then her future husband was at her side, his face as genial as before, an expression she later understood was a mask, not a sign of infatuation with his new bride-to-be.

Only in hindsight did she understand that this was the moment she said goodbye to her old life.

Chapter Nine

On the train, Batya lay curled on the seat in the private compartment. Just yesterday she would have felt awed to travel by train, let alone ensconced in the luxury of leather-upholstered seats and curtained windows. Now she didn't care.

"Sit up," Moskowitz said.

Batya shook her head.

"Look," he said quietly. Nothing about his voice was menacing, nothing in its tone indicated the brutality he had displayed during the night. "You know about marital life, don't you?"

She shook her head again. The seat beneath her cheek felt sticky, unclean, used. Like her.

He sighed. "Your mother should have instructed you. It's in the Bible: The way a man and a wife are. It says, 'He would cleave unto her.'"

Don't quote the Bible to me, she wanted to scream. That was her father's domain, and her father would never ever do such "cleaving" to her mother. *Don't tell me that God decreed such filth.*

As if it were happening now, she felt Moskowitz's naked body crushing hers, her private parts violated, his lips sucking her neck. She had seen dogs copulating, and once, when a neighbor brought a bull to impregnate his cow, heard the trumpeting sounds of the beast, even though her mother kept her inside until it was over. But dogs and cattle were animals. Humans had been created in God's image and were therefore above such acts. It was implausible that her mother had conceived so many times in this disgraceful way.

The sudden screeching of the axles beneath Batya was accompanied by a yanking of the train car, followed by a slow, shuddering jerk. Batya sat up, wiped her cheeks with the back of her hand, and fixed her gaze outside as the train began to move out of the huge station, with its palatial glass domed roof as high as a mountain.

She placed her palm on the windowpane, as if to hold on to the receding station before being carried away, alone at the mercy of this horrible man.

She had become accustomed to the constant grumbling and swaying of the train, when it entered the belly of a mountain. The horn blared, the roar of the engine bounced off the walls, deafening, and instant darkness enveloped the car. Batya screamed. Her hands grabbed the seat; she was falling into the abyss, swallowed alive in the earth.

"It's only a tunnel," she heard Moskowitz say, and just then, yellow light flickered on in the cabin, turning the windowpane into a mirror in which her face reflected back. Her eyes seemed sunken, and twin hollows in her cheeks made her look ghostly.

It was only when they were speeding through open fields that a thought crossed Batya's head. She was the feisty Zelda's daughter, sister to two older girls who knew their minds and weren't timid about following their hearts. She raised her head, took a deep breath, and steeled herself to speak.

"You said—uh—that this is a man's way with his wife." She forced herself to look at Moskowitz's thin moustache so as not to see his watery blue eyes. "But I'm only your intended."

He sighed. "Please forgive me. You are so beautiful that I lost my head."

"We're not even permitted to touch."

He sighed again, leaned forward as if to take her hand, then pulled himself back. "It will be hard to wait two years."

Mixed emotions washed over her. Moskowitz didn't view her as spoiled goods; she still had the chance of helping her family one day. But it meant that she was destined for a lifelong nightmare of despicable acts. Tears came to Batya's eyes. She must be brave for her family's sake. For them, she would endure whatever she must.

The syncopated beats of the wheels pounded in Batya's head. Outside, only the horizon remained steady while villages with onion-shaped church steeples or wooden huts crouching below a hilltop manor house flew by. She should say no more to this man who knew the ways of the world. He shouldn't regard her as a shrew who badgered him.

Moskowitz rose to retrieve his leather suitcase from the top shelf, withdrew a ledger similar to the one the money changer used, and, to Batya's relief, busied himself making calculations with a pencil. The Yiddish newspaper he'd bought at the train station lay folded on the seat next to him, and words from the headlines jumped out at her: *Factory. Reactionaries. Workers. Czarina. Finance. War. Criminals. Russia.* She would have liked to read the newspaper, but since Moskowitz must believe her illiterate like most shtetl girls, she wouldn't reveal to him that she could read. It would be her secret, one he couldn't reach or violate.

The train's chugging lulled her, and she closed her eyes, only opening them when, with screeching wheels and banging axles, the train stopped at a station.

Moskowitz lowered the window and signaled a peddler to approach. He paid for a small packet wrapped in colorful paper, which he handed to Batya.

She wanted to refuse it, but curiosity got the better of her. She peeled back the paper to reveal a dark brown block.

"Bite on it," Moskowitz said, the kindness in his voice unchanged. "Chocolate."

Batya took a bite, and a heavenly taste melted on her tongue. It was like nothing she had ever tasted—like spiced honey, but richer. Sweetness spread through the whole of her. If she were an angel, this was what God's nectar would taste like.

She took another bite, and her awe almost made her forget the man who'd given it to her.

"I'm glad you like it." Moskowitz's eyes hooked into hers. "Where we're going you'll have chocolate every day."

At his words, the sweet pleasure turned bitter in her mouth.

Chapter Ten

*T*wo days later they stopped in a big city to wait for the ship to sail. Moskowitz took Batya to a shop where dresses that had already been cut, sewn, and pressed hung in three open armoires. Batya had never imagined that so many dresses, trimmed with lace and ribbons, would have been made without specific customers in mind.

The shop matron eyed Batya. "I have nothing for a child."

"I'm sure you can make something fit," Moskowitz said in his pleasant voice. "Let's see what you've got here." He rooted in the armoires and selected three dresses. "Only the best for my princess."

Batya didn't know how to react as the woman turned each dress toward her to inspect, their designs so utterly foreign. Even Batya's Purim costumes had been simple, made of painted newspapers and scraps of materials worn over her own shabby pinafore.

The first dress Batya tried on reached the floor and was made of baby-blue taffeta with a cinched waist and petticoats that bloomed out the bottom like an upside-down kiddush cup. Batya was afraid to move as the taffeta made a rustling noise. The other dresses were blessedly silent, made of fine cotton. One was white, trimmed with a lovely lace, but had a low scooped neckline. Trying it on, Batya's face burned when she saw in the mirror her upper torso exposed.

"In Buenos Aires, you'll cut off the long sleeves," Moskowitz told her. "This dress will be the only thing you'd want to wear in the heat of summer."

Perhaps rich matrons in America wore dresses that left so much skin exposed. Afraid to raise Moskowitz's ire, Batya said nothing.

The third dress was bright red and hugged the waistline closely. If such immodest dresses were what American women wore, she must get used to that, too, just as she was learning to allow Moskowitz to do those awful things to her body. On their two nights in the train, he'd climbed onto her berth, and he repeated the visits in the mornings, because of, he said when apologizing, his lack of control in the face of her beauty. Forever this would be the price she must pay in exchange for the life he was promising for her and her family. Batya did not speak as the shop owner bent to pin the hem and seams.

At sunset, in her hotel room, Batya untied the package of dresses that a steward had delivered, all refitted to her size. She gazed at each, hardly believing that she owned so many, delighting in them, yet apprehensive about looking beautiful. Of all her new dresses, the only one she felt comfortable wearing was the gray pinafore she had had on since the maid at the inn had handed it to her the first morning.

To her relief, Moskowitz didn't dine with her that evening. The maid who brought her food used a key to enter and, upon leaving, locked the room behind her. To keep her safe, Batya now understood. She couldn't miss noticing the strangers eyeing her in the hotel's foyer and dining hall.

Alone, with nothing to occupy her, Batya stripped a bed pillow of its case and, with the rope that had tied the package, created a new doll. The one Surale had given her must have been burned along with her lice-infested clothes. She should be above such girlish make-believe, yet hugging this improvised doll to her chest made the pogrom, Miriam, and her own agony melt away.

"No one will hurt you," she whispered. "I'll be your good mama."

The maid returned with a fresh pitcher of water and a small bar of soap. In a strange language that wasn't Russian, and using hand signals, she gestured for Batya to wash up. She retrieved the chamber pot and returned it empty.

Batya changed into her nightshirt and lay under the covers, hugging her doll. The dread that crept in with the thought of Moskowitz's return rose up her throat until she began to tremble. *Let it happen already so this fear will go away,* she told God. *If that's Your wish, I will obey You.*

"My beautiful wife," Moskowitz told her when he came in wearing a robe. In spite of her wish to obey God, Batya began to whimper and her body tried to wriggle away. Moskowitz grabbed both her wrists with one hand and pinned them over her head, while with the other he lifted her nightshirt. "Didn't your mama teach you to please your husband?"

She stopped her struggle. *You are not my husband. Not for two more years.* But there was no point in arguing. As if watching from the corner of the ceiling, she saw Moskowitz take his pleasure from her. His penetration wasn't as painful as the first couple of times, but the indignity of it made the Batya hovering above close her eyes.

In the morning, Moskowitz lingered over breakfast. Batya sat staring at her fingers as she clenched and unclenched her fists. In this man's presence, she couldn't eat a single morsel of the eggs, sausages, or toast.

"You've made promises to my parents," she finally said. "You are not my husband, and I am not your wife."

"It's only a matter of time. Didn't I say I'd wait until you'd look favorably upon me for marriage? It's up to you."

I'm only fourteen. In Batya's mind's eye, she saw her parents and Surale standing outside their hut, waving goodbye, crying, hoping . . .

Her untouched food didn't seem to dampen Moskowitz's chatty mood. "You'll love Buenos Aires. It's a beautiful city with wide boulevards and stately mansions. The many city plazas are decorated with huge sculptures and fountains, with gurgling water that's music to the ears. Of course, such a city has a large harbor, with ships coming and going from all over the world— the most eye-pleasing sight, if you ask me. People travel on street cars, called *tranvias*. Do you know what they are? Like trains, moving on tracks, but drawn by horses—except one that now has electric wires on top. These *tranvias* are smaller than the train we rode, and, naturally, not so fast; people can just jump on and off." He paused as if to let Batya visualize his words, then went on. "But the best parts are the open areas of the city, parks full of trees with flowers on them. Have you ever seen a purple tree?"

She raised her glance from her fingers and shook her head.

"Well, you're in for a wonderful surprise. They're called jacaranda, and when a whole street of them is in bloom it is a magnificent sight." He smiled. "There's another tree with a fat trunk, like a beer barrel. The legend says that the tree used to be a woman who devoted her love to a soldier. But he died in battle, and as the blood of her deceased lover spread through her fingers, it turned into flowers, and she became a tree. Beautiful red flowers this tree has.

"We also have concert halls and theaters that perform in Yiddish: drama, comedy, singing, you name it. Every night there are plays and musical productions and great dancing. The dance halls are like nowhere in the world. Everyone dances—not just the actors but all people."

He had a way with words. Batya couldn't help but be intrigued. Buenos Aires was a paradise city, and, Batya reminded herself, once she had made a life there with Moskowitz and he sent for her family, they would dance there together. Their only concern would be not to stub their toes on all the gems on the ground.

Breakfast over, Moskowitz brought a suitcase and showed Batya how to fold her new dresses to minimize wrinkling, then stood over her while she packed them.

She picked up her cloth bundle and, before placing it in the valise, rooted through it. Her fingers turned frantic as they searched through her menstrual rags. "My letter. The one with my uncle's address," she called out, panic rising. "I can't find it."

"Not to worry. We'll find your uncle without it. Jews always know one another, don't they?"

If Pittsburgh was like her parents' shtetl, or even as large a town as the ones she'd passed these past three days, everyone must know one another. Batya said no more as Moskowitz lifted her suitcase. She followed him to the stairwell and down the stairs.

He stopped on the last landing before the hotel lobby. "My business compels me to stay here for a few more weeks. My associate will take you to the ship and watch over you during the voyage."

Cold perspiration erupted on Batya's neck. Travel across the ocean alone? Without him? In spite of what he'd done to her, he was taking care of her just as he had promised. Her future husband was all she had in the frightening world away from her family's protection. Why hadn't he mentioned earlier his plans to leave her?

In the foyer, he led her to a nook where a big man was seated, his legs spread wide and his large gut spilling between them. "This is Dov-Ber Grabovsky," he said.

Batya shrank back. His given name was the Yiddish word for "bear," and this huge man, with thick dark hair and thick lips and thick fingers, was as frightening as encountering a bear in the woods.

Unsmiling, Grabovsky rose, lifted Batya's suitcase, and gave a quick gesture with his head for her to follow.

Batya felt the blood drain from her face. "I'm scared," she

whispered to Moskowitz, clutching on his arm. "I'm not supposed to travel without you."

"Nothing to worry about, my dear. My sister will fetch you at the port in Buenos Aires. The most extraordinary part of our life is yet to come."

"Will there be kosher food on the ship?"

He smiled. "You haven't been eating kosher for three days. Has lightning struck you?" Without waiting for her reply, he turned his back to the lobby and withdrew a small velvet box from his pocket. "While we are apart, I have something to remind you of our bright future." He opened the box, and Batya stared at the diamond ring.

"May I place this engagement ring on your finger?" he asked in a ceremonious voice, bowing from his waist.

She was too awed to speak. He gently grasped her hand, and in the brief moment before he placed the ring on her middle finger, she registered his soft skin and manicured nails against her calloused hands with chipped, bitten nails. Once again she reminded herself how lucky she was that this nobleman had chosen her for his bride over all the women in America.

"You've been my dream," Moskowitz continued, his voice sweet as honey. "You have such a good soul. I'll join you as soon as I can. I can't wait to show you my beautiful Buenos Aires."

Batya looked down at the ring as if from the moon. Her mother would cry with happiness to see such riches on her daughter's finger. Surale would dance to hide her envy. Her father would grin with the certainty of having made the right choice for his third daughter.

Moskowitz lifted Batya's chin, and his eyes bore into hers.

"Listen carefully. A woman cannot legally get a Russian passport, but Grabovsky was generous in agreeing to put you on his. *Farshteyst?*"

He released her chin, and she nodded her assent. Yes, she understood the words, but not what they meant.

"Say you understand," he said.

"I do." The words croaked.

"Good girl." He reached for her coat. "Take it off, please. You won't need it in Buenos Aires."

She recoiled. *It's mine. It was your gift.* Relenting, she released the buttons and stared as he draped the fine-wool coat over his arm—the coat that had been hers for less than three days.

He extracted from his pocket two wrapped packets of chocolate. "Here, my angel. For the journey."

Chapter Eleven

$\mathcal{T}$he cabin in the ship where Grabovsky settled her was decorated with gilded molding. A delicate crystal chandelier hung from the ceiling, and flowery brocade covered both the bed and the matching chair that stood by a table secured to the wall. In a tiny commode, the chamber pot was set into a wooden seat with a lid.

Grabovsky watched as Batya hung her dresses in the armoire. In the polished surface of the mahogany, she saw him behind her, yawning, and she hid her rag doll, afraid that he'd think it a *shmate,* a rag, and take it away.

"Wear this dress for dinner." He pointed at the blue taffeta. "I'll come get you."

After he closed the door behind him, she waited a moment, then reopened it and gazed out. To the left and the right stretched a long corridor with many doors. Two little boys in sailor suits peeked around the corner, before a hand on each one's shoulder pulled them back. The ship had seemed huge from the outside, and a valet had led them to this cabin by a long, circuitous route. If she left the cabin, she would never find her way back. Batya retreated and climbed to stand on the bed. She looked out the round window and glimpsed the bottom of two gangplanks, one of which she had crossed thirty minutes earlier.

On the pier, porters carried valises and trunks, and long-armed iron lifts hauled boxes and crates too big to be carried. It was all frenzied, exciting, and foreign. So much to look forward to in the coming weeks. She scanned her beautiful room. As much as she had wanted Reb Moskowitz's protection, here she would be free from his unwelcome visits.

The maid brought in bread, berry marmalade, and tea. Batya ate it slowly, trying to fill her time. The marmalade's sweetness reminded her of the chocolate Moskowitz had given her, and she regretted having gobbled it down immediately. The next time he gave her chocolate, she would savor it slowly, in small measures.

She looked at the ring on her finger, and her heart sang at the promise of a sparkling future for her family. *Betrothed. I am betrothed.*

She picked up her doll, imagining that one day she would care for a baby, or many more. Hopefully, five or six babies would be healthy enough to live to adulthood in the magical city of Buenos Aires.

"The first thing I'll do in Buenos Aires is plant a tree," she whispered to the doll. "A tree that will have a strong trunk and grow high and bear all the fruits of the Garden of Eden for my family and my children." Carrying the doll around the cabin, Batya showed it the beauty of the molding and the furniture, and pretended to feed it the good food she'd been served. "In our new home, in Buenos Aires," she told it, "the streets are laid with gold, and the sun shines so bright that it turns fruit orange."

Batya caught sight of herself in the mirror. What was she doing playing with a doll? She was a betrothed woman. She dropped the tied pillowcase on the bed and faced the mirror. There had been a small mirror in Miriam's home, and the two of them used to make faces into it, pulling their eyes wide, flattening their noses, and sticking out their tongues. If only Miriam were here with her now to idle the many hours away. But Miriam was dead. Dead.

Batya hoisted herself on the bed again and watched through the porthole until darkness fell.

At the sound of a knock on the door, she opened it, and a uniformed steward came in to turn a knob on a light fixture that didn't smell of kerosene. After he left, Batya pulled the chair to sit underneath the light and twisted her ring so the diamond sparkled in the yellow glow. What had her sisters felt before marriage? Neither had time for a ring or to prepare for a proper wedding. Each courtship had been secretive, and if one sister had confided in another, Batya was out of their whispering circle. Both Keyla and Hedi had fallen in love and, unlike her, had been eager to spend time with the man she had chosen.

She wished her mother and sisters were here to assure her, to guide her in the secrets of marriage. Her mother couldn't have loved her father before they had met for the first time under their chuppah. Their mutual fondness had surely happened later. Batya hoped that she, too, would learn to feel that fondness for her husband.

The back of the hairbrush on the table featured a graceful

maiden in a white gauzy dress. A virginal dress. Batya couldn't twist away from the shame as she brushed her hair and rebraided it. It was absurd—even blasphemous—to give a picture the power to embarrass her, she told herself. Yet her own face reflecting in the mirror seemed different, more angular. Her becoming a woman showed for the whole world to see.

The maid returned to help her with the light-blue taffeta dress, buttoning it up in the back. Stroking the rich folds of a skirt the color of the sky, Batya recalled that she had imagined such a dress for Queen Esther. She was already living the life of a wealthy matron, a woman who couldn't dress without help.

As the maid laced the silk cord at the front under the chest, Batya looked down. Her breasts had budded the previous year but had been hidden under the layers of her blouse, pinafore, and the bib of her apron. This bodice made them seem fuller.

The maid left the room, and Batya sat on the chair to wait for Grabovsky, her shoulders hunched to minimize her chest.

Chapter Twelve

*T*he ship jolted as it detached from the pier. A deep, distant rumble rose, and like a Leviathan, the ship turned slowly. Batya held on to the sides of the chair as a low hum vibrated through the walls. She lifted her skirt and climbed on her bed to look out. The lights on the pier were receding, while more ships glided into view, their hundreds of windows lit as though the starred night sky had fallen into the water.

Soon, those ships, too, were left behind.

A sense of desolation enveloped Batya. She was sailing to America all alone.

Only when they were in open sea, with nothing left to see outside but tar-like darkness, did Grabovsky return for her.

He crooked his finger. "Come," he ordered, not waiting for her as he marched away into the corridor.

Batya stood. The floor shifted beneath her, and she grabbed the bed for stability, then took careful steps through the cabin and braced herself against the doorframe. Grabovsky was already far ahead, so she closed the door behind her and hurried after him. She bounced against the wall, then regained her balance, only to bounce against another, as she followed him along the hallway, up a flight of steps, through another corridor.

In spite of his bulk, Grabovsky moved briskly. Batya's legs tangled in her petticoats, making it hard to keep up with him. Finally she caught her breath when he stopped in front of a pair of glass doors guarded by twin uniformed footmen. He lifted Batya's right hand onto his left arm, then placed his right hand over her fingers, locking her hand in place.

The footmen opened the doors simultaneously, and Grabovsky and Batya stepped into a vast dining hall. Elegant groups of people sat around tables covered with white tablecloths; the chandeliers above shone down on crystal glasses and silver bowls.

Stunned by the beauty of the room, Batya was taking it all in when a pinch of the underside of her arm made her yelp.

"Smile," Grabovsky hissed.

What for? As he squeezed even harder, she forced her lips to quirk up.

He strutted with her around tables of well-dressed diners, pinching her when her smile waned. Batya thought of the ballerina in the music box dancing to the turn of the key.

A white-uniformed servant led them to a table against the wall, and Grabovsky seated her on his side, both of them facing the room. Batya slid to the far end of her chair to distance herself from Grabovsky, but his heft spread over the edges of his seat, inescapably close.

She examined the women's fine dresses and jewelry. Their hair was brushed into rich hills of curls, while her tight braids wrapped around her head like a Russian peasant's. Dozens of curious eyes scanned her and her blue dress. She dropped her head.

"Look up and smile," Grabovsky commanded.

In Komarinoe there was a dimwitted Russian boy who smiled at strangers for no reason—even at Jews. Batya didn't want to appear stupid to this roomful of elegant people, but the threat of the pinch made her smile while she fixed her gaze on the back of someone's chair.

A waiter delivered a basket of freshly baked bread, and the warm aroma made her salivate. She quickly said a blessing in her head, reached over, and tore off a piece. She glanced at Grabovsky lest he disapprove, but he said nothing.

A bowl of green soup arrived. She lifted it up to her mouth and gulped.

"Put it down and use your soup spoon," he grumbled.

She did. When only a little soup coated the bottom of her bowl, she looked at him again for approval to soak it up with bread. He shook his head, and she lowered her chin in embarrassment.

Grabovsky handed her a stemmed glass of red wine. "Here. Drink."

She'd never drunk wine outside the sacred ritual of Shabbat and Passover. She sipped. It tasted bland, yet rich in a new way, so different from the syrupy kiddush wine. And instead of just a tiny ritual sip, this entire glass was hers.

The empty soup bowl was removed. Batya's head felt strange, as if the soup were sloshing inside it, but her attention was on a plate that appeared in front of her, with a portion of meat that could have fed her entire family. She recalled Moskowitz's warning to eat slowly and not use her fingers.

The potato piroshki were fluffy as clouds, accompanied by a rich blend of onions, mushrooms, and carrots boiled with tiny green leaves. A second glass of red wine made it taste even better. Drinking wine was like eating chocolate, Batya decided, but more acute: it made her sight clearer, the gilded room brighter. The disgrace of her recent wrongdoing melted away.

After the main course, Grabovsky seemed in no rush to leave. His stomach looked even larger than before. He motioned to the waiter to refill Batya's glass, leaned back, and ordered cognac and coffee for himself. He lit a cigar. Its bluish smoke made Batya cough but didn't distract her from the whipped chocolate over white meringue that materialized in front of her. A distant voice in her head warned her that the airy chocolate must have been whisked with cream and shouldn't be consumed in the same meal as meat, but she no longer cared. She savored the dessert's fluffy and crunchy sweetness, and joy flooded the whole of her. This was the life awaiting her when she married Moskowitz, dressing in finery and eating in a plush dining hall attended by servants. She drank the rest of the wine, and more happiness filled the spaces that had been occupied by dread.

At last, she stretched in contentment and yawned, her arms raised. The room pitched and swerved, and the lights of the crystal chandeliers doubled. The walls swayed. People's voices rose to a din, when something heaved inside her.

Then her dinner exploded all over the table.

"*Polaca.*" Grabovsky shook his head in disgust, then belched, and Batya wondered why he called her a "Pole" when he knew that she was a Jewess from Russia. Two waiters appeared, mumbling in that strange loud, high, clucking language the maid had spoken. They folded away the tablecloth, and one of them placed a glass of water in front of Batya. She sipped, and the water seemed to settle her stomach but did not cool her burning forehead. Grabovsky pushed the table away and rose, yanking her arm. When she tried to stand, her legs folded under her as if made of cheese.

He lifted her in his arms and carried her out a side door.

She felt her head loll as he moved swiftly along the many corridors and down the stairs, and finally dropped her like a log on the bed in her cabin.

The maid entered and released Batya from the confines of her dress and underthings. She helped her to the commode, where Batya retched again. The maid washed her face and had Batya rinse her mouth in the bowl with mint water, then slipped over her head a shift that was too thin for the chill in the room. Batya tried to tell her that there was a nightshirt in the drawer, but the mush in her head jumbled her tongue. Words turned into pebbles impossible to spit out even if the maid had understood Yiddish.

No sooner had Batya sunk into deep sleep when something rattled her foot. She opened her eyes a slit. Grabovsky stood by her bed, naked. In the light of the lamp on the dressing table, his belly was huge.

"No!" She tried to sit up, but the room swerved around her.

He slapped her face hard. She collapsed onto the pillow, shocked by the sting of his slap. He fell on top of her, knocking her breath out. "No!" she tried to scream into his vast chest. His hands pinched her bare buttocks as he lifted them and shoved himself into her.

Panting and grunting, he puffed his foul breath straight into Batya's nose and mouth. She screamed, and he silenced her mouth with his paw while he pounded, the pain tearing her with each thrust.

He left her coughing for air, sobbing. She curled into a ball, filled with hatred and self-loathing. Her head felt unanchored when she turned it, as if her brain had to be nudged to move along with her skull.

She was still wailing when a sailor entered her room. Batya's wine-laden limbs barely obeyed her as she scrambled to the corner of the cot. The sailor lifted her legs and spread them apart. His hand was like a steel vise as he held her down and unbuttoned the trousers of his cotton uniform with the other.

She screamed, then sank her teeth into his shoulder. He punched her jaw. She gathered what little force remained in her and bit again, and he laughed. She wrenched an arm free to scratch at his face, but he was already inside her, enjoying her struggles. Like a cat playing with a mouse, sometimes he let go of her arms, laughing as she flailed and hit him, then seizing them back in one swoop.

When he finally rose, she slumped over the side of the bed and retched. Only bile came up, burning her throat.

The door hadn't closed behind the sailor when Grabovsky re-entered. He slapped her again. "Stop the racket," he demanded, and slapped her other cheek.

She was in a drunken stupor when two more men, well-dressed gentlemen she recognized from the dining hall, joined her, one watching the other as each had his way with her body.

Batya woke up feeling her head bursting like an overripe gourd. The light streaming through the porthole pierced her eyes. She lay still, counting the different pains that racked her body. Head, eyes, arms, stomach, her private parts, her legs. Her heart was lead. She was a debased, sullied human being. Not even that. A filthy animal. A creature undeserving to walk on God's earth.

The maid who entered wasn't the one from the previous night. This woman shook her head in pity, crossed herself, and clucked words in her language. Her hands were tender as she cleaned Batya and gently massaged her sore body. She put ointment on Batya's opening, but it did little to soothe the pulsating pain inside her or the splitting headache. When Batya wept, the woman cradled her head in her lap and sang her a song in her strange language.

After a while she left, returning with a breakfast of salted herring, a soft-boiled egg, a slice of bread toasted and buttered on both sides, and a glass of milk. She tiptoed out, as if not to disturb Batya's regained calm, but Batya could hear the key turning on the other side of the door. If only the key had protected her last night.

Nausea filled Batya at the smell of the food. She raised herself with difficulty and looked out the porthole. A vast lead-colored sea under an overcast sky stretched to the horizon. Low waves broke, their foaming tops receding, rolling the ship along with the rising and falling of her head and stomach.

How could this happen to her? Batya felt sick with no fever, her head as empty and brainless as a butter churn. Her future with Moskowitz was destroyed. It was one thing for him to give in to his desire for her and entirely another to have a wife who'd been despoiled by other men. She had failed her parents. She would never be able to bring them and Surale to America as a respectable wife of a man of importance and means.

For the rest of the day she stayed in bed, hovering between wakefulness and sleep. She tried eating the noontime meal to fortify herself, but fear and self-loathing clogged her throat. She was undeserving of God's abundant good food.

And worse, facing three more weeks at sea, she was Grabovsky's captive.

When dusk came, Batya rose and put on her gray pinafore, hoping to get out of the cabin. If she could escape, she would find some good soul to beg for help.

Outside the porthole, the sky darkened and blended with the sea into one impenetrable inky blotch. Instead of Grabovsky bringing her to the dining hall, a male servant carried in a tray. As he took out the previous barely touched meal, he smirked and winked at her.

Batya forced small bites around her growing lump of fear. Then, after drinking her hot tea, she smashed the china cup against the wall. She took off her diamond ring and placed it in the closet drawer, then clutched the curved handle of the broken teacup between her fingers, its jagged edges sticking out. Her heart pounding in her ears, she curled up in the corner of the room, trapped. Waiting.

It was late when a man came in, waddled unsteadily toward her, and reached for her.

Gripping the broken cup handle, she slashed his cheek.

Chapter Thirteen

$\mathcal{T}$he vibrations of the ship shook Batya awake into complete darkness. Her entire body hurt, and when she breathed, something pierced her rib cage. Her stomach ached inside and out.

She retched bile.

The floor beneath her was coarse wooden slats. Her legs touched rough planks. Raising an arm with difficulty, she met more slats. Frantically, she felt about her: she was lying inside a crate.

In the noisy thrum of the ship's engines, rhythmic, metallic, and juddering, events of the night before rushed in—the men, the beating, being struck on the head.

She started to cry, but every breath sent that ice pick into her rib cage. Passing her hand over her neck, chest, and legs, she touched the tender bruises. Only then did she notice the lump of cloth next to her head. Her rag doll. She must have been clutching it when she was knocked unconscious and thrown in here. Batya hugged it, her sobs turning to a wail. *"God help me.*

Please! Hear me here, Your daughter Batyale. I was a good, obedient daughter to my parents and a devoted believer in You—"

"Crying will only make you weaker." The Yiddish words in a girl's voice were unmistakable. Batya turned her head, but could see nothing in the darkness. "Your name is Batyale?" the girl asked. "I'm Shayna."

"My family calls me that. I'm really Batya. Where are we?"

"You have a family?"

"Don't you?"

There was a long pause. When Shayna spoke, Batya had to strain to hear her voice over the din. "My parents were killed in a pogrom when I was four. My brothers and I grew up in a Jewish orphanage until soldiers came and conscripted all the boys into the czar's army." After another pause, Shayna went on, her voice stronger. "They did bad things to the girls. Took some away with them. Of the girls that remained, four of us were chosen for jobs. We're sailing to work as maids in good Jewish homes in Argentina."

"Where's that?"

"It's where this ship is heading."

"It's going to Buenos Aires."

"Buenos Aires is a city in Argentina, which is the country."

"The country is America," Batya said, certain in her one piece of knowledge.

"Argentina is a country in *South* America."

Something ran across Batya's leg. She yelped. The creature circled and came back. She screamed and batted at her leg.

"Those are just rats," Shayna said. "Are you wearing something to cover yourself? They bite."

Batya tucked up her legs under the bottom of her slip and undid the rag-doll pillowcase. She slid it over her head and shoulders and breathed through the fabric. *Merciful Father, have mercy on me. Don't make me live in this filth and degradation.*

The rat came again, sniffing her. She felt a sharp nip through her thin slip and screamed.

"Shhhhhhh. Let's pray," Shayna said. *"God, we are here, Shayna and Batya, and we need You to rescue us. Save us from evil. Heal our wounds."*

What were Shayna's wounds? Batya dared not ask. *"Yes, let us out. Take us back home,"* she cried. In her mind's eye she saw her beautiful cabin upstairs and recalled how good it had felt for just a few hours to have been a rich woman. Silently, she asked God, *Please bring Reb Moskowitz back to me. Even if he won't take me for his wife, make his kind heart show benevolence toward me.*

"How old are you?" Shayna asked.

"Fourteen. And you?"

"Almost sixteen."

For a while, neither spoke. The ship's engines droned. The swaying of the ship was unrelenting, unsettling Batya's empty stomach. A cockroach climbed up her thigh, and she yelped, batting it away. She mulled over what Shayna had told her. Batya had advantages over this girl: she had caring parents; she was under the protection of a man who'd mistakenly trusted his business associate; she also had an uncle living near their destination. When she arrived in Buenos Aires in that country, Argentina, that was in America, in the southern part of it, Moskowitz's sister would take her under her wing. Even if Batya could no longer be Moskowitz's wife, she could still become a hardworking maid.

Her thumb felt the inside of her middle finger for the ring Moskowitz had given her, and she remembered: it had been abandoned in her cabin. Moskowitz would be cross that she couldn't give it back.

Her bladder intruded on her thoughts. "I need to pee badly," she told Shayna.

"Might as well just do it. If you need to poop, scoot to the corner of your cage."

A new wave of incredulity contracted the hair on Batya's scalp. "How long have you been down here?"

"Since right after we sailed. How long has it been?"

The ship began to rock widely, and the rumbling noise rose to a new pitch. The ocean roared close by, and Batya felt herself rising and falling. She was hurled upward, then dropped down, as though the ship were a giant swing. She propped herself against the sides of her cage as her empty stomach heaved and retched.

Hours later, when the storm subsided, a door opened in the distance, and in the wan light filtering through the slats of Batya's crate she saw a slim figure holding a lantern.

"I was sent to bring you water," she heard a boy say in Yiddish. "How many of you are here?"

"Two," Shayna replied.

He approached and kneeled by Batya's cage. He rested the lantern on the floor and ladled water from a pail, then handed her the filled tin cup.

Batya took it with shaking hands and gulped quickly, then licked her lips to collect the droplets. "More, please." Her voice sounded like a croak to her own ears.

He refilled the cup, and she drank thirstily, then handed it back to him. He lifted his lantern, and she heard him move toward Shayna.

"What about food?" Shayna asked him.

"We are very hungry," Batya added. As poor as her family was, she had never gone a day without at least a potato or some root stew, and they always had milk and cheese.

The boy hesitated. "I'll try."

After he left there was nothing but dread of the dark, of the confinement, of the rats. Batya drifted in and out of consciousness. Hunger mixed with the pain in her rib cage with the ache in her limbs. When she peed, a needle of pain pierced her. The stench of her excrement stung her nostrils—but it also seemed to keep the rats at a distance. She breathed through her mouth and the pillowcase that covered her upper body.

The boy reappeared what seemed like a day later, this time with two apples and a hardtack, a dry flour cracker. "I've saved you my rations," he whispered, "and stolen the apples from the storage."

"Thank you." Batya gobbled down the cracker. "May God shower you with blessings for helping us."

"Why do you take the risk?" Shayna asked him.

"My sister sailed last year with her new husband but disappeared. So I got a job as a deck hand and have traveled to Buenos Aires twice to look for her. I can only stay as long as the ship docks. This is my third voyage. Maybe I'll have more luck this time. The rumors are growing."

"What rumors?" Batya asked.

"Men bring girls to Argentina by the dozens, then sell them."

He picked up his lantern, and as it threw light near Batya's cage, she saw cockroaches scattering away. "I must return to my shift."

"What did he mean by 'sell them'?" Batya asked Shayna after he'd left.

"That I'll be sent to a brothel." Shayna broke into a sob.

"What's that?"

But Shayna went on crying.

The days and nights passed with nothing to demarcate them other than the occasional break when a sailor brought water along with bread or a potato, supplemented by the boy's visits. The air became stifling and suffused with oil smoke, sending Batya and Shayna into coughing fits. Perspiration formed on Batya's skin and dripped down her body. She separated her limbs as far as she could to minimize the hot touch of her own skin. Images came and went: her family's hut burning; trees merging into a hot river that drowned her; diamonds growing into giant cockroaches. In moments of lucidity her mind figured that the heat meant that they were nearing America, where Reb Moskowitz's sister would be waiting for her.

God Almighty, she prayed. *Hear me down here. But don't tell my parents what happened. It would kill them. Just save me Yourself.*

Batya had no idea how many days or weeks had passed when her crate was pried open. A sailor pulled her out of the crate and, when she stumbled, pushed her against a wall with Shayna. Shielding her eyes against the sudden light, Batya saw her new friend for the first time, a girl taller and wider than she, with black curls caked with filth and brown eyes swollen from crying.

Against the swaying of the ship, Batya remained standing by pressing her back to the wall when a sudden spray of cold seawater hit her with a startling force. She slid down and covered her head, but there was no place to hide as the sailor directed the hose onto her hair and between her legs, stinging the old cuts and the newer rat bites, then sprayed Batya's head and face, where the salt water burned her eyes and lips.

When he stopped, Batya wrapped her arms around herself to hide her nakedness in the torn wet slip. The sailor sniggered, but the break from the crate and its rats was a relief, and the cold water a reprieve from the grime and heat. Despite the burning, the fast-drying salt was preferable to the filth.

The sailor handed each of them a sheet, and Batya draped hers around herself. Trembling, her eyes stinging from salt and blinking at the light, she followed his hand signal to climb up a metal ladder. Shayna lumbered a few rungs behind her, the sailor bringing up the rear. At the top, Batya forced her rubbery limbs to pull her through the hole, and she found herself on a small balcony from which rose a flight of stairs. The ship was moving on a calm sea, and no land was in sight.

The sun was too bright. Batya shielded her eyes, then shuffled around a neatly coiled rope. Just as she reached the first stair, she heard a yelp from the sailor. She turned to see his head and torso emerge from the top of the ladder at the same time as Shayna hurled herself from the balcony. Flailing arms and legs, she hit the water with a splash, then disappeared.

"No!" Batya screamed, and rushed to the railing.

In one push of arms and shoulders, the sailor hoisted himself off the ladder and onto the deck. He grabbed Batya from behind as her eyes searched the water, hoping for Shayna's head to rise. His arm gripped her neck, almost choking her, and pinned her spine to his chest. His knee pressed into her as he pushed her toward the stairs.

"No!" Batya screamed again. But Shayna was no more.

Chapter Fourteen

The cabin Batya was led to was nothing like the first. Lined in rough-hewn wood, the tiny space contained two narrow cots fixed into the wall, one above the other like shelves, a thin mattress and a sheet on top of each. There was no ladder to reach the top cot, and she was too weak to raise herself onto it.

On a hook she found one of her muslin slips but none of her dresses, and no shoes. In spite of the warmth of the cabin, Batya wrapped herself in the frayed sheet the sailor had given her, now dry and caked with salt, and sat on the bottom cot, rocking herself. How could she face Moskowitz's sister looking as she did, as stained with shame as she was? She wished she had followed Shayna into the water.

A pail stood in the corner, containing cloudy water. Batya lowered her head into the pail. The water seeped into her hair roots, and the image of Shayna jumping to her death gave Batya courage. She dunked her head fully and held her breath. Water filled her nostrils and bubbled into hidden paths behind her forehead, pressing. She fought the urge to breathe, but her body—or God—overpowered her and yanked her head out of the bucket. Sputtering water, she caught air. She tried again. Once more, her body betrayed her and pulled free, gasping for air.

A key turned in the lock, and a maid came in, carrying a tray containing a tin bowl of kasha with a piece of chicken and a hardtack. Despite her death wish, Batya wolfed it down, dipping the last piece of hardtack to soak up the remainder of her meal. The maid took out the tray and returned with a cup of warm tea. The cup, too, was made of tin. Batya sipped the tea, sweetened with sugar, breathing in its fragrance. Anything was better than the horror of being caged down below, but she wouldn't give up on her death wish, even if her body's instinct to live defied her soul's desire to escape her misery.

A few hours later, Grabovsky barged into the cabin. Batya hoisted herself to the top shelf and scooted to the corner, shrinking her body into a ball.

"You want to cause more trouble and stay belowdecks?" He pulled her down and threw her on the bottom cot. "Is that what you want?"

Clammy fingers of dread crawled from Batya's neck down her spine. Whimpering, she shook her head. She could never again face the rats, the cockroaches, and the confines of the cage in the darkness.

"Let's see, then." His gaze hooked on her as he unbuckled his belt.

She shut her eyes tight, feeling tears escaping. Expecting the assault, her body began to shake.

"Open your eyes. No man wants to fuck a corpse." He slapped

her so hard that it felt as if a rock bounced inside her skull. "Open your eyes, I said."

She forced her eyes open to see his bulbous nose and the hair growing out of his nostrils even as she shut down her soul and deadened her heart.

Two days later, the ship reached harbor. It anchored at a distance from the piers, where it bobbed on ripples of waves. The engines fell silent.

A maid brought a clean pail of water and a bar of soap. Batya could barely wash herself. She felt feverish, and in spite of the heat she shivered. Impatient with Batya's sluggish movements, the maid grabbed the sponge from her hand and swiped it across Batya's shoulders and back and down her thighs. She handed her a brush, but Batya's head hurt as if a barrel hoop were tightening it, and her arms were too weak to fight the knots in her hair.

The maid placed wooden clogs on the floor and laid out Batya's white dress. The sleeves had indeed been cut off. Batya put it on, and, after the maid had departed, raised herself to the porthole and saw in the distance a bustling pier with long rows of windowless redbrick buildings. A gigantic steel arm lifted massive crates from a nearby barge. Farther down, the end of the pier was enclosed by a high iron-bar fence with a gate. A huge crowd of people looking like the shtetl poor—men in dark, shabby vests and coats, heads covered in black felt hats, and women in flowered headscarves, bundles slung over their shoulders—pushed and waved papers. Policemen shoved back the crowd and separated them into lines that fell apart as the crowd pressed forward again.

Somewhere, past the fence, Moskowitz's sister was waiting for her. But how would the woman recognize Batya? How would Batya even manage to ask for her? In his hasty departure, Moskowitz had forgotten to tell her his sister's married name.

Batya dropped down from the porthole. Once she left the port with Grabovsky, she would look for a lady waiting in a carriage. If necessary, she would scream to get her attention. Someone would help her.

The hours passed, and the air in the cabin heated up. Batya was being cooked alive. Moskowitz had said it was hot in Buenos Aires, but who ever imagined such sweltering heat? She lay on the cot, her head light, perspiration dripping from her body onto the mattress. A sudden wave of shivers made her teeth chatter. Thirst dried her mouth and felted her tongue. She was sick, she realized. Death would finally find her. *Just make it come fast,* she prayed. *Take pity on me.*

When Grabovsky opened the door, carrying her valise, the gust of air that entered with him revived Batya enough for her to try to sit up. She dragged herself after him up the stairs, through air that remained as hot and damp as steam rising from a samovar.

"For the officials, you're my wife," Grabovsky said. "Understood?"

She lowered her eyes in assent.

"And raise your head. Don't look so sick, or they won't allow you in."

Chapter Fifteen

A sailor picked up Batya under her arms and handed her down to another who stood in a bobbing wooden boat. Grabovsky followed, as did other passengers and their luggage. When the boat was full, the sailors rowed it the length of the harbor to the pier.

The steady ground under Batya's feet felt as if it bucked and swayed. She tried walking on legs that refused to move in a straight line. Her insides were on fire. Grabovsky's arm wrapped around her waist, too tightly, forcing her forward. Before they reached the crowd pressing on the fence, he pushed her through the side door of a building. In a huge hall, behind a row of tables at the far end, sat officials in short-sleeved, khaki-colored uniforms. Without hesitation, Grabovsky approached a short man with bushy eyebrows whose desk was angled so he could supervise the others. Speaking in that strange language, Grabovsky presented his papers. The man raised his glance at Batya and unfolded the papers. Batya saw him slipping the money tucked in the document onto his lap before he sent a look of understanding to Grabovsky.

Outside, they walked onto a long, busy ramp paved in a black substance and crisscrossed above by metal beams and hooked ropes. The stench of rotting fish and sea salt filled the air.

Batya gathered all her strength to keep walking. In a few minutes she would say goodbye to her captor. Passing a row of warehouses, she and Grabovsky moved along with a bustling crowd of people wending their way around horse-drawn carriages and porters pushing carts heaped with boxes. All around, people spoke Yiddish or that clucking, high-pitched language.

Her head swimming, Batya searched the awaiting carriages, but no woman waved to her. "I must wait for Reb Moskowitz's sister," she managed to say. "She's supposed to meet me here."

He let out a chuckle. "I'm taking you to her."

Batya shook her head. No way was she going with this man beyond this spot. She scanned the street as he tugged at her arm.

"You want some police officer should take you to jail?" Grabovsky hissed. "Let's go."

If the police were like the ones in Russia, they must be avoided; nothing good ever came of them, especially if she had no passport. Batya sniffled. She was sick, didn't speak the language, and had no money. Her only valuable possession, her diamond ring, was stashed in a drawer in some plush cabin on the ship. She relaxed her resistance; this was the very last time she would listen to Grabovsky.

As she allowed him to pull her forward, pain gripped her abdomen and she doubled over.

He muttered a Russian curse. "Next thing you die on me?" He motioned to the nearest coachman and shoved Batya up into the carriage.

The bench in the carriage was hard, but sitting offered a reprieve. Batya shrank to its farthest end. As much as she tried to disappear, Grabovsky's thick thigh still rested against hers.

The carriage meandered along alleys through run-down buildings before stopping in front of a house that was nothing like the manor Moskowitz had described. Rather than the large polished-stone home of Batya's daydreams, with grand stairs and ornate columns, it was a low, decaying clapboard structure.

Grabovsky tossed the coachman a coin and prodded Batya down.

The tiny entrance had no windows, only a cutout above the door. Inside, it was dark and reeked of fried food and an open latrine. All Batya could see was a narrow, dark corridor off of which were rough wood partitions with dirty curtains that served as doors. A straw mat lay over the packed-mud floor, like in her Komarinoe home.

Batya's eye sockets throbbed, and she pressed her hands against them to ease the pressure.

A woman with a scar across her right cheek came from one of the rooms, spraying rosewater that failed to mask the stink in the air. She grinned, and the scar twisted her mouth. Batya recoiled against Grabovsky. The woman laughed, and the scar pulled down her lower lid to reveal the eye's reddish part.

Another woman turned away from a sink set in a nook and wiped her hands on her apron. She nudged the scarred woman away. "Welcome," she said to Batya. "I'm Nina."

"Are you Yitzik Moskowitz's sister?" Batya asked. Every fiber in her body hurt.

Nina's eyes were cold as she examined her face, and chills ran down Batya's spine. "She's sick," she said to Grabovsky.

"Make her better," he retorted.

"What is this, a hospital?" But Nina's lips pulled up in a smile toward Batya, a smile that failed to bunch up her cheek. "Come, *meydele*. I'll show you to your chamber." She picked a long yellow fruit from the shelf by the sink and peeled off a part of its skin. "This is a banana. Eat."

Too ill to refuse or argue, Batya simply wanted to lie down. Holding the hewn wooden planks of the corridor for support, she followed Nina while taking small bites of the fruit. Sick as she felt, she couldn't resist savoring its sweetness and creamy texture. Like the cheesy filling of a blintze, but better, it must have come from the Garden of Eden.

Chapter Sixteen

The thin walls and the canvas curtain doors offered no privacy. Starting in the afternoon and stretching throughout the night, from the chambers on both sides, Batya heard men grunting and moaning. Feverish, she pressed her hands to her ears to block the crying of girls like her.

Now the words she'd heard from the kind boy on the ship became clear. She had been sold! Grabovsky had kidnapped her from Moskowitz and sold her to Nina. These groaning men—like the men who'd exploited her on the ship—were all paying customers. Horrified anew, Batya curled up, trembling in fear. Only when the house quieted and no man entered her chamber did sleep finally take over.

The sun was high, and the ceiling's corrugated tin radiated heat on her by the time she woke up. It took Batya a few moments to get her bearings. Her head hurt as it had when she had been inebriated. She pulled herself to the chamber pot, and when she peed, that needle of pain had worsened, spreading upward.

She was also leaking something thick and yellow that smelled as bad as the wound that her father's old horse had once developed on his hind leg.

The scarred woman poked her head through the curtain. "Come get your tea."

Clutching her stomach and leaning on the rough wooden walls of the short corridor, Batya followed her to the kitchen nook. A large woman with skin so black that it had a blue sheen was doling out what looked like thin pancakes. As she placed some on Batya's plate, Batya eyed the two girls next to her, who wore only slips, their hair disheveled and their exposed chests and shoulders showing open cuts and bruises. She poured herself tea from the kettle, not daring to speak.

"Now take it back to your chamber," the scarred woman said.

Batya sat on the bed, balancing her mug and plate on her knees. Her stomach rumbled. She picked up a pancake and chewed slowly. Could she escape this house? Where would she go to find Moskowitz's sister? Even if she found her, would the woman still take her in after all Batya had done?

By midday, the temperature in the airless house had risen, and with it the putrid fermentation of sewer. Baking in the heat, swatting the flies that entered through the cutout by the ceiling, Batya missed the cold of Russia. Feeling too vulnerable in only her slip, she dared not take off her dress, and she lay on her cot, her perspiration soaking it through.

A girl a few years older than Batya came in. Unlike the disheveled girls in the house, this one wore a new-looking flowery summer dress, her dark hair was brushed, and she smelled of lavender.

Batya sat up.

"I'm Rochel." The girl smiled, and twin dimples puckered her cheeks. She touched Batya's forehead with lovely long and cool fingers to feel her temperature, and Batya wished they'd stay there.

Rochel examined Batya's bruises and stroked her back. "Poor thing," she murmured. She withdrew out of her bag a vial of ointment. "Use it between your legs."

Batya grabbed her hand. "I must get out of here," she whispered. She motioned with her head toward the wall. "I'm not— I'm not that kind of a girl."

Rochel shook her head. "You're sick, and Nina doesn't want you dying on her. But as soon as you are better, they expect you to work—"

"Never!"

Rochel's tone was soft. "This is America. Their customs are very different from ours." She dabbed Batya's face with a rose-scented handkerchief. "You think this is bad? It can be worse. Come. Let me show you."

She helped Batya up and led her to the front door, where she pointed down the street to tin huts. "Do you see those crates closest to the river?" She moved a dirty tendril of hair from Batya's face. "Instead of holding cargo, they are brothels. God help the girls working there. Those units—you can't call them houses—are as hot as Gehenom, and the clients are the poorest men, paying only two pesos, using those girls like a toilet, without even letting them wash between clients. There're not even partitions inside, only curtains; everyone's crowded together. On weekends, these girls must take as many as seventy men a day." She paused to let her words sink in. "It's called La Boca. The mouth. It is the mouth of hell."

Batya pressed a closed fist into her mouth and began crying. She was already in hell.

Rochel led her back to her chamber. "Look, prostitution is legal here. Everyone is either a prostitute, a pimp, or a client. And the government gets its cut."

Batya's sobs turned into hiccups. Rochel retrieved a mug of water from the kitchen nook. She brought it close to Batya's mouth. "Shhhhhhh," she whispered over and over. "You want to run away. I know. But you'll never get far. You don't have a passport, right? You probably entered as someone's wife."

Batya nodded. "Grabovsky's."

"It gets easier. Really. I promise. This is the training house. They purposely bring the worst of men here—sailors with overgrown, crooked nails; street cleaners stinking of garbage; poor construction laborers with calloused hands. But if you behave, they'll move you to a better home. You'll have the good men, the ones that smell nice, get manicures, and pay well. Then you can save some money, too." She waved her hand somewhere outside. "Many of us have regulars—judges, journalists, politicians."

Us? Batya's mind couldn't reconcile this clean-smelling and caring Rochel with accepting being a prostitute. "How can such things get easier?" she cried out.

"I learned to play by their rules. Believe me, it's better." Rochel swatted two flies circling her head. Her gaze traveled around the chamber, and Batya felt her pity at the dim and hot surroundings.

"You're pretty—and blond," Rochel said, stroking Batya's

hair as if it weren't knotted with filth. "Just do as they tell you, and everything will be all right."

Batya shook her head. "I can't," she whispered.

"What would you do if you saved some money?"

"I'd send for my parents. That's why I came here." Batya thought of Moskowitz. If she could only find him, perhaps he would allow her to work as a maid in his big fancy house. Such a life was still a hundred times better than the poverty of the shtetl, and thousands of times better than the future of which Rochel was speaking.

Rochel hugged Batya. "Think of me as your big sister. You are not alone." She stepped out, and through the canvas door curtain Batya heard her speak to Nina. "Don't waste the investment. What could you get for her here, two to three pesos each, like for a black or creole girl?"

"A blonde brings more."

"That's what I mean. You'd do much better if you moved her to our house."

"She's beyond saving," Nina said. "Did you smell her?"

"She's sick. It will be on both our heads if she dies."

Batya clapped her hands over her ears so she wouldn't hear any more. *God, is that Your world order?* she asked. *Is this what You've ordained for me?*

Then she remembered her mother saying that it made no sense to complain to God about Himself.

Chapter Seventeen

This Buenos Aires was Sodom and Gomorrah, the biblical cities of sin, which God had decreed must be destroyed by the flood. How could Moskowitz have allowed his young fiancée to venture here alone, to travel to a city where such immorality and brutality existed? There must be another Buenos Aires, his beautiful city with tree-lined boulevards, bubbling fountains, and stately mansions. The cunning Grabovsky must have taken her to another city.

Batya closed her eyes. Her only hope was that Moskowitz would find her and take pity on her even though she had been sullied. She must hold on to that hope or she'd go mad.

In spite of the constant pain that had spread throughout her abdomen, Batya forced herself to leave the bed in the morning. She retrieved her food from the kitchen nook. As she hobbled back with her plate, she caught sight of a girl in the chamber adjacent to hers seated on her bed and balancing a plate on her knees. They made eye contact, and the girl gave a minute wave. Batya entered, and the girl slid down her bed to make room for Batya.

The girl turned to show Batya two deep gashes on her back. "Look what he did with his belt buckle. If you lick them, it will make them better."

Lick them? Batya gasped at the open wounds and the suggestion. She spit on her fingers and tentatively touched each of the gashes. "I'm Batya," she said.

The girl didn't turn back. She gestured to Batya to continue her ministering. "I am a *polaca*. That's what they call all prostitutes from Eastern Europe. I am a *kurve* to the Jewish men and a *puta* to the Spaniards and Portuguese."

"Were you—eh—a prostitute back home?"

The girl shook her head and turned toward Batya. "I was too ugly for that."

Batya took in the broad forehead, flat nose, and bowed legs. "You have lovely brown eyes," she said.

"Who'll bother to look at them when I'm on my back?"

Nina burst in. "What are you whispering about?" she demanded.

Batya lowered her head. She wanted to ask the girl whether she, too, missed Russia, her family's hut, the mud in the road, the soot from the stove. The cold. Whether she missed the Russian language the goyim spoke. Anything in Russia was better than this. Even the czar's vicious edicts.

"Don't contaminate her with your attitude," Nina ordered, and Batya slunk back to her chamber.

Outside Nina's brothel the bright light sent a sharp pain into Batya's skull. She had forgotten how blinding the sun could be, although she knew well its trapped heat. That morning, Rochel had passed by and told Batya to expect to be moved to her home. Batya didn't want to go there either, especially when Grabovsky came to fetch her.

Batya hugged herself, sadness clutching her. The alley was bustling with people—peddlers, pushcarts, coachmen and horses. Did they all eat a chicken every day, or did all those men visit prostitutes as Rochel had said?

Death was her best solution, Batya thought as she spotted a body of water at the end of the alley. Her eyes searched for a break between boats where she could hurl herself into the river. Once in, she would run deeper, and when her feet lost the bottom, she would drown. *Courage.* She looked down at the oversized, open rubber sandals that Grabovsky had brought. To escape, she must sprint barefoot in the debris, but even this small movement deepened the pain in her belly. Grabovsky would catch her. Then it would be his belt—or another rat-filled dungeon.

When he poked her rib, she followed him, attempting to keep up with his fast pace. But her legs were weak, and the sandals kept slipping off. Even the touch of the dress on her skin made it feel raw. The sun's heat and its pulsating brightness caused her head to swoon. She stopped, doubling in pain. The blood rushed to her lowered head.

Grabovsky's steel fingers clutched her arm. "If you faint, I'll take you back to Nina."

She took a deep breath, then another, and fought to straighten up. Rochel and her warmth beckoned her.

Soon they were on a wide street, where a horse-drawn tram traveled on tracks in its center, just as Moskowitz had described, and passengers jumped on and off. When Grabovsky pushed

Batya to climb in, she grabbed a handle for support and swung inside. To her relief, a passenger seated nearby rose to jump off. She fell into his seat.

From the tram window she saw dilapidated two- and three-story houses, laundry hanging from every window. Bedraggled men wearing yarmulkes lugged baskets, carried water pails, fixed broken stairs, or offered meager belongings for sale. A band of filthy children hit empty cans with sticks, then set upon an emaciated dog, laughing as they whacked its bony back and ribs. Through ground-floor windows Batya noticed women in headscarves hunched over sewing machines, while above them women with painted faces leaned out second- and third-floor windows, calling out to passersby. One of them dangled huge breasts, barely covered, over the windowsill.

Life seemed to be lived outside: A cobbler hammered shoe soles; a barber pulled a screaming client's tooth to the guffaws of onlookers; women cooked on balconies; men played cards on rickety tables between houses; a tinsmith soldered a broken pot over a fire. A knife sharpener pumped a foot pedal to turn his stone, and its screech prickled the hair roots on Batya's arms.

Some of the ground floors of houses served as shops. Through their doors, Batya glimpsed mounds of rolled cloth, meat and chicken hanging on hooks, housewares piled on shelves. Yiddish signs announced a bakery, a tailor's shop, a bookstore, a tobacco store, and an apothecary. A moneylender sat outside his shop at a small table, a lockbox at his elbow. A woman bargained loudly with a yarmulke-wearing vegetable vendor. Farther down another street, three women rooted through a pile of *alte-zachen* on the cart of a ragman. Two men hauled boxes of produce, and two others unloaded furniture. Occasionally, Batya glimpsed through an open gate a shabby courtyard filled with stoves, a water well, barrels, and piles of lumber beneath the ever-present sagging laundry lines.

The houses, made of clay and stone with buckling walls and peeling plaster, were so different from the low mud-and-straw huts of the shtetl, and even from the better ones built of wood planks. Yet, for all their differences, the filth and poverty had the familiar feel of the world she'd left behind. This place was as far from the Buenos Aires of Moskowitz's description as Russia's snowy hills.

At Grabovsky's shout, the driver stopped the tram. Grabovsky jumped off, pulling Batya with him. Standing in the shade of a building, he withdrew a handkerchief from his trouser pocket and wiped his sweating brow. Batya was thirsty. In her eagerness to escape Nina's house, she had not drunk any water from the pail a boy had brought to the brothel. Her father would never believe there were water carriers in America. Water here was supposed to flow from pipe faucets, like the ones her father had reported seeing in the homes of Bobruevo's rich.

Grabovsky rounded the corner into a cleaner residential street of two-storied houses that touched one another, creating an impenetrable front. He stopped in front of one painted in muted sunset orange. A climbing vine with magenta flowers twisted around the iron grilles of its second-floor verandas. Batya glanced up at the bright blue window frames that gave the house a fairy-tale look.

Grabovsky's thick finger poked her spine and prodded her inside.

The door opened into a large room with a floor paved like a carpet in small, colorful tiles. The geometric pattern stretched unbroken onto a spacious patio bordered by planters with fantastical blooming shrubs—large, voluptuous flowers in riotous colors, looking like mythical birds in one of Batya's mother's stories.

The indoor and outdoor were separated by open floor-to-ceiling windows, their gauzy curtains swaying in the breeze. In the pavilion, long swathes of colorful fabric were strung along the tops of the walls and gathered in places by decorative masks and gilded plaques. The air was suffused with flowery perfume, aromatic cooking, and cigar smoke. The beat of music sounded, though Batya couldn't see the musicians.

Men and women flowed out of the pavilion to the patio and back. The women were in various states of undress—some, to Batya's embarrassment, with breasts fully exposed. A few women danced with each other. Men played cards, two of them with young women seated on their knees. Batya felt that she had dropped into an obscene version of a Purim carnival, the joyous Jewish holiday when everyone wore costumes and many imbibed. But this festivity wasn't make-believe; these people seemed to be celebrating a trouble-free, happy life.

A few meters away, on a round sofa, sat several half-clad women with painted faces. One of them rose and sauntered languorously toward Batya, her hips swaying. She held a cigarette in a long holder. She kissed Batya on both cheeks and wrapped her in a hug like a long-lost relative. "I'm so glad you're here."

"Rochel?" Batya was bewildered by the transformation. Only the voice remained the same.

"Who else?" Rochel laughed, the twin dimples punctuating her cheeks. "You're hot." With a flick of her wrist she flipped open what looked like a stiff lace handkerchief shaped like a half-moon. She waved it in front of Batya's burning face, then handed her the device. "This is a fan. It will help you bear the heat, but you can also use it in a most feminine way." She crushed her cigarette in an ashtray and took Batya's hand. "Come meet the sisters. We're one big family."

Batya turned back to seek Grabovsky's approval and saw him disappear through a side door.

Deep inside the pavilion, she spotted the source of the music: one klezmer played a violin, and two others played instruments she'd never seen—one an oddly shaped stringed instrument and the other a rectangular bellow-like device with dozens of buttons on both sides. The melody was strange, and the girls dancing to it thrust their hips and tossed their torsos so their long hair flew. The kicks of their legs barely missed each other's shins. The way they held their spines like haughty ladies of means while they alternated between challenging glances and resting their cheeks against each other was both haunting and brazen.

"That's tango," Rochel said. "A Buenos Aires specialty. A lot of it is about lovers and heartbreak. Very romantic."

Romantic. Batya had forgotten that she and Miriam used to wonder about the nature of that mysterious emotion. Now that she knew about the degrading way of men with women she also understood that romance was for stories, not real life.

Rochel led her to a sofa where more women with painted faces chatted and fanned themselves. "Meet Batya, my new little sister," Rochel declared. As each of the girls rose to kiss Batya's cheeks, three men came over. Batya cringed, hating their heady smell of tobacco and cognac, but Rochel seemed to enjoy their presence; she laughed and batted her eyelashes at them. "Checking out the new merchandise? Not yet. The poor thing has just arrived from Paris and needs to rest."

"Paris?" A man chuckled, and said in Yiddish, "You all wish you were like the Parisian courtesans. They're the best. But give me my old-fashioned Jewish girls, with a bit of horseradish."

"You like your gefilte fish, all right," Rochel cooed, and hit him playfully with a second fan she had withdrawn from between the sofa cushions. "You're naughty, but I like you."

Batya blushed at the bantering.

"Dimples," the man said to Rochel, "I'm your slave as long as you pull those tricks on me."

"Wait for me, then," she replied. "Don't go cheating on me with anyone else." She laced her fingers in Batya's. "Let me show you to your room."

Upstairs, she led Batya to a tiny chamber with a pink-flowered quilt covering the bed, lace curtains on the windows, and clean towels next to a ceramic washbasin on the dresser. Batya's blue taffeta and red dresses hung from hooks on the wall.

"We even have a lavatory inside the house, and a shower right here." Rochel led her down the hall and demonstrated how to start the shower by turning a lever. She gave Batya a bar of soap and a bottle of almond oil to use after she soaped her hair to untangle the knots. "Don't try eating or swallowing these. It won't do you any good, only give you a terrible stomachache." She pointed to a basket of sliced yellow fruit. "These are lemons. Squeeze some juice and brush it onto your hair every day. It will give it a gorgeous blond shine." She kissed both Batya's cheeks. "I wish I could stay to wash your hair, but I must work. Freda will be here shortly. She's the matron here, the manager. She's out at the market now. She barks, but her bites are not too bad. Just do as she tells you and you'll be fine."

"Thank you," Batya said, and held out the fan to Rochel.

"It's yours to keep. Open it."

Batya opened the fan and could now see the cream-colored ribs, each carved in a delicate flower design, separating silky cloth on which two exquisite turquoise and yellow birds faced each other, their wings spread. "It's magnificent," she whispered with awe.

"Ivory." Rochel pointed at the ribs. "From elephants in Africa."

What's an elephant, and where is Africa? The words seemed so foreign. There was so much Batya didn't know.

Rochel kissed both her cheeks and darted away.

Alone, Batya took off her clothes and stepped into the shower stall. The water was cold and soothing as morning dew and eased the pressure of the soup-like air. She let the water run over her. Her fingers were in the roots of her hair when she realized that to remove the filth, to cleanse herself from the sins that had stuck to her flesh, only immersion in a *mikveh* would do. Unmarried women—virgins—did not use the communal ritual bath, but she was neither married nor a virgin.

Batya tried to recall a prayer her mother uttered before immersing. God would understand that all she had was this running water. *"Dear God,"* Batya improvised, *"You created the world from a womb of water. You made me in Your image, pure and holy, according to Your will. As I immerse in the* mikveh *waters, I know that my life is sustained by Your mercy. Please pu-*

rify my life from pain and sorrow, from bad influences, from my own faults and inadequacies. As these waters embrace me, dear God, may I embrace Your presence at all times and in all space, Amen."

She was sobbing now, and her tears mingled with the water running over her. It took all her strength to wash her hair and brush the oil through it. Exhausted, in pain, and craving the inviting bed with its pink cover, she skipped the lemon treatment.

Upon returning to her room, Batya found a tray of warm food. The knish stuffed with chopped meat was like her mother's, only meatier. The fatty soup was thickened with red beans, but its spices stung her mouth. The grainy bread was fresh, and the chicken must have been cooked in a coal oven, as it carried its savory smoke flavor. Root vegetables she didn't recognize were heaped next to it, and when Batya tasted each, wary of the hot spice that had suffused the soup, they turned out to be delicious.

She had just lain down when a short, squat woman with dark skin, scraggy hair, and eyes buried under sagging lids brought her a slice of cinnamon cake and a cup of fragrant tea. No milk, of course. At least breaking this rule of kashrut wasn't one more sin on Batya's list. After she swallowed the cake, Batya prayed again. *"God, please make sure that one day soon I'll share the bounty of such food with my parents, Koppel and Zelda, and my sisters Keyla and Surale."* She would never mention Hedi the ghost along with the names of the living, or she'd draw the evil eye to them. *"Instead of my next meal, I ask that, in Your mighty power, You take my tray and fly it to them. I would be forever grateful. Amen."*

It was still light outside, and the house was filled with music and laughter, not crying like in Nina's house. Batya closed her eyes, dejected but curious about this new world. Had it been less than four weeks since she'd left Komarinoe? She hugged her pillow, trying to ignore the pulsating pain in her abdomen and praying that her parents would know the hug was meant for them.

Chapter Eighteen

*T*he next morning, after Batya's breakfast, a big-boned woman entered her room without knocking. Her hair was tied in a top bun so tight it pulled smooth the wrinkles around her eyes and on her forehead, while the bottom of her face remained grooved and slack.

"So you are the new girl? I hear that you're very sick." She sniffed as if testing the air in the room.

Batya sat up. This must be Freda.

"You're still a child." Freda's eyes raked Batya's body, then she tilted her head sideways as if assessing her. "Will you give me any trouble?"

Batya shook her head.

"Well, then. Come." She led Batya to a side kitchen yard separated by a wooden partition from the main back garden and its mosaic-paved terrace. A pot of melted wax sat on a charcoal brazier, and eight girls, their hair gathered and knotted on top of their heads, were busy grooming.

"Take care of her," Freda said to no one in particular, and walked away.

"Welcome," said one.

"You're Rochel's new little sister," said another.

"I'll be with you in a few minutes," said a plump girl in a cheerful voice.

Batya watched the nearest girl spread wax on another's leg, tap and blow on it for a few seconds, then yank it off to the shrieks of that girl and the laughter of the others. One girl with dark hair, whom the others called "the Armenian," had dark fuzz felting the entire length of her legs and arms. When her friend had her lie on her stomach and pull down her bloomers, Batya saw that the Armenian's buttocks, too, were hairy, like a man's. From the bantering, Batya understood that this girl required a full-body waxing every week.

Batya had never given the blond fuzz on her shins any thought until the plump girl bent down to examine her legs. She smiled at Batya as her fingers felt her leg hair. "Only from the knees down. We'll do your pubic hair after the doctor checks for bugs."

"Bugs?" Batya recalled with alarm the cockroaches in the bowels of the ship. "What kind of bugs?"

"*Mendeveshkes.* Pubic lice." The girl giggled. "They're so tiny you can't really see them. Do you itch?"

Batya shook her head. Her abdominal pain wasn't an itch. She shivered at the new dread. If bugs hid in the hair on her body, she wanted it all removed at once.

"I'm Nettie. Sit down here." The girl collected wax on a wooden stick. "You're beautiful."

Tears sprouted to Batya's eyes. After the cruelty of her recent days, the kindness of yet another stranger soothed her despair. "You're beautiful, too," she replied. Nettie's breasts were large and her limbs long. Her gray eyes smiled even when her mouth didn't. Batya liked her instantly. "Where are you from?"

"From a place I'd rather forget." Nettie spread warm wax on Batya's legs. "Aren't we all?"

Batya shook her head. "I miss my mother and father. And my sisters—"

Nettie cut her off. "My father sold me through a matchmaker, may her name be burned with that of Haman."

"The matchmaker helped sell you?"

"She knew that this man was a swine." Nettie yanked on the cooled wax, and Batya yelped. Nettie pressed her hand on the raw spot to soothe it. "Better?"

Her touch felt good. "Maybe the matchmaker lied to your father," Batya ventured. "They always try to make their clients look better."

"She told my father that the swine would pay *him* to take me as his 'wife.' Ha! What a joke! Everyone in the village had seen the man before. I was the third such 'wife' this matchmaker found for him. My father knew it when he brought two witnesses and without a rabbi gave me a worthless *shtile chuppah*. He took the money and was on his way to the tavern even before I left with my new 'groom.'"

Your father couldn't have imagined that your fate would be so bad, Batya wanted to say. Her father, too, had accepted Moskowitz's money, but he had been awed by the worldly man who would pull her out of their persecuted life. Even her no-nonsense mother had believed Batya would have a great future in America. And Batya would have, had it not been for Grabovsky.

Nettie broke into a whistle, and Batya looked at her puckered lips. She'd heard only *shaygetz,* non-Jewish scoundrels, whistling, never a maiden. Nettie grinned and pointed at her teeth. They were white and square, with a gap between the two front ones. "This is how I do it." She kept whistling, seemingly unperturbed by her memories, and Batya thought of Shayna's tragic orphanhood. She'd be careful not to ask Rochel about her past.

The girls turned their attention to their underarms and were soon squealing at the pain, laughing as they pulled off each other's hair.

At their shrieks, a window opened on the second floor of the house next door, and a woman shouted in that high-pitched clucking language. Before Batya knew what was happening, the woman had emptied a bucket of dirty water on them. Batya was hit in the face, and Nettie, with her back to that house, had her hair drenched. In the altercation that ensued, Batya guessed that the woman was complaining about the prostitutes. The houses were close to each other, and from her spot above, the woman must have been able to witness the goings-on in the patio and hear the activities in the bedrooms through the windows kept open in the summer heat.

A part of Batya's brain hung back, still numb and confused, as she rinsed and watched the girls hose themselves down. A few minutes later, their chatter and hilarity resumed. These girls were so different from the ones in Nina's training house. No shadow of her own self-loathing seemed to hang over them; no great suffering was embedded in their eyes or in a hunching of shoulders. No one seemed to prefer death.

When one of the girls turned to a new task—waxing off the Armenian's moustache and sideburns—Nettie produced a pair of tweezers. "Your eyebrows," she said to Batya.

"You're going to take off my eyebrows?" Batya asked.

"Just some areas. They are wild and unfashionable." Nettie smiled. "Wait till you see yourself after I'm done."

After ten minutes of plucking and yelping from Batya, Nettie presented her with a mirror. Batya stared at the young woman with thin arched eyebrows that indeed framed her eyes, making the green in them shine. As the sisters gathered to admire the results, Batya didn't dare say that she hated looking appealing to any man. She blushed at the attention, and tears threatened to erupt yet again. Pulling down her hair, she let it fall over her face to hide it.

Before noon a doctor arrived, and two dozen girls who weren't working lined up in front of one of the rooms. Freda led Batya to the head of the line and, once inside, instructed her to lie on the bed, legs splayed. To Batya's relief, Rochel came in to hold her hand.

The doctor stationed himself on a low stool at the bottom of the bed, adjusted a monocle into his eye socket, and looked between Batya's legs. A wave of humiliation swept over Batya at this new violation, and she brought her knees together. Without a word, the doctor swatted them apart and dug his fingers into her. He palpated soft spots inside, and Batya cried out at the searing pain.

"Tsk, tsk." The doctor shook his head sadly. "What do we have here?"

"She's leaking puss," Rochel said.

"I thought so," Freda said. "She stinks."

The doctor shook his head, ignoring Batya's cries of pain. He gave her thigh a light slap. "Stop moving."

Freda placed a short rope between Batya's teeth to bite on, and the doctor inserted something hard deep inside her. A moment later, fire exploded in her abdomen. Batya screamed and clutched her stomach.

Rochel grabbed her arms and raised them over her head. "Let him do his job," she whispered.

"Abscess." The doctor leaned back. "This requires surgery."

"It will cost too much. I'll just get her auctioned off," Freda replied.

"No, please!" Rochel grasped her hands in supplication. "Please. I'll pay."

Freda shrugged. "If you want." She opened the door and left.

"I need to finish seeing the others," the doctor said to Rochel. "I'll come back after the siesta."

"Shouldn't she be in the hospital?" Rochel asked.

"If you want to wait two or three months for surgery." He wrapped a felt piece around his monocle and placed it in a small case. "The infection is already spreading through her abdomen, as her fever indicates."

"Please come after your siesta." Rochel's tone turned playful. "I'll make sure it will be worth your while."

He pinched her cheek, stroked her buttock, and left.

The next few hours of waiting were excruciating as Batya's

fear swelled. At last, after a clock somewhere struck four, Rochel led her back into the same room where the doctor had checked her. He was laying instruments on a white cloth. Batya sat on the bed, a towel underneath her. She breathed hard through her mouth; her own stench was undeniable, but the doctor's instruments frightened her.

"Lie down," he ordered, and she used the last drop of her courage to obey. He raised her legs and buckled them to a metal frame with leather straps. Against her determination, she began to weep and shake.

"Can't you give her something?" Rochel asked the doctor.

"Opium will cost you." He filled a thimble-sized cup from a vial and handed it to her. "Have her drink this."

The tincture smelled like the sap Batya used to collect from the bark of trees in Russia to make glue, and its taste was bitter. She scrunched up her face, coughed, and pushed Rochel's hand away.

"I don't have all day." The doctor removed his monocle and glared at Batya. "You'd better drink it, or I'll go where I'm needed."

"Please," Rochel said to her. "You're lucky to have a doctor."

Batya swallowed the medicine, then rested her head back. Sniffling, she closed her eyes, awaiting the wave of pain.

Chapter Nineteen

*S*he wavered between consciousness and hallucination. It was daytime, then night. She heard the sounds of cicadas and the melody of haunting musical chords, maybe played by angels. Constellations of stars danced in the sky. She shivered in the Russian winter and burned in the Buenos Aires heat. Somewhere women laughed, chatted, argued, until the Siberian wind swept their voices away. She panicked in the bowels of the ship; rats and darkness attacked her, cut off her windpipe. Only the cool hand on her burning cheek comforted her. Her mother! She changed wet compresses on Batya's forehead and stuffed her private parts with cotton. She made Batya drink that bitter opium and promised she would be healed. Then Batya was Miriam, cut open, blood seeping from every rat's bite and pooling on soil too frozen to absorb it. Miriam, the friend she hadn't sufficiently mourned, laughing at Batya. "Who's better off?" Batya had felt guilty for surviving, until life wasn't worth surviving, and now she envied Miriam, murdered at the end of her ordeal.

Standing behind the flames of their burning home, levitating with the smoke, Hedi the ghost waved and cried out, "You must live to pull Mama and Papa out of their Russian hell. I was never given that choice." Her voice became Freda's. "We employ here only good prostitutes who are healthy and whole. This house has a reputation to uphold; we can't pass diseases to our clients."

Finally there was silence and comfort as all voices receded and Batya's body became so light that it floated up until God emerged from a lit tunnel. In the sudden respite from pain, He laid Batya's body on a bed of clouds, and she heard her father chat with Him. "I am Koppel, and I thank You for watching over my third daughter, my Batyale. The daughter You and I share."

A wave of shame washed over Batya at hearing her father's voice. She ordered him back to Russia, to never see his child in this state, in this place.

As Batya's fever subsided, she became aware of Rochel supporting her head and feeding her spoonfuls of chicken soup with *kneidlach*. And when Batya managed to swallow more, Rochel cut each airy matzo ball into tiny pieces and placed them in Batya's mouth. One day Nettie fed her cooked carrots mashed with butter, and a soft egg.

Then there was the day that Batya opened her eyes, her mind aligned to the present, and saw Rochel seated by her bed, her mouth moving in what seemed like a prayer.

"You're awake." Rochel squeezed her fingers. "Any pain?"

Batya shook her head. Her body was light with the absence of pain. In the periphery of her vision, a river of anguish drifted, but for the moment she couldn't recall what it was about.

"The doctor cut off the abscess. A sac of it, you poor thing, but now you'll have no more leaking pus," Rochel said. "Luckily, he said, there was no chancre—that's a sore that indicates that you've caught the French disease."

"What's that?" Batya's voice was a whisper.

"You shouldn't know from it. First it consumes your body with sores, then turns you *meshuge*." She paused. "Girls who catch it are sent away, and when they become mad, they're just left to die."

"I can't thank you for your kindness. Only God will be able to repay you." A quiver ran in Batya's voice. "But you should have let me die."

Rochel stroked Batya's hair. "It's not a bad life here. The sisters will help you adjust. We cook together, take care of one another, we laugh, we dance." Batya was about to drift back into her oblivion, when Rochel's next words jolted her back. "You were also pregnant. From now on, we'll make sure your clients use a safeguard."

Pregnant? Of course. Her monthly flow hadn't arrived in the bowels of the ship. Grief swept over Batya. A baby—most likely Moskowitz's—had started growing inside her. It had been alive and was now dead. If only she could have died with it, because if Moskowitz was ever to forgive her sins and rescue her, this was one he could never overlook.

A couple of hours later, Batya woke up again, to pain. "Please, make the pain go away," she wept to Nettie, now at her bedside. "Please ask Rochel to give me that miraculous bitter potion."

Rochel came in and looked down at Batya, as if assessing her, then produced the tiny vial. Very little of the tincture was left. As Batya licked her lips for every drop, Rochel said, "This is the last opium I give you, or your body will get too used to it. It costs a fortune."

Batya put her head back as the effect of the few drops spread through her.

When the doctor came to check on her a couple of days later, he palpated her insides.

Freda crossed her arms over her large belly. "Is she ready to work?"

"The entry is almost healed, but she's not ready inside. Her young body fought the infection once. We don't want her getting infected again, do we?" He still didn't address Batya. "I'll remove the stitches next week. We'll see then."

Batya had no time to be grateful for the small reprieve. Freda fixed an angry stare on her. "Before you waste any more time, cost us food, and bring nothing but disruption to this house, we'll use the time to instruct you."

At lunchtime, Rochel entered, bringing a tray of corn empanadas and a piece of meat doused with green sauce. "You must eat meat to enrich your blood. It will make you heal faster." She pointed to the green sauce. "Eat this, too. It's called chimichurri and it's made of healing herbs."

There was also a new vegetable, eggplant, whose smoky flavor Batya liked.

"Nettie and I, we'll teach you all the tricks," Rochel said, while Batya ate. "In time, you'll have your regulars."

Batya stopped chewing. She looked at her new friend. Rochel had been so kind, so caring—even paying with her own money for the surgery and the opium.

"I'm not going to do it," she whispered. She glanced toward the door to ensure that Rochel had closed it. "I have—I had—a fiancé. He'll come for me soon."

"You do?" Rochel eyed her, doubt written in her raised brow. "And would he still come for you after he learns of—of everything?"

Batya shrugged, unsure of the answer. She inserted into her voice all the conviction she could muster as she said, "He's kind. At least he'll take me out of here and get me a decent job. But if I 'play by the rules,' as you call it, he will think it's in my character."

Rochel stroked her hair. "Until he comes to rescue you, give this house a chance. In time you'll learn Spanish and—"

"What's that?"

"What's what?"

"Spanish."

"Silly. That's the language they speak here in Argentina. You'll learn it from the clients, from the merchants, from the neighbors. In time you'll forget about your life in the shtetl."

"I'll never forget my parents!" Batya cried out wildly. "I'm supposed to bring them here, with my youngest sister."

"If you work hard and are nice to your clients, you can save money." Rochel stood up and extended her hand. "After you wash up, get dressed and come downstairs to meet the sisters."

"May I have opium first?"

Rochel shook her head. "I gave it to you for pain. It's very expensive. Now you must either earn enough to buy it yourself or force your body to forget about it. If you want my advice, it's bad for you."

Batya dropped her face into her hands. She craved the lightness that opium brought her, when she forgot both the clients awaiting her and her death wish because of them. But if she ever had any money, she would need it to get her parents out of Russia.

When she still claimed to be too weak to rise from her bed, Rochel said, "Let me give you a sponge bath." Gently, she helped Batya out of her nightshirt, then, with a small touch, indicated for her to lie back.

She left the room briefly and returned with a bowl of warm soapy water. Before she began washing Batya, she passed the tips of her fingers along Batya's arm. Then the other. "It feels nice, doesn't it?" With the lightest touch she stroked Batya's legs, down her thighs and shins, and ended at her toes.

She pressed a round yellow sponge to Batya's cheek, so she could feel its softness, then dipped it in the water, squeezed out the excess, and passed it along Batya's collarbones. She stroked down her middle, then circled her breasts, staying away from the hardened nipples.

New sensations rose in Batya's body. Urging, confusing. She willed them to stop as Rochel's ministering continued, never reaching any of the parts violated by the men.

The water in the bowl chilled. Rochel covered Batya's body with a sheet, then bent toward her. "It's enough for now," she whispered. Her puff of breath in Batya's ear was warm, sending a shiver of pleasure through her body. When Batya opened her eyes, Rochel extended her hand. "Ready to get up?"

Batya sat up and took Rochel's hand. Pressing it to her face, she took comfort in the touch of security and friendship.

Chapter Twenty

*I*t was ten more days before the doctor declared Batya well. In those long days and nights, Batya was instructed in the ways of the flesh, learning from her own sensations what would please another person. "There's so much to the body," Rochel said, and took turns with Nettie explaining and demonstrating ways to delight men.

Every day Nettie covered Batya's hair with lemon pulp to lighten it, and had her sit in the sun for an hour before rinsing it off. While Batya was outside, Nettie made sure that the rest of her body was covered so that the sun wouldn't darken her porcelain-pale skin. Nevertheless, Batya's cheeks, now filled from good food, acquired a warm glow.

Nettie's cheerfulness seemed unbounded. She was always whistling or chattering. "You can break your back in Russia working in the field from dawn to dusk or, if you're lucky, be shackled to a sewing machine in a dark sweatshop, choking on lint, not even allowed to talk." She paused. "I knew a girl who lost her arm in a factory. Is that what you want?" She brushed Batya's hair in long strokes to make the blond streaks shine. "Or you can have fun in Buenos Aires and dance every day. You can have your own room, get your siesta, and chat and laugh. You can eat mangos and bananas and sing along with the birds." Her voice turned to a whisper. "Not only do you make money, but you get gifts. When in our old lives did we imagine such wealth?"

Still standing behind Batya, Nettie hugged her from behind, and the ache of Batya's loneliness on the ship felt as if it had taken place eons before.

One afternoon, Freda summoned Batya and walked her past some girls lining up in front of an office off the corridor on the ground floor. Batya noticed the excitement as the girls chattered, but she had no time to ask questions as Freda led her inside.

A long-limbed man with a shock of gray hair, whose spectacles rested on his hooked nose, sat at the desk. In front of him rested an inkwell and a plume like the one the scribe in the shtetl had used.

"The Professor will write a letter for you to your family," Freda said. "Give him their address so we can also send them money."

Send them money! The words were sweet to Batya's ears. "Will you give them my address so they can write me back?" She hoped her family hadn't moved again, or she'd never find them.

"I'll take care of it," the Professor replied.

Doubt hit her. "What will you tell them?"

"Only good things," Freda said, and escorted Batya out.

"Next time you'll be allowed to dictate the letter to your family," Rochel told her. "He'll embellish it beautifully."

She had no good news, Batya thought. Whatever was happening to her needed more than embellishment.

One night, as she lay in bed, listening to the exotic music that rose from below, the laughter of the sisters, the groans and sighs from other rooms, a thought hit Batya. How would Moskowitz be able to track her down? Grabovsky wouldn't be forthcoming in revealing what he'd done. She must seek out the city rabbi, who would no doubt know Yitzik Moskowitz, a most prominent citizen. Maybe the rabbi would hide her until her former fiancé—hopefully still her benefactor—arrived. Moskowitz would surely reward him, just as he had donated so generously to the synagogue in the Russian shtetl.

How could she find the rabbi? Even if she snuck out of the house, she couldn't venture alone into the frightening maze of this foreign city. She would have no idea which way to go, and no way to ask for directions to the real Buenos Aires.

Right after the afternoon siesta—the rest time most of the girls took during the hottest hours of the afternoon unless occupied by clients—the sisters were drinking yerba maté tea, which Batya was growing to like. The musicians had just arrived and were tuning their instruments. Rochel gestured to Batya, and the two of them took their gourds of drink to the patio, along with plates of cakes drenched with dulce de leche that tasted as delicious as the chocolate Moskowitz had introduced her to.

The two of them settled at a round metal table with a tiled top, and Rochel lit a cigarette. "Want one?" She offered the gold case to Batya.

Batya adored the elegant way Rochel held her cigarette at the end of her long ivory holder, but the two times Batya had tried smoking, she had broken into coughing fits that brought up bile. "No, thanks." She sucked her maté through its straw and pondered which she liked more, this bitter tea or the strong coffee with its grainy texture sweetened by three spoons of sugar.

"Smoking is good for your digestion. It also improves the skin tone and dries up pimples." Rochel puffed out practiced rings of smoke.

"Maybe later." Batya eyed the clay planters along the garden fence, with their gigantic flowers in luscious reds, yellows, and oranges. Beyond them, in the soil by the fence, grew low leafy plants in various shades of green, some with long, striped leaves, others with rounded clusters in dark hues. She wished she were permitted to help the Chinese gardener who came every morning to weed and water. She would have loved to feel the moist earth between her fingers, to plant seedlings that would grow into magnificent plants.

Everything here was beautiful. The flowers, the food, the songbirds, the pavilion, her chamber, the friendships. If only the price weren't beyond her capability. She looked across the table at her friend. "It's my great-grandmother's yahrzeit," she began, "and I would like to ask the rabbi to say a prayer for the anniversary of her death."

Rochel burst out laughing, and her dark curls bounced on her shoulders. "I was wondering how long it would take you." As Batya felt her eyes narrow in confusion, Rochel explained. "Every other girl who arrives here looks for an excuse to see a rabbi." She reached over and held Batya's hand, pity in her eyes. "There are more rabbis in this city than synagogues. There are some wretched rabbis whose congregations were destroyed by pogroms, who are now roaming the streets and muttering to themselves, as if God would finally listen to them. You'd think they would have sympathy for us, God's lost sheep, right? Wrong. None want anything to do with the likes of us. We're *tme'ot*. Sullied." She chuckled. "Though not polluted enough to keep at least two of them from coming here regularly to dip in our honey."

So much for her new plan. "Don't they have wives?" Batya asked.

"This is a country of men. Hundreds of thousands of them arrive alone to make their fortunes here. Italian. Spanish. Jewish. *Compadritos,* you name them." Rochel tossed her hair back in a gesture Batya now recognized. "Some leave wives and children behind. Most are still single. Some men have wives who are just tired or are too busy with children. No matter. They all need women, and we are here."

Batya thought of her father. There must be decent men like him here, too. "Don't they think it is immoral?"

Rochel laughed. "I've told you that this is America. It's a modern culture, not backward like Russia. Get it into your head that things here are much more advanced." She paused. "Thirty years ago, prostitutes here were all black- and brown-skinned women. But men prefer us, white women from Eastern Europe. Some businessmen saw an opportunity and began kidnapping girls." She reached across the table and fluffed the ends of Batya's hair, which fell past her shoulders. "You are blond. The most in demand."

Batya sipped her maté. There were so many new things of

which to make sense. She thought of Nettie's story. She thought of Grabovsky stealing her from Moskowitz, who would never find her. "All the sisters here were kidnapped?"

Rochel shrugged. "Some arrived on their own, alone, seeking husbands, adventures, jobs, or gold in the street. What difference does it make? We all end up in the same place. There's nothing else for a woman alone. What's important is *what* we do with what fate deals us."

Nettie approached their table, whistling a tune. Her full mane of hair was held back by a dozen small clips fashioned with butterflies, birds, and flowers. A medallion shaped like a bird hung from her neck, its long tail nestled in her generous cleavage. Nettie, who had no family, had not only accepted this life but was happy through every moment of it.

"Come. Dance with me." She extended her hand to Batya and led her inside, to the center of the room. As the musician played, she taught Batya the first square step of the brazen dance Batya had observed the day of her arrival. "We call the Yiddish version of tango *tangele*," she said. "It's a dance not only of the feet but of your entire body, of your soul." Nettie adjusted Batya's torso, shoulders, and lower spine. "Control your posture, follow the lead of my chest, and put nuance into your hips. Keep your shoulders square, and use your stomach muscles to transfer energy into your legs."

"All at the same time?"

Nettie smiled. "One, two, three, four, five, six, seven, eight." She showed Batya the basic walk in all directions, and then, holding Batya close, began to sing along with the band.

On a clear summer's day.
As always so beautifully sunny.
When nature filled with so much charm.
Birds were singing on treetops
Cheerfully hopped about,
While we were ordered into exile.

"Are we dancing to a pogrom song?" Batya asked, struggling to keep up. "We should be crying."

Nettie giggled. "It's our new version of Yiddish culture in Argentina. Forward, back, step to the right, now left. Stay close to me so you can feel what I do—"

"Rochel said that tango songs are romantic—about lovers and heartbreaks."

"That, too." Nettie went on singing as the music gathered force.

Oh, we knew not what would become of us!
We understood all is lost.
Our pleas were of no help
Asking for friends to rescue us,
We had to flee our home.

With each line, Nettie changed direction. She indicated to Batya to whirl halfway around, caught her, then moved her in a half circle the other way. "Make a figure eight with your feet," she told Batya. "It's called *ocho*."

When the song ended, Batya asked, "How can the murdering of Jews be sung and danced to?"

"This is what happens to sadness once it reaches Argentina.

We can either cry about the past or laugh about the future. So we drown out the old pain in dance. A good lesson, don't you think?" The side of Nettie's foot pressed against Batya's, and she showed her how to interpret the cue by responding with a half pivot. "Stay connected to the leader—that's me—and let the music flow through you."

Over the next few days, Batya found herself looking forward to the afternoon. Rotating bands of musicians brought to the pavilion the new quick sounds of polka violin, driving flamenco guitar, and the strange mournful jangle of the banjo. In the poor shtetl, no one could afford klezmers. This music, the first to fill her life, was an opulence of America that no one had spoken of when they'd fantasized about streets paved with gold.

Batya savored this richness as she did the many sweet cakes. Tango had order and discipline. In her chaotic new life, she could control her steps, even though within every exuberant move there loomed the certainty that this freedom would soon end.

Chapter Twenty-One

*T*onight would be her debut. There was no escaping it. She had been living in the brothel and had heard enough to know that if she refused to work, Grabovsky would show up to discipline her or, worse, Freda would sell her to one of the miserable brothels somewhere in vast Argentina. She would be separated from her new friends, lonely and anchorless as she'd been since leaving her parents. One nauseating choice chased another nauseating choice, with no cure for either.

"Stop crying," Rochel told Batya when she came into her room. "You can't have swollen eyes." She hugged her, then placed compresses of chamomile tea on Batya's lids.

Freda entered, holding a pencil. "Show me how you hold it."

Batya blushed, understanding the house matron's meaning; Rochel and Nettie had had her practice.

"Well? I don't have all day."

Batya peeled off her bloomers, accepted the pencil and tucked it up inside her. She squeezed hard. The pencil didn't fall to the floor.

"Walk," Freda ordered, and Batya complied. The pencil stayed put.

Freda rose, extended her hand for the pencil. "Each client will give you a token he buys from me. That's your receipt for service. Every week you give me the tokens and I give you a share of your earnings." To Rochel she said, "Get her ready."

As soon as she closed the door behind her, Rochel burst out laughing. "She wouldn't pass the test herself, that old hag."

Batya forced a smile. Nothing about what awaited her was amusing.

Rochel pulled a candle and a box of matches from a cloth bag. She lit the first match, blew it out, waited a few seconds, then began to paint a line along Batya's upper right eyelid. She continued burning matches and painting until Batya's eyelids stung from the ash. Rochel took a step back. "Gorgeous," she declared. "Wait till you see yourself in the mirror—but not yet." She opened a small jar and dabbed red powder on Batya's cheeks, then, using a thin brush and some waxy substance, painted her lips.

When she finally permitted Batya to peer in the mirror, she grinned so widely with pride that Batya suppressed her shock at the woman—not a girl—who stared back at her. She wanted to wipe the paint off her face. "It's not me," she whispered.

"Better that you feel this way. You'll be able to distance yourself." Rochel spread Batya's blue taffeta dress on the floor and opened its center. "Pretend you're an actress onstage. You can also choose a different name."

Batya had never seen an actress, nor a stage. "What kind of a different name?"

"Something Spanish. Let's find a name that's not already taken." She ticked off a list of strange names as she helped Batya into her dress. "I got it. Esperanza. We haven't had an Esperanza for a while. It means 'hope.'"

Hope was a good word. "Es-pe-ran-za," Batya said slowly, uttering the unfamiliar syllables. "Esperanza."

Nettie entered to check on their progress, carrying a feather boa.

"Meet Esperanza," Rochel said.

Nettie twirled the boa around herself and pivoted twice. "A good name. With a name like Batya, Jewish men would think they're screwing their mother or sisters."

Rochel sighed. "She's gained weight. I can't button the dress."

Nettie dropped her boa around Rochel's neck and pulled at Batya's dress herself. "Let me see what I can do." She left and returned moments later with scissors, a suicide tool that was never left unattended around Batya, and a wide silk ribbon. She slit the back of the waist to release the fabric and tied the ribbon as a belt to cover the gap. Then she adjusted the front, lifting most of Batya's breasts out of the confines of the dress to form a cleavage Batya had never had before.

"Go get them," Nettie said, and clapped her hands.

"Make money to bring your family out of Russia," Rochel whispered.

Her first evening. Not a captive chained to the bed, but a captive nonetheless.

Batya thought of the lessons her friends had taught her—how

to tie a man down with silk scarves, or disrobe playfully—and couldn't reconcile them with the person she was. She certainly would never use her tongue and fingers all at once the way the sisters had shown her. Perhaps Esperanza would be able to initiate such acts. It would be Batya, though, who would remember to douche with vinegar between clients, to cleanse herself of the filth.

She stood at the bottom of the stairs, clutching the railing. The pavilion was in her full view, yet her feet refused to move toward it. *I can't do it.*

A slap on her bottom jolted her, and she heard Freda's gravelly voice behind her. "Get going."

Cold fear radiated from Batya's center. She walked to the sofa and sat down, angling herself toward the window to dry the perspiration forming on her back, forehead, and underarms. At least she was wearing a dress, marking her as the new addition to the house. The sisters wore skimpier clothing, mostly silk bloomers and short slips that hid little or nothing, or chains of beads that streamed from necks to navels over exposed breasts.

"I got a virgin for you," she heard Freda tell a man with a bald head, dressed in a cream-colored suit. He glanced in Batya's direction and nodded. Though he looked like an average man of means, he seemed frightening. During the negotiation that ensued out of Batya's earshot, she pressed her back to the corner of the couch, wishing to make herself invisible.

Freda must have asked too much, because the man declined and moved on to select another sister. Freda shot Batya a look, elongating her own neck to indicate that Batya should straighten up. The matron had been the one to teach her about the reusable rubber prophylactic she sold to new customers who failed to bring their own, custom-fashioned by their physicians. "If anyone refuses to use it, you call me," Freda had instructed. "We don't allow diseases in this house."

Rochel poked Batya gently. "Smile," she whispered, and pulled her lips wide, deepening her dimples. "Make your eyes bright. Look interested."

"I'm so scared," Batya replied from behind her fan. She must have been fanning not in the beguiling way she'd been taught, because Rochel touched her wrist to slow her down.

Just then a huge bug flew into Batya's face. She screamed and swatted it onto the floor. A wave of panic climbed up her throat. Cockroaches, each as large as a man's thumb, had been turning up on the kitchen floor; she'd seen them skittering in and out of the street sewer from her second-floor window. They brought her back to the darkness in the bowels of the ship, except that this Buenos Aires breed could also fly.

At Freda's warning glance, Batya composed herself. She searched the floor for the bug and was lifting her feet to avoid it when a man approached. He bent and caught the cockroach, then, holding it in front of Batya's face, crushed it between his fingers. The scrunching sound and greenish juice brought bile up Batya's throat, but when the man leered and put the dead, oozing bug on his tongue, she blanched and clamped her hand on her mouth to stop herself from vomiting.

She had barely collected herself when the man exchanged a quick word with Freda, and then returned and extended his hand to Batya.

Batya remained rooted to her spot, terror filling her head with images. Having just eaten the bug, would the man kiss her on the mouth?

Rochel gently elbowed Batya's side. "Pretend you don't mind about the cockroaches or he'll torture you with them," her friend whispered in Yiddish as Batya rose to her feet.

Rochel wasn't in the pavilion when Batya descended the steps, but Nettie handed her a glass of chilled, sweetened lemonade with mint leaves. Batya took a sip, then rolled the cold glass against her burning forehead.

She had cried when she cleansed herself not only from the cockroaches running on her naked body, but more so from the man's delight at torturing her. No token was worth it. She hated having to treat him pleasantly when every fiber in her body recoiled, when all she wanted, yet again, was to die.

Four sisters embraced her and led her to the sofa. Batya drank a second glass of lemonade to push down waves of nausea and fought back another bout of tears. Freda was watching her.

For the sake of the men around them, the girls pretended to giggle. Batya lowered her head and reached her arm up, as if she were fixing her hair, her elbow blocking Freda from her view.

"Everyone knows this client, and she charged him double the rate." Nettie stroked Batya's arm. "He enjoys the uninitiated girls who show fear. Pretend you like it until the next new girl takes him off your hands."

"Don't mind Freda. The old hag wishes she could have a man between her legs," a sister whispered in Batya's ear.

"She pays the delivery boys to service her," chimed another.

Their gossip was interrupted by a joyful squealing. Batya looked up. A man who'd just entered the room was surrounded by a group of welcoming sisters. Sitting low, Batya had only the view of their backs—until he stepped forward.

It was Moskowitz. He had found her!

Batya jumped off her seat, almost spilling her drink, and was about to rush over when she stopped in her tracks. She had just been initiated with her own consent. She had allowed her soul to be sullied. Yet, looking at him before he'd spotted her, his solicitous smile directed at the girls around him, she knew that she'd never stopped believing that he was her salvation. Compared with the brutality she'd suffered since their separation, his violation of her seemed mild—and had been accompanied by kindness. Even the dress she was wearing now had been his gift.

"Reb Moskowitz! Reb Moskowitz!" she cried out, returning to the honorific "reb" she hadn't used since their first night on the road. Pushing through the circle of girls, Batya flung herself onto him.

"My dear." He guided her into the corridor, away from everyone's sight. "You look beautiful."

No, she didn't. She felt both her eyes and nose running, smearing her makeup. It no longer mattered. What was important now was to convince him to take her away from here. She wiped her nose with the back of her hand and clutched his arm. "I must tell you what happened. It's not my fault—I was beaten and locked up and—"

"But you're all right now, right?" The sound of his familiar, honeyed voice warmed her heart. "Have you been well-fed, as I promised?"

"Yes, but— No!" she cried out. "Let me explain—"

"My dear, everything will be all right now."

She tried to control the panic in her voice. "I understand why you no longer want to marry me, but I beg you to take me to your sister's house. I'll be a good maid. You saw how I worked at the tavern." Her voice was shrill to her own ears.

"Shhhhhhh. Listen to me." He pulled her into the office where the Professor had written the letters, put both arms on her shoulders, and looked deep into her eyes. "I've had a business reversal. I owe money. Would you mind helping me?"

"Me?" She was relieved that he talked to her, that he wasn't shunning her. He even sought her help! "Anything."

"Good. Stay here, then."

"Stay here? In this house of prostitution?" At that moment— one she would recall many times later—it dawned on her that many of the sisters had greeted him. They knew him. He knew this place well. Yet, shouldn't it be expected from a healthy man still searching for a bride?

He touched her cheek with the tips of his fingers. "Just for a while, until I get my affairs in order."

The genial smile, the concern in his eyes, hadn't dimmed. Did he believe that she was like the rest of these women? He knew that she had come from a good home—poor but decent, where both her parents had been lucky to still be alive. How could he wish her to be a prostitute?

Batya's head was buzzing. Of all the scenarios she'd churned in her imagination, none had involved Reb Moskowitz knowing what would happen to her. Even now, her mind refused to accept what it was telling her. Reb Moskowitz couldn't have initiated her kidnapping. Of course he couldn't have. Yet— "Where's that rich sister of yours?" she asked.

"Freda is my sister. Hasn't she been teaching you, just as I promised?"

Batya swatted away the hand resting on her shoulder and stepped back from him, her palms rising in front of her to fend off the evil eye. Her throat constricted. "You knew?" she whispered, still hoping he would deny it.

His hand swept toward the pavilion past the corridor. "All these girls? I took them out of the hell of Poland, Latvia, Ukraine, Belarus, Lithuania, Hungary, and Russia, and gave each one of them a better life. They are all grateful, and so should you be. For the first time in your life you aren't starving, right?"

Batya's mind ticked off the women she'd met. Nettie had told her about "the swine" who'd taken her as his third wife. Others had hinted at being tricked with the promises of jobs in the homes of Jewish families. Rochel said women had been kidnapped. Others had been "married" in a worthless *shtile chuppah* without a rabbi. All to Moskowitz?

A wave of despair took Batya's breath away, and she crumpled to the floor.

Part II

Buenos Aires, 1893–1894

The night gleams at me in the dark,
Gray and cold;
Terrifying corpse-shadows
Fill up my void soul.

Fearful of death, I look all around
For a glimmer, a spark somewhere!
I stare and, creeping, crawl
Ever nearer to the door.

—Yiddish poem by Zelda Knizhnik, 1900

Chapter Twenty-Two

Spring 1893

$\mathscr{B}$etter that I should open the letter for you," Freda said to Batya, holding a stained envelope that, like all the letters before it, had been passed through many hands over many months. "I should read it for you."

Batya trembled with the desire to grab the letter and rush to her room. She still couldn't—wouldn't—reveal that she could read. That secret had grown larger these past four years. It dwelled where her true self resided, untouched, her last hold of pride—and a thread of a promise. It was the part of her that clung to life against all the many hours of despair.

A letter from her family reminded her why she was still alive.

Sisters crowded around her. News was news, and a letter—no matter from whom it came and to whom it was addressed—was exciting and so rare. Many girls had lost touch with their families in Eastern Europe. The victims of frequent pogroms, families dispersed or perished, never to be heard from again.

Without waiting for Batya's approval, Freda snaked a thick finger under the fold of one side and tore into the paper. Batya cringed. *Careful,* she wanted to say, but didn't dare.

The sisters squeezed closer as Freda's eyes scanned the page. She sighed. "Your mother died."

"What?" The word sent a lightning rod through Batya. *Died?* "How? What happened?"

"In childbirth. Five months ago. You have a baby sister. Vida. Congratulations."

Died. Too stunned to cry, Batya took the letter and stumbled upstairs. When Rochel took a step to accompany her, Batya shook her head. "Later."

In her room, finally alone, she read the letter. Her father's familiar handwriting spoke to her through his grief. Clutching the single page, Batya fell on the bed. Her tears soaked her pillow until she thought she had none left.

Five months earlier. All this time she'd had no premonition. No tingling down her neck had signaled that her mother was watching her from above.

She needed to pray, to plead with God for her mother's departed soul. Girls didn't say kaddish, the prayer for the dead, but there had been another women's prayer her mother had recited for her own deceased mother from her collection of Yiddish women's prayers, *tkhines.* Yet the words were elusive. For four years Batya had been trying to remember some of her mother's utterings. She had been too young or too busy—or, Batya now admitted, too uninterested—to have memorized them. She had failed to anticipate how short her time with her mother would be. Now she regretted her ignorance.

She walked to her dresser and withdrew a small packet of letters tied in a red ribbon. Had she not kept the letters in her dresser, a snooping sister might suspect another hiding place. Six letters in all had come through these past four years, and probably as many others had been lost. She braced herself as she took out the one letter she had read only once, for she couldn't bear the pain of it. Her refusal to bring Surale to Buenos Aires had left her father baffled, but her mother didn't save her tongue when she asked her husband to admonish the daughter who had dashed their hopes, all the while bragging about her good fortune.

Your mother asks how you can deny your sister the chance to find happiness and riches with a good husband like yours. I know that you are not selfish, but your mother can see no other reason for your denying your flesh and blood. You know Surale's good heart, as pure as the fresh snow and as generous as late summer dandelions. As the Good Book says, she would have turned mountains on their heads to help you.

Batya had cried then, and cried again now. "Forgive me, Mama. Now that you are in heaven, you see for yourself. You know the truth of the fate I wanted to spare my little sister. I risked your wrath out of my love for her. Please forgive me and love me again, wherever you are now."

When Rochel knocked on the door, Batya let her in and fell into her arms. "I need to pray for my mother's soul but don't know how."

"But I do. We'll have our own minyan."

Encroaching on men's spiritual territory was heretical. Women weren't allowed to imitate the religious service that required ten men for public prayer, but Batya needed all her friends' comfort. Clutching her father's latest letter, on which the ink had smeared from his tears—and now from her own—she could hardly speak her gratitude.

It was late afternoon, and clients were filling the pavilion below. Rochel managed to gather eight more sisters in Batya's room.

"Where's Nettie?" Batya asked her.

"Resting. Let's begin."

Recently, the light had dimmed in Nettie's eyes. For weeks she had been forlorn, her joyful whistle silenced. Sometimes her mouth slackened; other times, her breath slowed down and she seemed confused. Just the week before Batya had noticed that one of Nettie's regulars had selected a newcomer, Ariana, a petite blue-eyed girl who exhibited the vivaciousness Batya had always appreciated in Nettie.

In spite of Batya's entreaties, Nettie had refused to see a doctor. She was fine, she insisted.

There was no time to get Nettie now. In a few minutes the sisters must rush back to work.

Rochel began chanting. *"May God remember the soul of Batya's mother, Zelda, daughter of Tova, who has gone to the next world. May her soul be bound with the souls of our Mothers—Sarah, Rebekah, Rachel, and Leah. May she not be judged by her daughter's wanton ways and be permitted to join all the righteous men and women in the Garden of Eden. Amen."*

"Amen."

The sisters scattered when Freda arrived. To Batya's surprise, Freda, who checked a girl's menstruation pads to allow a single-day break only if the flow was heavy enough to upset the clients, pronounced that Batya must take the week off for the decreed shiva, seven days of mourning. "It's a mitzvah never to be broken," she said, and handed Batya a modest black dress with a black collar. "Tear only the collar to show your grief," she ordered, "not the rest of the dress."

Batya covered the mirror in her chamber and folded blankets on the floor for visiting sisters to sit down on, as mourners weren't supposed to enjoy the comfort of chairs. Relishing the feel of being fully covered by the black dress, she curled up on the blankets. Fresh tears streamed down the side of her face. It was liberating to no longer keep secrets from her mother. Now that Rochel had performed the ceremony and her mother had been accepted in heaven, Batya felt less alone.

Lying in the semidarkness, for once certain that no client would enter her chamber, she was free to transmit questions to her mother on subjects never before even hinted at. Had her mother ever felt the sexual rapture that Batya had grown to enjoy? Not with all clients, certainly, but in her first year, with Rochel's and Nettie's guidance to her body's secrets, with the sisters' frank talks about their trade and the sensuous and seductive tango, something had bloomed in Batya. By the time she celebrated her sixteenth birthday, sometimes passion rose in her to an unimaginably pleasurable pitch.

Clients often complained about their unresponsive wives, and the sisters speculated that married women were given to other pleasures in their lives to make up for the drought of their flesh. Had her mother's body, forever burdened by worries and exhausted by physical labor, ever experienced sexual sensations underneath the layers of clothing she removed only in the *mikveh*—a body her mother had never even glimpsed in a mirror?

Hours later, Batya stood at the open window, unable to sleep. The monotonous screeching of cicadas was broken by the hoot of an owl. The full moon, now on her side of the sky, bathed the street in silver, and she imagined her father and sisters watching the same moon even though it wasn't possible, not in this upside-down world called Argentina. Dawn in the southern hemisphere, Rochel had long explained, was dusk in Russia. Perhaps in a few hours, in Russia, when the moon shone full and yellow like a wheel of cheese, her father and Surale would be thinking of her, comforting themselves with the myth that she was the only one of them living a *tsures*-free life, that no troubles plagued her. With Keyla in Siberia still visiting her husband once a month and Hedi forever the ghost, Surale must be the one taking care of the orphaned Vida and managing their father's house. Five months ago, they had been united in their sorrow, but by now they were back to their daily struggles. Batya was alone in her grief.

She replaced the letter in the stack and reread the first one to have arrived. How well she remembered that day, Passover eve— her fifteenth birthday. The Seder was the first time she'd seen the house closed for business. Huge tables were set in the pavilion for all the sisters, and a wayward rabbi invited to retell the story of the Jews' exodus from Egypt. Together, they chanted the familiar songs of deliverance. The decreed bitter herbs of slavery Batya had eaten that night were the most bitter she had tasted, and the *charoset* the sweetest, as her heart had shared both of these symbols with her family.

Thank you for your gift of money, that first letter read. *We were able to buy a new stove, thank Hashem, and a traveling rabbi has blessed it, so it should serve us faithfully until the age of one hundred and twenty. I mean, your mother's and my one twenty, of course, not the stove's.*

There's another matter I consulted the Good Lord whether to tell you, and He advised me to do so. You see, your intended, the revered Reb Moskowitz, has fallen victim to a crook, and I ask that you warn him: When I finally found a money changer willing to break down the one-hundred ruble bill that Reb Moskowitz had forced upon me and your good mother, the money changer laughed us out of his store. The bill was fake. Please warn your groom that when it comes to his business associates, he should remember to employ the "honor him, yet suspect him" rule, as the Good Book teaches us.

An old lump swelled up in Batya's throat. Her hatred toward Moskowitz had long grown as big as if it were another organ in her body. A curse she had heard her mother direct at the czar surfaced: *May he hang himself with a sugar rope and have a sweet death.* The man had no soul. If she could yank out his heart and throw it to the dogs, it would have still failed to satisfy her desire for retribution.

For her second letter home, months later, Batya had sat with the Professor and told him to write that she was in good health and eating well. Batya regretted that when Fishke had run off with Keyla too soon, it had left her able to read but not yet ready to write full sentences. Indeed, when the Professor read Batya's letter back to her, his lyrical descriptions of her well-being and rich food were written in a flowery language she would never have been able to emulate. In subsequent letters, the Professor reported about her marriage—earlier than initially planned, at fifteen. The Professor built fantastic tales of her successful union with the devoted groom who covered her in silk gowns and jewels, of her pantries filled with provisions she shared generously with the poor, and of the Garden of Eden–like beauty of Buenos Aires.

Batya had been grateful for the fables, even if she could never be forgiven for the lies. Telling her parents the truth would have killed them. There was nothing her simple dairyman father could have done to help her from across mountains and oceans.

Batya had long figured out that letters like hers, sent all over Eastern Europe and accompanied by gifts of money, ensured that word of the girls' good fortune would spread. The pimps, who called their organization Zwi Migdal, often traveled back to their home countries to offer poor Jewish women great jobs as shopgirls, governesses for children, or companions for aging Jewish matrons—or better yet, to "marry" them. Batya suspected that her mother's envious tales of Pesha's daughter, who had lived in Germany in luxury and bathed in hot springs, had made her mother more inclined to accept Moskowitz's offer. *May a fish bone get stuck in his throat.* No wonder Pesha's daughter sent money to her mother but never brought her out of Russia to live with her.

Batya reread her father's latest letter, mourning his wife. *What is a wife for if not to keep a man in his place?* he wrote, and Batya thought with fondness about her parents' constant bickering. With all their differences—and her mother's complaints about their financial woes—they had been suited for each other. Now Batya also understood the connection the two had shared in the dark. In the long, cold Russian winter nights of her childhood, while the family slept together on the wide loft built above the stone stove, she had heard their muffled moaning and believed it was the aches in their joints from the hard labor they endured all day. Come summertime, there had been evenings when her parents insisted on relieving their daughters from milking duties and took their time returning from the cowshed. How else had her mother been able to conceive time and again?

Batya tied the letters with the ribbon and put them back. *"God of great mercy, please protect my naïve father."* She wished she knew more prayers. Without a script, she was merely speaking to God instead of reciting the words He had prescribed for His followers. If she heard the prayers recited aloud at any of the synagogues in town, the forgotten sentences might jolt her memory. Maybe the women's section had that *tkhines* book she so wanted.

The moon moved to the other side of the house, and Batya turned away from the window. She sank back on the blanket on the floor. Moskowitz wouldn't permit her to attend a service at the synagogue. Maybe Freda, who respected the shiva, would have, except that for all her religious adherence, the matron never attended a service herself. Better not ask. If her jailers withheld their permission, Batya would have to defy them. She'd do better to figure out a way to just go.

Chapter Twenty-Three

*B*efore dawn, when the house had quieted down, Batya went to check on Nettie. She found her friend already asleep. Probably exhausted after hours of entertaining customers, Nettie hadn't bothered to remove her smeared makeup. With her eyes closed, in the dim light of the kerosene lamp she had neglected to turn off, her beautiful face seemed ghostly. Batya registered that Nettie's formerly full figure had lost its curves, and her hair, spread over the pillow, seemed thinner.

"You need to see a doctor," Batya said to the sleeping girl. "In the morning I'm taking you. No more arguments about it."

Nettie moaned. Perhaps she'd heard her. Batya touched her friend's forehead. It was cool. No fever marked the mysterious illness that seemed to be eating her from within.

Midmorning, though, Nettie knocked on Batya's door, waking her up.

"I went to the doctor only so you'll stop nudging me." Her

old warm smile flickered on her face before it disappeared again. "He found nothing wrong with me."

"Did you tell him you're not eating?" Batya asked.

"He gave me an elixir to increase my appetite." Nettie withdrew a small bottle from the folds of her skirt. "A few drops every day should do it."

Batya smiled with relief. Nettie had to get better, or Freda might sell her off. "Keep your regulars from Ariana. She may be new here, but not to the profession. Her mother trained her in Hungary."

"I'm taking care of my clients," Nettie said, but Batya was unsure if the confidence was genuine or forced.

She rose and kissed Nettie on both cheeks, testing the temperature of the skin. It was normal. "And hide your jewelry. Those Hungarians have fast fingers."

Nettie laughed her old laughter. "Will you stop fretting over me like a mother hen?"

Her worries assuaged, Batya put on the black dress and walked down the back staircase that opened to the recently extended corridor. Moskowitz had acquired two buildings next door, each a *casa chorizo,* a sausage-like row of rooms. He had refurbished the two parallel dwellings into more than a dozen new chambers, all accessible from a center portico. During the renovations he had also gutted a few rooms on the main house's ground floor to enlarge the pavilion. In the new extra space he added nooks with upholstered raised platforms and countless pillows. Separated by sheer curtains from the main hall, the nooks offered a modicum of privacy so the girls could warm up their clients. By the time the men were eager to go upstairs to satisfy their desires, they were willing to pay more.

The other end of the corridor connected to the pavilion just past Moskowitz's office. Batya walked in to gather his discarded newspapers, a daily task Freda had assigned her a couple of years before, to cut them up for use in the latrine. The scent of Moskowitz's French cologne permeated the air. As he had instructed her, Batya picked up only the newspapers on the floor, never those on his chair. She rooted in his wastebasket and found a discarded pencil stub no bigger than her pinky, and she tucked it into her pocket so she could copy words in the margins of the newspapers. She hadn't dared buy a notebook for fear of discovery—if not by Freda, then by a snooping sister.

Batya wasn't supposed to linger in the office, only to take the papers to her room to cut, which gave her the privacy needed to improve her Yiddish reading.

Upon leaving the office she was startled when from behind her came the cry of Glikel, a brown-eyed beauty with unruly curly hair. "I was coming to get the newspapers!"

Batya swiveled on her heel. Glikel never volunteered her help, and only performed her assigned household tasks under threats. "How come?" Batya asked.

"Freda said I could cut them up this week," Glikel replied in a defiant tone.

"Well, it will keep me busy." Batya started toward the stairs.

"You were never his wife, so you shouldn't have any privileges," Glikel said to Batya's back.

"You're talking nonsense," Batya said to Glikel. "What's eating you?"

Without waiting for a reply, she continued to walk. No one thought cutting newspapers for the latrine was a privilege, nor did anyone in the house claim a superior status for having been "married" to Moskowitz in one of those make-believe *shtile chuppahs* like Nettie's. Many of the sisters, though, delighted when he visited them in their chambers, as if singled out for a special honor.

In spite of all Batya had learned about Moskowitz, she had still been surprised to discover that at the time he kidnapped her, he had a legitimate wife and three children. Now the oldest was soon to be bar mitzvahed. Batya had overheard Moskowitz boasting to Freda that when his son turned fourteen the following year, he planned to send him to a boarding school in Switzerland. "He should receive the education of a gentleman in a school where European nobility send their children," he had said. "Yitzik's son will carry no traces of the shtetl in his French and English pronunciations."

Batya's foot was on the first step when she heard Glikel's demanding voice: "Give me the newspapers."

With the girls' tragic histories, it was a wonder there weren't more *meshugenahs* in the house. Batya turned and pushed the newspapers into Glikel's middle. "Here you are."

Glikel didn't reach to take them, and the papers fell to the ground. "I've changed my mind." She snickered with an air of superiority and sauntered away.

Seething, Batya picked up the newspapers. She began to climb the stairs.

"Wait!" Glikel called. "Wait!"

Batya allowed herself half a turn. She let out a low breath to keep her temper in check. "What now?"

Glikel's gaze traveled over Batya's black dress, as if noticing it for the first time. "Sorry about your mother. May her soul rest in peace."

"Thank you." Batya set her foot on the next step.

"Would you do me a favor? Please?"

"What kind?"

"Ask your mother to send my regards to my parents, they, too, should rest in peace. Their names are Sigmund and Hilda Gottstein."

"My mother is really busy sending regards to a lot of parents," Batya said, and added with emphasis, "Parents of my *friends*."

"Please. Just two more. Sigmund and Hilda Gottstein."

There seemed no end to Glikel's audacity. Batya looked down at the pleading face. "You'll have to pay for it." She pointed at Glikel's opal ring, gleaming in blues and greens. "With this."

Chapter Twenty-Four

*T*he eight days of Chanukah filled the week following Batya's shiva for her mother, with their late spring afternoons in which Freda presided over the candle lighting. For fifteen minutes each evening at dusk, Batya stood with the sisters and peered into the menorah and its flickering candles. She sang the Chanukah songs she remembered from home, ate jelly-filled *punchkes* sprinkled with powdered sugar, and felt the bond of shared traditions with these girls who had replaced her family and whose closeness had sustained her in the days of mourning.

The first Friday evening after Chanukah presented no chance to try to visit a synagogue. The brothel was busy. Now that a gas line had been snaked to the street corner to illuminate the lampposts, Moskowitz had installed colorful lights on the house's outside wall facing the street. The klezmers stationed by the window played as much for the clients inside as for the men roaming the street, deciding which house to enter. Some Jewish men arrived early in the afternoon, allowing themselves time with the impure *kurves* before cleansing from the mundane in the *mikveh* so they could properly receive the holy Shabbat. Many others snuck out of their homes after the family's festive dinner and welcomed Shabbat not by doing the mitzvah of satisfying their wives as ordained by the Talmud but by attending to their favorite prostitutes.

Since Freda forbade the sisters to leave lit Shabbat candles in their rooms—and tradition forbade blowing out these sacred candles—each of the girls had to light hers in the kitchen. Many sisters had invested in silver candlesticks; Batya's were brass, to remind her of her mother's. She struck a match, brought the flame to each of the two wicks, then covered her face. Saying her prayer, she communed with her mother and with all Jewish women throughout history who had suffered strife yet survived. Even if it cost her her life, she swore yet again, she would get her family out of poverty and misery, out of pogroms and repeated exiles.

The non-Jewish clients sat around the pavilion and the patio, drinking Quilmes beer and bitter *aperitivos,* joking, listening to the music, and conducting business. They played cards for hours, seemingly not in a great hurry to take their turns in the private chambers. The smoke of their cigars, cigarettes, and opium swirled around their heads. Batya inhaled it; tobacco was good for one's health even if her lungs couldn't tolerate smoking it. She loved how these smells mixed with the aroma of boiling coffee and heady perfume. She hated how they turned stale on her clients' breath.

The musicians broke into a tango, and Ovad, a swarthy Moroccan Jew, a building contractor, nodded at her from across the room. She sauntered toward him, her hand fanning her blond hair over her right shoulder, her eyes locked in his while he stepped forward. The music swept through Batya as Ovad took her hand and held her in a close *abrazo*. She didn't like Ovad the hairy client, but she enjoyed Ovad the dancer. Her full breasts pressing against his torso, she gave herself to the illusion of romance, closed her eyes, and immersed herself in the harmony of their moves. Her sharp yet fluid steps exposed her skin through the Spanish shawl tied like a skirt, its long fringes swaying with each swivel. When she danced, her body was hers alone, and in the flow of the music, Ovad let her shine.

From the corner of her eye she saw Freda exchanging clients' money for the tokens they would leave with the prostitutes. Every week, when Batya handed Freda her tokens, the matron deducted food and rent, leaving her just enough to entice her to continue working. The first year of Batya's bondage, Freda had deducted the cost of her ocean passage from Russia. At least now Batya was free of that debt.

After two songs, Batya stopped dancing and gestured toward the stairs. She had to work. Besides the token, she knew Ovad would leave her a gift of money.

Half an hour later, she came downstairs to find that her new favorite regular had arrived. She took Ulmann's hand, and the smile on her lips was genuine. A jeweler in his late thirties, Ulmann had bland facial features but hadn't yet gone to fat as many men did, flaunting their good fortunes. He was blessed with a gentle soul: he neither drank nor danced, and cigars gave him headaches. All he wanted was to be alone with her in her chamber—and mostly talk.

Heavy rain had washed the city at dawn, and at eight o'clock
the air was still cool and fragrant, before garbage would bake on
the streets in the spring sun. As Batya left the front yard, a jacaranda tree weighed down by its purple flowers leaned toward
her in protective blessing. A large woolen shawl covered Batya's
shoulders and arms, both against the chill and for modesty. She
couldn't help the revealing, colorful dress—she owned no modest clothing—but she had tightened her shawl with a mother-
of-pearl brooch given to her by a client. Her wide-brimmed
hat, though, with its swath of tulle, was finer than any common
woman could afford, marking Batya as a prostitute.

Saturday mornings, she was permitted to visit the Mercado
de Abasto, where farmers displayed their produce and vendors
paraded soap and candles, perfume and makeup, lace and fine
linens. Batya no longer required supervision after she'd learned,
like many sisters before her, that there was no place to run to, no
place to hide, and no better means of employment to be found in
this growing city of men and immigrants. She had proven herself adept not only at learning Spanish but also at negotiating
on price, so Freda trusted her to purchase provisions to supple-
ment the meals delivered from the mess halls. The matron was
especially appreciative that the butcher made it a practice to give
Batya a *yapa,* a bonus piece of meat.

Batya looked forward all week to her walk through the market. Shabbat in Buenos Aires was nothing like Shabbat at the
shtetl. Like everything else in this new world, the prohibition of
labor or handling money was merely a memory. Batya was par-
ticularly fascinated by healers who offered herbs and ointments
along with magic words meant to cure a baby from the cholera,

capture the heart of an indifferent would-be lover, or find a pot of gold.

She had only once spent her hard-earned money on a secret wish. She had hoped to be miraculously carried back to Russia, to the shtetl, to her parents' arms, to the sour scent of dairy products on her father's beard. Even if they would all live in a hut whose rat-infested walls were covered with mildew and soot, whose thatched roof crawled with insects, and whose stove sputtered and smoked, they would be together. She had been disappointed when the magic words accomplished nothing, even though the soothsayer who had sold them explained that the key to their success was persistence: more secret words would bring about the magic. Batya refused to part with more money.

Batya had been toying with the idea of praying in the Sephardi synagogue where Ovad worshipped, and where there was no chance she'd encounter Zwi Migdal pimps who'd come from Eastern Europe. She entered San Telmo with its dilapidated, soot-covered tenements, sarcastically called *conventillos,* small convents. The hordes of poor immigrants living there—Jews and goyim alike—were no better off than they had been in Europe. The buildings with sagging staircases and walls swarming with rats and vermin were so crowded that families not only shared beds, but fifty families shared two lavatories. Unlike the good food Batya ate—though every morsel was deducted from her pay—these people lived on potatoes and hardtack.

Batya quickened her pace, careful to protect her good shoes from the open channel of sewage running along the street. She chased away a pack of children with filthy faces and heads speckled with lice eggs, begging her for pennies. There was nothing here to indicate it was Shabbat, she thought. Through the window of one of the *conventillos,* she glimpsed men smoking opium through bamboo pipes. She breathed in the wafting sweet smell, so different from the bitter tincture she had been given during her surgery and recovery. She wished she could buy some to float her down that river of dreams and forgetfulness, but it cost its weight in real silver, an indulgence she wouldn't allow. Opium, she had learned, made its users lose all their money in pursuit of it.

She hurried on, ignoring the prostitutes who leaned against doorways or bent out of second-floor windows. In this overcrowded neighborhood, most operated out of rooms rented in families' small flats or ran brothels on roofs, with only straw partitions separating each woman and her groaning, panting client from the next. Despite the squalid conditions, many of these sisters were independent, not subjugated as she was, though rumor had it that Zwi Migdal extorted protection fees from these women, too.

When she reached the Sephardi synagogue, she stood in front of the building with its ornate arched façade. Only then did it occur to her that since Ovad's people had emigrated from Morocco, not only did they not speak Yiddish, but their Hebrew pronunciation of the prayers must be incomprehensible. For all she knew, God didn't understand it either and wouldn't listen to such prayers any more than He would to prayers coming from a church. She must make her way to the Ashkenazi synagogue that had been opened recently near Vella Crespo, where merchants and government clerks built villas for their lawful wives.

She would go there first, she decided, then return to San

Telmo to complete her market shopping. In spite of Shabbat, she hailed a carriage to take her the twenty-five blocks' distance.

During the ride, Batya removed her hat and pinned her hair up with four tortoiseshell combs. However, when she put the wide-brimmed hat back on, it failed to block a view of her hair, so unlike the tight head coverings married women wore in the synagogue. Virgins didn't cover their heads, but what was the rule of *halacha* for a woman who was neither married nor a virgin? If Batya raised her shawl to fully cover her head, would she be deceptive, pretending to God that she was a respectable married woman? He knew well that she was the lowest of all humans in His vast universe.

Or maybe He knew differently. Maybe for Him, she was forever Batya, "God's daughter," His child. It was Esperanza, the other girl, who engaged in filth.

When Batya arrived, the Shabbat morning services were just starting. She entered the building, her eyes downcast to avoid catching the eyes of men she knew—not only her own clients but also those who frequented other sisters in the house.

Immediately to the left of the entrance rose a staircase that must lead to the women's section. The circular wooden stairs were hard to navigate with her ample skirt. She had to lift it above her ankles and wondered how women with little children could make their way up.

Upstairs, only five women sat on the backless wooden benches. A mother and a teenage daughter huddled, the mother's arm around her child, and from their heaving shoulders Batya guessed that they were praying for a sick relative or for the soul of a recently departed loved one. The other three women sat far away from one another, each with her eyes shut while her lips moved in a silent prayer. All were dressed in simple, dark clothes, and the stark contrast to her own colorful, high-quality attire made Batya want to shrink and disappear.

In a bin at the entrance, she spotted several bound books and was delighted to find the *tkhines*. Below, in the main sanctuary, some men had already started davening, their bodies swaying back and forth under their prayer shawls. Afraid to contaminate them with her gaze, she settled in the back row with her book, too far to hear, but out of the line of vision of the other women. She wished that, like the men, she could close herself to the world and hide under a talis, that white silk cloth lined with gold and silver threads and edged with fringes, the number of strands of each representing a symbol. Under a talis she could convene with God as if He were close to her, like the friend her father had found in Him. But it was God's wish that prayer shawls be the province of men only.

Do not focus on human inadequacies or on the injustices God unleashed upon the world for reasons He saw fit, Batya told herself. What mattered at this stolen hour was that she was in a house of purity, of sanctity, of holiness. From here, her prayers could be heard by Him, He who had forgotten her existence.

She was flipping through the book to find the right page when it was yanked out of her hand.

"What do you think you're doing?" The words were hissed at her in Yiddish by a woman whose burgundy-colored kerchief twisted tight around her head.

Batya's face flushed.

"You're impure." The woman's blue eyes darkened in anger. "How dare you bring your filth to a house of worship?"

"He's my God, too." The heat of humiliation deepened in Batya's cheeks. Who was she next to a truly pious woman, one who must have shaved her head for modesty under that kerchief? Batya's voice took on a begging tone: "I must talk to Him."

"*Tme'ah,*" the woman yelled in a loud whisper. "Impure!"

At the sound of her voice, the other women turned around and stared.

"You want to contaminate our holy books with your muck?" The woman swung her hands to encompass the whole building. "To corrupt the virgin brides before their weddings?"

The other women rose to their feet, shock and disgust on their faces.

"Leave!" one spat.

"Get out before you pollute the air in the synagogue!" called another, not attempting to keep her voice down.

"Shame on you," the mother huddling with her daughter yelled. "The chutzpah of the likes of you to come here!"

Not since her family had been chased from Komarinoe had Batya felt such naked hatred. Her taunters this time, though, were Jews. Her head bowed, she slunk toward the exit and almost tripped onto the circular staircase, since she could barely see through the tears misting her eyes.

At her back, she heard, "And don't you ever dare come back!"

Chapter Twenty-Five

$\mathcal{T}$wo evenings later, Batya sat on the lap of a card player at the pavilion, a man whose pile of money was growing. Later, after she'd brought him good luck and he'd shown his gratitude with a few coins, she strutted in front of a newcomer who seemed confused by the large selection of women. Ever since the incident in the synagogue she'd made an extra effort to lure one man after another. Anything to please Moskowitz in case he'd heard about what she'd done.

Thankfully, no reaction came from him. Until several months ago, he had spent hours prowling the streets for male passersby, soliciting them to try his wide offering of pleasures. Lately, though, he'd hired two hustlers to fill this role and had shut himself off from women's squabbles to work on his abacus. When Batya walked past his office, she heard the sounds of his counting tool as he swiped the wooden beads over the metal rods, and through the open door she glimpsed him filling the pages of a ledger. The month before, three men had brought in an iron vault and a three-drawer filing cabinet. When Batya retrieved the newspapers from the floor, she had noticed the letterhead of Zwi Migdal among the stacks of papers on his desk.

Now fanning herself, she caught sight of Ulmann approaching, his shoulders stooped from long hours over his jewelry creations. "I've missed you," she purred, and meant it. His visits had become an oasis of tranquility in her hectic evenings.

He looked down at her with tender eyes. *"Mayn sheyn meydele,"* he said, my pretty girl.

She led him upstairs, where he removed his jacket and sat on her bed. While he took off his shoes, she stroked his head, neck, and back. Her hand moved down the length of his arm. "How was your day?" she asked. "Your week?"

He sighed and lay down, still clothed. She unbuttoned his shirt while he spoke. "The clients, the suppliers, they are all one big pain in the *tuches*." He smiled at her. "Just the thought that I'd see you tonight made me happy."

She kissed his cheek, then buried her face in his neck. His arm wrapped around her and brought her closer.

"You have no idea how lonely I am."

She nodded into his shoulder. "Your wife?" she ventured, knowing the story of his poor wife who was sick in both body and soul, but whom Ulmann could never divorce because she was his second cousin. Such shirking of responsibilities would make him a pariah in his family. His three sons needed a father who was a role model, a man who wouldn't desert a wife in her time of greatest need.

"Loyalty to family," he repeated now. "It's the foundation of being Jewish. It means sacrificing one's happiness for the sake of the others to whom one is related." He sighed, and his free hand covered his face. "But I'm so miserable."

"You're here, now, with me," she whispered, her hand moving downward. "I'm your friend."

At the end of the hour, Freda knocked on the door to indicate that Ulmann's time was up. Batya rose slowly so not to rouse him as he rested under the light cover. He opened his eyes to a slit, smiled at Batya, and motioned toward his jacket on the chair. "Another hour, although God knows I should watch my spending."

Batya took money out of the pocket, opened the door a crack, and exchanged it for a second token. When she returned to the bed, Ulmann bent toward his pants on the floor and fished out a booklet so thin it was folded in half.

"I want to read you a poem that tells how I feel about my life," he said, leafing through the pages.

She snuggled up to him so she could read the printed Yiddish words without revealing her secret.

"It's by a poetess named Pessi Hirschfeld-Pomerantz."

His voice became melodious:

> *Sun, O sun!*
> *I'd like to wander*
> *in the open fields*
> *and drink up the light*
> *all day, so my eyes*
> *would radiate*
> *your light, your warmth.*

Between narrow walls
my eyes look dull.
Between narrow walls
I speak angrily to people—
the path they walk
seems too confining for me.

"It's beautiful." She planted a kiss on his chest. He kissed her head in return, then raised her face so their lips met.

"As beautiful as you are." He rose toward his jacket. "I'd like to ask your advice about something." He took out a small notebook with drawings. "Some pieces I'm designing. As a woman of the world you must know what other women want."

Doubting her ability to judge what jewelry virtuous women wanted, Batya bent toward his notebook as he turned the pages. The drawings, some with splashes of color marking a precious stone or the brightness of a diamond, were exquisite. "You are truly an artist," she said, and brought his hand to her lips. "I didn't know these fingers were as skilled with a pencil as without it." Then she pointed to some images. "The leaf on this ring might snag on clothes, and for this choker, maybe you could add a couple more rubies on each side of the medallion?"

"Thank you. Great ideas." He let out a laugh, the anguish that had accompanied his arrival clearly gone. It pleased her to have made him happy.

After he left, Batya washed up and thought how many sisters would have exploited the chance to root through a client's pocket to palm some coins for themselves. Ulmann always rewarded her with a little cash and, on holidays, a piece of jewelry, albeit light in its gold content—a hatpin, or the tiniest pair of delicately shaped earrings.

Most important, she enjoyed the warmth of his visits. As inconceivable as it was for a *polaca* to hope for a patron, she let herself daydream. Maybe one day Ulmann would take her out of here.

Monday morning, Batya queued with the other girls in the kitchen to receive her share of the money she had earned for the house. Her eyes searched for Nettie, but there was no sign of her friend.

"Have you seen Nettie?" Batya asked the girl in front of her.

"Not since last night."

Batya rushed to Nettie's room. There was no answer to her knock. She opened the door.

Nettie was slumped over the side of her bed, head down, vomit pooling on the floor, her hair streaming into it.

"Help!" Batya shouted. She lifted the listless body back onto the bed. It was distressingly light. She touched her friend's wrist to feel the pulse. It was there, albeit faint. She ran to the door. "Help! Help!"

Thirty minutes later, two men loaded Nettie on a wagon to take her to the hospital. "You can visit her later," Freda told Batya and Rochel. "We've wasted too much time. I must finish the accounting."

"What do you think is the matter with Nettie?" Batya asked Rochel after Freda waddled her heft down the stairs. "The doctor told her she was fine."

"She's sick with sorrow." Rochel's voice sounded resigned.

Sorrow gnawed at all of them, Batya thought. She recalled the vivaciousness with which Nettie had once faced her situation, whistling songs through the gap between her teeth. Batya didn't wonder what had made Nettie's exuberance ebb. Grief underpinned their lives.

"What will happen with her regulars?" Batya whispered to Rochel. One of them was the man with the appetite for cockroaches. Another relished tying Nettie to the bedpost and flogging her. Batya never understood how Nettie withstood these cruelties.

Rochel shrugged. "It's in God's hands."

Batya lowered her head in reverence for God and His will, while her heart sank. It wasn't like Rochel to be so accepting of a sister's illness; she had fought so hard for Batya's life. Weariness must be settling inside Rochel, too. Like the rest of them, Rochel hadn't escaped pogroms; she had just survived untold losses, then gathered the threads of her strength to forge on. Only once she told Batya of the two little brothers she had raised alone in Krakow after their parents had been killed, until one day, when she came back from foraging for food to the coal cellar where they lived, the boys weren't there—and never returned. Rochel acted as if the past could truly be buried, as if her heart didn't agonize with worry every day, tortured by questions about the boys' fates. When Batya and Rochel again took their spots at the payment queue, Batya held her friend's hand, concerned that like Nettie Rochel might break down.

And how long could she herself go on? Many of the girls in Freda's house were in their teens. Nettie and Rochel, in their

early twenties, were considered "mature." In this city full of prostitutes, few lived to old age. If they didn't die of disease or kill
themselves in their youth, they were forced out of the brothels
once their bodies outlived their usefulness. On their own, with
no other means of employment—and denied charity by the formal
Jewish benevolent organizations—they often died of starvation.

Through the open door, Batya heard Glikel arguing with
Freda about her deducted pesos. "I had stomach problems. I ate
no chicken all week, only rice." The third time Glikel raised her
voice, Freda slapped her face. "Take it, or go elsewhere. Many
girls will be grateful to take your room in this house."

When it was Batya's turn, she spread her tokens on the table
and waited while Freda compared their accuracy against the records in her notebook. At last Freda raised her head, and her
finger punched the page. "You've been keeping the light on in
your room. You're wasting kerosene." Her pale blue eyes were
sharp. "And now that you dance so much, it's only fair that you
pay more for the musicians."

"I can't afford that," Batya blurted out. With such deductions,
she would end up owing the house money.

"Who should pay that?" Freda retorted. "And you had two
pieces of cake at the café last week—"

"Your brother took me there!"

"Did he eat the cakes, or did you? And here's the doctor's bill
for this month."

Batya swallowed. The doctor had renewed the certificate testifying that she was free of disease. For an added barrier to the
clients' use of rubber, he had fitted her with a small protective

cup even though her scarred uterus could no longer produce "work accidents" in the form of pregnancies. Every day, inserting it was a ritual that separated Batya from Esperanza.

Batya took the pesos Freda pushed in her direction and rose to leave.

"You didn't say thank you," Freda called from the door to Batya's back. "Ungrateful bitch."

"Thank you," Batya tossed over her shoulder, and in her head added, *A* farshlepte plog, *a chronic plague.*

She skipped mealtime and rushed to the bank where she safeguarded her money before its doors closed for siesta. Most sisters had no concept of a future and spent all their earnings on new clothes, hats, and toiletries. No doubt Moskowitz was aware that a few of his *kurves* saved money in the local banks. His tacit silence on the matter, Batya suspected, was because these savings might buy a *kurve* who had outlived her usefulness her freedom from him, or if she died, he'd inherit it, as was the pimps' union rule.

The British bank was one of the foreign banks that had sprouted in the growing city of Buenos Aires, an institution that Batya hoped was immune to Zwi Migdal's influence. The bank clerk she favored, a fumbling and pedantic aging bachelor with fingers stained with ink, had issued Batya a small savings book in which he recorded each of her deposits. Should it ever get lost, he explained, blushing when he raised his eyes to her, her deposits were also logged in his ledger. Today again, he made sure to show Batya his meticulous entries, and the respect with which he treated her touched her anew.

Leaving the bank, she hugged the savings book to her chest,

then tucked it in her skirt pocket. She dashed over to the hospital to visit Nettie.

The sentry at the door stopped her. "We have enough diseases here without someone like you bringing in more," he said.

"Please check on my friend," Batya said. "Nettie Blum. She was brought in earlier."

But the sentry waved her away.

Batya stepped back. The only places she wasn't shunned were the ones to which she brought her money—the market, the seamstress, and the bank. She'd have to wait until Freda found time to come here to inquire. The matron would, if only to check on her property. At least Nettie's free medical treatment in the public hospital wasn't costing the house.

Back in her chamber, Batya slid under the bed and pushed aside a small trunk in which she kept mementos and what might be perceived by snooping eyes as her most important treasures: a cloth napkin with the name of the café embroidered in gold, a peacock feather, a wooden dreidel engraved with the four magic letters of Chanukah, two beaded necklaces, a beautiful lace ribbon she sometimes tied around her forehead, a red flower made of silk, and her brass Shabbat candlesticks.

The trunk served to deflect suspicion that she had another hiding place. Batya removed the loose brick in the stone wall facing the street. Her hand snaked through the opening and felt the interior hole she had carved by removing mortar. She pulled out a cloth pouch and tucked the bankbook in the hole, then retreated to unwrap her collection of jewelry. She bathed her eyes in Glikel's opal ring, felt the coolness of a pearl pendant on a gold chain, and stroked the ivory silhouette of a gentlewoman on a cameo made of onyx. The silver necklace a sea captain had brought her from a place called India had its own leather bag. She put it on, rose to look at it in the mirror, and admired its fine filigree curlicues dotted with coral and aqua stones.

Some sisters who saved their money invested in pelts they stored under their beds. Hides were available, albeit expensive. The impracticality of storing such bulk in a small room that soon reeked of it—especially in hot weather—made no sense to Batya, and, as it turned out, neither to Freda, who ordered the pelts removed. Unlike pelts, jewelry and precious stones were small and never aged. One day, she would bring her family over and leave Buenos Aires. She would cash in her treasures to open a store far away from Moskowitz's reach. She would also take her father on a trip to Pittsburgh to search for his brother.

Batya tucked her jewelry back into the pouch and returned it to the hiding place. She still wanted to obtain the book of *tkhines*—more so now that she must pray for Nettie's recovery. She should buy one. Since Freda hadn't mentioned the incident at the synagogue, it was safe enough for Batya to try again, if she could figure out where. The Judaica store must carry the book, but she wouldn't dare bring sin to a place filled with sacred texts. Surely the bookseller and his clerks would chase her away, humiliate her as the women in the synagogue had done.

Her musings were interrupted when she heard her name called from down the corridor. She opened the door to see Glikel smirking. "Moskowitz wants to see you."

Dread climbed Batya's throat. News of Nettie? Or was Moskowitz about to punish her after all? Bracing herself, Batya descended the steps, forcing her feet to move faster than they wanted to. If there was no thug in Moskowitz's office to beat her, he wouldn't do that dirty work himself. Maybe he would slap her a bit, pull her hair. Unlike some obtuse pimps who damaged their goods, he had boasted that his *kurves* never exhibited marks that hurt their ability to work.

Chapter Twenty-Six

*B*atya entered Moskowitz's office to find him and Freda flanking a girl hunched on a chair, her face in her hands. Batya could see only the girl's unwashed hair falling forward and black and blue marks on her exposed neck and upper back. The small bumps of the girl's upper spine and her shoulder bones jutted through the bruised, emaciated skin.

"Take care of her," Moskowitz told Batya. "You know what to do."

"If she commits suicide, you'll reimburse us the price we paid at the auction," Freda added.

Auctioned naked, paraded and probed. The hair roots on Batya's arms pricked with hatred. She looked at the girl, and a pang of her own memories hit her. She crouched and touched the girl's arm. It was so thin, it felt like the limb of a bird.

"What's your name?" she asked.

The girl responded with a jerk of her shoulder.

"She asked you for your name," Freda said, her tone ominous.

The girl mumbled something.

"Speak up!" Freda hit the girl's back, jolting the body.

"Dora." Her voice was only one notch above a whisper.

"Well, Dora, you'd better listen to Batya."

Dora dropped her head farther toward her bony knees.

"*Farshteyst?* Understand?" Freda hit her again.

"Let me take her upstairs," Batya said to Moskowitz. She kept her tone low as she turned to Freda. "Which is her room?"

Freda gave her a key to a tiny chamber diagonally across from Batya's. It had recently been evacuated by a girl whose French disease must have been dormant until she started losing her mind. "Clean her up, and always lock the door," Freda said.

Batya put her hands together in supplication. "Will you please find out about Nettie?"

"She'll stay in the hospital until she's better."

Batya suspected that, visiting the auction, Freda hadn't checked on Nettie. "Please send her my warmest blessings when you visit her *again*," she said with emphasis. Worry gnawed at her, but for now Dora must be her priority. "Come with me," she said softly to the girl. She would comfort Dora the way Rochel had offered her warmth and compassion in the hours of her greatest despair. "You must be hungry. Let's feed you."

At the mention of food, Dora rose to her feet and, without looking at Freda and Moskowitz, allowed Batya to prop her up as they walked upstairs.

"Where are you from?" Batya asked.

Dora only shook her head.

Batya understood. In time, after she gained Dora's trust, they would talk.

When Batya brought up a tray, Dora ate hungrily, using her fingers. Following the meal, Batya led Dora to the shower. She used her own quinoa soap bar, which bubbled up when applied to the hair, to rinse away the filth of the ship. She wrapped Dora in a soft cotton sheet, then led her to the bed and tucked her in, tightening the light blanket around her as if in a hug. Dora wept, and Batya sang her a Yiddish lullaby until she fell asleep. Although Dora had surely been raped repeatedly during her ocean crossing and probably locked up and starved, she had been lucky to be auctioned off directly upon arriving rather than passing through Nina's training brothel.

In her sleep, the girl cried and kicked. Sitting on the edge of Dora's bed, Batya recalled how she, too, had been a suicide risk and could have died from the infection that had spread through her abdomen. By now Batya knew that Rochel had been ordered under threat to see that Batya lived and be broken into the profession, yet her friend's ministering had been genuine; Rochel's kindness came from a well of humanity that hadn't been dried up by cynicism and betrayals. Batya must succeed with Dora the same way.

The girl slept on. Midday rain poured down, then stopped, but the sky remained overcast. At siesta time, the house and street quieted down. Batya watched Dora sleep and wondered if she had a family, and the thought led Batya to her own sister. In her latest letter, written through a scribe, Surale had reported that their father was aging. Aggie had long stopped producing milk, but he didn't have the heart to sell her to the butcher, so the task had fallen upon Surale.

A commotion from the street drew Batya to the window. The

chamber assigned to Dora faced a side courtyard. Batya opened the window and squeezed her head out between the twin bars crossing it. A man wearing a skullcap—a modern Jew—stumbled into view in the alley past the courtyard, clearly drunk. "I'm tired of being lumped in with all of you ruffians and *kurves!*" he shouted. "I lost a business deal because of you! The goyim think all Jews are *ganefs*—but I'm not a thief like you, filth of the earth!"

Batya closed the window and returned to Dora's bed. This time she stretched next to her, hoping to catch some sleep before her late afternoon and long evening's work. She thought about the drunkard's anguished words. Just last week, Rochel had been booed when she had gone to the Jewish theater with Moskowitz. When confiding in Batya, Rochel's eyes brimmed with tears, and she explained that the pimps' union faced harsh criticism from the leaders of the Jewish community.

"My client said that the upstanding Jews of Argentina and Brazil blame the *caftans* for the rising anti-Semitism," she said. *Caftan,* the Spanish word for a pimp, originated from the Orthodox men's garb. Rochel had a regular weekly engagement at an out-of-town private villa owned by a wealthy merchant who entertained government associates away from the public eye. She had explained to Batya that Zwi Migdal worked diligently to widen opportunities for its members. The stronger it became and the greater its holdings across South America, the greater were the bribes Zwi Migdal distributed all around. The organization—legally unionized—was the source of corruption at all levels of government and police.

When Batya went to the kitchen to fetch lemonade and cake

for Dora after her siesta, Rochel was there, chatting with other sisters about the incident. "That drunkard? He used to be rich, from an important Sephardi family that has been here since before the Warsaw gang arrived. Now he lost his construction contracts to goyim because they don't know the difference."

Batya hurried out of the kitchen to bring Dora her treat and lock her up so she herself could get ready for work. She couldn't stop thinking about how she had been hated by the women at the synagogue. By Jewesses. Now, like in Russia, Jews were hated by goyim, too.

Just before sunset, in the pavilion, Moskowitz crooked his finger at Batya to join two influential clients he was entertaining on the patio. She sat with them as they, too, were discussing the afternoon's incident. "A loser that can't handle his own stupidity," Moskowitz said to the customers. "Who gives the tailors in town the best business? The cobblers, the milliners, and the haberdashers their livelihood? What about the jewelers and the bankers? Who buys carriages and hires the coaches? Who builds new houses and pays for the cultural institutions? We are the businessmen that drive the economy of Buenos Aires. We bring the money in, and we spend it generously. We are the heart and the pulse of this city."

"Let's drink to that!" One of the men raised his glass.

"Lechayim," said Moskowitz, clinking his glass with both men's.

Batya smiled sweetly, but her hands closed into fists of despair.

On Saturday, after Batya had brought Dora breakfast, she tended to her kitchen chores. Wiping the breakfast mess off the large wooden table, she prayed for God's help. *Save us all, guide us with Your wisdom. Bless my sick friend Nettie with a full recovery, and relieve Dora's suffering.* She rushed through the rest of the cleaning, looking forward to the market and its concert of colors and sounds, the freedom to move about, even as she still cringed at the notion of handling money on the sacred day of decreed rest.

Moskowitz had arrived early, dressed in the cream-colored suit he wore when going to the synagogue with some of his neighbors, owners of other brothels. He never started his day without first collecting the previous night's money from Freda. Having deposited it in his vault, he now stopped in front of the mirror in the foyer. Batya watched from the corner of her eye as he smoothed his hair, styled by an Italian barber, and adjusted his Shabbat hat. He admired his diamond ring, then pulled from his pocket a new gold watch, larger than his previous one. To Batya's amusement, he repeated the gesture in the mirror as if practicing the impression it would create, then tapped on his belly with both palms, approving the paunch of a respectable man.

Moskowitz had started toward the door when two of his fellow pimps burst in. "They take our money to fix the roof," Enrico, a corpulent bald man, thundered with indignation. "They take our money to buy a new Torah. They take our money to pay the rabbi's salary, but we're not good enough to pray with them?"

"What are you talking about?" Moskowitz asked. "I'm getting the honor of an *aliyah* to the Torah this morning—"

"No, you're not. None of us does, today or ever." The second man, an influential brothel owner who had changed his Jewish name, Peretz, to Pedro, calmed down enough to speak. He was dressed in a plaid purple jacket with a green butterfly tie. "The leaders of the Jewish community have conspired against us. They teamed up to block us from attending services in every synagogue in town!"

"They hired security forces." Enrico pulled out a handkerchief and wiped his sweaty brow. "You should have seen these goons standing at the door of each synagogue, preventing us from entering."

"I've sent for the chief of police." Pedro waved his index finger in the air above his head. "He'll teach them a lesson—"

"I have a better idea." Moskowitz made for the door. "Follow me."

In the mayhem, two dozen sisters trailed out after the men. More girls streamed out of the houses up the street, and soon more pimps merged with their colleagues as they all headed toward the center of town. Batya couldn't resist following, and within minutes she was swept along behind one hundred *caftans* and twice as many prostitutes.

To her surprise, Moskowitz's destination was the Judaica store. As expected, the store was closed for Shabbat. Moskowitz kicked gently at the door to protect the polish of his lacquered shoes, but his gesture served as a signal to two other men, who unleashed their fury on the stubborn door until it crashed in.

Once inside, Moskowitz headed to the locked glass display case behind the counter, where a large Torah scroll stood upright, exhibited in all its glory with its heavily carved silver posts peeking through a velvet sheath embroidered in gold. It took a *sofer* painstaking years to hand-scribe a parchment, Batya knew, and it cost a fortune. None of the synagogues in the shtetls had been able to afford such a holy Torah.

"Break it," Moskowitz directed, and the man standing next to him smashed his handgun into the glass, splintering the case to a million pieces. Moskowitz grabbed the Torah and the additional double silver crown resting beside it, decorated with precious stones.

The mob behind him cheered as they marched out. On the street, Moskowitz danced with the holy scroll as if this were the festive holiday of Simchat Torah.

Batya hung back until the store emptied of people. She stood still, disbelieving her good luck, then rushed to the floor-to-ceiling bookcase. In the hundreds of thick leather-bound, gold-embossed spines she was unable to locate the simpler, smaller *tkhines* book.

God, please show me the way, so I can recite for You Your words of prayer. Please give me a sign that You will accept my prayers, me, Your humble Batya who's sinned so much. Please show me that You know that my soul is still as pure as it was on the day I was stolen from my parents' home.

Scanning more rows of books, she kept speaking to Him. She couldn't leave without the book. Failure would mean that God had indeed turned away from her forever.

The minutes ticked by on the huge wall clock, the pendulum marking every other beat of Batya's pounding heart. *Hurry up,* she told herself. Running along the bookcase on her left, she examined every shelf, then retraced her steps to view each with more care. *Hurry up!* If she was the only person here when the police arrived, she would be accused of the double crime of vandalizing the store and stealing the precious Torah scroll. Her fingers shook as she passed them over the wooden shelves, her eyes searching. Cold perspiration formed at the back of her neck.

The strike of a bell jolted her: the chime of the clock marking the half hour. More minutes ticked past. In a corner toward the back of the store, near a bolted back door, she found a stack of volumes with torn covers resting on a table next to pots of glue, brushes, and sheets of pulp paper.

At last, next to the table, on a low bookshelf, Batya recognized the small burgundy spine. Blood pulsated in her temples as she grabbed the book and quickly leafed through its pages to verify that it was what she thought it was. It was! She tucked it in the pocket of her skirt and rushed out, her heart singing.

Just before rounding the corner, she heard the siren of a police carriage entering the street from its far end. She broke into a run.

Back home she discovered that Moskowitz, for the first time other than for the Passover Seder, had emptied the house of its clients. One of his colleagues, formerly a chazzan, a cantor who'd found a new calling as the pimp of his wife and sister-in-law, began to conduct the Shabbat services right there in the pavilion.

The sisters gathered in the courtyard, peering at the backs of the men inside. Their eyes were bright; for once they were permitted to hear God's holy words.

Batya squeezed through the sisters. Walking slowly to avoid attracting attention, she climbed the stairs to the second floor. She sat on her bed and pressed her book to her chest, then kissed it, happiness filling her. Even without the prayer shawl men used, she could wrap herself in solitude with God, commune with Him. No matter what happened to her body, from now on she could keep her soul pure.

From below came the voices of the men repeating some sentences after the chazzan. Moskowitz didn't get the honor of an *aliyah* today. Batya smiled with satisfaction. The one thing Yitzik the Pitzik craved remained out of his reach: respectability among the upstanding Jews.

Chapter Twenty-Seven

*I*n Flores Cemetery, they weren't allowed in the Jewish section. No prostitute—alive or dead—was to contaminate the Jews buried there. The few sisters from the house Freda had permitted to participate in the sacred act of accompanying Nettie to her last resting place congregated outside the fenced-off section.

Batya covered her head with the lace scarf she'd brought. A few meters away stood a one-room structure. Since the Chevra Kadisha, the official Jewish burial society, shunned the *tme'ot*, the two elderly women who formed the prostitutes' burial sisterhood had retrieved Nettie's body from the hospital and brought it here to wash and purify. Now Batya and Rochel volunteered to carry out the stretcher on which she lay, wrapped in white shrouds. Her body seemed so small that Batya couldn't reconcile it with the full-bodied friend she had first met.

Outside the fence, one of the two aging prostitutes gestured to rest the stretcher on a flat stone bench. Perspiration made the woman's flowery dress stick to her body, and the powdered skin of her face drooped under its two painted blotches of red. Yet there was fervor in her hooded eyes as she addressed the small group of mourners. "Whatever happens to us, we must always remember one thing: we're Jewish. We may neglect most of our Jewish traditions—even forget many—but the *tahara,* purification of the body in preparation for burial, is one thing we should never ever give up."

"Amen," murmured the sisters.

"Today, the *tahara* allows your sister Nettie to meet her Maker with the utmost respect and dignity. She may be banned by people of our tribe from being buried among them, but the gates of heaven will open to her no matter. There she will wait, pure, with all other departed holy souls of our people, until the Resurrection of the Dead with the arrival of the Messiah."

"Amen," murmured the sisters.

"And after we're gone," the woman went on, pointing at herself and the other sister, a small-boned woman with a birdlike face whose sagging breasts reached her protruding belly, "you must take over this very important tradition. It's a mitzvah that will grant you a special spot at God's feet."

As the sisters nodded, Batya nodded, too, wishing that she had such benevolence in her heart to wash and cleanse dead bodies. For the first time in a while she thought of Miriam, who had been deprived of the last rites of purification and burial. Had her young friend's soul been punished yet again by being turned away from the gates of heaven? Could God be this unfair? At least Nettie was again as pure as the child she had once been. *Goodbye, Nettie, my beloved friend,* Batya said in her head. *May the Good Spirit envelop you.*

Juliet and Clara, sisters always eager to help, took over the carrying of the stretcher, and the procession walked along the outside periphery of the cemetery, where small tombstones listed the names of pimps and prostitutes, forever outcast.

"The curse of consumption," Batya said to Rochel.

"Not consumption," Rochel murmured. "She poisoned herself."

"What?"

"She swallowed drops of rat poison. She's been doing it for months to avoid drinking carbolic acid all at once."

A chill ran through Batya. Drinking liquid carbolic acid, as many prostitutes did, caused agonizing pain. So many had tried it that the hospital and the police dubbed it "blue-fingers death." Freda read aloud the newspapers' detailed descriptions so all the girls understood what was awaiting them if they attempted it. The mouth, esophagus, and stomach lining burned off, followed by convulsions, uncontrolled vomiting, and fingers and lips turning blue before one died in excruciating pain. "You'll be lying in your vomit," Freda had warned, "writhing like a worm, with the pain of hell's sulfur eating your mouth and throat so you can't even scream."

"You knew?" Batya asked Rochel. Nettie had lied when she said she'd seen a doctor, and the bottle she'd shown Batya hadn't been an elixir for appetite.

"I suspected."

And you didn't stop her?

They reached the freshly dug grave, where a burly Spanish man stood beside the gaping hole.

Nettie's shrouded body was lowered to the bottom of the grave. There was no man to say kaddish for the soul of the departed, so the two elderly women recited this prayer while the laborer shoved the earth back. The thump of the earth dropping on top of Nettie's body jolted Batya with the finality of her friend's life. With a new burst of tears, she joined the sisters in reciting the sacred words. *"O God, full of compassion, who dwells on high, grant true rest upon the wings of the Divine Presence, in the exalted spheres of the holy and pure, who shine as the resplendence of the firmament, for the soul of Nettie who has gone to her supernal world."*

The prayer ended before the grave was fully filled. Each sister picked up a fistful of earth and threw it into the hole. When it was Batya's turn, she scooped earth with both her hands, threw it, then scooped more, digging her fingers deep in the warm soil. *Rest in peace,* she cried silently, not merely full of grief over her friend's death but filled with fury over their life. Like Rochel, who had done nothing to stop Nettie, she, too, understood why Nettie had reached the end of the road. Were Batya not holding on to the hope of someday bringing her family over, she could very well have done the same.

The grave covered, each of the sisters lit a candle, stuck it in the freshly turned earth, and asked Nettie to carry her regards to her deceased loved ones.

Nettie, please send my love to my mother, Zelda, daughter of Tova. Please ask her to watch over me. Batya placed a small stone on top of the grave, then forced herself to turn away.

She walked with Rochel, their arms around each other under a dense cloud of sadness. They spoke little as they made their way back to the house.

At last, Rochel broke the silence in a voice that was uncharacteristically angry. "Although she was purified, Nettie was still *tme'ah* and had to be buried outside the fence."

"Even if she weren't a prostitute, committing suicide is killing God's image. That alone would have excluded her from being buried inside the fence. But God should have made an exception." Batya raised her head heavenward. "Don't You see that living as we do is more of a desecration of Your image than killing it?" She caught herself. She was becoming like her father, telling God how He should run His world.

She felt Rochel's shoulders heave and wondered how many times her friend, too, had wished to die.

Just then, the sky opened. Rain poured down like buckets of water drained from heaven to shower dust off the trees and houses, to wash Nettie's sins into the earth. Holding Rochel's hand, Batya ran.

Freda stood at the door of the house, counting the sisters as they entered, as though any of them might dare take the opportunity to escape.

Chapter Twenty-Eight

*B*ack home, Batya checked on Dora, who was still curled on her bed and not speaking. Batya assumed that she was granted days rather than weeks to break through to the girl, and was saddened that once again her entreaties bore no results. Dora sulked and remained unresponsive, until Batya just left the tray and returned to her room.

She picked up her *tkhines* book, hoping that even when they were read from a stolen book, God would accept her prayers for Nettie's departed soul and for Dora's tortured heart. Outside her window a family of pigeons had settled in the gutter. Maybe, somehow, the pigeons would fly sky-high with her words, and God would pluck her pleas from the air . . .

She opened the book at random. *"May my dough be blessed as the blessing hovered over the dough of our Mothers Sarah, Rebekah, Rachel, and Leah,"* she quoted the kitchen blessing uttered by generations of women before her.

No matter that she didn't have a kitchen. From now on, she,

too, would learn the many blessings that governed every minute action performed by women in their daily lives. She would say them as she washed her laundry, chopped vegetables, or cared for a sore on a sister's foot. To begin, she walked to the window and thanked God for the pigeons' company, for the moment of forgetfulness they offered.

Heavy steps outside the door interrupted her, and Batya quickly tucked the book under her mattress an instant before the door opened. Freda must have heard her moving about; Batya couldn't feign taking the rest of her siesta.

"Every moment you're not on your back is a moment lost." Freda untied the string that gathered the fabric of Batya's shirt above her chest, then yanked it open to expose her shoulders and the tops of her breasts. She slapped Batya's backside toward the window and thrust a red rose at her. "Sit there, and if no one comes up within fifteen minutes, I'll report you to my brother."

Instantly, Batya closed herself off, becoming Esperanza. She settled by the window. Back in Russia, Moskowitz had told Surale that in Buenos Aires there were one hundred men for each woman. In truth, there were thousands to one, and men's sexual appetites were insatiable. Satisfied one day, they came back for more the next—or as soon as they obtained more money.

Smiling toward the street, Batya stroked her cheek with the rose's petals and trailed the flower down toward her cleavage. She took deep gulps of air to tamp down the fear and disgust she felt at the prospect of yet another unpredictable stranger.

In the coming hours she hardened her heart to endure the humping, sweating, panting men who pawed at her buttocks and breasts, who kissed her mouth with slathered onion- and tobacco-stinking saliva, whose rough, unshaven faces scratched her cheeks, neck, and chest, whose bodies smelled of acrid sweat and stale sugarcane alcohol. Some wanted to watch themselves climax onto her breasts. Some paid Freda extra to climax in Batya's mouth. *God, keep my soul pure,* Batya thought. *Even if worms are eating my heart, please keep it pure, as it is Yours.*

The hardest men to ignore were those who enjoyed slapping and biting until her skin was black and blue. There had been men who tied her to the bedposts or even choked her. As soon as Batya detected such needs, she would make a quick flamenco dance move, banging her heels on the floor. That summoned Freda, who then charged the client for the additional services before he could proceed.

Batya preferred the younger boys, the ones she inducted into the mystery of women's bodies. They were confused or embarrassed, eager but always gentle, so unlike some judges, journalists, policemen, lawyers, businessmen, and politicians. Once the boys were hers, they often became regulars who paid for her time as frequently as they could afford. Invariably, they told her about conflicts in their families and shared with her the anguish and joys of their studies or emerging careers. Unlike some old men who appreciated when she revived their aging bodies but expected no more from a prostitute, the young men improved her Spanish.

Like Ulmann, who shared his feelings with the eagerness of a youth, no one ever inquired about her. No one guessed that she was a prisoner, shackled to her bed even if no chains were visible. Even Batya's excursions to the market for shopping were good for business. Other than washwomen and domestic helpers, honest women never left their houses unchaperoned. Moskowitz and Freda were confident that a seasoned girl like Batya knew that there was no place to run to and that she would return with a trail of hungry men following her.

Batya washed between men and chewed mint leaves to refresh her breath. At dusk, she took a permitted break to rest, eat a light supper, and redo her makeup and hair. At least she knew what to expect from regulars, who showed up mostly in the evenings. The more income she produced from her regulars, the more she could avoid the perverts. *"God, keep my soul pure,"* she mumbled her refrain. *"God, please show me a sign that You hear me. Save me from this hell."*

Glad as Batya was to have the *tkhines* book, its theft weighed on her. On her subsequent excursions to the market, she distributed pesos among amputees exposing stumps, dark-skinned native women begging with babies tied to their chests, ancient people with no hair or teeth, and street urchins whose bellies were distended from hunger.

But no matter how many coins she distributed, her conscience wouldn't be sated. Her mother's watching from above made her sin visible. While her mother might be crying with Batya over her fate, she would be unforgiving when it came to the voluntary offense of theft. Her mother was also watching Batya gobble down an abundance of food, while their relations in Russia starved. For all of Batya's careful saving, she was a long way from having enough money to pay for passports and travel tickets for her father, Surale, baby Vida—and, if she was inclined to join them, Keyla. From Siberia, Keyla had written to their father that she'd had twins, a boy and a girl. She hadn't mentioned that Fishke was the father, even as she continued to visit him monthly in prison, and Batya feared that her sister had been violated, all alone in that frosty wasteland of men.

"Help me, Mama, to get my father and my sisters out of Russia. You are closer to God. Maybe He'll listen to you. I know that I'm their only hope. So far, I've failed them. I've failed all of you."

The following week Batya accompanied Moskowitz on his late afternoon outing. They walked up Calle Corrientes, lined with cafés and stores that were out of the reach of the poor immigrants who lived in this mixed neighborhood. The late afternoon sun still shone high in the sky, while the pale, humble moon hung at a distance, awaiting its turn.

Just being outside at this time, when the house was becoming busy with its hilarity and debauchery, was a privilege. Moskowitz settled down at his favorite café, joining a table with three other pimps and their women. As much as she despised Moskowitz, Batya liked being chosen to sit at this café, so elegant that the waiters wore white gloves and where, like the wives of government ministers who met after their siestas, she sipped strong coffee and ate a delicious meringue and whipped-cream cake. She had labored hard to earn this special gift of reprieve.

Yet she was here to work. Rearranging the bottom of her dress to flow in a feminine way, she raised her hem above one ankle. She straightened her back to exhibit her long neck and exposed cleavage. If patrons from the café came to the house asking for her, they would likely be higher-class, generous customers.

She caught the eyes of a sister across the table and smiled. She didn't know the woman's name, and they couldn't chat over the men's conversation, but the bond of shared tragic history was a fine spiderweb that tied them together. Batya fixed her wide-brimmed, pinkish hat to uncover one side of her face and threw long glances at a corpulent man with kind brown eyes. His female companion selected a chocolate éclair from the passing tray, ignoring her man as she savored it. A waiter moved in front of the woman, leaving Batya visible only to the man. No doubt Moskowitz rewarded the waiter for this special service.

Silently, Batya continued to work the crowd at the nearby tables. The café was large, and tables in other sections hosted other pimps and their *kurves,* as if the competitors had divided the territory. It was easy to distinguish the pimps from other businessmen by their meticulous haircuts—probably by the same Italian barber Moskowitz used—and their manicured, buffed nails that shone with clear polish. Moskowitz's clean hands were a source of pride for him, a sign of his higher social standing. "My hands never get dirty in menial work," he liked to say when he delegated the beatings and cigarette burnings to others.

The conversation around her table flowed as the men sipped peppermint water or brandy, joked, and discussed business matters they considered to be beyond their female companions' grasp. "When a *kurve* becomes ill or pregnant, it affects the cash flow," Moskowitz said, puffing both his cigarette and his chest. "Frequent medical inspection is imperative to maintaining your investment."

"What about the new law that requires all our *kurves* be checked three times a week?" asked Pedro. He was wearing his plaid purple jacket but had replaced the green butterfly tie with an orange one.

Moskowitz laughed. "Unrealistic even for the best house. Ignore it."

Batya sent a shy smile to a man across the room. The man's moustache twitched in response. She batted her lashes, when her attention was arrested by a turn in the conversation.

"I didn't steal that Torah scroll," Moskowitz declared, laughing. "When the Judaica store reopened on Sunday, I showed up early and paid for it. I also paid for the damage of the broken door, and then some, for goodwill." He shook a finger at his companions. "No one would ever say that Yitzik Moskowitz is a thief."

Her *tkhines* book was paid for! A wave of relief washed over Batya. Smiling, she bent over her cake to allow herself a few seconds alone to bask in this discovery. The payment Moskowitz had made to the Judaica store was from money he'd extorted from her. God knew it.

"It's time we build our own synagogue," Moskowitz went on. "Why depend on the stuck-up Jews allowing us in? They are colluding against us? Well then, we'll show them what we're made of. We're as good Jews as they are. Our synagogue will be grand. We'll hire the best rabbi and the best chazzan."

"They'll come crawling back to us for our donations," said the corpulent Enrico, who had been Aharon in the old country.

"There's an empty lot on Guemes Street," Pedro said.

"If the owner will sell to us," Enrico replied.

"It's owned by a Frenchman's widow living in the south of France." Pedro winked. "I'll make sure she'll be happy to sell to us."

"If we want to move our offices there, too, there's a larger lot on Córdoba 3280," Moskowitz said. "We can build a mansion so that all those who scorn us will know whom they're dealing with: the best businessmen in this country, the smartest, shrewdest capitalists in all of South America."

"I'll drink to that." Pedro signaled the waiter, who brought over a bottle of champagne, popped the cork with great ceremony, and poured it. "I'll donate the most beautiful crystal chandelier you've ever seen," Pedro declared.

"I will donate the curtains for the arc," said Enrico.

"Two Torah scrolls." Moskowitz sniggered. "One I already own."

The men went on to discuss who would donate what furnishing, decor, and funds, but Batya stopped listening. Rather than suffering God's wrath for his sins, Moskowitz only continued to rise in the ranks of Zwi Migdal.

Chapter Twenty-Nine

Summer 1893–1894

*S*he was forever wrapping her head around the fact that while summer was in full force in Buenos Aires, in Russia winter was holding on to the earth and sky, merging them into one icy substance. It had been as hard to breathe in Russia's freezing air as it was to breathe here in the humid heat.

At least in her room, the stone wall stayed cool. Batya leaned her back against it, fanning herself, and contemplated what her chatty morning client had just revealed.

He was a gaucho, a rancher of cattle, dressed in leather leggings with a gun tucked in the back of his brown-black belt, but his white shirt was clean. To her astonishment, he spoke Yiddish. She'd never heard of a Jewish gaucho, a Jew who rode a horse rather than harnessing it to a peddler's cart. His name was Kolkowski, and he said he'd come down to Buenos Aires

to greet Jewish immigrants arriving from Odessa as guests of
the Baron.

"What baron?" Batya had asked, thinking it was a game.

"Baron de Hirsch. Maurice—Moses de Hirsch." When Batya
seemed confused, Kolkowski added, "Haven't you heard of his
initiative?"

No, she hadn't. "Teach me your game," she cooed.

"I'm serious. This Jewish German baron lives in Paris and
has decided to save the Jews of Eastern Europe by establishing
farming communities in Argentina. He's already built many agricultural colonies in Santa Fe, Entre Ríos, and La Pampa, with
synagogues and yeshivas. He's bringing over shiploads of Jews."

Batya had known that there were vast empty areas beyond
Buenos Aires, but she hadn't heard of anyone choosing to live
there. "What will they do there?"

"Resettle in the ranches. What else? Moïseville, Mauricio,
these are Jewish colonies in the Pampas. We teach them agriculture, mainly, but also how to raise cattle." Probably seeing Batya's
skeptical expression, Kolkowski added, "The Baron is paying
the czar to let the Jews leave. He wants to empty Russia of the
Jews and bring them all here."

She couldn't hold her laughter. The man was delusional. "Like
Exodus? Does God also split the ocean for you all to cross?"

"Not God, but the Jewish Colonization Association does.
That's the Baron's project for resettlement," Kolkowski replied,
seemingly unperturbed by her ridicule. "One million Jews. You'll
see soon."

There was no point in arguing with a madman. "Let my people
go," Batya intoned, and broke into a dance.

"Really. The Argentine government wants people from all over the world to come here, to help build the country. Jews are good at commerce. The Baron—"

She had stopped Kolkowski by placing her hand playfully on his mouth while the other traveled downward. He'd paid for a short visit but was wasting it on nonsense.

Now Batya rose, dressed, and checked the pavilion. No clients waited there. It was early, and the midday meal wouldn't be served for a while. Freda was occupied in the adjacent house. If Batya used the new tram—now electric—it would take her fifteen minutes to reach the port. She threw on her lightest dress and hat and ventured out. In spite of her disbelief in Kolkowski's tale, she wished to ascertain with her own eyes whether any part of it could be true.

She had just walked a block when an old woman clutched the bottom of her skirt, and Batya swiveled around.

"Please, señora," the woman pleaded, her eyes brimming with tears. "Let me launder your clothes."

Batya took in the cheeks blotched in caked rouge that failed to make them look healthy. Her tone soft, she asked, "Sister, what's your name?"

"Leila." The woman held on to Batya's skirt. "No one else allows me to touch their clothes. I'll do a good job. I'll wash and iron everything. Please—"

"Come to that house at siesta time," Batya replied, pointing. "Now I must rush."

She disembarked from the tram near the port's administration building and walked to the wide pier to examine the docking ships. Two women in flowery, ruffled dresses and kohl-blackened eyes approached her. "This is our spot," one yelled. "Move away."

Batya shrugged and crossed the road, where she still had a view of the customs gate. Unlike four years earlier, the ships now docked at the new pier, and hordes of immigrants carrying cardboard valises and canvas packages streamed down the ramps instead of being rowed in by small boats. Prodded by policemen into orderly lines, the newcomers joined the mass of humanity crowding behind the high gate. Children cried, men held packages over their heads, fistfights broke out, women called over the crowd to keep their families together. Batya stepped into the shade of a warehouse, afraid she would be seen by someone she knew from home.

But then again, no one would have recognized her now.

She watched as a pretty young woman carrying a carpetbag emerged from the customshouse, then stopped, bewildered. A matronly woman in a carriage called out to her in Yiddish, "Do you need a job? Do you have relatives to take you in?"

After a short exchange, the young woman climbed into the carriage to what Batya was certain would turn out to be a life of prostitution.

A monk marched out of the customs building with four teenage boys in tow. A policeman parted the way for him and let the monk—whom Batya recognized as an Italian pimp—walk out with his new entourage. Even from a distance she could tell that these were girls dressed as boys to fool the customs clerks. She was certain the policeman knew it, too.

And then she spotted him: Kolkowski emerged from the port's office ushering a group of mostly men, but also some families, all carrying bundles and boxes tied with ropes. They looked pale and emaciated in their bedraggled clothes. Most had taken off their coats and struggled with carrying them along with the rest of their belongings.

Batya counted fifty people. She followed them through the two short blocks to the expansive dormitories that made up the Immigrants' Hotel. This part of Kolkowski's story seemed true, as unlikely as it had first sounded. She followed him back to the port and took her post by the warehouse. He disappeared behind the gate, only to come out fifteen minutes later accompanying a smaller group.

Batya allowed a small hope to bloom in her chest. Might she have found a solution for her family? As she walked away, she saw two women in black mourning clothes and head scarves, with five little children between them, standing in the middle of the street, dazed as she had once been by the piercing bright, hot sun and disoriented in the unfamiliar surroundings. No men accompanied them. No relatives showed up to welcome them. These desperate widows, who must have come here seeking a better future for their children, would end up as destitute and resourceless as they had been in the old country. Batya wished she could warn them against the couple that was approaching them, a husband-wife team she was certain were pimps. The man made an attempt at respectability by wearing a shiny top hat that was incongruous with his frayed jacket. But Batya doubted that these confused, tired mothers would heed her warning against this benevolent-seeming couple who was handing the children chocolate and, in a few moments, would offer the mothers shelter for the week. Soon after, Batya knew, in order to feed their children, the women would be pressured into prostitution.

The idea of Jewish colonies in remote parts of Argentina stayed with Batya throughout her waking hours. In her dream that night she saw herself riding a horse and rounding up a herd of cows, all showing her beloved Aggie's black-and-white pattern. Her father welcomed her at the stable late in the afternoon and conversed with the horse in Yiddish, giving both the questions and the answers.

The next day, though, doubt about the story crept back. She was glad when Kolkowski came two days later, before returning to his village.

"Isn't farming difficult?" she asked, thinking about her father's aching back.

"Aren't Jews used to difficulties? When did we have it easy?"

She smiled and stroked Kolkowski's back, letting her nails hypnotize him into talking.

He went on. "In the Baron's villages, Jews are learning new forms of agriculture. We give them equipment, instructions, and even credit, so one day they can own the land."

She would have a vegetable garden, she thought. Having discovered tomatoes, a couple of years earlier she had planted a tomato plant in the kitchen yard behind the concrete trough where they scrubbed clothes. Freda had thought it was a waste of Batya's working time. She poured the soapy water on the plant, killing it. More important, Batya thought, she would plant a tree. Permanency was symbolized by a tree planting, by the confidence that one would always be there to watch it grow.

"Did you say Jewish schools?" Batya asked Kolkowski.

He nodded. "The Argentine government doesn't forbid Jewish studies, and certainly doesn't kidnap the students for the army."

Her father had been delighted to have only daughters, free from this danger that loomed over boys. Forcefully conscripted before their bar mitzvahs and reeducated in military schools, they served in the czar's army for twenty-five years. By then they were no longer Jewish. "Your Baron really plans a mass exodus?" Batya asked. "A million Jews?"

"It's already started. We have an office here, in Buenos Aires. Señor Farbstein, who runs it, buys the land, sends experts to show our people how to ranch, and hires teachers for the Jewish schools. No one calls them 'dirty Jews,' and no priest accuses them of killing Jesus."

Her family's salvation was right here in Buenos Aires! Señor Farbstein. Batya rolled the name on her tongue. She could taste the hope.

The next morning, she snuck out again, this time straight to the Immigrants' Hotel, and watched as the newcomers, still wearing their too-heavy peasant clothes, loaded valises onto wagons. Batya approached a woman sitting on a bench and nursing an infant under a cape. "Where are you all going?"

"To the train station, to take us to Moïseville."

Moïseville. A new Moses, like his namesake who had led the Israelites out of Egypt, was freeing the Jews from the czar and his incessant edicts. Decent people like her father could rise from abject poverty to farm in peace. Could it be true?

"Just one more question, please," Batya said as the woman rearranged herself and picked up a large bag. "Who paid for your ocean passage?"

"The Baron. May his name be linked to the greatest *tzaddikim's*. That's who."

Batya skipped on the broken sidewalk on her way back to the house. Moïseville. Her family's salvation. Her own safe haven. It had a name. Once there, never again would a man come near her body. Never again would she dress and paint her face, sit at her window, and smile at passersby.

Batya completed her morning chores, retreated to her room, and opened her *tkhines* book. She prayed for the Baron, for his good health and long life. The new Moses. Miracles happened after all.

Chapter Thirty

$\mathcal{B}$atya sat at the table in a client's mother's home. She watched as Efram, a young Talmudic scholar and one of her regulars, dipped his pen in the inkwell, checked the amount of ink at the tip, then dabbed it against the blotter. Today she wasn't employing the services of the Professor, who was the favorite among the *caftans* to write their prostitutes' letters. Her father appreciated the Professor's Yiddish-language prose. *His flourishing words are a feast to my eyes and ears, every description a masterpiece of literature that tells me of your good luck,* he had written. *When we are finally united in Buenos Aires, this is the man with whom I would be honored to have a Talmudic debate.*

Unlike the scribes in the service of the pimps' organization, Efram would fear turning her in for this infraction; he knew as well as she did the wrath of Zwi Migdal against anyone who'd steal from a member his just earnings, and indeed Batya would pay Efram with a private, unauthorized reward. Luckily, Efram's mother's house was not far from the market, and Batya would make up for the stolen time by shopping fast and seducing a couple of merchants to come see her at the house.

The lace curtains in Efram's mother's parlor were drawn to block neighbors' curious eyes, but the large window had to be kept open to let in fresh air, which nevertheless did little to relieve the heat of the day, as the audacious summer was refusing to give way to the next season. Across the street, a sweets seller was rearranging his display of dried fruits, caramelized walnuts, and sugar crystallized on miniature sticks. Batya spotted a large earthenware jug whose clay sides kept liquid cooled. She fanned herself. She could almost taste the chill of the almond drink she would buy as soon as she left.

That cold, sweet drink had to wait. She turned her attention back to Efram, hunched over his letter. He wound his long, reddish *peyes*, corkscrew sidelocks, around his ears to keep them from dropping onto the paper and smearing the ink. His mother was visiting some cousins for a few days, and, by prior arrangement, Efram feigned a stomach illness so he could stay home from his yeshiva, the Jewish religious school. Batya had waited a whole week for this opportunity.

Efram read to her what he'd written, having embellished her dictation almost as well as the Professor would have. *"I want to share my bounty with all of you. I beg you, my dear father, help me make it happen. Please travel to Odessa to register with the Jewish Colonization Association for resettlement here in Argentina,"* he finished, raising his ginger-colored eyes to Batya.

He adored her now, but soon, when he turned eighteen, he'd

be married off by his rabbi. Orthodox Jews, concerned about their youngsters' sexual urges, married them off in a hurry. Efram would turn his back on the prostitute who had made him a man.

Efram dipped his pen in the inkwell. "This resettlement program needs more explaining," he said to her. As eager as he was to conclude this part of their exchange so they could retreat to his bedroom, he also seemed to want to do well by her. Such a sweet boy. She trailed her fingers on the back of his neck and felt him shiver in response. He went on speaking while writing. *"The Baron de Hirsch from France, may he be blessed with a long and healthy life, envisions farming in Argentina to end Jewish blood flowing in the streets of Eastern Europe."*

"That's very good." Batya smiled, wondering how much of her plans Efram had guessed. Her father had often said, "A Jew shouldn't trust even his own dog."

"I like your face when you think hard," Efram said, and closed the small distance between their heads. He kissed her on the lips. "Let's finish this letter," he whispered, his breathing heavy.

"Yes, we must." She licked his ear. "Please add to the letter, *You and my dear beloved sisters, Keyla and Surale, whom I miss terribly, will be safe here.*"

Was it right to convince Keyla to join them here, now that Fishke had died in the gulag? Her father had written that Keyla and her children were *starving three times a day*. With the money Batya would be sending, her sister must find a way to make the dangerous way west with two toddlers. Keyla had been breaking her back in the fields as a hired hand for years and could work just as hard in the new Argentine settlement. But a widow would be a target for pimps.

She'd leave it to God, Batya decided. The proof that He'd already determined the outcome for His people was that He'd sent this second Moses.

"You will all be transported to a newly built village," Efram went on, *"where you'll start a new life free of discrimination and strife. My nephews will attend yeshivas and bring us all honor."*

Batya waited while Efram dabbed the blotter on the first written page and set it aside to dry. As soon as she mailed the letter, she'd find a way to speak to Señor Farbstein. She took a deep breath as she began to dictate the second page. *"Papa, you know your way with both horses and cows. You will be of great help to your fellow Jews. They will look up to you."* If nothing else, her father cared about being respected. This might be the incentive he needed.

First, though, her father must agree to take the necessary steps on his end. Now that Surale had a husband who could also register with the Colonization Association, her sister might be out of danger of being snared into a brothel. In fact, a healthy young man in the family would surely add to its appeal for the Baron's agents, Batya figured. Upon her family's arrival, she would escape to join them deep in the vast land of Argentina. The farther they lived from any main city, the safer she would be.

It was a daring dream; she'd never heard of a prostitute who had escaped Zwi Migdal—certainly not lately, when its network, which stretched throughout the entire South American continent—seemed to be getting bigger and richer. But the Baron's project was surely clear of Zwi Migdal's influence. She must secure its protection.

"Tell my father to be careful with his money," Batya told

Efram, thinking of the forged one-hundred-ruble bill Moskowitz had once given him. "He's quite gullible."

Efram read back to her. *"Please do not trust any agent other than the Baron's. Some desperate emigrants fall victim to unscrupulous crooks posing as agents who offer to get their documents in order. They get falsified passports while the 'agents' disappear with all their savings. Believe no one but the Baron's representative—"*

Batya cut him off. "Inside—Efram, please emphasize this word—*inside* the Baron's office, not even right outside its front door. And tell him I'm enclosing three money certificates." She dictated, *"The first, send to Keyla. Cash the second one at a reputable money changer to pay for your trip to Odessa. Save the third one from robbers on the road until you are ready, in Odessa, to pay for the passports for you, my sisters, and their families."*

"You won't be able to see your family. The colonies are very far away," Efram said. "Argentina is as big as Russia. You can't just travel easily from place to place."

"Knowing that they're out of danger will be enough," Batya replied, inserting into her tone all the sweetness she could muster. Maybe even Hedi might change her mind and join them. Her goy husband might have turned out to be no less a drunkard than most Russian men. If Batya had an address, or even just the name of the village where her sister lived, she would write to her and offer her this chance to join the family. Maybe her children, raised Christians, wouldn't be taught to hate Jews, wouldn't be told that Jews deserved torture and death.

Efram finished writing the letter and showed it to Batya. "Your handwriting looks so beautiful," she purred, her hand on the inside of his thigh, moving upward. "You must be the best Talmudic scholar in your yeshiva." She bent over his chair and rubbed her breasts against his sunken chest. "It's been a while since you spoke Spanish to me. Tell me what you want me to do to your body."

His Adam's apple bobbed, and his face flushed when the bulge in his trousers grew. She buried her face in his neck, enjoying the fresh smell of his skin, unsullied by tobacco or alcohol.

She loved the closeness after lovemaking, which happened with only a few of her regulars. The glow of Efram's satisfaction was combined with the gratefulness he showed her. But she couldn't bask in it now. She couldn't even linger in the luxury of the bathtub in the white-tiled room, the second such bath in her life. Her letter in her pocket, Batya left Efram's home. She must figure out how to mail it from a post agent not under the control of Zwi Migdal—surely not one in the center of Buenos Aires.

Within moments outside, in the humidity of this midday hour, perspiration formed on Batya's upper lip and underarms. She was ready for that chilled almond drink.

As she started across the street, she noticed a commotion around the sweets seller's cart. Four teenagers were stealing from him in broad daylight, and rather than fleeing with their loot, they taunted him—hopping around him, shoving fistfuls of his sweets into their mouths. Red-faced, his moustache trembling, the man begged them to leave him alone. He didn't shout or raise a club to fight them off. He cried and pleaded with his tormentors.

The man's powerlessness pulsated under Batya's skin. In her mind's eye she saw her father's goods stolen by cruel goyim who had ordered cheese, buttermilk, and cream but, when he delivered, sent him away with no pay. She saw the czar's soldiers confiscating all the butter she and her mother and sisters had churned for hours.

Passersby had stopped to watch, leering, enjoying the scene. Without thinking, Batya rushed into the fray. She swung her arms, slapping, shoving, punching. When a boy turned to her, astonishment on his face, she raised her knee into his groin. He fell to the ground clutching his private parts while his friends fled.

Some spectators clapped; others, aware of her status, shouted lewd remarks. Blood rushed to Batya's face at her public humiliation. She gathered her courage to ignore them. "I'll have the almond drink, please," she said to the sweets seller, who stood stupefied. At Batya's feet, the youngster writhed and groaned.

Concern spreading over his brow, the sweets seller leaned across his cart to watch the boy. Up close, Batya saw that the man was a simpleton, his tongue too large for his mouth, his round eyes bewildered.

To Batya's relief, the young attacker crawled to his feet and scrambled away. The small crowd dispersed. The show was over.

The sweets seller turned to fill the tin cup from the earthenware jar shaded under a canvas stretched with three poles.

"You must be so smart to know how to make all these sweets," Batya said in Spanish.

"The almonds, they are from my family's orchard." His eyes were drawn to the ample skin showing above her breasts.

She passed the tips of her fingers lazily down her neck to her cleavage. "And where is that place where this orchard grows almonds?"

He named a village she'd never heard of, adding, "The sugar, too, is from my village. From sugarcanes." He handed her the cup. His hand shook.

She sipped. "It's so good. The best ever!" She licked her lips slowly. "What's your name? I'm Esperanza."

"Rafael."

"That's a good name. In the Bible it means 'God heals.'"

"It does?" His round eyes grew rounder. She noted the creases in his forehead and the dryness of his skin. His gums were gray with disease. He was older than he'd first looked, like that old man in her shtetl whose simplicity made the worries of the world slide away before they could mark his face.

She fished in her purse for a coin.

"Oh, no." He waved her coin away. "You are a good woman."

A good woman. She was warmed by the compliment; no one had ever referred to her as *good*. "Thank you. You are a good man yourself." She dropped the coin back in her purse and sipped more. "Is your village far? How do you get there?"

"Every two weeks, my brother comes with a horse to take me back to our mother." Rafael pointed to the end of the cart, where two long shafts were propped by wood blocks.

She smiled. "I like you. Can we be friends?"

God was on her side, showing her the way. This was how she would get her letter mailed.

Chapter Thirty-One

*I*n the pavilion, Batya sat in rapt attention as Rochel, who had been to the Yiddish theater the night before, regaled the sisters with the details of her adventure. Of all the sisters chosen by Moskowitz to accompany him to the theater, Rochel was the best raconteur. She could reenact the jokes, the singing, even entire scenes.

Batya had never been to the theater, and these reenactments fired her imagination and lit a spark of envy. She was grateful when Moskowitz took her to cafés, but he spread theater outings among his other prostitutes. Even Rochel, who had been invited often, said she didn't know why he favored her.

Rochel's story this morning was about a maid who had been accused of stealing her mistress's jewelry. It turned out that the mistress had sold them in order to give the money to her elusive lover. Unbeknownst to her, that man was in love with her maid, with whom he had conspired to elope.

"Batya, stand up," Rochel ordered. "You're the lover, a dashing Spaniard. Repeat the sentences I tell you, then when I quote mine, you say yours. It's called a dialogue. *Farshteyst?*"

Batya, whose mind was also on the promise in the Baron's project, stumbled on her lines, which seemed unrelated to one another. The sisters laughed, but when Rochel interjected her sentences between Batya's, the sequence made sense. Encouraged, Batya refocused and repeated her lines with pathos. The scene of misunderstandings and double-talk sounded hilarious.

When she and Rochel finished, the sisters clapped and cheered. Batya loved the applause. It gave her the same joy that fueled her muscles when she performed tango in front of a crowd of sisters and clients.

"Now for the thief's song," Rochel announced. "It's a Yiddish tango, so the rhythm is one-two-three-four, one-two-three-four."

> *I am Salve, the thief,*
> *Four brothers are we;*
> *One is hungry, the other well fed,*
> *But thieves all four are we.*
> *One is a pickpocket,*
> *The second a pimp, a handsome fellow;*
> *One is a hijacker on the lookout for packages,*
> *And I am a house thief.*

The sisters joined in, repeating the lines. Some rose to dance, entangling and disentangling their legs in the tango steps.

Freda interrupted the merriment. "Every moment that you sit

or stand is a moment lost," she snapped. "Rochel, you to your window. Batya, you to the kitchen. Glikel, go help the wash-woman hang the sheets. She's too short to reach the lines."

Batya retreated to the kitchen, humming the new song. Facing the sink, she yelped when she felt Moskowitz's warm breath on her neck.

"It's only me." He cupped her breast.

Her mouth was dry. She forced her lips to smile. "I missed you."

"No, you didn't, but you're quite convincing." He snaked his other hand over her other breast and gyrated his hips against her buttocks. "How about the theater tonight?"

Theater? Her tongue stuck to the roof of her mouth. She nodded, then found her voice. "Thank you."

He laughed. "Forever the polite little girl, aren't you?" He released her and walked out.

The blood pulsed in Batya's ears with a mixture of hatred and excitement. She arranged a breakfast tray—making sure the coffee was only lukewarm—and took it upstairs to Dora. She knocked on the door before using her key, knowing that nothing lessened the girl's dread about who was entering. Freda's patience with Batya's failure had reached a breaking point, and she had announced that it was time to sell this bad investment.

Dora sat curled on the floor in the corner. She didn't raise her head.

"Good morning. Are you hungry?" Batya trilled, hoping yet again for a response that she doubted would be forthcoming.

When the girl made no sign that she even saw her, Batya sat

down on the floor facing her and crossed her legs. "Look at this food, at this room. You can have a good life. What difference does it make where you work?" She took Dora's hand. "Dora, if you do housecleaning, you will work just as hard, but it will take you ten years to make what you can make here in a month."

Dora let out a guttural sound, more like an angry animal's than a human's.

Batya pulled the tray closer. "Only rich matrons are blessed with a good life. Most women are dirt-poor, and they hate the drudgery of their lives as much as you do prostitution. But it can get a lot worse for you if you continue to resist. I'd like to help you."

When Dora still refused to acknowledge her, Batya left the room and locked it. There was no use. If Dora committed suicide, the cost of it would fall on Batya, yet in her heart Batya admitted that ending her life might be the better option for Dora.

Back in the kitchen, as she finished her chores, the excitement of the upcoming evening's adventure returned. Batya renewed her singing and was wiping dishes and stacking them when three sisters entered the kitchen for their cooking duties.

"Why are you singing?" Glikel asked Batya, her eyes glazed. Glikel's affinity for opium had increased; Freda and Moskowitz didn't begrudge sisters who spent their earnings on it, since it motivated them to better serve clients.

"I'm going to the theater tonight!" Batya grabbed a broom as her partner and danced while humming the thief's Yiddish tango.

Glikel interrupted. "It's my turn to go to the theater, but you stole it from me with that new dress of yours."

Batya stopped, tossed a glance at the girl, and put the broom away. She hated the bickering, the jealousy, the competition among some girls. Glikel was beautiful and had more generous regulars than most. Even before the opium, she had no reason to be spiteful.

"It's Batya's turn," replied Juliet, a delicate, flat-chested girl with cropped hair who catered to men who wouldn't admit to preferring boys. "She hasn't been to the theater yet. You went twice this year. After Batya, it's my turn."

"Go present Yitzik Moskowitz with a list of whose turn it is and see what he says," said Clara, so named for her very clear skin, eyes, and hair, as though God had painted her with a one-color brush before sending her out into the world.

Annoyed, Batya walked out to the kitchen yard to hang a sponge to dry and collect her underthings from the line. She ran a finger over her chin to feel the pimples, hoping that by the evening the yeast she'd applied would dry them. It was true that Batya had overcome her frugality and replaced her outgrown dress with a new mint-green organza creation. It wasn't the first time she had needed new clothes; the abundant food continued to fill her, and, to her surprise, she had also grown taller—taller than her parents or her older sisters had been. She no longer needed to pretend to look like a woman; she was one.

That evening, Rochel helped Batya step into her new dress. "It brings out the green in your eyes," she gushed, fluffing the rows of ruffles that layered the sleeves and also ran above the skirt's hem. She gathered Batya's hair loosely on top, allowing some tendrils to escape, and tucked peach-colored rosebuds between the curls. Then she kissed Batya's cheek and smiled. Batya loved seeing those twin dimples deepen, her friend's sign of approval.

"You look like a French courtesan," Rochel said. "All you need is a fluffy white dog."

Chapter Thirty-Two

*R*iding in the horse-drawn open carriage, Batya still couldn't believe her good fortune. She straightened her back, imagining herself the wealthy woman she had been falsely promised she would become, and looked around as the horses trotted past magnificent buildings into the newly widened boulevard of Avenida de Mayo. She turned her finger to reflect the light off the opal ring she had acquired from Glikel and touched the mother-of-pearl brooch that clasped her shawl. Made of the same mint-green fabric as the dress, the sheer organza wrap still permitted a view of her thin waist while offering some modesty. She wouldn't wear her better jewelry, only the pieces that the sisters had seen. The rest were her secret. She hoped that Ulmann, whose drawings she was helping improve, would soon reward her with one of those more substantial creations. Beyond the weight of the gold, such a gift would strengthen the delicate tie that was forming between them—one she wished to nurture.

Next to her, Moskowitz wore a fine black suit, with tails that ran down to the back of his knees. Before sitting in the carriage, he had rearranged them the way she did her long dress. The suit's shiny silk collar matched the band of silk running along the sides of his trousers. His pointed, lacquered shoes shone as brightly as his top hat. Diamonds sparkled in his cuff links and in each of his shirt buttons.

Signs of construction were everywhere; just ahead stretched a series of high mounds of broken brick, tin, and lumber—the remains of hundreds of huts and houses demolished to make room for the widening of the boulevard.

"Do you know why this boulevard is called 'de Mayo'?" Moskowitz asked, and then, assuming her ignorance, answered, "To commemorate the May Revolution of 1810. That's when Argentina became independent from Spain."

It had taken a revolution to achieve freedom, she thought. Fishke's ideas about a Russian revolution landed him in prison, but here another revolution had succeeded. An insane thought flashed through Batya's head: Could the thousands of Buenos Aires's prostitutes unite to rebel?

"So, you haven't guessed where we're going?" Moskowitz asked her.

She shook her head. Most of the Yiddish theaters were in Once, Spanish for "eleven," named after the neighborhood's Once de Septiembre train station, not in this most elegant part of town. If Moskowitz hadn't dressed so lavishly, she would have assumed that he was about to deposit her at a private party in a *casita*. "Where?" she asked.

Up ahead, more horse-drawn open carriages and even two

horseless automobiles carried well-dressed people, the privileged high class, all heading in the same direction.

"We're going to Teatro Colón, of course," Moskowitz said, and ordered the coachman to slow down. Then, as if pulled by invisible strings, his shoulders straightened and his neck stretched. He lit a cigarette and, in a slow, calculated gesture, placed it between his lips. His eyes glanced sideways without turning his head, as if to check the impression he was projecting.

Teatro Colón! Batya dared not speak and reveal her excitement.

Moskowitz went on. "The Italian patron who financed the renovations of the theater died twenty years ago. The city had no money to finish this grand project, but guess who solved the problem? The Warsaw gang. Zwi Migdal. That's who. We make the business engine of this city run, and now, with our support, culture will make Buenos Aires the most prominent city in all of South America."

You feed the engine with the meat of our bodies. Moskowitz probably expected her to say some words of adulation about how influential he was, but Batya couldn't bring herself to give him the satisfaction.

The carriage stopped in front of the theater, and Batya gasped. The mass of scaffolding she had seen whenever she passed here was gone, and instead there appeared an imposing palace. The giant busts and bas-reliefs on the façade seemed poised to jump off the building.

"Wait until you see the inside," Moskowitz said with pride. "It's as palatial as any grand opera house in Europe."

Batya smiled, although his comparison meant nothing to her; she'd never seen either a palace or an opera house. Nor did she know what "opera" meant. She waited till the coachman opened the side door and placed a small stool on the ground, then she climbed down, lifting her dress to keep it off the sidewalk in what she hoped was an elegant gesture.

Moskowitz walked slowly, taking his time to cover the short distance between the curb and the entrance. He tilted his head in salutation to acquaintances, each with one or two young women hanging on his arms.

Entering the theater with her arm looped into Moskowitz's didn't dampen Batya's excitement or suppress her grin. They stepped into an enormous vestibule with marble columns reaching up to a huge stained-glass dome. Batya heard her own intake of breath at the sight of the immense lobby, with an endless row of massive crystal chandeliers multiplying in the mirrors on both sides.

Moskowitz's fingers on the small of her back guided her protectively as if she were his wife, not his *kurve,* toward a grand marble staircase as wide as a street and flanked by commanding pillars. She raised the hem of her dress and stepped on the first stair, laying her hand on the balustrade. It felt luxuriously cool to her fingers. *Marble.* The word rang of opulence, as did the hued veins running through the stone, delicate serpentine streaks of color that hinted at their depth.

Moskowitz stopped at the first landing and looked around like a proprietor. Scanning the vestibule below, Batya could view the women's dresses of lustrous silk, gossamer, or organza embroidered with pearls. Swathes of lace or Spanish shawls embroidered with sensuous flowers in red, purple, and yellow covered the women's shoulders, and when the lights ignited their diamonds and precious stones, their collective brilliance blinded Batya with their class statement. Yet, with all their fine fashion and elaborate hairstyles, these women were devoid of makeup other than a discreet touch of cheek rouge, the well-placed black dot of a faux beauty mark, or perhaps the finest rice powder to lighten the skin. Batya wished she could wipe the bright red from her lips and erase the charcoal with which Rochel had accentuated her eyes.

After more greetings, Moskowitz guided her to the third floor, where a uniformed usher bowed. "Your box seat is ready, señor." He pulled the brass handle of a heavy mahogany door and led them into a small enclosed area, where he drew open a double-layered curtain. Batya glimpsed eight chairs set neatly in two rows facing an upholstered railing.

She caught her breath yet again at the sight of the vast theater below and the horseshoe-shaped galleries above. She touched the plush scarlet velvet of a chair. Her eyes drank in the gilded molding that framed the balconies, columns, and entrances. Every centimeter was decorated with either red or gold.

"Sit," Moskowitz ordered.

Batya hesitated, uncertain whether someone like her was permitted to sit on such a beautiful chair.

"Sit, I said, and close your mouth," he repeated. "You look like a stupid *polaca,* gawking like this."

She winced at the term and sat down. Leaning forward, she dared look over the railing. In the main hall, men and women seemed to be in no rush to take their seats as they crowded the aisles, the women giggling modestly behind their fans. A heavy curtain blocked what Batya assumed was the stage, framed by a huge border of decorative paintings. Outside the box balconies ringing the theater, hundreds of crystal sconces cast a dim yet rich glow.

She must memorize every detail to report to the sisters in the house. She counted six floors of spectators, and above them all, rising like the canopy of God's sky, a grand cupola painted with beautiful scenes of crowds following musicians.

The cacophony of voices was drowned out when dozens of musicians broke into a discordant concert like an army of night insects. *Is this opera?* Batya wondered, then figured that like the klezmers, they were only tuning up. She pointed her finger and began counting the men.

"You can't count over a hundred," Moskowitz sneered. "This orchestra pit holds one hundred and twenty musicians. Like the best of the European opera houses!"

Batya dared not ask him what "opera" was. So much of the world was still beyond her grasp.

A hush fell over the theater. Here and there a throat cleared and taffeta rustled. Then the orchestra began to play. The harmonious sounds spread like buckets of pearls tumbling from the sky, yet instead of falling, they were carried by a playful wind. They picked up Batya and transported her to a place where only dreams could live.

At first, the sisters didn't believe her story. Horses and camels onstage? Pyramids and a whole army of soldiers and another army of servants?

"The opera is called *Aida*." Batya repeated the running explanation Moskowitz had provided the night before. "It's about a

Nubian princess captured and enslaved in Egypt by Pharaoh—"
Batya stopped, almost choking with the recollection of how she
had identified with Aida, except that the beautiful chocolate-
skinned princess had lived inside the magic of the dazzling stage
rather than in Batya's nightmare, made more real by Moskowitz's chattering. "The Egyptian military commander falls in
love with her, but Pharaoh's daughter is in love with him. Aida's
father, the Nubian king, plans to invade Egypt to rescue his beloved daughter—"

The excitement around the breakfast table was palpable. This
morning, instead of each group of sisters clearing their plates before the next took its turn, dozens of girls crowded the kitchen
and the yard, interrupting Batya with so many questions that she
had to repeat the details of the frescos and the women's dresses
and restart the story of Aida yet again—never reaching the most
significant part of the evening: the singers' voices, which had even
shut up Moskowitz. Like the voices of angels, who had floated
down from heaven only for the evening before flying back up to
sit at the feet of God. How could Batya describe such sounds
emanating from the throats of humans, the women's high, like
magic flutes, the men's as sonorous as the roar of the ocean?

She was in her fourth telling when mayhem broke out. A police
carriage stopped in front of the house, and two officers dragged
Dora in through the door, the girl screaming and kicking.

Batya felt her stomach flip. The night before, in her excitement
after the opera, she had briefly checked on Dora and verified that
the girl had eaten. Then Batya fell asleep happy, the sights and
sounds of the opera pulling her into a dream in which an Egyp-

tian commander dressed in a leather tunic rode his horse across the desert toward her.

It took only a few minutes for the officers to unfold the story to Freda and Moskowitz: Sometime near dawn, Dora had climbed out her window—probably had wriggled out between the twin bars—jumped on the roof of an adjacent lean-to, and run off to the police station. There, in Yiddish mixed with a smattering of Spanish, she begged and cried and asked for protection. She tried telling the officer of her entrapment, of the beatings, of the auction. With several policemen snickering at the *polaca*'s distress, the officer told her in Spanish that she must obey the law, that prostitution was legal, and that the law said she must obey her husband. Dora, of course, didn't understand any of it, but the officer who dragged her back to the house filled in the details as he handed her back to Moskowitz. Batya watched as their jailer, not attempting to be surreptitious, tucked a gray banknote into the policeman's palm. One hundred pesos!

During the following days, Dora was beaten, starved, and confined in a hole under the kitchen yard, where sewage seeped through the walls and cockroaches swarmed. The sisters moved in silence through their morning chores of cleaning, laundering, mending, and cooking. The lesson for disobedience and betrayal was meant to reverberate in their hearts. Indeed, while doing her kitchen duty, Batya could hear Dora's moans through the floorboards. No one but Freda was allowed to open the top of the hole, into which, once a day, she lowered a pail of water and some bread.

The descriptions of *Aida* that Batya had cultivated in her

head throughout the evening at Teatro Colón turned sour in her mouth. Images of the fantastically elaborate stage sets of palaces and pyramids in a vast, sunbathed desert melted into the image of Dora in the hole. The haunting beauty of the singing drowned in the muck of the girl's loud suffering.

Four days later, Dora was brought up right after breakfast. She was dropped on a chair, splayed like a rag doll, head lolling, arms dangling at her sides, legs apart. The wild yet vacant look in her eyes told Batya that the girl had gone mad, and in a way Batya was glad for her. Escaping the torture through madness was better than feeling every iota of it.

Two hundred prostitutes from nearby houses were rounded up in the pavilion, courtyard, and kitchen. The Professor, who had been seated in Moskowitz's office, came out to address them. He adjusted his glasses and stood silent until all the whispering died down. With great flair that matched his florid prose, his long fingers unfolded a letter he'd written to Dora's family. Dora could no longer comprehend the words, but the sisters could.

Instead of the flowery sentences describing Dora drinking the nectar of exotic flowers, her queenly chair fashioned out of ivory from African elephants and upholstered in silk from butterflies in China, or her brilliant husband whose scholarly words were strings of pearls the whole Jewish community gathered to collect from around his feet, this letter regretfully informed Dora's family that she had lost her virtue. Their wayward daughter had fallen in love with a Negro criminal who'd enticed her to work as a prostitute. No amount of begging by her loving husband, Yitzik Moskowitz, who had first tried to take her back, and the rabbi, who attempted to put sense into her contaminated mind, had convinced Dora to change her wanton behavior. Insatiable with lust, she was overcome by the dybbuk of Satan. All she could think about was taking more and more men into her bed.

"Your daughter is lost forever," the Professor concluded in a theatrical voice. *"You should sit shiva for her soul."*

The sisters stood squeezed together in silent shock, their expressions somber. For once, old enemies didn't bicker; grievances were pushed aside. Close friends held each other, soul to soul connected in shared horror. Batya had known of this practice, yet hearing the words turned her blood cold.

"Such a letter will be sent to the family of any girl who tries to pull that stunt," Freda informed the sisters. "And if your parents are deceased, it will be sent to the elders of your home shtetl or to relatives, shaming your mother's and father's memories." Her glance took in the entire crowd and stopped on Moskowitz, who stood silently, his arms folded. When he nodded, she went on. "Who would say kaddish on the yahrzeit of people whose daughter veered so far from the righteous way befitting a Jewish woman?"

Before noon, Dora was sold to a brothel located far away, near a coal mine, where prostitutes were not even permitted to get up as they served, for a pittance, hordes of poor, dirty miners and even poorer, foul-smelling farmhands. Clients there weren't protected. Before long, she would be infected by the French disease.

Batya's ache for Dora mixed with guilt over her own failure to convince the girl of her one better option. She hoped that Dora

would be able to commit suicide, although Nettie's experience—
and her own in her early days—had shown that dying could be
as hard to accomplish as living.

As distraught as Batya was for Dora's fate, she was also distressed by the fact that for the next year or two she must repay
Moskowitz the cost of buying Dora. So much for saving more
money for her family's rescue.

Chapter Thirty-Three

Winter 1894

*O*n Batya's way to Efram's house she passed a house with a large patio. Two dozen unkempt laborers congregated out front, no doubt waiting for their turn with the prostitutes. They passed around a jug of what Batya assumed was cheap cachaça, sugarcane alcohol. Someone played a mandolin, and the men passed the time by tangoing with each other. Their aggressive gyrating and strong hips bumping revealed their anticipation of what was ahead.

The cloud that had hovered over Batya since Dora's episode two months earlier tightened around her like a cold blanket of air.

Before she had given Rafael her letter, Batya had to wait for Efram yet again so he could pencil on the back in Spanish, *Postmaster: Please add your return address.* It had been three months since Rafael had said he'd mailed her letter, and Batya hoped that the postmaster in his village had indeed complied with her request. She would know only if and when her father's reply arrived, perhaps in a few more months.

The wait was maddening. "It will take time for my sister Keyla to receive my father's letter with the money, and a lot more if she even decides to make her way from Siberia to join the family," Batya told Efram when they sat down at his mother's dining table. "Just in case my father hasn't received the previous letter, let's write another one. And if he did receive it, this one should urge him to act." Without her father, a man who could work, it was likely that her sisters and their children—and now Vida—wouldn't be accepted into the Baron's program.

Efram put his hands to his ears. "What you're doing is dangerous."

"What is?" She pretended not to understand. "I want the letter to be short."

He looked at her. "These secret letters. I don't like it."

She pressed herself against him. "Would you rather that I don't come here for extra visits? Do you want to wait for your monthly stipend?"

After leaving his home with the letter in her pocket, she crossed the street to Rafael's cart. She had visited him twice in the makeshift tent he created at night by throwing a large canvas over his cart and unrolling a thin mattress on the ground underneath. It had taken an effort for Batya to drag herself out of the house at dawn, after her night work ended and Freda had retired to bed, but Rafael had become her lifeline; God must have put him in her path to help save her family.

Rafael smiled when he saw her. He recognized her, of course, but she was never certain whether he remembered having sent a letter for her.

"Maybe you could do me a grand favor?" she asked, as if posing the question for the first time.

"Anything." He craved her. She didn't need to lower her eyes to check.

She repeated the instructions she'd given him last time. "I need you to mail a letter for me. My fiancé should never know, so it must be from the post office in your village." When he nodded his head vigorously, she added, "Can you keep a secret? Our secret? No one is to know, no matter what they say to you." She touched the back of his hand, and her fingers grazed, as if unintentionally, the front of his cotton pants. "I'll bring it shortly."

She rushed to the bank, where she converted money into two more certificates only her father could cash. She walked to a side table and, with her back to the lobby, put them in the envelope Efram had already addressed in Russian.

Then, shaking with apprehension and worry, Batya asked the clerk to write in Spanish on the back, *Postmaster: Please add your return address,* before sealing her letter with his red wax stamp.

Although winter in Argentina wasn't as freezing as it had been in Russia, it was nevertheless rainy and windy—and often cold. The many rooms of the house had no heat. The open public spaces had been constructed to serve long months of hot, humid weather, and the coal stove in the corner of the pavilion failed to offer relief from the chill that blew in through the large, loosely fitting windows. The stone wall in the front of the house helped curb the heat but was porous to the moist cold that penetrated the bones. In Batya's room, only the sheepskin rug she threw on the stone floor kept her feet—and the clients'—warm.

Standing in front of the heater in the pavilion, now empty, Batya rubbed her hands. It was summer in Russia, and she wondered what her father was doing. It was maddening to wait for his response; she must find out what could be done on her end to start the process. It was time she spoke with the Baron de Hirsch's emissary, Señor Farbstein.

The opportunity came merely an hour later, when Freda sent her to the apothecary for ointment for her aching knees. Wearing her red coat—the only one she owned—Batya set out to also see Señor Farbstein. His name had become an incantation that could bring her family out of poverty. The man had acquired an ethereal quality when Efram reported that not only had Señor Farbstein never been seen entering a brothel, but he had joined the chorus of Jews who berated the community for allowing the pimps to support the Yiddish theaters and to subsidize the synagogues where, in return, they were given the honor of *aliyahs* on Shabbat.

"I heard Señor Farbstein speak in our synagogue. He's not afraid to say that he wants to destroy Zwi Migdal's empire. It's a moral cesspool, he said."

Batya cringed at these words. She was part of that cesspool. "Will he?" Batya asked.

"This corruption and graft has been going for almost thirty years," Efram replied. "My father says that no district attorney or judge would dare tackle it. Everyone knows that the men who run the country and its civic law—the police, the judges, and the politicians—are all on Zwi Migdal's payroll."

Walking toward Señor Farbstein's office, Batya told herself that he wouldn't want to talk to her. She should just turn around before being humiliated. Just then, like an apparition, the image of her mother appeared before her, reminding Batya of her obligations. "You must give it a try," her mother whispered as though she were nearby.

Pretending to stroll at leisure, Batya walked slowly toward the Jewish Colonization Association office. It would take a horde of righteous people from within the sex industry to bring down Zwi Migdal, she thought. The pimps would never speak against themselves, so only the prostitutes could reveal the truth. But who would dare? And who would listen to a girl in bondage? Both were as unlikely as snow in Buenos Aires. Anyone speaking out would be murdered before anything could be accomplished.

The Baron's office was in Recoleta, the most stylish district of the city. The northeast part of the neighborhood was home to private mansions built in European styles. In its center stretched a grand cemetery, where generations of nobles and the landowning elite rested in their families' crypts and mausoleums. The wealthier section of Junín Street passed through the heart of Recoleta and was lined with expensive stores and outdoor cafés serving the most prominent members of Buenos Aires society.

From a café-turned–dance hall wafted the music of a tango band. These dance halls, *milongas,* had sprouted in La Boca, but this was the first time Batya had encountered one in a fancy neighborhood. She was further astonished to see that, like in the brothel, tango was danced here in the middle of the day.

She leaned on the railing outside and watched through the large windows the silhouettes of the dancers. Unlike her favorite skimpy dance costume, the women wore long, dark dresses whose flouncing fabric allowed no hint of the bodies swaying underneath. Batya could only guess at the women's steps, yet her muscles tightened as her body recognized the familiar rhythm.

Three men leered at her, an unchaperoned woman, and Batya was jolted from the near trance of the music. She tightened her coat and moved on until, a few blocks farther, she stopped at the sight of the Parisien building, where, she could tell by the street activity, an auction of recently captured girls was taking place on the second floor above the opulent café. Half hidden by large displays of flower arrangements that two sellers offered visitors to the cemetery, Batya watched, and cold perspiration erupted on her neck at the sight of pimps she recognized. One, a fat-bellied man in a silk shirt and striped blue suit, a diamond pin sparkling on his tie, wore a top hat and carried a walking stick that made him look distinguished. His companion, no doubt the helper who did his dirty work, had broad shoulders, his open-collared shirt and unpressed trousers revealing months of oil and food stains. The two men shook hands with a third who wore the long black caftan of an Orthodox Jew, along with dangling *peyes*. Like Dora before them, girls would be hauled off the boats with fake marriage documents, broken by rapes and beatings. On this cold day they were being paraded naked, their private parts probed as if they were horses sold in the market.

Batya bit her lower lip and raised her eyes to heaven. *Please hit the place with a bolt of lightning. Spare the girls my life, or worse.*

The men turned into a side entrance of the building, where

a staircase led directly to the second floor. As Batya was about to resume her walk, a horseless carriage driven by a uniformed chauffeur stopped a few steps away. Two men descended, and from their cream-colored suits, fine straw hats, and dark skin color Batya guessed that they were Argentine judges or politicians arriving for a preview of the new merchandise. Unlike the auction conducted over Brutkevich's barbershop, or even the one in Zitnisky's restaurant, the Parisien auction attracted elite customers.

The flower sellers where Batya loitered sent her questioning looks. If she weren't heading to Señor Farbstein's office, she would have bought a red flower and tucked it in her hair. Not today. She crossed the road and entered a smaller street, whose shops were as fashionable as those of Junín Street but less flashy. She dabbed off her red lipstick and scanned the street and its shoppers. No one seemed to be spying on the JCA's building. She approached its entrance, aware of how out of place she must look with her flaming-red coat. At the door, she paused, glanced about her, then touched the small brass plaque carrying the organization's name and brought her fingers to her lips, as if the plaque were a mezuzah blessed with divine powers. So much of her family's future depended upon this moment.

She stepped into the foyer, climbed up the first flight of wide steps, and knocked on the double door. A secretary dressed in a black mourning skirt and a lace-adorned black blouse opened the door. A pair of spectacles hung from her neck by a gold chain.

The woman's smile faded, and she glared at Batya. "What do you want?"

"I'm here to see Señor Farbstein." Batya replied, using her most polite tone.

"He won't see the likes of you." The secretary pushed the door to slam it.

Batya stuck her foot in the threshold. "Please." She clasped her hands in supplication. "Please—"

"Go away."

"I beg you—"

"Leave, or I'll call the police."

Batya lowered her head and took two steps back. If the police came, her visit to this office would be reported to Moskowitz. She turned and walked down the stairs.

There was no place to hide while she lingered across the street, desperate to catch Señor Farbstein when he left the building for his midday meal at home. Men gawked; women sneered at her and fluttered their elegant fans as if she emitted a putrid smell. Batya shrank under their gaze, yet was certain that their husbands visited prostitutes. It had become a cultural norm, a common pastime that penetrated deep into Argentine society.

The clock in the nearby church marked the passing of the quarter hour. With the fourth strike of the clock, Batya threw a last look up at the building and its many windows, wishing she knew which one was Señor Farbstein's.

After picking up Freda's ointment at the apothecary, Batya ambled back to the house, swaying her hips, and was rewarded when a pleasant young man followed her inside.

Chapter Thirty-Four

*B*atya waited two months after sending her second secret letter with Rafael, then checked with him every two weeks before his brother collected him for a home visit. Each time she reminded him to take a stroll to the local post office and inquire about a letter for her, yet he must tell no one. After Rafael's return, even when rain poured for hours and she'd find him huddled under his canvas-covered cart, she made sure to go over, forever concerned that he might not remember what she had asked him to do or, if a letter had arrived, keep it secret. *God, please watch over Rafael.* So much of her life was at the mercy of a person with a limited brain.

One day, upon seeing her crossing the street, Rafael waved an envelope in the air. Quickly, Batya took the letter from him, touched his cheek in thanks, and tucked the envelope in her skirt pocket. *Thank you, God!* Walking away, she couldn't bear the thought of waiting until she reached the privacy of her

chamber to read it. She stepped into the space between two
houses and, standing under a line of wet laundry, tore open
the seal.

> *Why should I apply for hard work through the Baron*
> *when I have a rich daughter who wears pearls and*
> *whose house—a mansion with broad stairs—can keep*
> *us all bathing in butter? I can see you roaming with*
> *a key ring through all those rooms, with clocks every-*
> *where and alcoves that hold fine tchotchkes. I imagine*
> *the pantries you've described, stocked with goose liver,*
> *cured beef, jars filled with jam and schmaltz. And those*
> *rows of pickled cucumbers and sauerkraut are waiting*
> *for me to feast every day! I can't wait to fill my belly*
> *with them.*

Batya wanted to stamp her feet in frustration. *Oh, no. Please
don't,* she begged, then read on.

> *Every time I think of the wonderful life the Master of*
> *the Universe has blessed you with, my heart expands*
> *like in a holiday. I can't wait to have all my teeth*
> *capped in gold, as I've heard is the custom in America.*
> *I count the days until I'll see you again, may they be as*
> *numbered as the coins in my pocket.*

Attached to her father's letter was a note from Surale, written
by a scribe:

Dear Most Esteemed Sister Batya,

All our prayers are with you, my darling sister. May your beauty shine through the universe the way it fills my heart with light. Please remember us, your loving family, with your very generous heart. For the blessed memory of our beloved mother we beg you to send us the passage tickets you promised so long ago.

A detailed list of the nine names and dates of birth of each family member followed. Batya sighed. The dates in the Jewish lunar calendar were useless for the issuing of official documents. When the time came, Efram would have to convert them to the Gregorian calendar. Most important, Keyla and her children were listed, which meant that Surale had reached her in Siberia. Batya also learned from the list that Surale must have given birth to two boys, but her baby girl had died. Poor Surale. God should protect Surale's sons.

Batya picked up the second page of her sister's letter and read its closing paragraph.

To my great distress, our beloved papa, may he be blessed with long life, is ill. His cough is getting worse. Every night I pray that he will survive the coming winter. He laughs it away and says, "A Jew lives and breathes with one foot in the grave." You know how Papa is, never losing faith with our Father God in Heaven. My husband, Duvid, is a very good man willing to take

any work, except that there is none. With babies in the
house, they should be blessed, and nothing to feed them
and no coal to heat our bones, I am sinning gravely by
losing hope. Please hurry up and rescue us.

Batya returned to Rafael's cart. His coconut drink failed to revive her spirit. "I'll visit you in the dark," she whispered to him, hating to have to pay with her body, telling herself it was a mitzvah to give this simple good man what he needed.

What else could she do but try again to speak with Señor Farbstein? In the following ten days she visited his office twice more, only to be turned away by the secretary. In spite of the risk of being seen in the street, Batya waited outside each time with the hope of catching Señor Farbstein as he entered or left. She noticed the stream of people that entered the building: some with the dress and demeanor of recent Jewish immigrants, some gauchos with horse-bowed legs, some Argentine officials arriving in carriages driven by uniformed coachmen, but no one who might be Señor Farbstein.

Her plan to meet the Baron's emissary was not to be. Batya had to face the fact that she must find another way to compel her father to act. Since her fairy tale about her wonderful married life had worked against her, she must tear apart this story to get her father to apply for the resettlement program.

If only Efram would overcome his discomfort with her letters. It would be another week before he received his monthly allowance and, she hoped, visited her. Waiting, all she could do was pray that the Baron's project in Odessa would still accept her father, sick and old as he was. Duvid should help tilt the balance in the family's favor; one young man and one useless old man with seven dependents. Nine passages for which she'd stopped saving since Freda had begun to deduct payments for Dora's purchase price.

It was siesta time, and the house was quiet when Efram arrived, probably cutting classes. He paid Freda the fee, and Batya led him by the hand to her chamber.

"Where are your paper and ink?" she asked as she helped him unbutton his shirt.

"How could I bring them? I'm in the midst of a studying day."

"Don't you write there?"

"We only read and recite, or argue Talmudic points."

"For twelve hours?"

"That's what Torah studies are."

Twenty minutes later, spent, they lay quietly with their limbs tangled. He fingered her hair, then kissed one blond tendril after another.

She smiled to herself and stretched lazily. "When can I come over to your house?" she whispered.

"My mother is ill," he whispered back. "She hasn't left our home in weeks. Two maids and a cock service her. The house is never empty."

"Then you must come back here. This week. Bring paper and ink."

"I can't until my next allowance."

Batya sauntered to the dresser, feeling his eyes on her bare buttocks. She liked this passionate boy-turned-passionate man more than she should, even more than she did Ulmann, as much as she enjoyed the jeweler's company. She retrieved a banknote from her linen drawer and tucked it in the pocket of Efram's black caftan, thrown on the chair.

She returned to the bed and kissed him hard on the mouth. "Promise you'll come back before Friday. With ink and paper."

He didn't return her kiss. Instead, he flung his legs off the bed and stood up.

"What's the matter?" she asked, her heart sinking.

"These letters of yours. You'll get yourself killed. Or me."

She laughed, pretending that disappointment wasn't crawling in her rib cage. "There's nothing to worry about."

She helped him button his shirt, her fingers grazing reddish chest hair. His body had filled out since she'd first met him. His ginger-colored beard was thicker, and he moved with certainty, as if his proven manhood with Batya bestowed confidence in other areas of his life.

She rubbed her breasts against his chest, and, pacified again, Efram buried his face in her neck. *"If she is a wall, we will build towers of silver on her. If she is a door, we will enclose her with panels of cedar,"* he quoted from Psalms. His hug was possessive, tight.

Batya savored the words of endearment as she guided him to the door. Very soon, the rabbi would marry him off. At least for a while, until she became pregnant, Efram's wife would satisfy him.

Batya was relieved when he returned a week later. After paying Freda with Batya's money, he stood by Batya's dresser with paper and ink at the ready. "This is the last one," he said, leveling his gaze at her, the gaze of a man who knew his mind. "I came because you'd given me the money, and I, in my weakness, God should forgive me, didn't refuse as I should have."

This was it, then. Her last chance to convince her father.

"A great disaster has befallen me," she dictated. *"My beloved husband, Reb Yitzik Moskowitz, has died unexpectedly after a bout of high fever. His sister, Freda, whom I had considered my only friend and family here, turned against me overnight. Through her attorneys, not only did she throw me out into the street, but with the help of her husband—whom Reb Moskowitz had generously employed—she has captured all his businesses. They've left me with almost nothing."*

Efram put the pen down. "I can't be a part of this."

"You know I can't tell them what I really do."

"It's not the lying. The sages would be on your side, saving your family from angst. It's the danger to me."

"Who will know?" She stroked his back. "This is the last one. I promise." She picked up the pen again and placed it back between his fingers, then dictated:

"I'm sending you my last money, for Keyla, too. My only hope now is for you all to come here. Together we will start a new life in one of the esteemed Baron's new settlements. Will you do that for me even with your last breath?"

When Efram readied to leave, she combed his red hair with her fingers. His face closed up, and when she brought her mouth to his, he returned a perfunctory brushing of the lips. She swallowed and forced a smile. She had pressured him too much; their liaison was no longer just fun for him. Her heart hoped it wasn't the last time she saw him, knowing it was.

She closed the door behind him and let silent tears fall.

Part III

Buenos Aires, 1894–1895

When you buy a Hebrew slave, he shall serve six years,
and in the seventh he shall go out free, for nothing.

—Exodus 21:2

Chapter Thirty-Five

Summer 1894–1895

*T*he new client sat alone at a small side table in the pavilion, smoking. He sipped his Italian-imported limoncello in measured movements while examining the room. His white linen trousers were clean, their center crease pressed, and his black boots shone as bright as his onyx eyes. The coconut oil with which he'd slicked back his hair gave it a blue-black sheen. His sharply trimmed sideburns reached the center of his cheeks, looking painted, as did his thin black moustache. When approached by two sisters, he turned them away with only a slight wave of his long fingers, then continued to study the room from under a lowered brow.

The sisters huddling on the sofa with Batya speculated. "A ship captain?" "A tax collector?"

"Ship captains are a hungry lot; he wouldn't wait this long." Batya chuckled. "And tax collectors dress shabbily."

"Tax people are paid handsomely by Zwi Migdal. They wouldn't bother its members," said Rochel.

"I bet he's a poet," Clara said.

"Look at his long fingers. Like a painter's," Glikel said. She took Batya's hand. "Let's show him something."

Glikel was trying to get the intriguing stranger's attention by choosing the best tango partner among the girls, Batya knew. She'd give it to her, and then some. Tango relied on improvising, and she had become expert in teasing the moody, deeply sentimental melodies to life. Now, as she swiveled halfway back and forth in a series of *ochos,* the long fringes of the shawl tied around her hips revealed her legs in stockings held up by garters. Across the room, observing her, the new man tapped his foot to the music.

It took two songs for him to rise and walk over to her. Cutting Glikel out, he extended his hand to Batya.

From his first smooth square step she knew he was an expert dancer, a professional whose tall, lithe figure moved with ease and grace. His torso rigid with an open embrace that allowed space between their chests, he guided her with the certitude of a man in full control. Batya let herself surrender and follow as their bodies conversed in an emotional harmony. The stranger swept her around the dance floor, holding her back as she double-stepped and swerved over his extended leg. The feel of his thigh guided her to kick while avoiding his shins before he broke the turn to spin her in the opposite direction.

The song ended, and the man dipped her so low that both

their bodies leaned dangerously close to the floor. His arm supported her shoulder blade while applause erupted.

Batya straightened and smiled into his face, but his expression remained solemn, his gaze piercing. For the first time since Efram's exit from her life eight months earlier, Batya felt a sexual heat rising.

Before the clapping and whooping subsided, the musicians broke into a new song, and the stranger nodded an invitation to her. Just as she accepted, another man stepped forward. He wore sunglasses so dark that Batya couldn't see his eyes, and his bald head was covered by a hard felt hat. He cut in, challenging the handsome stranger, who performed a minute of solo dance before cutting back into their embrace. As the three of them dominated the floor, the two men wooed Batya, fighting over her in a choreography in which she was the prize. At the end, she would choose the winner. For the duration of the dance, she was in charge.

She let the alluring stranger win. He paid Freda, then followed Batya toward the stairs. Upon reaching the staircase, still in full view of the pavilion, he cupped her buttocks. She glanced down, and he grinned, revealing straight white teeth.

In her room, he sat down on the upholstered chair. She untied her shawl, let it drop to the floor, and sauntered toward him. She reached to loosen the top of his shirt, but he grabbed her wrist and shook his head. Smiling, she tried again, as if his game was a play-out of their dance downstairs.

"No, please," he said in Spanish. "I'm not here for what you think."

"How do you know what I think?" She let out the girlish giggle men liked.

"I have a pretty good idea," he replied, this time in Yiddish. "But I'm not here for that."

Batya stared at him, stupefied. He looked Spanish through and through, not at all like a Jew. "Well, thank you for a great dance," she replied in Yiddish, her mind buzzing with the possibilities of what he had in mind. A pervert? He hadn't paid Freda extra. "What can I do for you?" she purred.

Still seated, he pulled her down to perch on his knees. She smelled the raw heat of his body, the aftermath of his exertion on the dance floor, mixed with his clover-scented cologne. His mouth was next to her ear, and his breath smelled of mint and tobacco.

"Is anyone listening?" he asked.

She shook her head, wondering what his game was, and touched the tip of her tongue to his earlobe.

He put his hand up to block her mouth. "I'm serious. I have a business proposal to discuss with you."

Batya searched the new man's face, and something in her dislodged, like the wheel of a cart finally extricating itself from a groove in the mud. Some extremely lucky sisters found a patron to take them out of the brothel and install them in their own apartments as mistresses. Such good luck happened mostly to the French courtesans, the ones with haughty mannerisms, who peppered their conversation with French words and who strutted their wares by walking down the boulevards with little white dogs called poodles. It had become prestigious for a man of influence to flaunt a French mistress around town.

This luck didn't happen to *polacas*. Even the devoted Ulmann, who was visiting more often, was tight with his gifts. In spite of

Batya's hope, he had made no overture toward anchoring their relationship.

A business proposal. This could be a turn of her fate. She stilled her heart and fluttered her eyelashes. "It's safe here," she whispered back. Sooner or later, though, some love sounds must come from her room.

"You've tried to see Señor Farbstein."

Her back straightened as if lashed, and she jumped to her feet. Dread filled her. Was this man collaborating with Moskowitz? Would he torture her to extract a confession?

"It's all right," he whispered in his husky voice, and extended his hand to pull her back onto his lap.

She remained standing. She wouldn't fall into a trap set by Zwi Migdal. "Let's get into what you've paid for," she purred. "Got your token?"

He handed it to her. "I'm here on Señor Farbstein's behalf."

Señor Farbstein's secretary had never asked for Batya's name, and Batya would not have given it to her for fear of retribution. "I don't know what you're talking about," she murmured.

"Please don't be afraid. One of our men followed you here," the stranger whispered.

"You can pay to dance with me or to have sex with me. Which one is it?"

"My name is Sergio Rosenberg."

A Jewish last name. That made him just as likely to be colluding with Moskowitz as with Señor Farbstein. Batya walked to the dresser, dipped her fingers in the bowl of water, and touched them to her forehead. Her head swimming in confusion, she turned to look at him and his strong, dark features. He was taller

than most Spaniards, probably a descendant of Cossacks. His
ancestors, Slavs mixed with Tartars, might have been warriors
who had swept through the Eurasian Steppes, raided shtetls, and
raped Jewish women, passing on to their offspring their ferocity
along with the high cheekbones and olive skin.

"What is it that you wanted to speak to Señor Farbstein
about?" he asked, still whispering. "Is it about your family?"

Batya could barely find her voice. "You're sure you're Jewish?"

"I won't drop my pantaloons to prove it to you," he replied
in Yiddish, then began to chant a prayer, "*Baruch ata Adonai,
Eloheinu*—how is that for proof?"

She couldn't help smiling. Yet she mustn't fall for his charm—
or Zwi Migdal's trap. "How do I know that you really work for
Señor Farbstein?"

"I swear." He raised his hand, and his stretched fingers split
into two pairs in the manner of the Jewish priests in the days of
the Temple in biblical times. "Let's talk more and you'll understand." Again he extended to her his other hand. This time she
accepted it, resettling on his knees. "What would you like our
office to do for you?" he asked.

Her mouth was dry. She chose her words so they could be
open to interpretation. "My father and my sisters. And their families. They're all in Russia." It was awkward to sit so close yet
whisper a conversation that wasn't seductive.

He looked at her with his raisin-black eyes, waiting for her to
continue.

She was silent for a moment, wrestling with doubt, then said,
"I want them to sign up for the resettlement program. But my
father is stubborn. He doesn't understand, uh, why I can't just

bring him over myself." She cleared her throat. "He's really good with horses and cows. He's been a dairyman all his life—" She halted, feeling foolish.

"So you would like the Baron's agents to reach out to him?"

The conversation made no sense. Why would a professional tango dancer, who looked like a Cossack, pretend to be a client yet be an employee of the Baron's emissary and come here to ask about her family? Batya bit her lip. "There must be hundreds—thousands—of people asking Señor Farbstein for his help."

Before he had a chance to reply, a light knock sounded on the door. "Is everything all right?" Freda asked.

"Yes, superb," Batya replied. She rose to her feet. To Señor Rosenberg she whispered, "We must pretend to make love—unless you wish not to pretend, of course."

"We'll pretend." He sat on the bed and bounced a bit. "Come lie down," he said, and placed his head on the pillow.

She stretched out next to him, their faces close. He pressed his foot against the bedpost and kicked it in a repetitive rhythm. "You need the Baron's office to help get your father's papers and all the documents for your family—and bring them here?"

She blushed. "That's asking a lot. I know. Why would you bother with me?"

His whisper was even lower as he enunciated every word. "To put it simply: we are trying to bring down Zwi Migdal."

She felt a twitch in her eyelid. "Not possible. No one can fight them."

"We could—with help from the inside."

She sat up, fear gripping her stomach so hard that she felt nauseated. "Why me?" she finally asked.

"You're the only prostitute courageous enough to try to see Señor Farbstein. More than once or twice, right? We believe that you have more of that valor hidden inside of you."

We. This man and Señor Farbstein and God knows who else. Batya looked down at her fingers, clasped together so hard her knuckles were white, then remembered to bounce on the bed, making the springs creak.

"Were you lured away from your family with lies?" Señor Rosenberg asked.

She nodded.

"How old were you then?"

"Fourteen."

"How old are you now?"

"Sixty." When he showed no reaction to her joke, she said, "Nineteen."

"What was your name before Esperanza?"

"Batya."

"Daughter of God." He paused. "Why are you still alive?"

She glanced at him. "You mean why haven't I died from the beatings? Or from disease?"

"That, too. Or why have you not committed suicide?"

It astonished her that he understood. None of the men in this bedroom had ever hinted at grasping the truth that glared in their faces. Each should have suspected that a Jewish girl wouldn't stoop to prostitution unless destitute or coerced.

Tears filled Batya's eyes. "Because of my family. I promised to get them out. So far, I've done nothing. My mother died disappointed in me."

"Well, here's your chance." His finger wiped away a tear rolling down Batya's cheek.

She sniffled. "What would I need to do?"

He grabbed the headboard and shook it. "Testify. There's an uncorrupted prosecutor who works with us. He needs someone like you to come forward."

"Testify?" She thought of Rochel's description of a scene in a play—a trial in front of lawyers, a judge, and a roomful of spectators.

"Tell the judge what happened to you. What you've seen happening to others."

Shame curdled Batya's stomach. How could she reveal her degradations to the whole world? "Everyone must know what's going on. Ask any ten-year-old boy."

"Knowing something is not the same as first-person testimony. You telling the judge your story carries legal ramifications that are different from mere rumors."

"Just a judge, no one else?"

"Our prosecutor will first talk to you."

Batya's head buzzed with confusion. "What is this to you and Señor Farbstein?"

Señor Rosenberg put his arms behind his head, crossed his ankles, and stared at the ceiling. "The reputation of the entire Jewish community. The Baron de Hirsch wants to build more agricultural villages here. He plans to bring hundreds of thousands of Jews from Eastern Europe. It's the largest charitable project in human history carried out by one man. It's his vision and his passion. But how can he save Jews from anti-Semitism in Russia if some Jews in Argentina bring the same hatred upon us all?"

She took a long moment to compose herself, bouncing the bed as she did so. "How will the Baron's plans change life for us, the *tme'ot*? If he's bringing over more men than women, more girls must be captured to serve them."

"We aim to bring down the entire Zwi Migdal operation. To abolish prostitution run by Jews. The Baron holds that the white slave trade debases not only the Jewish community but all of Argentine morality."

White slave. The words hit Batya with the force of a gale. "Slave" was a word reserved for Negroes, not for a fair-skinned, green-eyed, blond Jewish girl. Batya sat up and hugged her knees. "Tell me who cares if I get killed before I even utter a single word to that prosecutor of yours."

He touched her arm lightly, then withdrew it. "The word has gotten out, and many people have begun to care about women in your situation. A new benevolent group, Ezrat Nashim, now works to save girls before they are lured and trapped. You may have seen their representatives—usually mature women—trying to intercept girls at the port here before some pimp gets to them. These charitable women also work the train stations and ports in Europe and speak with the girls before they embark on trains or ships."

Batya let out an acerbic laugh. "Some pimps are mature women. How would a naïve girl know the difference? Both must be telling her the same story. 'Don't trust anyone but me,'" she imitated in a mocking voice. She recalled the matronly woman in a carriage at the port, luring a young woman. Her intentions were revealed with the first question, "Do you need a job?"

Señor Rosenberg let out a loud series of groans, then with a last gasp rose from the bed. He bent toward Batya. "We'll get your family out and place you under our protection. In hiding. Think about it. I'll be back in a few days." He smiled. "Have your dance shoes ready."

Chapter Thirty-Six

*B*atya waited for Moskowitz to finish counting his money. She heard the familiar click of his vault opening, then the sound of it closing and locking. As he left his office, Moskowitz brushed against her at the door, but made no sign of acknowledgment. He knew she was coming to collect the old newspaper for the lavatory, and for him she was no more than a piece of useful furniture. Even an obedient dog occasionally received an affectionate stroke. *A slave.*

Since Señor Rosenberg had uttered the word, she'd been searching the newspapers for mentions of slavery. She hadn't encountered slaves in Argentina but now learned that the Negroes she'd seen were Africans who had, for centuries, been captured in droves and shipped to North America and other places whose names she didn't recognize. There, each person was bought and legally owned by someone. Like she had been.

Slave. That night, at last alone in her bed and after the new streetlamp wired for gas went off, the word burst again in her head. *A slave*. It shocked her to the core. She wasn't God's daughter but *a slave*. Her mind resisted accepting it, yet as she mulled over the word, her limbs numb with fatigue, her private parts chafed, she had to face the truth. Her philosophizing father would have quoted the Passover Haggadah, that the opposite of slavery was freedom. Indeed, while she was granted permission to walk outside—she had no chains on her legs like the Hebrew slaves in Egypt—she was bound to Freda and Moskowitz body and soul.

In Batya's first year, Freda had taken her to the municipal magistrate to record Batya as belonging to her. Rochel had explained that the law allowed only women to operate brothels that employed underage prostitutes. Now nineteen, Batya was still a minor for two more years, and still belonged to Freda. Nor would she be freed or gain legal rights as a free adult once she reached her majority. The only difference would be that Moskowitz could replace Freda as her lawful owner.

She was *owned* forever. Like an African slave registered to her owner she could be exploited—or tortured if she rebelled. Then again, if the slaves in North America had become free, maybe so could she.

Now in Moskowitz's office, she glanced at the newspaper on his chair. Still neatly folded, it hadn't yet been read. Since she was supposed to pick up only the newspapers thrown on the floor, she must wait a day or two until she could follow up on another story that had caught her interest.

She touched the bold letters of the headline, "Alfred Dreyfus Is Facing Trial," then examined the grainy photo of the Frenchman in his military uniform, wearing a hard-edged hat. The accused man's face looked gentle, his gaze straightforward. There was none of the hardness about him that she had learned to expect from officer clients. Nor was his expression menacing or devious as a spy's must be.

Of course, he was Jewish, and a Jew could be as unscrupulous as any goy. Yet this man's eyes seemed innocent. How could a powerful man, an officer, be trapped in a net of lies, as his attorney claimed? The answer came as soon as she asked it. France was in Europe, and Europe was bad for the Jews.

Batya sighed and crouched to collect the older papers from the floor, refolding each page slowly in order to steal glances at the headlines. In Australia—was that the country near Germany?—women demanded the right to vote for something called parliament. The bubonic plague broke out in Hong Kong, wherever that was. Such a plague had once killed most of Argentina's Negroes, she'd heard, which was why there were so few of them now. If such a plague were to arrive here, it would seek new victims and might find them in the Jews of Buenos Aires.

Batya rose and listened for sounds from the corridor. Hearing none, she scanned the neat stacks of papers on Moskowitz's desk. Most were tucked between cardboard covers held together by thin leather strips. On top of the right-hand pile rested a letter, like many others she'd seen, from one of Moskowitz's colleagues in Europe regarding a new shipment of girls. The folder next to it had to do with Zwi Migdal. She leafed through pages: boring reports from meetings, with phrases such as "allocation of mutual credit fund," which she didn't comprehend. But she understood the parts about money that financed members' travels back to Europe to recruit more girls. She'd seen these reports

since last year, when Moskowitz had become even more prominent in the organization.

The folder to the far left contained something new. The document inside listed two rows of names. By the fourth line Batya
understood: the names were of the dead pimps and prostitutes
buried in the Barracas Al Sur cemetery, the one Zwi Migdal had
recently purchased. She thought of Nettie, an outcast buried
outside the fence before this acquisition of the special cemetery
for the *tme'yim*. The column next to the names noted how much
Zwi Migdal paid for headstones for its members, the pimps. The
dead girls had none, of course. The one time Batya had visited
Nettie's grave, on the thirtieth day of her passing, the name on
the wooden sign had already been washed off by rain.

Batya forced herself to close the file before she risked being
caught. She checked the corridor and, seeing no one there, returned to root in the wastebasket for a discarded pencil under
the sheets of carbon paper Moskowitz had crumpled and some
letters he had torn in half. Finding no pencil, Batya was about
to return the garbage back to the wastebasket when she changed
her mind and tucked a handful inside the newspapers she was
taking away.

In the privacy of her room she checked her loot. It wasn't hard
to put together the few torn letters and to smooth out two pale used
carbon papers showing Moskowitz's handwriting. Batya couldn't
see anything of interest in these documents, but they might help
her curry favor with Señor Rosenberg. She rolled the pages and
wrapped them in a handkerchief, then crawled under her bed
and squeezed the roll of letters into the tight space in the wall.

A week later, Batya paused at the top of the stairs to examine the goings-on in the pavilion. She felt a smile taking over her face at the sight of Señor Rosenberg sitting alone at the same table he'd occupied the first time.

He was back!

Batya touched her forehead as if she'd forgotten something and rushed back to her room. She must retrieve the roll of papers while he wasn't there to learn of her hiding place. Praying that no one would search her room in the coming thirty minutes when she would be dancing, Batya tucked the papers in a slit in the mattress where she sometimes placed gifts of money until she was alone and could hide it.

"Have you given some thought to my proposal?" he asked her later, when they were shaking her bed—he fully dressed, she in her lace bustier, with her Spanish shawl still tied around her hips.

"How can you get to my father? Their shtetl is very remote." In fact, she had no idea where the family's new shtetl was. They had been forced to move yet again, and the name of the village on her father's second envelope that had arrived through Rafael meant nothing.

"Our Odessa office will take care of it."

"A letter to them takes months."

He rocked the bed so hard it banged the wall. "You let me know that you are willing to cooperate with us, and I will contact our office by telegraph."

"What's that?"

"A new invention. A person sends a message in one country, and another office in another country receives it without a piece of paper ever being mailed."

She turned her back to him in anger. "You think that I'm just a stupid *polaca* that you can tell me such ridiculous tales?"

"You don't have to believe me. Go see with your own eyes in the central post office. They send signals instead of words." He made some clicking sounds. "Once they reach across the Atlantic, the signals get translated back into words."

"So what will I see in the post office, an empty air into which people click their tongues?"

He shrugged. "Actually, there are lots of wires."

"Wires going over the ocean from here to Odessa? I don't believe it."

"Look, I don't exactly know how it works, but it does."

"So if I want to speak with God, I click into this apparatus?"

He laughed. "Only if God has the matching apparatus to catch your transmission."

"He's God. He's invented your apparatus. Of course He'd have one."

Her cooperation with Señor Rosenberg would bring about the use of this miraculous apparatus. Her resistance melting, Batya turned toward Señor Rosenberg again, then traced his sideburn, admiring its neat edges. She trailed her hand down to his chest.

He removed her hand gently.

"Don't you like me? Don't I look pretty to you?" she asked.

"You are beautiful, and I like you very much. But I will not take advantage of you."

Batya hadn't heard of a healthy man who didn't possess a robust appetite. No sister would have believed it.

"I have something to show you," she said, and immediately regretted it. She would reward Señor Rosenberg's kindness by handing him garbage. Blushing, she reached into the mattress and pulled out the roll of papers. "Sorry. It's really nothing. Don't be insulted that I thought you might be interested—"

He sat up, took the papers, and unrolled them. His eyes opened wide. "Where did you get these?"

Her blush deepened. "I'm sorry, it's only junk."

"No, it's not." He flipped through the pages. The carbon paper rustled as he held it up against the light from the window. "How did you get them?"

"From Moskowitz's wastebasket."

"Do you know what these are?" His dark eyes sparkled. "If you could read, you'd understand that these papers are very important."

She bit her lip.

"I knew you were different," he said. "Señor Farbstein thought your courage was remarkable. Now I see that you're also smart." He grabbed her hands. "We will need all of this 'garbage' in the coming months."

"Months? How long until you take me out of here?"

He waved the papers. "This information is critical. It will establish our case. Can you get more?"

"Every day. Except maybe on Shabbat."

He flipped through the letters and pointed to the one with Zwi Migdal's emblem. "You see this? These are the ones we need the most."

"When will you get my family out?" Batya countered.

"We'll telegraph the Baron's office in Paris tomorrow. That office can telegraph Odessa. Do you have your father's address?"

She banged the headboard against the wall for good measure,

then walked to her dresser. She slid out the top envelope from under the red ribbon that contained all her father's letters. Then she thought about her uncle's lost envelope so long ago. She rooted in her drawer, found a pencil stub, and handed it to Señor Rosenberg. "Copy the address."

He copied it at the edge of one of the documents, then said, "You continue to get us these papers, and your wish will come true. But be careful."

After he left, Batya retrieved her father's letter and pressed it against her lips. "Very soon, Papa. Very soon."

Chapter Thirty-Seven

$\mathcal{I}$'m not going to eat this dreck!" Glikel shouted.

"You eat what's there to eat," Freda shouted back.

Batya emerged from the kitchen yard, where she'd hung her underthings to dry. The shouting also drew Moskowitz out of his office, so she stepped back.

"Who do you think you are?" Moskowitz said to Glikel, not raising his voice.

"Look! I'm losing weight because I can't eat this shit!"

"Did your *kurve* mother eat better?"

"My mother was an honest woman," Glikel screamed. "You're the son of a *kurve* yourself!"

Moskowitz slapped her face.

"Calm down," Freda ordered her. "Get back to your office," she told her brother, as several sisters gathered to watch the scene. "I'll handle her."

"You taste the dreck they're sending us from the food halls,"

Glikel screamed at her. "We used to have good food. Jewish cooking, Argentine meat—"

"You tell me how we can cook here for so many girls," Freda replied. "Most brothels have the midday meals delivered."

"Delivered with cockroaches floating in grease," Glikel spat. "Right, sisters?" When no one dared agree, she went on. "You can't tell a potato from a chicken's *pulke*. They won't feed it to the pigs. Soon, we'll all be so skinny that the clients will go to houses where the girls are plump and pretty. We'll get poisoned from this dreck and die—"

Moskowitz peeked out of his office again. "Stop the racket, or you'll go with no food at all."

Batya pulled back into the yard and touched her middle. Her stomach's softness had indeed melted away in recent months.

Glikel's final points had hit where it counted. Two days later, Freda hired two cooks. Due to the large quantities of provisions they required, farmers delivered produce to the house a few times a week, which meant that Freda didn't send Batya to the market as frequently, cutting into Batya's daily excursions outside the house.

Now that she was venturing out only twice a week, the highlights of Batya's days were Ulmann's weekly visits and the times she tangoed in the pavilion, practicing with a sister, or especially when her partner was Señor Rosenberg. He still refused to use his tokens for what they were supposed to buy him, but on the dance floor he displayed Batya's beauty as if she were his prize mistress. She became acquainted with his body, the minute shift of his firm torso or the press of his right palm on her back. Her body followed his as he led her backward and sideways, whirled and dipped her. In his arms, she became confident enough to point one leg to the sky, draw an imaginary wide arc, and land it gracefully far behind her.

How she loved the applause!

"Bravo!" a man had shouted recently as he clapped his hands. "You should enter the competitions."

"I might do that," Señor Rosenberg had replied, bowing. "With this fine partner here we will even win."

For two months now, Batya had been collecting trash from Moskowitz's wastebasket and giving it to him, yet no word from her family had reached her.

"They were contacted," Señor Rosenberg finally told her on his next visit. "They have been in touch with your sister Keyla, and she'll get on her way to them when summer arrives."

It was hard to imagine that the freezing winter was now reigning in Russia while the sweltering heat in Buenos Aires didn't seem to let up. Even when the icy Siberian roads would finally melt, a woman alone with two toddlers would be at risk from robbers and God knows what else. *God, please watch my sister Keyla, daughter of Zelda, on her dangerous travels.*

Batya handed Señor Rosenberg more documents. "Maybe the rest of the family should wait for Keyla in Odessa? It's safer from pogroms, right?"

Señor Rosenberg nodded. "We can arrange that."

Batya recalled her family's exile five years earlier. They had been only four people then. This time, though, her family would take no furniture or household items, and she was certain that none had a change of clothes.

Three weeks later, while rhythmically kicking the bedpost, Señor Rosenberg whispered to Batya that her family was in Odessa, at a hotel.

If only Keyla hurried up, in a few months, Batya could see them all again! A sudden urge to meet little Vida rose in her. She would adopt and raise her as the daughter that her scarred uterus could never produce. A wave of protectiveness came over Batya. She recalled two big cities where she had stayed with Moskowitz overnight. Had she sailed from Constantinople or Odessa? She'd been too awed and shy then to ask. By now she knew that both had ports from which ships sailed all the way to South America. They were safer from pogroms, but how could her father manage in such a place, waiting for weeks on end? The peasant Surale would be as overwhelmed as Batya had been at fourteen, too paralyzed with fear to even cross the street.

"How do they eat?" Batya asked. "Where do they live? Are they warm enough?"

"We house and feed them. Don't worry."

She sighed. "You know about my family's whereabouts while I can't even get a letter from my father for months. I want to hear from him directly."

"I'll ask that one is sent through our own courier." Señor Rosenberg smiled at her. "Do you have more documents for me?"

Another month passed, another hot, sticky month in which she hated the string of men she had to please. She recalled Nettie's argument: Did factory or sweatshop workers have it better, chained to their machines all their waking hours? Life was survival, and survival was hard work.

At least Batya's time with Ulmann no longer felt like work. His conversation and neediness made her feel valuable, all the more so when he asked her opinion about his artistic designs. For her attention, he rewarded her with a measure of humanity and self-respect.

Moskowitz surprised her one day when he asked her to accompany him to lunch rather than an after-siesta outing. Unlike cafés that served only drinks and desserts, Calle Florida was a restaurant that roasted a whole cow on a rotating grille right in the street. The smoky smell welcomed Batya and made her mouth water. She sat down with great anticipation for the feast of succulent red meat.

"Remember your table manners," Moskowitz told her, just before he was joined by two uniformed military officers and soon by Pedro in his colorful plaid jacket and two other pimps whose names Batya didn't know. "Act like a French whore, not a *polaca*," Moskowitz added, and she lengthened her neck to assume a queenly posture.

When the slabs of juice-dripping meat were placed in front of the men, Batya received a small, empty plate. Moskowitz sliced off a morsel of his steak and dropped it on her plate, while Pedro and the other men went on to suck on fatty bones, laughing and chatting, never acknowledging Batya's presence. She took dainty bites of her tiny piece of meat, feeling more like a stray dog that had come begging than a desired high-class French courtesan.

Recalling that Freda deducted the cost of the cakes Batya had eaten at the café, she decided it was better not to be charged for this sumptuous meal.

Lunch over, Moskowitz gestured to Batya to climb into the carriage of the two officers, who took her to a *casita*.

Chapter Thirty-Eight

*M*idmorning, Batya was about to enter Moskowitz's office to collect the newspapers when she stopped at the sound of Señor Rosenberg's voice. She hadn't seen him in a couple of weeks, had been anxious to receive more news of her family, but now, peeking in, she glimpsed him seated in the guest chair, seemingly in the middle of a friendly chat. Moskowitz laughed at something as Señor Rosenberg gestured with a lit cigarette.

No! Her heart beat so hard she heard it. Señor Rosenberg had betrayed her. Batya pressed her back against the wall, her head cocked to one side to hear better.

"Our profession is not for everyone," Moskowitz said. "Yes, anyone can sell his wife's services to make a few pesos, maybe recruit one more girl to work for him. But to be a successful businessman, one needs to be both shrewd and charismatic; seductive, while exercising self-control; a skilled manager and a comforter of hysterical females." He paused. "You need to teach these girls manners, how to save their money, how to make something of themselves. It brings them joy, while you increase their value. It's a profession that demands the whole of you— your character, your perseverance, and your expertise in many areas, from finance to personal hygiene."

The hair stood on Batya's arms. Was Señor Rosenberg becoming a *caftan*?

"You are very proud of your business," he said.

"Why shouldn't I be? Me, Yitzik the Pitzik Moskowitz, a *pisherke,* a little pisser—a nobody from a poor shtetl, beaten by my father, by my older brothers, by the horse master, by the tavern keeper, you name it. Always beaten and left to rot in the mud. Now, here, every day, when I'm called upon by important people in government, in academia, in the police, I'm showing them all who I really am. 'Here comes Yitzik Moskowitz,' they say up and down the street, wherever I go." His voice as he uttered his own name was deep with self-importance. "They even talk about me in Berlin and New York. And all of this because of what? Because of my entrepreneurial spirit, because of my vision, my clear-eyed ability to smell where the dog is buried. That means having a sixth sense about the market and being able to pick the choice merchandise to meet its demand."

Señor Rosenberg let out a chuckle. "And I thought that pimping was easy money. So many people are entering into it."

"Don't call us that. 'Pimp' is a name for criminals, not for my kind of entrepreneurs. We help the economy, which in turn strengthens the government, which is the foundation of stability. We are gentlemen with a strong moral code of mutual aid. We support and help one another. The loans Zwi Migdal gives? We do that by a handshake only; no one signs a piece of paper the way a bank requires you to do. We want our members to succeed, because when the individual becomes stronger and gets *respect* for his honest dealings, our union becomes stronger and gets more respect."

"By 'respect' you mean from the goyim?"

Moskowitz took a deep breath. "I see what you're hinting at. You're saying that we have a problem with the stuck-up Jews here? Not really. It's just talk. They don't utter a peep of protest when we give them business. The tailors, the jewelers, the importers of silk and brocade, the merchants of the fine china and crystal we buy for our wives—they all bow when we enter their shops. And what about artisans of cabinet and furniture making? The masons and the marble carvers? You name one Jewish business that doesn't benefit from our largesse."

Señor Rosenberg made a noncommittal "Hmm."

When Moskowitz spoke again there was delight in his voice. "As far as the goyim are concerned, who do you think finished the renovations of Teatro Colón? Zwi Migdal saw the need, and Zwi Migdal has come to the rescue. You tell me now, how can they not *respect* us, when we help bring culture and glory to Buenos Aires?" Batya heard the rustling of papers, then Moskowitz went on. "Look. Read it yourself, a letter from the largest yeshiva in Jerusalem. I personally support them. I personally pay for a dozen soup kitchens, hospitals, and immigrants' charities in Buenos Aires, Rio, and Montevideo—and the Holy Land. You name them, they all come to Yitzik Moskowitz, and Yitzik Moskowitz never turns away any worthy cause."

Batya was about to slide away into the depth of the corridor when she heard Freda's footsteps coming down the back staircase. In a few seconds, she'd be caught eavesdropping. Having no choice, Batya stepped up to the door for her original purpose, to collect the newspapers.

"Here you are," Moskowitz said to her. These past couple of years he'd gained weight, and his previously rounded face was now pulled down by his jowls. His blue eyes sank between bags of fatty skin. He smiled, and cold sweat erupted on Batya's back. She'd known that smile, of the snake before it struck. In her mind's eye, she saw the hole in the kitchen yard, the one Dora had been thrown into.

Señor Rosenberg turned and let out a plume of bluish smoke. "Oh, I'm glad you're here. Come in."

Her feet were lead, and she held on to the doorframe for support.

"Señor Sergio Rosenberg here is making an offer." Moskowitz licked his lips.

An offer? Batya clamped her hand over her mouth to stifle a yelp of sorrow. She had been gullible to trust Señor Rosenberg. Now she would become his first prostitute in his new enterprise. She'd be taken away from this house, separated from the sisters she loved, to work at some dingy apartment all alone.

Her new enslaver wasn't looking at her as he spoke but regarded Moskowitz as if for approval. "I told him that I would like you to join me as my dance partner in a competition." Señor Rosenberg turned his head toward Batya. "If you want to, of course."

Batya's glance traveled from one man to the other, her emotions ricocheting. His dance partner, not prostitute. Why would Moskowitz allow her out of the pavilion or away from her window?

Responding to her unasked question, Moskowitz gestured with both arms magnanimously. "You will bring honor to our house."

She looked down at her toes in pink house slippers and tried to make sense of it all. She must think fast. Perhaps Señor Rosenberg had promised to pay for her lost earnings, and her public appearance would draw more men back here. If Señor Rosenberg won his competition, Moskowitz would have a higher-class prostitute for whose services he could charge more.

When she didn't respond, Señor Rosenberg asked her, "What do you say?"

She fought the tears gathering in her throat; crying would only annoy Moskowitz. She shrugged.

"It's decided, then." Moskowitz rose from his chair and extended his hand to Señor Rosenberg. "You can take her for your practice today, as long as she's back right after siesta time."

Confused by this new development, Batya went to her room to change. *On the other hand,* she told God, *at least I'll be out of the house, doing something I love. But missing my midday meal and my siesta? I'll be tired all evening. How is that for a reward?*

She put on her ankle-length black skirt and her red blouse, tightening the string that gathered up the scooped neck so the fabric covered her chest rather than exposed her cleavage. She had danced only in her Spanish shawl, which barely concealed her nakedness. At least now she would practice in clothes.

Chapter Thirty-Nine

*W*alking next to Señor Rosenberg, Batya seethed. He had deceived her with false promises to take her away. Now he made sure to keep her in Buenos Aires. It was her fault for having trusted him. She kept her gaze straight.

They entered the Jewish barrio Once and passed through crowded streets filled with synagogues, *mikvehs,* and brothels and lined with vendors' carts. Among the eclectic mix of Jews from Eastern Europe mingling with Jews from Morocco and Syria, no one paid attention to Batya, and, in spite of her frustration at Señor Rosenberg, she enjoyed being chaperoned even if her clothes indicated that she was a prostitute. Having a man at her side—and one so imposing—gave her an air of respectability that kept other men from making lewd remarks and women from raising their noses with superiority.

"Thank you for agreeing to be my dance partner. Officially, that is." Señor Rosenberg glanced at her. "This is all part of the plan."

"I'm a stupid *polaca*. Explain to me what you're doing and why I'm still in Buenos Aires."

"I thought I had. Sorry if I wasn't clear." In the lull of foot traffic, he stopped. Facing her, he put both hands on her shoulders. His voice was just above a whisper. "Moskowitz has admitted to me directly what he's been doing. I'm getting closer to being able to destroy him. In the meantime, we'll participate in tango competitions. These are my excuses to get you out of the house."

Someone emptied kitchen garbage out a third-floor window, and the neighbor below poked her head out and screamed upward, waving her fist.

Batya looked around to make sure no one was close enough to hear, and whispered through clenched teeth. "If you want me to believe you, just take me away from Buenos Aires."

"I promise again that I will—after you tell your story to the prosecutor."

She stomped her foot. "After I get killed?"

A group of youngsters in school uniforms burst from a building for their midday break. Señor Rosenberg resumed his walk, and Batya followed. When no one could eavesdrop, he murmured, "You and your identity will be kept strictly confidential. I give you my word on that as well."

They passed a section where many tall buildings were under construction, their iron protrusions making the area look like a petrified Siberian forest. Hundreds of laborers perched on scaffolding. Come evening, these downtrodden immigrants—exhausted, disillusioned with life, and resigned to their low status—would shun their crowded bedrooms, spending their money instead on cheap beer while waiting in long queues for their turns with the poorest, most wretched prostitutes of La Boca. That could be Batya's fate when she aged out of Freda's brothel or became sick.

Señor Rosenberg stopped by a vendor seated on the ground who roasted chestnuts on top of a charcoal brazier. He ordered a dozen, and the vendor placed them in a torn newspaper rolled into a cone.

Batya glanced at the stack of square-cut newspapers by the vendor's side, then stared. On the top was a caricature of Alfred Dreyfus, showing him as a rabbit with an exaggerated hooked nose. The rabbit sat in a copper cooking pot, about to be stewed. One word, in a foreign language, was posted on the pot.

Noticing her stare, Señor Rosenberg picked up the top paper and nodded his head sadly as he handed it to her. "This is why we mustn't allow anti-Semitism to spread here in Argentina the way it has in Europe."

"Poor man," Batya mumbled. "What does the word say?"

"Traitor, in French."

"He's innocent. He's an honorable man." Batya felt hot with indignation. "May I keep this?" she asked the seller, and after he shrugged, Batya folded the edges around the drawing and tucked the caricature in her pocket.

Señor Rosenberg paid the vendor and accepted the chestnuts. He handed Batya the packet, then asked, "May I?" before helping himself to one.

As they resumed walking, Batya sucked on a meaty chestnut, savoring its earthy, yam-like taste, but the image of the French officer burned in her pocket. She had seen Jewish caricatures

in Russia, had cut them away when she and Surale used newspapers to make their Purim costumes.

"We're fighting anti-Semitism by draining out the pus in our
midst," Señor Rosenberg continued. "Your testimony will go a
long way toward making that happen. It is the key to opening
new channels in our investigation."

It was ludicrous to think that the words of one prostitute—of a
white slave—could be the key to halting anti-Semitism in Argentina. Batya said no more as they entered the wealthy district of
Recoleta. She wished that Señor Rosenberg would slow his long
stride so she could examine the large private family homes with
arched windows, breezy porticos, and lush trees peeking over
high walls. This was the life Moskowitz had falsely promised her.

A matron and her daughter passed by in a carriage. As soon as
the mother's gaze fell upon Batya, she put her hand over the girl's
eyes, forcing her head away. Batya cringed. If Señor Rosenberg
had noticed, he gave no sign of it as he turned into a side street. A
block away, he indicated a building with heavy wooden double
doors. "Here we are."

The doors opened into a *milonga,* dimly lit by red lamps.
Only a half dozen couples danced at this midday hour to music
played on the small piano.

Batya stopped in her tracks at the sight of the musical instrument. There was no musician. The keys were moving of their
own accord.

"A ghost!" She held her palms forward to ward off the bad
spirit.

"It's a pianola." Señor Rosenberg pointed to the side of the
instrument. "You see that perforated paper roll? It pulls the keys

down from the inside. No ghosts in this building." He nodded his head to the proprietor at the bar and led Batya to a staircase.

Feeling foolish, she followed him up the two flights to a large loft that extended across the length of the building. He threw open the shutters of the windows at both ends. As a pleasant breeze glided in, he walked to a small table in the corner where an earthenware jug sat and poured two glasses of water. He handed one to her.

Tears filled her eyes.

"Is everything all right?" he asked. "Not another ghost?"

She shook her head, busying herself with the drink to hide how grateful she felt. How could she tell him how much the simple act of handing her a glass of water meant to her? Clients offered her wine or fruity liqueur, but not as a gesture of kindness. Even when she visited Rafael, she always asked for his almond drink; the simpleton never thought of it on his own. The last time a man had shown her such a basic courtesy was in the bowels of the ship, the water brought by the boy looking for his lost sister, whose fate Batya now understood.

A small, dark man appeared at the door, wiping perspiration from his face after the difficult climb. He unpacked from its case his *bandoneón* and, at Señor Rosenberg's gesture, began to pump this accordion-like instrument, his fingers running over the keys on both sides.

"First, now that we are official partners, call me Sergio."

Batya placed the empty glass on the table and shrugged as if it were all the same to her, but it wasn't. He was a man, like all others. Keeping the honorific "señor" would remind her not to fully trust him. "Sergio," she murmured.

He took her palm in his. "We'll prepare three dances. One you already know, but we'll add *adornos,* embellishments to our performance. I'll lift you up in the air, and you'll help me by vaulting into position." He demonstrated his part and then marked hers. "Let's try it."

It took a couple of fumbling attempts before Batya had enough confidence in both herself and him to jump and stay up, held aloft. "Hold your arms straight up; curve your spine back," he instructed once she stayed in place. He supported one leg and told her to extend the other. When he brought her down, his fingers above her head sent her into a double spin.

"Wow." She smiled. How she loved the freedom of being airborne!

He worked with her on a quick succession of steps that required her full concentration—a brisk tapping against her own shin, front and back; the hook of her leg on his; wrapping her bent leg around his hip; and the scissoring of her feet between his.

"Splendid," he said. "Stretch and practice on your own between lessons."

He gestured to the musician to start another song and laid his hand on Batya's shoulder bone in an *abrazo.* The music rushed through Batya, down to her toes. All her muscles were taut, and passion surged through her limbs. Yet as Sergio guided her into a series of syncopated grapevine steps, she avoided responding to the challenge of his smoldering stare, to his masculine authority. While she gave her body to the dance and her cheek touched Sergio's in a simulation of romance, she held back from giving her heart to the longing for another life and love. It would only weaken her.

An hour had passed when two well-dressed men entered the room. *These must be the organizers of the dance competition,* Batya thought, looking at Sergio for an explanation. He danced her toward them. Stopping, he bowed to the older gentleman, and then pointed the younger man toward the table in the corner. The younger man, with pink cheeks and wearing a brown suit, pulled the table away from the wall and set up two chairs on each side.

"Take a seat, please," the older man said to Batya. He was dressed in black and had silver hair that, although oiled, fanned out like a dandelion.

Sergio nodded his assent. "Meet the Honorable Joaquin Ramos, the prosecutor," he said to Batya in Yiddish. "He wants to ask you a few questions."

They spoke little on the way back. Batya was emotionally drained from reliving the horrors of her initial captivity, from articulating its experiences in words. Señor Joaquin Ramos's probing questions—asked kindly but unrelentingly—brought back the fear and agony of those early days five years before. The rapes, starvation, caging, and beatings rushed back with all their force. At one point, she bolted from her seat and, gagging, ran to the spittoon in the corner of the room.

While she was vomiting, a cool palm pressed her forehead, and she glimpsed the bottom of Sergio's pressed white trousers. When she straightened, coughing, he let go of her and went out to the stairwell, where he called down an order for a meat sandwich, tea, and cake.

Once she had revived, though, the questions continued.

Now, walking in the streets, her legs felt as weak as if she had danced those two hours of interrogation. Hopefully, she could salvage a half hour's siesta before the late afternoon work, which wouldn't end until just before dawn.

Her cheeks ached from speaking Spanish; she had never used that language for more than flirting with a client, bargaining with a vendor, or instructing the house helpers who handled the heavy laundry and lavatory cleaning. When she stumbled or was at a loss for words, Sergio came to her rescue. She told him the Yiddish words and he translated them for her, but for the young man taking notes, it was required that she utter the Spanish herself.

Señor Ramos must have been dissatisfied with her story, because he kept grilling her for more details. Just the recollection of how he had made her repeat or expand on every moment of her suffering had made her feel exploited all over again. Sergio's presence nearby, hearing everything—well-meaning though he was—magnified her disgrace.

At the end of the session, the young man asked Batya to sign every page of his large notepad. How proud she was when, presented with an ink pad for her fingerprint, she instead courageously took his pen and signed her name. She knew how to do it only in Yiddish, not in Spanish—and had never held a pen. The ink smeared while her hand moved over the letters from right to left, but it was her name. She'd written it herself in ink!

"A signature is a signature, and we are witnesses," Joaquin Ramos had said.

Now she and Sergio rounded the corner onto a tree-lined street, and he finally spoke. "Thank you for telling it all. I knew you women suffered, yet I didn't imagine how much."

Batya placed her hand on her heart to still it. With all her reporting, she hadn't really told how bad it was. She had been unable to express the feelings on the ship, when she'd wake from a stupor as more men mauled her nipples and kneaded her flesh; how their rough-skinned hands pawed her and how they tore into her small body while she screamed, only to be beaten for crying. She recalled, but had not spoken of, passing out, only to wake to that throbbing pain deep in her gut, that burning below, that degradation of the person she had once been. She had reported wishing to die, to follow Shayna into the ocean, but not her frustration at hearing the ocean's blessed roar just outside the steel walls, out of her reach.

That roar suddenly filled her head, and the world shifted. Batya stumbled.

Sergio caught and steadied her. "Are you all right?"

"No." She took in a deep breath. "And I won't be until I'm out of here." She took a tentative step forward.

His hand still held her arm. "You understand why I can't be one of those men in your chamber?"

She glanced at him and was astonished to see his reddened eyes. She took another step and then, feeling secure on her feet, marched on.

Sergio's tone was soft when he spoke again. "Your testimony will be a great service for the entire Jewish community."

"Was that a testimony? I thought that it would take place in a courtroom."

"In a courtroom you'd be exposed."

And murdered by nightfall. She snorted. "What will Señor Ramos do with what I've said? Prostitution is legal."

"Prostitution may be legal, but not kidnapping and enslavement, nor is the use of brutal force. And corruption of officials is definitely against the law."

"Zwi Migdal has spies everywhere. Moskowitz will find out what you're doing—what I'm doing—"

"Very few people know about this investigation. Our cover—training for competitions—is good. I promise." As he had done before, he raised his hand, his fingers split into two pairs, like a biblical Jewish priest. "In the meantime, I have news to cheer you up: your sister Keyla is making the journey to join your family."

"By train?"

"There's no train in Siberia. She's probably traveling by various coaches across the endless steppes, over rivers and through forests and swamps." He paused. "It might be shorter to travel the other direction, through Shanghai, but not less complicated and grueling."

A surge of worry swept over Batya. "She's a woman alone. Can't your Baron do something?"

"We aren't in contact with her. Your father only knows to wait for her because of one letter he received." Batya barely had a moment to rejoice when Sergio went on. "In the meantime, you are helping not only the entire Jewish community but also the many thousands of Jewish refugees who will arrive here soon."

She stopped in her tracks and faced him. "You talk about your Jewish reputation. The good reputation of those kosher Jews who snub women like me, who think that we are the dirt of the earth." Her hand swept to encompass the city. "Let's say you free the prostitutes. What will happen to them—to us? There are thousands of us in Buenos Aires. How are we going to live? Who's going to employ us—and in what jobs?"

He touched her elbow to indicate that they should resume walking. She took a long step ahead of him, her anger percolating. When he caught up with her, she spat, "Would your wife employ a former prostitute in your home? Would your married sister bring one into her house? What about your mother—wouldn't she be worried that your father would crawl into the new maid's bed?"

"I don't have a wife or a sister, and my father is deceased, so my mother wouldn't be harboring such thoughts." He paused. "But I see your point."

"I know a woman, Leila. She used all her savings to buy her freedom from her pimp and planned to take in laundry to wash and iron for clients. No one would let her touch their soiled clothes. She was starving. Finally, she had no choice but to beg her pimp to take her back."

Sergio was silent for a moment as they continued to walk. "You're right. We'll need to think of a solution, but with so many women I can't imagine what it could be."

Chapter Forty

Fall 1895

*U*lmann rested on Batya's bed. He'd been in her chamber for almost two hours; lately he made sure to purchase from Freda enough tokens to satisfy his need for Batya's companionship.

"You have no idea how it feels to spend every evening sitting alone in my house with not a soul to talk to," he said, as if Batya hadn't heard it before. "My boys are busy doing their homework, and my wife is like a mummy wrapped in sheets, lying in her room with her night maid knitting by her bed." He wiped a tear from the corner of his eye. "The more I read literature and poetry, the more loneliness is eating me up."

He passed his hands over Batya's naked back and asked her to emulate his movements with her hands on his bare skin. "The human touch," he whispered. "No soul can survive without this very simple need being fulfilled. Thank you for bringing me back to life."

After he got dressed, he lingered, a pleasant smile on his face. "I've brought you a poem I know will touch you." He settled on the upholstered chair, had Batya perch on his knees, and pulled out a folded sheet of paper typeset in Yiddish. "It's called 'The Circus Lady,' by Celia Dropkin."

I'm a circus lady,
I dance between the knives
standing in the ring,
tips pointing up.
My lightly bending body
avoids death from falling
by brushing lightly, lightly against the blades.

Breathless, they watch me dance
and someone prays for me.
Before my eyes the points
flash in a fiery wheel,—
and no one knows how I want to fall.

I'm tired of dancing between
you, cold steel knives.
I want my blood to scald you,
I want to fall
on your naked tips.

Tears had gathered in Batya's eyes even before he was done. Did a client finally understand?

He touched her face and kissed her mouth. Then, still seated, he reached into his pocket and pulled out a key and dangled it in front of her face.

"What's this?" she asked.

"What does it look like?"

"A key." Her heart gave a flip. Was it finally happening?

"That's right. I've purchased an apartment in Barrio Norte, and I am asking you to live there." His voice lost its force. "If you want me, of course."

She couldn't believe her good luck. Yet— "Your poor wife. Will she get better?"

He shook his head. "The doctors agree that she's deteriorating."

Batya dropped down to her knees, closing her arms around his waist. "Of course I want you." She tilted her head back and, using her sweetest tone, said, "You'll talk to Moskowitz?"

"I'm prepared to pay him. I am a man of comfortable means, but not wealthy. My store is small, and my expenses are high, what with my wife's medical bills and my saving for my boys' education. The oldest is about to leave for boarding school in England." Ulmann held both of Batya's hands in his and brought the tips of her fingers to his lips. "I can guarantee you a small stipend, enough to pay for your food and those little things you women find so charming. Also some clothes—nothing extravagant, but of the style you can wear to accompany me to the theater."

Her heart sang. Ulmann didn't need to add that he would be her only man. She would be done with her life of prostitution. Being a mistress was a thousand times better—and there could never be a more gentle, more considerate patron.

"Thank you," she whispered, and planted little kisses all over his face. "I will make you very happy."

"What was your given name, your Jewish name before Esperanza?"

"Batya."

"Batya," he repeated. "I'm Bernardo. Baruch at the synagogue, but call me Bernie."

Baruch meant "blessed." He was her blessing. "Bernie," she whispered.

"My Batya." He looked deeply into her eyes. "Of all the letters of the alphabet, both our names begin with *bet*. We're meant for each other."

The moment felt ceremonial. Batya, not Esperanza, was being chosen. She smiled, unable to find more words of gratitude.

He drew her close and spoke into her hair. "Will you be my lifelong companion? It's settled, then?"

Gently, she pulled back and cleared her throat. "There's just one thing."

"Moskowitz. I know. I'll take care of it."

She swallowed. "I'm saving to bring my family out of Russia."

"Your parents?"

"My father and two sisters." She couldn't even mention their families. Nor Vida, the orphan baby sister she wanted to adopt. "Will you help me do that?"

Ulmann rose to his feet and looked down at her. "So you will be encumbered by taking care of them? That would negate the whole point of our arrangement."

She felt herself falling off a cliff. *Please, God, don't let him rescind his offer. I can't lose this good man.* She stood up to face Ulmann. Her voice was sore to her own ears as she said, "Will you give me time to make the arrangements?"

He nodded, but the magic seemed to have evaporated from the room.

The next morning, Batya stood in her window, holding in her palm Ulmann's promise—she still couldn't think of him as Bernie. Her key to freedom. She closed her fist on it, feeling its long, cold shaft and its cluster of sharp teeth. How much time would he give her? His emotional needs would surely pressure her into a decision.

This was her one and only chance for happiness; there would never be another. The comfortable middle-class neighborhood of Barrio Norte wasn't the expensive Recoleta, where some wealthy patrons installed their French mistresses, but the prospects of the new life awaiting Batya in her own home—a lifelong companion of only one man, a most pleasant gentleman—far exceeded the dreams of any *polaca*. Even if Ulmann wasn't handsome, he dwelled in a world of beauty through his love of poetry and his exquisite jewelry. When she looked at him, she no longer saw his bland features, but rather his insightful soul that appreciated subtlety. In his sensitivity, Ulmann must have seen the purity of her heart—of Batya's, not Esperanza's. And even if he wasn't wealthy, he seemed to have just enough to support both his family and a mistress. He was still young. With her encouragement, he would expand his business.

But unlike Ulmann, Sergio had promised to bring her family over. How could she let down poor Keyla, who suffered so much and was struggling through the wild, vast Siberia to make her way here? And Vida, for whom Batya already felt deep love? Sergio's words, though, were only that—words, and any prostitute who believed in promises was a fool. For all Batya knew, his scheme might come to naught, and in her gullibility she would miss her only chance to break away from Moskowitz's shackles.

There was no one to consult, to help her untangle all the speculations crowding her head. What would Rochel do if, by a miracle, she had the chance to find and rescue her two young brothers? Would she forsake them and selfishly choose a new, comfortable life for herself? Batya couldn't ask her friend. As close as the two of them were, their hearts were isolated islands, each floating in its own ocean of grief. And a betrayal of Moskowitz was too frightening to reveal to anyone.

She raised her head to heaven. "Mama, you've seen how hard I've tried to save money for them. You've seen what hell my life has been. Haven't I done enough? Isn't it time I free at least myself?"

The pigeons in the gutter cooed an incomprehensible response.

A couple of days later, just after breakfast, Moskowitz ordered Batya to put on her organza dress. Getting ready in her chamber, Batya wondered what kind of party was being held this early in the day, but when she descended from the carriage twenty minutes later, she learned that Moskowitz was taking her to a photographer to have an image taken of her holding a tango position.

The next day, proud of his rising star, Moskowitz hung grainy copies of her picture at the entrance to the house and pinned them to fences around the neighborhood—and probably far beyond. In the following days and evenings, while Batya serviced a string of new men who came in response to Moskowitz's hype, Ulmann's offer became unbearably tempting. It was hers to grab—now, and not sometime in the vague future like Sergio's plan. A long time ago, Batya recalled, she had been lured by death. Now she was being lured by life. Then, she had chosen to live only so she could get her family out of Russia. Now she must decide whether to live for her own sake.

Chapter Forty-One

*A*nother month had passed when her family in Russia celebrated Passover, while in Argentina summer refused to leave and its humid heat pressed on Batya like the lead cape of her dilemma. In his weekly visits, Ulmann had repeated the sweetest words Batya had ever heard, "I want you to be my lifelong companion," to which she mumbled that this was what she wanted most in her life. "You know it takes time to get the papers in order," she said.

He never asked the obvious question, whether she had saved enough to pay for the ocean crossings for her family. She wouldn't have had a positive answer: her bank account hadn't grown since Freda had begun deducting Dora's cost. Nor did he ask what would happen when her family arrived. She alone existed for him, detached from her relatives, and Batya guessed that, wrapped as he was in his need, he assumed that they'd fend for themselves as all immigrant families did.

Her only escape from her predicament and the men visiting her chamber was her dance practice sessions in the upstairs hall above the *milonga,* where the *bandoneón* player pumped his instrument and the music swept Batya into forgetting, at least for a little while, the pros and cons that kept churning in her head. How she loved the daring new combinations Sergio taught her! He had given names to the steps she already knew. *Palanca* was levering her during a jump. *Tijeras* were the foot or legs scissoring. *Quebrada,* the sudden body twist. At dawn, before falling asleep, Batya forced her mind off her burning quandary by envisioning their choreographed dances.

Twice more the prosecutor showed up at her rehearsals to interrogate Batya, going over endless details. He showed Batya photographs of pimps, asking her to identify those she knew. When and where she'd seen each, why she remembered the occasion, and what she had heard in café conversations.

"What about Restaurant Calle Florida? Have you ever been there?"

She let out a derisive chuckle. "Oh, yes."

"Who were the *caftans* you met there?"

"One was in jail at the time but got permission to get out to see his dentist. Instead, he came to Calle Florida for a gourmet feast."

"What was his name?"

"I don't know. But I heard him tell the others that his judge had stored his own late mother's furniture in the jail. Then, when his palm was greased—"

"Explain please what you mean by 'greased'?"

"Bribed. The judge ordered the warden to furnish the pimp's cell with his mother's beautiful furniture."

Señor Ramos took a moment to look at his notes. "The procurers. Whom do you know?"

"Procurers?"

"*Alfonsos*. Those who work in Europe for the pimps but don't run the brothels."

She shrugged. "They are young and make a very good impression." She thought of Moskowitz's first appearance in her life. He no longer traveled to Eastern Europe. In his mid-thirties and tending to fat, he might be suspected of being a widower with children; younger men had better luck with teenage maidens. "They look for *agunot,* too," she added, "and—"

Señor Ramos raised his hand to stop her. "Agu—what?"

"Married women abandoned by their husbands," Sergio interjected. "They can't remarry without a Jewish divorce, called a *get.* In their extremely poor society, without financial support, they have no means of survival."

Batya added, "Some matchmakers give the *alfonsos* lists of *agunot* in their villages, so they can offer these women jobs here. If an *aguna* has a daughter, it's a double coup. They call the girl 'lightweight.'"

"Thank you." Señor Ramos leaned forward on his elbows and looked into Batya's eyes. "Do you know of any other woman in your situation who might talk to me?"

Batya pretended to consider the question, knowing the answer. She wouldn't approach Rochel. Since Nettie's death, Rochel, too, had changed, as if some light had dimmed in her and had been replaced by sadness. Or perhaps it was just fatigue. Batya also was exhausted from this life, but at least she had hope to sustain her. "There's no way for me to know," Batya finally said.

"What about someone who seems brazen, who talks back to Moskowitz?"

Glikel could never be trusted. Batya shook her head.

"Please say 'yes' or 'no,' so my clerk can write down your responses."

"No."

"How about someone from another house who fights with her pimp?"

"No."

"Let me get it straight: You do not know of any girl—in your house or elsewhere—who fights with her pimp?"

Batya shrugged. "Many fight with their pimps. They are family. Fighting doesn't mean anything."

"Explain that, please?"

"They make up. The women give in. What's their other option?" Annoyance crept up Batya's spine at having to spell out the obvious. "We are told many times not to go to the authorities, because prostitution is legal. We are legally registered, so you know who we are. The police regard our pimps as our husbands and don't get involved in 'domestic disputes.'"

Señor Ramos scribbled something in his notepad. "You've heard conversations about the Jewish community ostracizing Zwi Migdal?"

"Sure. They lump the *caftans* and the *kurves* together. As if we—I—have a choice."

"What about antislavery organizations. Any talk about those?"

Batya thought of the matrons Sergio had mentioned. She let out a puff of air in dismissal. "Those do-gooders are only interested in saving girls *before* they are trapped. They wouldn't help someone like me. Anyway, Zwi Migdal has spies everywhere."

"Spies. Any names you suspect?"

Lying on her back was easier than these endless probing questions. Esperanza could tolerate a lot more than Batya could. She should accept Ulmann's offer and be done with all of this.

"No." Batya yawned, not bothering to cover her mouth as Moskowitz had insisted women should do. "I'm missing my siesta."

"Let's take a break," Señor Ramos said.

Sergio ordered a cool ginger drink and a plate of *media lunas,* flaky, crunchy cookies shaped like half-moons and sprinkled with white confectioner's sugar. While Batya ate the pastry and drank the spicy drink, she half listened to the honorable prosecutor and his clerk chat with Sergio.

"The Italian community and the French don't have a problem living with pimps and prostitutes," the young man said to Sergio. "Why the difference?"

"We have a strong moral zeal. One of our decrees is that 'all Israel is responsible for one another.' We are one people." Sergio paused. "Also, because the Jews are a majority in this business, we are facing a new wave of anti-Semitism. Argentina should be a safe haven for us, not another source of hatred."

"We'll take them down one at a time," the older man said. "All these criminals, not just the Jews, are staining our country's reputation, just when we are moving forward and developing at such a fast pace."

The future of Argentina and its Jewish community had nothing to do with her, Batya thought. She was tired. If she were with clients, she would have faked interest in their talk. No need to expend such effort now. She pushed her plate away. "How much longer?"

"Forty-five minutes?" Señor Ramos pulled out a file crammed with papers, opened it, and showed her some of the letters she had stolen. The Yiddish letters were marked with asterisks and numbers corresponding to a list of comments in Spanish on another sheet, which the prosecutor consulted. He pointed to names of associates in Europe, showed her photographs from another file, and questioned which of them she had met personally or had heard about from other prostitutes.

At the repeated questions—asked from new angles but returning to the same points—Batya's patience ran thin. "I don't know him, or him, or him," she said, poking each photograph in front of her. She regretted having provided the letters.

She turned to Sergio and said in Yiddish, "You said you wanted to destroy Moskowitz. How many more pimps do you need to investigate before you take me away from here?"

"Sorry, but it is all part of the same plan. Bring down Zwi Migdal."

Batya thought of Ulmann's dwindling patience. If Sergio wanted to investigate every pimp in Buenos Aires, she'd be stuck slaving for Moskowitz for years.

Señor Ramos waited through the exchange, then, responding to a nod from Sergio, handed a Yiddish letter to Sergio. "Please read it to her."

Pretending to be illiterate only took more of Batya's time. She put out a hand to the prosecutor. "I can read it myself."

"You can?" Sergio blurted out, then, as if regretting his outburst, leaned back in his chair.

"Before your arrival I've already prepared for you clothes made of silk." Batya raised her head and looked at Señor Ramos's

bushy white eyebrows. "It's from a husband who plans to bring his wife from the old country to work here for him."

"As a prostitute?"

"What else?"

"Why was the letter in Moskowitz's possession if it was between a husband and his wife?"

Batya pointed at the letter's heading. "It has no woman's name," she said. "Zwi Migdal sets the husband up in business by loaning him money to buy a girl at an auction, then it helps the husband bring the wife over to work so she can help her husband pay his debt."

"Please let's be clear: Zwi Migdal writes these letters for a husband to send to his wife? Does he know that she will have to prostitute herself here?"

"Of course. That's his new plan."

"Allow me to explain," Sergio said to Señor Ramos. "A man leaves the old country with the intention of finding honest work, to earn money and send for his family. He discovers that he can't pluck gold fruits off trees, and without Spanish or work skills he's unable to earn a living. Zwi Migdal convinces him that in the New World pimping is a form of good business—and that he is already blessed with a potential income in the form of a wife waiting to be brought over." He paused. "The divorce rate in such cases is high, and our community tries to help these wives when they arrive and learn the truth."

And then what do these divorced women do? How do they feed their children? Too exhausted, Batya kept her mouth shut. Cooperating in this investigation for months, she was helping neither her family nor herself, only assuming an enormous risk.

Back in the house, Glikel interrogated Batya about her outing. "Such a handsome man must be cutting Moskowitz off from his earnings." Laughing, she made crude remarks about Sergio's anatomy.

"You're just jealous." Batya turned her back to her. Just the week before, exiting the dance hall with Sergio, she thought she'd caught Glikel's silhouette next to a vendor's cart. It turned out to be a woman selling vegetables. But that night in Batya's dream, men stuck pins under her nails and burned her with cigarettes. Then one man waved a sword and stuck it in her belly. Batya woke with a start and sat up, her heart pounding.

She had slid out of bed and pulled out the trunk. She lit a candle instead of the kerosene lamp, so no light would be seen from her window while she examined the caricature of Dreyfus. Her finger stroked his face. The plight of this man across the ocean had touched her because, like her, he was trapped in a web of lies; like her, he'd lost his freedom. Like her, he didn't know who his real friends were.

The next morning, Moskowitz had asked her, "How is your dance practice coming along?"

Batya's heart skipped a beat. She shrugged. What if he came by to watch? The fact that she hadn't yet been caught giving her testimony to Señor Joaquin Ramos was a miracle.

But miracles never happened to her. Ulmann wouldn't bring her family over, and if she were murdered by Zwi Migdal's thugs, her family wouldn't be rescued either. If she were to continue working with Sergio, something must change.

Chapter Forty-Two

Winter 1895

*W*inter arrived with barely the benefit of autumn, and the sunlight that washed the world dimmed. For days, rain came down with no reprieve, driving into the windowpanes, and chill burrowed into the porous walls and penetrated the bones.

Ulmann hadn't been to the house for two weeks. Maybe he was busy with the upcoming Rosh Hashanah orders, sitting by a table at the back of his store late into the night, fashioning fine jewelry for rich customers. Or perhaps he was ill; so many people suffered from severe coughs. Having sent three girls to the hospital, Freda refused clients who obviously posed a health risk.

Batya stood in the corridor outside her chamber. Winter wind blew in from the patio and whistled an eerie music through the cracks around the ill-fitting window frames, and it echoed through the corridor, as if an evil eye were searching for a soul to capture. Batya buttoned up the green cardigan that Glikel had knit for her as what had at first seemed like an olive branch. Batya had purchased the wool according to Glikel's instructions, but when she completed the cardigan, Glikel requested payment for her labor. Her opium consumption had increased and with it her need for money.

Batya tucked her hands into the cardigan's deep pockets, fearing Glikel's mean spirit knitted into each stitch. She preferred the warmth of her magenta-colored velvet robe, which flowed luxuriously down to the floor, but the pretty robe had to be kept pristine, worn only when she worked. From the top of the stairs she confirmed that no client was waiting in the pavilion, so she descended and made her way through to stop by the coal-burning stove. Later in the afternoon, the musicians would station themselves in front of it in order to keep their fingers nimble.

She was rubbing her hands together to maintain the warmth when she entered Moskowitz's office to take out his old newspapers. He was still in, later than usual, dressed in his travel suit. He stood in front of his open vault, rummaging through its contents and depositing selected documents into a small trunk at his feet.

Batya turned to leave just as Freda entered with a cup of coffee. "I'll come back later," Batya murmured. Outside the office, she halted and pressed her ear to the wall to eavesdrop. Right by her face, hanging along the side of a painting, she noticed a key. Probably to Moskowitz's door. In a houseful of illiterate prostitutes, he rarely locked it.

"How long will you be in Rio?" she heard Freda ask her brother.

"A week." Moskowitz took a noisy sip of coffee, something he forbade Batya to do in public. "Important members of Zwi Migdal will be coming from all over to vote."

"God will bless you, you should be elected president."

"Pedro won't relinquish his throne so easily. If I don't get all the pledged votes, next year is only a year away." He chuckled at his own joke. "Pedro hates that I'm the treasurer; I have more say than he does as president. He must go through me for every expense, so who's in charge?"

"Even as a little boy our Yitzik was a math professor." Freda laughed. "There's no situation you can't handle."

He chuckled again, and Batya walked away. She wouldn't get the newspapers for a whole week; she'd miss reading about Alfred Dreyfus's fate.

An hour later, feeling gloomy, she looked down from her window at the rainwater flowing along the street. A covered carriage was parked in front of the house, the horses' heads lowered under the heavy rain. From the commotion that reached Batya from inside the house, she figured that a horde of girls was gathering in the vestibule for a big sendoff.

She descended the back stairs, intending to get herself a cup of hot coffee and then, after Moskowitz had left, join the sisters in the pavilion, since few customers would be around in this weather.

As she passed the office, her glance caught Moskowitz's leather briefcase still resting on the chair next to his gray felt hat, a walking stick with a silver handle leaning against it. His wool coat was draped on the second chair, but the trunk with the documents must have been carried out to the carriage; Moskowitz was probably making a last stop at the lavatory before collecting his personal belongings.

Without thinking, Batya entered, unbuckled the briefcase, and looked inside, unsure what she hoped to find.

There was the ledger.

She pulled it out, slid it under her cardigan, and quickly rebuckled the briefcase. She hugged the book to her chest and, heart pounding, slipped through the back corridor up to her room.

Minutes later, she watched from her window as, surrounded by giggling sisters sharing umbrellas, Moskowitz stepped outside, wearing his hat. Freda carried his leather briefcase and handed it to him once he was settled in the carriage.

Batya knew what she had in her possession: Zwi Migdal's accounting book. But she wouldn't give it to Sergio until he liberated her and her family from their respective hells.

Or unless Ulmann forced her hand—whatever happened first.

The evening after Moskowitz's departure to Rio de Janeiro seemed interminable. Batya danced and serviced long into the dawn hours, but when she finally curled up in bed alone, every joint in her body aching, fear kept her awake. The ledger was tucked between her dresser and the wall. If Moskowitz discovered the theft early enough, he would take the train back to search the house. His men would wreak havoc in every room, turn every piece of furniture upside down, empty the contents of every drawer until they found it.

Batya struggled with dread another full day, until it occurred to her the following night that one place Moskowitz wouldn't turn upside down was his office. She secured the ledger to her waist with a belt and crept downstairs; if she bumped into anyone, she'd say she was heading to the kitchen to warm a glass of milk against the chill.

The skeleton key to Moskowitz's office—similar to the one Ulmann had given her—was hanging where she'd seen it.

Careful not to make any noise, Batya unlocked the door, slipped into the dark room, and felt her way to the bookcase. She stretched to the highest shelf she could reach and, in the predawn light streaming from the window, tucked the ledger among a row of books.

Chapter Forty-Three

*F*rom what Batya gathered later, when Moskowitz thundered out the story to Freda, he blamed the theft of the ledger on the train's conductor or one of his cabin mates. The thief had also relieved him of a bundle of cash, he told Freda—one hundred thousand pesos—and Batya figured that Moskowitz had added this lie to prove to the members of Zwi Migdal his own personal loss in this debacle.

"They will see who Yitzik is," he ranted. "Not only did I lose the election, but they've fired me from my position as treasurer! No one was ever as good at this job!" He cursed Pedro and the rest of the members. "Imagine they dared call me Yitzik the Pitzik? After all I've accomplished—and after all I've done for them and for our community? But wait and see. I have big plans. They will all see who Yitzik is. They'll come crawling back to me, begging me to take over the presidency."

When Batya entered his office the day after his return, eager to collect the newspapers and read about Señor Dreyfus, she dared not raise her eyes to the shelf where the ledger was placed. Would Moskowitz notice it up there? Its brown spine was as unadorned as the other volumes, yet, without looking, she knew that it was lighter and thinner than the bindings of the books on either side. If Moskowitz found it in this unlikely spot—and Freda would deny ever placing it there—the search for the true culprit would be focused on the sisters. Batya didn't want to think what methods Moskowitz's thugs might use to extract a confession from each of them.

For now, all she could do was pick up the newspapers and rush back to her chamber to catch up on the news. An article told of someone by the name of Emile Zola who had written an essay in a French newspaper that was causing a great stir in France. Titled "I Accuse," it denounced the French government for its anti-Semitism and the unlawful jailing of Alfred Dreyfus. Zola's letter wasn't included in the newspaper Batya held in her hands, but the article hailed the author for his courage. Batya tore out the article and put it away next to Dreyfus's picture and caricature.

Moskowitz's return from Rio de Janeiro marked a change in the house. He was upgrading his operation, he announced to the sisters. Only the most beautiful and alluring, most creative and productive prostitutes would be entitled to work in his new deluxe brothel, so the girls who were slacking had better shape up.

He proceeded to acquire the building adjacent to the house, a former mansion that had long been converted into a rooming house with families crowding every floor. In three days all the tenants who had cooked on open fires in the verandas and had strung laundry lines between them were gone—either after accepting cash payments or, if they demanded too much, forcibly evicted by Moskowitz's thugs. On the fourth day, construction crews arrived to demolish the beehive of temporary interior partitions, remove piles of accumulated debris, and scrape the outside walls of layers of mold and crude paint until the building's fine original carvings were exposed.

Over Freda's objections, Moskowitz engaged Rochel to help him in his plans. Rochel, who had been forlorn and remote for months, seemed revived. She spent hours in Moskowitz's office, poring with him over blueprints an architect brought over.

A week later, Rochel approached Batya in the kitchen yard, where Batya was washing her underthings. The winter day was dry and warm, and Batya liked the feel of the sun on her back.

"Moskowitz is elevating my status," Rochel whispered.

Batya turned to look at her. "Elevating it to what?"

"For the past two years, I've been urging him to design a fancy, specialized brothel in which each bedroom would have a motif and the girl working that room would playact a scene based upon it."

That was why Moskowitz took Rochel to the theater so often, Batya realized. Rochel had never admitted it. She had kept secrets, just as Batya had.

Rochel went on. "I convinced him that simply acquiring more girls, when the many he had were already hard for Freda to manage, wasn't as profitable as converting one of his brothels into a more high-class enterprise." Rochel smiled, and the twin dimples that Batya hadn't seen for months returned. "Buenos Aires is hungry for entertainment, not only for sex." Facing the crisis with his colleagues, she went on to explain, Moskowitz finally saw the value of a unique approach to his business.

Rochel giggled. "The walls of the African room will be painted with elephants and giraffes. Stuffed monkeys will swivel from tree branches that will create a canopy over the bed. Maybe we'll even have a real trained monkey observe the action in the room. What do you think?" Without waiting for Batya's response, she continued to gush. "The girl working there will have a fake gun and will hunt the client, tie him in a net, and gag him until he does as she orders him to." Rochel's voice was as animated as in the mornings when she had recounted the plays she had attended. "The Chinese room will have red lanterns, and its walls will depict bubbling springs, with paintings of delicate virgins crouching by the pond, cherry blossoms in their hair. Weeping willow branches will create a canopy over the bed, where a girl wearing a kimono will serve tea—"

"That's a Japanese girl," Batya interrupted, showing off what she, too, had learned from her clients. "Just the first part is Chinese, I think."

"They both drink tea from tiny cups and wear kimonos, right?"

Batya scrubbed the laundry, which was already clean. "The men won't know the difference."

"But it's a good idea to have a Japanese room, too. I'll ask the architect to bring books with pictures of Japan so I can see the difference."

Batya tried to digest what she was hearing. Would Rochel work in any of the rooms, or would she become the matron running the place? Batya pushed away her apprehensions. "How about an Indian room?" She thought of her necklace with the filigree work and the description she'd heard from a sea captain about that mysterious country. "They wear saris made of long swaths of silk shot through with gold and silver threads." She turned away from the sink, wiped her hands on a towel, and demonstrated in languid dance movements the allure of peeling such fabric away from her body. "You could also drape silk of all colors of the rainbow all over the room to turn it into a giant tent."

Rochel nodded enthusiastically. "That's why I'm telling you this secret plan. You can work with me, especially now that you'll be dancing professionally. We'll decorate a room for you based on *One Thousand and One Nights*."

"What's that?"

"I heard about it from a storyteller in the market. It will be an Arab desert room, and we'll have girls trained in belly dancing perform either alone or in a group of three. You can take a few lessons in belly dancing." Rochel smiled at her. "It's your chance to raise your status. The new brothel will be the best in all of Buenos Aires and will attract only the wealthiest and most influential clients."

Batya lowered her head to hide the horror that was seeping into her heart. For her part in building this new brothel, Rochel would surely be rewarded with becoming the matron. She would receive a share of the profits. Before long, she might be accepted as a member of Zwi Migdal, which had women, too, among its hundreds of pimps.

Rochel went on. "You know those clients that want to be tortured? The ones Nettie used to whip?" She laughed. "There will be a torture room for them, complete with chains, handcuffs, and leather straps hanging from the wall. Also a cot made of nails."

Batya dipped her hands back in the water to hide their tremor. Rochel had always been practical about their circumstances, had always adjusted to make the best of it. Yet this?

"I got a real French girl, too," Rochel whispered. "Not even Jewish."

Batya turned to look at her. "How?"

"One of the *alfonsos* roams churches in the French countryside. In one he saw a well-dressed girl lighting a candle, praying to Jesus and Maria and crying her eyes out. So he knew that she'd lost her virginity."

"How did he figure that out?"

Rochel opened her arms as if the answer was self-evident. "For these Christian girls, it's the end of the world."

"It was for me." *And I'm sure for you, too.*

"It's not the same. They get hell and fire for eternity, or something like that. This girl must have fallen in love with a boy. She let herself go, and an hour later regretted it. My *alfonso* offered to help her run away from home to hide her shame."

The hair roots rose on Batya's arms. Losing her virginity in the French countryside to a boy she loved shouldn't be a girl's direct route to prostitution in Argentina. "Where is she now?" she asked.

"In training." Rochel went on. "The French room will be decorated like a Parisian bordello, with red velvet-covered walls and gilt molding. The girl will speak French and act like a true high-class courtesan."

Batya placed her wet lingerie in the wringer so she wouldn't have to face her friend. The poor French girl was now being beaten and raped in order to coerce her into acquiescence—and Rochel knew it. The compassionate friend Batya had known had been replaced by a cynical pimp wearing Rochel's face.

"Do you want to hear what else is different about our new brothel?" Rochel chattered on. "The girls will continue to live in this house but will go to the new house to work, just as if they had a job in a store. They won't occupy these expensive rooms. We'll train a few girls for each role. This way the clients will have a selection of girls. What do you think?"

Batya swallowed. How lucky she was not to have revealed to Rochel her true relationship with Sergio—and her betrayal of Moskowitz.

Chapter Forty-Four

Spring 1895

*K*eyla had finally arrived in Odessa, Sergio reported, and Batya let out air that had been trapped in her lungs all these many months of worry. "Are they ready to sail then?"

He shook his head. "They are being processed. Getting the passports and travel documents."

"Why do they need to wait if the Baron himself is vouching for them?"

"The Russian authority must issue the passports for the adults and the travel permits for the children. It takes time."

How long would Ulmann wait? "Can't you bribe someone?" Batya asked.

"We can only push the Russians so far about specific individuals before they start piling on new demands."

At least they were all together, and safe. Keyla would have a chance to recover from the arduous journey before taking the next difficult part. She and her children would be fed.

Batya thought of the ledger, still hiding in Moskowitz's office. She peeked at it when coming to collect the newspaper and steal discarded documents from the wastebasket. As long as Sergio seemed to be following up on his end of the bargain, she would save her last bargaining chip. In the meantime, he was excited about the competition coming up in a few weeks, recounting past such events, and there was genuine delight in his voice when he spoke about the judges' surprise when watching an unknown perform so well. If Batya was apprehensive about performing in front of a crowd, the upside was that the rehearsals had taken her out of the house and away from the string of men.

Ulmann was planning a trip to Montevideo to take special orders and sell his excess inventory. "You could have come with me," he said, making no attempt to hide his irritation. "Am I to understand that you prefer having many clients over being my one true companion?" His voice was uncharacteristically incensed. "Or are you waiting for a higher bidder?"

"That's not it. I—I—"

He cut her off. "I'm sure that you've received offers such as mine before and you'll receive more in the future, what with all these men around you." He dropped his face into his hands, and his tone softened. "Am I a fool to hope that you'll give up all your admirers?"

Batya was touched that he believed his offer wasn't a once-in-a-lifetime chance for her. "I want to live with you," she responded, "but also I am very close to my family. I promised to bring them out of Russia. My mother, may her soul rest in peace, is watching me while I let my sisters and their families down—"

"Your sisters have families? How many people are you talking about?"

"Nine. But five are children; they don't eat much—"

"Nine? And where would you put up nine people? You want that our little apartment should be a home to nine more people?"

"They can all live in one room." They did in the shtetl, and many families were similarly crowded in many sections of Buenos Aires.

"This is Barrio Norte, not the slums of San Telmo or Once." Ulmann's tone was indignant. "Who will feed these nine people? Me? And don't these children need schooling, and clothes and doctors—as if I don't have three of my own to worry about?" He shook his head in exasperation.

"They could go live in one of the new colonies," Batya said.

"With five children? How many strong men are among your four adults?"

One strong and one feeble. She looked at her fingers and said nothing. Her heart ached at the thought of having to forgo mothering Vida—or give up Ulmann.

Despite his annoyance, Ulmann let her calm him down, soothe his ego yet again, and nurture his soul with her murmurs and touches. An hour later, acting as though their conversation hadn't taken a turn, he showed her new drawings of jewelry and asked her opinion. When he left, he didn't ask for his key back.

In the morning, when she was spreading bread crumbs for the pigeons, Batya imagined herself doing so in the Barrio Norte apartment. She would fill the veranda with planters and grow flowers, herbs, and even a few tomato plants. Every day she would dust the furniture, scrub the toilet, and wash the tile floors; she would never assign the tasks to a maid. Everything in that small apartment—she now knew that it had only one bedroom and a separate sitting room—would be hers to take care of alone, symbols of her freedom. In her own kitchen, she would learn to cook for Ulmann, so when he arrived at night after tucking his boys into bed, she would show him her gratitude.

The dream was hers to pluck like a ripe fruit from a tree. It was so close she could taste it.

Her time for making a decision was running out.

Approaching the venue for her first competition, Batya treaded with caution on the unfinished sidewalk, trepidation and excitement fighting inside her. She hadn't expected to still be in Buenos Aires when spring was pushing winter away, and if she and Sergio won tonight, there would be a second round of competition, then another. When and how was he planning to hide her if he was making her famous?

From nearby came melodious waltz music, and she hurried toward the ice-skating rink that had opened recently to serve the city's insatiable hunger for amusement. Glikel, who had been invited to a private party of city officials, had reported about this miraculous arena. The officials had closed the venue one afternoon for their exclusive use and requested that Moskowitz send them *polacas*. Having no experience with ice, the men assumed that these prostitutes who came from snowy countries would know how to glide on it. Glikel told the sisters later that someone had attached blades to her shoes and pushed her onto the ice, where she kept sliding and falling. She showed the sisters the blue and purple bruises on her ample hips and thighs, which had cushioned her bones and protected them from cracking. Unfortunately, they hadn't protected her from the disappointment of the clients, who sneered at her failure and sent her back without the gift of cash she had expected.

Batya peeked through the open side of the warehouse-like structure. Several well-dressed people glided inside a fenced area. The swooshing scrape of their blades on the ice accompanied the music. She bent down and snaked her hand through the railing to touch the ice. The skin of her fingers stuck to it; after years of being away from it, she had forgotten that it could burn.

She straightened and rushed on to her appointment. Rather than pick her up, Sergio had secured Moskowitz's permission for Batya to go by herself to the costume store. It would take two hours to get her dressed and ready.

Batya walked into a shop filled with gowns made of layers of flowing chiffon and dotted with glittering sequins.

The shop matron's eyes raked over Batya. "So you are Señor Rosenberg's new *metziah*?" she sneered, and then, as if Batya weren't around, said to her helper, "Where else would he find a dancer but in a brothel? Take her to the storage room so our good clients don't see her trying on our dresses, or we won't be able to sell them."

The insult felt stale, like chewing on old bread. "Maybe I should go elsewhere to rent a dress," Batya said, pretending to start for the door.

The matron grabbed Batya's hand. "But I have the perfect

one for you." Her bluff called out, the woman's tone changed to pleading. "Just take a look." She removed a magnificent pink dress from a rack and nudged Batya to a dressing room whose walls were upholstered in cream velvet.

"Pin and sew the hem," Batya ordered when she put on the dress. "I don't want to catch it with my heels."

After selecting a pair of shoes with medium-height heels, Batya sat down and gave herself over to the ministering of the assistant.

The young woman parted Batya's hair in a straight line two centimeters off the middle and pulled it tight into a severe chignon, then smoothed down with coconut oil any stray strands. Using a soft black pencil, she lined Batya's eyes, elongating them almost to her temples, and then darkened the light-brown eyebrows into black arches. To finish the look, she wet the tip of the pencil with her tongue and dotted a beauty mark on Batya's cheekbone. "Don't look yet," she told Batya, and secured a pink hibiscus flower in her hair.

The proprietor returned with Batya's hemmed dress and helped her into it. Batya turned to look at herself in the mirror. The woman who stared back at her had little resemblance to the woman she'd known as herself—or even as Esperanza. *That's better,* she thought. Like in prostitution, hiding behind a mask helped her fight her trepidation about performing for a large audience and being judged.

The assistant held the hem of Batya's dress off the dust as she led her through an alley to the back entrance of the dance hall.

Upon seeing her, Sergio's eyes lit up with a sparkle of approval. "We're going to win," he said, a rare smile on his face. He looked dashing in his matador costume. The epaulettes of the short black jacket were embroidered in elaborate gold stitching that swirled into leaves on the rest of the jacket. His tight black pants emphasized the manhood he never let her glimpse.

All around them, backstage, couples were marking dance moves; women were checking themselves in the mirror and silently evaluating one another's sparkling dresses. Under their heavy makeup, Batya couldn't tell who they were—prostitutes or daughters of rich families. They all looked beautiful, and they had to be fabulous dancers. Why was Sergio so confident that the two of them would win? He could be equally wrong in assessing the outcome of the investigation.

Batya touched his arm. "Win or lose, there will be no more. I want out of Buenos Aires."

He looked at her silently, then said, "Let's not talk about it now."

"There's nothing more to say about it," she replied.

Half an hour later, waiting on one side of the stage while Sergio was on the other, Batya took in the audience. Men chatted and women rearranged their dresses in the seats. Sergio hadn't warned her about the stage lights, which nearly blinded her when they burst on. Shielding her eyes, she could see that the large crowd wasn't distracted by drinking or card playing, as they were in the pavilion. Everyone was looking at her! Nothing in her rehearsals had prepared her for this.

Then she remembered her mask. No one saw her, Batya-Esperanza—except Moskowitz. She felt him somewhere in the hall, his gaze slithering in her veins. This competition, she reminded herself, was a sham—a cover-up of her treachery meant to bring him down.

The band broke into the first song. Batya thrust one hip

forward as she stepped to meet Sergio halfway, and he arched his arm high and took hold of her opposite hand. Resting her head on his shoulder, she heard a murmur ripple through the crowd. Swirling in her magnificent dress, she fought the attraction and romance of the *caballero* Sergio portrayed, while she danced her lament for a love she would never have. Together, she and Sergio finished the first round in a double turn.

Triumph coursed through her with the applause and the shouts of "Bravo! Brava!" She curtsied, feeling more feminine and desired than she'd ever felt when naked.

At the conclusion of the first round, some competing couples were eliminated. The excitement in the audience was palpable as they cheered and clapped upon the entrance of each of the remaining couples for the second round. When Batya and Sergio remained in the competition for the final round with two other couples, Batya hoped that she'd stumble and fall and they'd lose. Within moments, though, as the music flooded her, and with Sergio's arm on her back guiding her in long, fluid steps across the dance floor, her feet became light, and she double-stepped and swerved, loving showing off that she wasn't merely a prostitute, the *metziah* that the store matron had dismissed.

The judges took a short break to cast their votes. Batya was catching her breath in the back, drinking water, when the three couples were summoned again to the stage.

To her disbelief, the chief judge declared that Sergio and his rising star partner, Esperanza, had won.

During the dreamlike party that followed, with food and champagne and words of adulation, Batya cast away all that troubled her. She had caught sight of Ulmann after her performance, when she was swept off the stage by the other competing couples, who offered their congratulations—the men more genuinely than the women. When she met Ulmann's eyes, he winked at her, then, not one to enjoy a festivity, turned to leave. She liked that he'd watched her dance. *My man,* she thought, surprising herself with the words. If only accepting him didn't mean rejecting her family.

Moskowitz worked the room, eyeing the men who eyed her, dropping hints and open invitations. Before the party was over, he signaled to Batya that it was time to return to the house.

Sergio took her palms in his. "Thank you," he said. "I'm sorry that you must leave. I'll come see you in two days."

The shop owner's assistant waited in the wings to accompany the dress and Batya back to the shop. With a pang of sorrow, Batya changed into her own clothes. The flower in her hair had wilted, but the theatrical makeup stayed on.

It was only ten o'clock when she returned to the pavilion. Clients were awaiting the new star, and Moskowitz raised the fees paid for her services.

Chapter Forty-Five

$\mathcal{T}$he pressure from Ulmann's dilemma was dwarfed by the weight of the stolen ledger. Moskowitz was bound to discover Batya's ticket to freedom hiding in plain sight. The more her dream of escaping felt within her reach, the more desperate she became about her slavery. Some days, she vomited after yet another physical contact with a stranger. Securing the ledger somewhere safe would ease one worry.

The only place outside the house she could access was Rafael's sweets cart. She retrieved the ledger in the morning when collecting the newspapers and tucked it back in her chamber between the dresser and the wall. The many hours the ledger was in her possession stretched on. Batya jumped at the sudden noise of a copper pot dropped on the tiled floor, at the odd note from a musician adjusting his violin strings, and at the screech of a bird.

She was relieved when the house quieted before dawn. She tore off a page and hid it in the wall, then slipped out of the house, the ledger secured under her skirt with a belt. Its edges pinched her skin with every step.

The streets were quiet at this hour, when the music in the cafés and *milongas* had stopped, drunkards lay asleep on the curbs, and more respectable customers were home in their comfortable beds. Stray dogs slept, the milkmen hadn't yet begun their rounds, and laborers were still inside their makeshift huts erected at construction sites. Batya was exhausted, but the chilled night air was fresh and fragrant with the scent of flowers and herb gardens. The moon at the edge of the canopied sky hung above as if it were her private protector.

She stopped a distance from Rafael's corner to verify that he had stretched out his nightly canvas to create a tent. Approaching, she listened through the canvas to Rafael's uneven breathing.

The shafts of the cart were raised onto wood blocks to keep the cart bed level. Batya crouched and reached under the canvas to feel the cross beams, like the ones that had reinforced her father's cart. They were narrower than she had anticipated. The ledger couldn't be secured there. She straightened and stood still for a minute, her hand resting against the cart's leather-upholstered bench.

A rooster crowed, and its cock-a-doodle-do reverberated over the houses, reminding Batya that the night was lifting. In an empty lot nearby, someone lit a small fire and began boiling coffee. Its aroma wafted toward her, teasing her. Soon, the municipal street sweepers with their two-wheeled carts would come out to collect debris. Batya contemplated her options. Her fingers searched the leather covering the seat—and detected a spot in the back where it had come undone. She raised the loosened section, careful not to pop out more nails, and explored the cavity. The bench had been constructed as crudely as the rest of the cart, and Batya's fingers found a large enough gap between the planks forming the seat's frame.

Without waking Rafael, she tucked the ledger into it and snuck away.

Ulmann produced a small gift box. Inside was a gold ring. Batya's breath caught in her throat at the sight of the two intertwined Hebrew letters; at the center of each a tiny diamond chip indicated that the letters were *bet* and not *vet*. The identical initials of both their names.

"Please tell me you want me to speak with Moskowitz," he said, and slipped it on her middle finger. "I'm so lonely without you."

Her heart was too full to answer. She'd never been loved. She hugged him. "Thank you. It's beautiful!"

"I saw you with your dance partner. I want you to be like that with me."

She rested her head on his shoulder as she did in a dance and, checking that he could watch her in the mirror, closed her eyes as if in a romantic trance. "It's just a game. Pretend." She raised her hand, the ring turned toward him. "This is real."

"I want you all for myself." His fingers combed through the mass of her hair as though he were admiring spun gold. "Be *my* Batya."

"You know what I must do first," she said, making her voice as gentle as she could. "As soon as I finalize arrangements for my family—"

"No more waiting," he said.

She could no longer put him off. Nor lose him. If only she could earn money while living with him, she might still save to pay for her family's passages. Even in the poverty of San Telmo they would be living no worse than they did now in Russia. "Will you let me work in your store?" she asked. "I'm good with numbers. I can draw the salary you're now paying your saleslady."

He scratched his head. "Isabella. she worked for my father. She knows all the customers." He paused. "But she's not young and said something about wanting to live with her son in Córdoba. I'll speak with her."

"Thank you," Batya whispered. Their lips met, and when they parted, she looked into his kind eyes, her heart light with possibilities and heavy with the unresolved issues.

"I'll talk to Moskowitz in the morning," he said, grinning as he left.

Batya had just hidden the new ring—she couldn't risk answering questions before Ulmann had negotiated with Moskowitz—when there was a knock on her door.

When she opened it, she was astonished to see Sergio. For months she'd seen him only during the day. Now he came late at night as a client in her chamber.

Batya closed the door behind them, and he glanced at it as if to ensure that it was secure, then pulled out of his jacket pocket a wad of gray-colored money—hundred-peso bills. "I had to pay Moskowitz a third of my winnings," he said, "so it's only fair that you get half of what's left."

She gulped at the thickness of the wad. It would have taken her two years to accumulate this much after all of Freda's deductions. "I'm grateful," she whispered, her voice brimming with emotion. This money would set up her father in his own store in the new colony.

Sergio dropped into the chair, and she settled on a sheepskin rug. "I have something else for you." He withdrew an envelope from his inside pocket and held it up. The stamp was from Russia.

Batya's heart sang, even as she recognized that the handwriting wasn't her father's. Surale must have paid a scribe. With trembling fingers, Batya took the letter. The seal was already broken. She unfolded the single piece of paper. It was written on both sides of the page, so the ink seeped through and stained some words.

My very dear sister, the most beloved Batya,

I hope that this letter finds you in good health, that your troubles as an impoverished widow are over, and that your local council has ruled in favor of you to receive your just share of your late husband's estate, including your mansion.

The good news, thank Hashem, is that Keyla is with us. Her son was very sick the year before, which delayed her departure, and his constitution is still poor. Please mention his name in your prayers: Shlomo, son of Keyla. The not good news is that our papa has taken ill. His cough became worse since our arrival in

*Odessa. The doctor says that his blood is thin. Luckily,
the Jewish Colonization Association has been extremely
generous. We had been terrified that, with our head
of household sick, they would send all of us back, but
where would that be? Where was home? Bless Hashem,
the JCA has arranged for Papa to be admitted to the
hospital! A real hospital, a big building with beds with
white sheets and real nurses, although if you ask Papa,
most of them are shiksas who would just as soon poison
a Jew as cure him. We praise Hashem for having delivered Papa from the crisis, although he is weak and
still coughs. He contends that his deliverance was due
to the fact that his soul couldn't die until he reunited
with you. I tell him that he was saved because God sent
us a doctor who had been trained in Paris.*

A wave of love for her family washed over Batya. How could
she have entertained merely an hour ago the idea of selfishly com-
promising her efforts to save them—not knowing if she could
work in Ulmann's store, and how much she could earn? Yet she
had. As if to apologize to Surale, Batya kissed the letter, then went
on reading.

*Nevertheless, we must delay our departure. First, be-
cause no ship captain will take Papa for fear of infect-
ing other passengers, even though the doctor says that
Papa's consumption is not of a contagious nature. Second, because the good doctor plans to send Papa to a*

convalescence clinic that our revered liaison from the JCA has graciously arranged. Imagine Papa, like a rich landowner from Bobruevo, being served all his meals while he lounges all day in the sun! We only hope that there will be other people to speak to, because Papa is regaining his chattering spirit—

Batya raised her gaze to Sergio. "Your organization is taking good care of my father, I see," she said. "Thank you so very much."

He smiled. "Didn't I promise to repay your great help?"

Her heart expanded. A real doctor, rather than a traveling folk healer selling elixir. A hospital. A convalescence clinic. Who would have ever thought that these were possible for her father, who hadn't known a day of rest in his life? "But they can't leave." She wiped a tear with the back of her hand, then read on.

Since our stay at the hotel was never meant to be long, we have obtained the right to a room in an apartment shared by two other families. My dear Duvid has found a job as an apprentice carpenter, a profession that will serve him well wherever we go next. He's learning fast. In the meanwhile, he brings home a few kopeks each day that he works, and we eat our meals in a soup kitchen run by good Jewish souls, may they be blessed with long and healthy lives. The only worms that gnaw our hearts are missing you, Keyla's recuperating boy, and the worry over Papa's health.

I will write to you when we are ready to take the long journey to meet you, may it be before winter, God willing. In the meanwhile, I hope that you will keep your good health and prepare your mansion for our arrival.

Your very loving sister,
Surale (and Keyla, who is home
now, joins me with her blessings)

Batya was crying openly as she folded the letter. She imagined Surale and her husband and two children, with Keyla and her two orphans, as well as the toddler Vida, all in one room. Yet Surale, with her good nature, was happy with the few kopeks her husband earned and the soup kitchen that provided them with more food than they must have had in years. But Surale's refusal to accept Batya's story that she no longer lived a life of comfort was exasperating. Rather than facing the harsh realities of agricultural labor awaiting them in Moïseville, Surale still imagined that they would be delivered into a life of luxury that had never existed. She was probably feeding Keyla the same illusions.

Sergio led Batya to the bed, and she appreciated that he took charge as he stretched out and rocked, while she covered her face and let the tears flow. Why was she trying so hard to bring them if, upon arrival, they would be sorely disappointed? She was offering them in this new land merely another version of their poverty and strife, and they would be furious about her years of deception. And if they lived in San Telmo, sooner or later someone would reveal to them that Batya was no more than a lowly *kurve*.

"What if my father doesn't get better?" Batya asked Sergio at last. "Will your organization still bring the rest of them, with only one healthy man, and settle them in a colony?"

Sergio patted her arm, careful not to touch her breasts, while he kicked the bedpost rhythmically. "We've promised to take care of them, and we're doing it."

"I'm grateful." Batya sat up. "But I can't stay here. I can't keep doing what I have to do!"

He sat up, too. "Let's wait until we hear about your father's progress."

She looked at him, and a rush of suspicion that he needed her here to spy—his prime concern, not her well-being—filled her head. He didn't care that she had to prostitute. She had known all along not to trust promises. "I told you, no more," she finally said, heat of anger rising in her. "I have another offer and I'm taking it."

"What kind of an offer?"

"I'll be gone tomorrow or the day after."

He pointed at the letter resting on the dresser. "I've held up my part of the deal."

"And I mine." Batya bit her lip, thinking of the ring. Dear Ulmann. He would speak with Moskowitz in the morning. "Send me to one of your villages immediately. When my family arrives, they'll join me."

Sergio let out a deep breath, but stared at the ceiling as if the answer were written on it.

"Well?" she demanded. "You need me in Buenos Aires to steal more documents?"

He sighed, then gave the bedpost a series of kicks. "Your family's delay complicates things. I can't send you to one of the colonies."

"Why not?"

"A woman alone? There are some young families there, but the majority of settlers are men."

"I can work the land as hard as any man. Just give me a chance."

The furrow between his eyes deepened. "The committee will regard an unchaperoned woman as a scandal. And a former prostitute sent to a village filled with lone men?" Sergio shook his head as if hearing the voices of argument. "It's a question of morals. You may put this life behind you, but others might not view you the same way. We must be careful to help build a society of the highest principled values, and it might seem to some—"

Cold, sharp pain constricted Batya's rib cage. She cut him off, her tone bitter. "It might seem to some that I will contaminate the village?" This was no different from her visit to the women's section in the synagogue. For the "good" Jews, she would be forever *tme'ah*.

"Only if you are alone there. I'm concerned about your safety." He looked at her. "Also, until twenty-one you're not even of emancipated age. We're not sending unaccompanied minors—"

"It's settled then." She could barely suppress the fury in her voice. After all these months he was letting her down. "I'm taking the other offer."

"Please don't. Give me two weeks."

She felt a roar in her head. "Ten days. Not a day more." Her heart contracted at the recollection of the ring and its intertwined letters. She must find a way to buy this time extension out of Ulmann. She stuck her hand inside the mattress, retrieved the page she had torn from the ledger, and handed it to Sergio. "Or you'll never see the rest of this."

Chapter Forty-Six

$\mathcal{T}$he next morning Batya woke up earlier than her usual late morning habit. Skipping breakfast, she seated herself at her window, her shawl covering her shoulders, in order to catch Ulmann before he spoke with Moskowitz. Her anxiety mounted at the thought that by the end of the day she could be free and installed in Ulmann's apartment, but instead she must beg him for ten more days. Ten more days in which strange men would use her body and she must pretend to enjoy their foul nearness.

And Surale's words in her letter kept pushing at her guilt. Every one of her family members would be disillusioned, either in the farming colonies or in a Buenos Aires slum. When Freda sent her to the market today, Batya would visit the bank and ask the clerk to help her mail to Surale the succinct response she had managed to scribble by herself: *I told you how things are for me. Now act.*

On top of it all, there was no twisting away from the fact that she was willing to deceive Ulmann when keeping both his ring and her options open. Her good, honest man deserved better, except that she couldn't figure out what else she could do.

To Batya's surprise, she caught sight of him exiting the house, having missed his arrival. Even with the padded coat, his shoulders seemed to gather downward.

"Ulmann!" she called out. "You're not coming to see me?"

He turned to look at her, his brow contorted in pain.

Her heart sank. "Please come up." She pouted her lips to mouth the word "Please."

When he handed her the token he'd just purchased from Freda, Batya slipped it right back into his pocket. "Keep it. Just talk to me." She removed his coat and led him to the upholstered chair, then settled on the sheepskin rug. Resting her chin on Ulmann's knees, she looked up.

"I can't pay him enough." His voice broke as he stroked her hair. "His share of your winnings in the competition has made him greedy."

Batya's stomach clenched. How could she let this gentle, beautiful-souled man vanish? If her family was going to be stuck in Odessa all winter and Sergio wouldn't send her to the colonies alone, Ulmann was her only lifeline. She pressed her breasts against his legs. "Couldn't you take a loan?"

"And then what? I'll have to pay it back." He shook his head sadly. "I've calculated my expenses carefully."

The money Sergio had given her was for her family. Afterward, though, she might be able to help. "What if I continue to participate in the tango competitions?" Batya asked Ulmann. "Many are taking place all over Argentina. If I win when we live together, my share will be yours to pay back."

He shook his head again. "I won't be your pimp. Even if I can't make you an honorable married woman, I must still treat both of us with the respect you and I deserve."

Didn't he see that by treating her with respect, he was condemning her to the degradation of prostitution? Batya rose to her knees and took his face between her palms. "Listen," she whispered, "dancing is reputable."

He frowned. "Your winning is not guaranteed. I'll be in debt if you don't."

Would he ask for his ring back? Batya racked her brain for something to say to convince Ulmann to hold on to their dream. In her mind's eye, she saw the apartment and her plant-filled veranda. There was no visual picture of the obscure future Sergio still dangled in front of her. "Do you know why I'm not encouraging offers from other suitors?" she asked Ulmann. "Because I want the same thing you do—for us to be together."

He let her comfort him in her bed. It was Batya, not Esperanza, who made love to him, Batya who didn't need to insert her protection cup, trusting that Ulmann wasn't carrying diseases from other women.

When he was about to leave, he hugged her tightly and buried his face in her hair. "Cherish our ring and remember that this is the last time I'll be traveling to Montevideo without you."

So he'd still try to figure out a way to buy her from Moskowitz. With tears brimming in her eyes, Batya hugged him back.

Sergio returned a few days later. "There's a tango competition coming up in Río Negro. That's south of here, a long train ride that will require an overnight stay," he told Batya in her chamber. "I've secured Moskowitz's permission."

"No more, I said."

He let out a small smile. "Instead of heading south, though, we'll go north, to Santa Fe. It will take Moskowitz two days to realize that you're gone."

This was it. What she had prayed for. Yet with the sudden exhilaration came the pang of never seeing Ulmann again, of the fantasy of their life together evaporating—and the ugliness of her deception. "What will happen when I don't return? Zwi Migdal will come down on you."

"As soon as I return I'll report that you ran away. Got off at one of the stops."

She stared at him. "They'll look for me. I'll be forever a fugitive, wanted by the police for escaping my 'husband.' I'm registered with the city as belonging to Freda." *Her slave.*

"Because you're still a minor, you'll be adopted by a recent widow. You will officially become her daughter under a new name, and you'll live in her house."

Fear crept into Batya's heart. For the second time in her life, she would accompany a man to some destination of which she knew almost nothing, and instead of starting a new life as a mistress of her own home, she would become someone's child, or, more likely, her unpaid maid.

For now, she and Sergio had to re-create their make-believe sex. Batya moved on the mattress, creaking the springs beneath. "When?" she asked.

"The competition, which we'll miss, is scheduled for Friday night. We will leave Thursday afternoon so we can arrive in

Moïseville before Shabbat. The only thing I need from you to finalize the arrangements is the ledger."

It was Monday. Only three more days of servicing men. "I don't keep it with me here."

"Where is it?" His tone was sharp.

"Hidden in a safe place."

"I must have it."

"I'll bring it to the train with me."

He stiffened. "Don't you trust me?"

"I trust my mother in heaven and my father, may his name remain with the living." She wasn't sure whether she trusted God, the way He'd failed her.

Sergio swung his legs off the bed. "You're sure it is safe, wherever it is?"

"Yes." She ignored the flash of anger on Sergio's face. "You asked me to trust your promise. Now I ask that you trust mine."

For a while he said nothing while she rocked the bed. "Don't think that we are not grateful for what you've done," he said. "It took courage. You took risks for the Jews that you dislike—"

"Jews that *despise* me and the likes of me," she corrected, then paused. "I have an idea for when you bring Zwi Migdal down. About all the sisters you will release from bondage."

"What is that?"

"A women's village. No men. Just women working in agriculture. While your Baron is liberating Jews from across the ocean, how about the thousands of us who could be liberated here? We'll learn new skills and start a new life."

A twinkle of a smile flitted in Sergio's coal-dark eyes. "Not a bad idea, but quite impractical," he said. "Who will teach women the agricultural skills if we don't allow men in the village? We need the help of the gauchos and other experts, and sadly, none of them are women."

"For one thing, I will have a head start. I could be learning some of these skills very soon."

He laughed. "It takes years to become an expert at irrigation, land management, and husbandry."

"We are a tough bunch. We've been through a lot. Try us." Her hand swept the outside of the room. "What hasn't killed us has made us stronger."

Chapter Forty-Seven

She was finally leaving. Rescued. How Batya wished she could say goodbye to her friends. The sisters had become her family; even the bellicose Glikel was a part of her emotional landscape. How could she just walk away forever, never to see the sisters again?

Not forever, she reminded herself. When the Honorable Joaquin Ramos proceeded with his prosecution, the enslaved prostitutes in this city and beyond would be set free. She imagined herself on the train back to Buenos Aires, arriving just as Kolkowski had done, to pick up the first group to settle in their own women's village.

Unlike the bewildered Jews whom Kolkowski had led to the train, the sisters would laugh and sing all the way to Moïseville, and from there to her village. Esperanzaville. To her village of hope. Batya giggled at the play on her name. In their gardens, the sisters would plant vegetables. They would grow their own cucumbers, beets, carrots, peppers—and those other odd vegetables Batya had learned to like in Argentina: squash, tomatoes, and eggplants.

The sisters mistook the smile gracing Batya's face as she moved about her chores for their own excitement about the upcoming second competition. Batya would win, they all agreed, and they shared advice about hair and makeup. Glikel insisted that Batya take her carpetbag for her overnight trip, because it would bring Glikel good luck. After a polite refusal, Batya had to accept it, knowing that she wouldn't be returning it. Sergio had warned that she wasn't to raise suspicion by packing all her belongings, only one outfit and a change of underthings. At the last moment, she would remove her bank savings book, her family's letters, and the hidden jewelry.

As she watched her friends as if from a distance, it occurred to Batya that she had been so engrossed in her dreams that she had deluded herself that they all craved freedom. But Rochel had just charted a new future for herself. Glikel, like many other sisters accustomed to this life, enjoyed her opium and the privileges that came with earning money—pretty clothes, jewelry, café and theater outings, wine and champagne, abundant food, and nightly parties. Why replace such a fun-filled life with one of hard homestead labor? Not unlike the way many sisters failed to save their earnings for the future, they failed to face the transient nature of this lifestyle.

The following days passed in a haze. Ulmann had left on his trip, and she would not be saying goodbye to him. Dear Ulmann, who wanted her only, not her large family, and she understood. Whoever heard of a man taking on someone's parents and children? Batya regretted breaking his heart, but they would both get over their shattered dream, she told herself. In the meantime, she worked hard to lure clients so Moskowitz and Freda wouldn't find an excuse to pose a last-minute obstacle to her travel. Rochel was watching her, too, assessing her candidacy for the new brothel. Going through her chores, servicing the clients, Batya transported her thoughts toward her new life. At long last, it was close.

Thursday morning, after a rainy night, Freda sent her to the market early to shop. Batya headed first to Rafael's cart. But when she rounded the corner into his street, she stopped in her tracks and stared, stupefied.

The cart wasn't in its usual spot.

Batya's eyes grazed the empty space, her heart sinking. She walked to the nearest vendor, who sold pineapples. His hands moved quickly as he sliced.

"Have you seen the sweets seller?" she asked.

"He's not here."

"I know he's not here. I've come for my almond drink. Where is he?"

The pineapple vendor shrugged. "His brother took him away two days ago."

"The doctor said I must have my almond drink. Wasn't he supposed to be going home only on alternate weekends?"

"Brother was angry."

"Angry about what?"

"What am I, their mother?" Two customers reached for slices of pineapple, and the vendor made an impatient gesture with his knife. "Señorita, buy or move."

Her heart pounding in panic, Batya bought a slice, trying to figure out what to do. This afternoon Sergio would pick her up. Only when they arrived at the train would he learn that the promised ledger was gone. She would explain, apologize, and beg not to be sent back.

Yet he might do just that.

Her stomach knotted, and her apprehension mounting, Batya returned to the house. She had just dismissed the boy she'd hired in the market to carry her baskets when she spotted Sergio in the pavilion, hours earlier than had been agreed upon. He wore a cream-colored travel suit and a white shirt, its collar open. Next to him rested a long cloth bag, out of which peeked her rented pink performance dress.

For a split second Batya thought that he'd found out about Rafael's disappearance.

"Are you ready?" he asked, smiling uncharacteristically widely, probably for Freda's sake.

"I thought you weren't leaving until later," the boyish Juliet piped from the depth of a sofa, where she sat with three other girls. They all rose up. "We've planned to give you a proper farewell."

"The train schedule has changed," Sergio interrupted, and his eyebrows zigzagged at Batya. She understood enough not to question him.

She ran up to her chamber to gather her belongings. Earlier, she had folded the change of dress into the carpetbag along with the baking soda with which she cleaned her teeth, her hairbrush, the eye kohl, cheek rouge, and lip coloring, and the cream she used to remove her makeup. Now she retrieved her father's letters from her dresser drawer and threw them into the bag, then slid under the bed, moved the trunk, yanked out the loose stone, and withdrew her treasures. She wondered whether she should leave Ulmann's ring behind, but there was no time to unfurl the jewelry pouch.

Just as she pushed the trunk back and scrambled to her feet, Glikel entered her room.

"What's down there?" Glikel's eyes darted from the bed to the packet in Batya's hand.

"None of your business. Leave my room." Batya tossed a last glance at the room, purposely left as if she had gone out on a stroll: her velvet robe that she so loved was thrown casually on the bed, her comfortable pink slippers strewn like neglected children by her dresser, where half her clothes remained. She pushed Glikel out and closed the door. Behind her she heard her door reopen, but there was no time to fight. In a minute, Glikel would crawl under the bed and find enough objects of desire in the trunk to sell for her opium consumption. It would make up for Batya's failure to return the carpetbag.

Tucking her jewelry pouch and bankbook in her skirt pockets, Batya rushed downstairs. A dozen sisters hugged her, offering prayers for the road and good wishes for the competition. When it was Rochel's turn, Batya held her tight, holding back tears.

"You're not scared of the competition, are you?" Rochel untangled herself and looked at Batya with concern. "Don't be. You'll be great!"

Batya nodded, glad that her friend had misinterpreted her

goodbye. To hide her misted eyes, she turned her head toward Sergio as he picked up her bag, and allowed herself to be led out, his hand on her lower back.

Giggling and chattering, the sisters followed them to the carriage that had been waiting. Once Batya was inside, the carpetbag in her lap, she smiled and waved at the sisters. She glanced up at the climbing vine reaching the blue shutters. She would never see this house again. A vision of Aida onstage flitted through her head. Like the Nubian princess, she was being rescued—if Sergio allowed her on the journey once he learned the truth.

The carriage pulled away. In a moment, Sergio would ask for the ledger. A tremor that had begun in Batya's lips traveled down her throat. She coughed.

Against the clip-clopping of the horse's hoofs, she heard the ringing bells of a fire wagon and moments later saw it rush by, followed by two more, each with a large water cylinder and pump at the back and uniformed firemen urging the horses in the front. At the loud ringing of their bells and shouts of the firemen instructing everyone in the street to open the path, Batya put her hand on her heart to still it.

Chapter Forty-Eight

At the train station, a tall, slim man in a European charcoal-gray suit and matching hat waited for them. He carried a bag, and now Batya noticed that Sergio had none, only her performance dress. The memory of Moskowitz transferring her to Grabovsky in the lobby of the hotel struck her, and she clutched Sergio's arm.

Without speaking, the man started along the platform, Batya and Sergio following. Suddenly, he glanced about, then turned abruptly into the nearest car. Batya rushed to climb in behind him, afraid to look back. With Sergio making way for her, they pushed through the car of high-backed wooden benches, under which passengers stacked packages, straw baskets, and suitcases. Children tried to run up and down the aisle, dodging people's legs.

Three cars later, Batya and her two companions entered a quieter car divided into private compartments, each with leather-upholstered seats facing each other. The man in the gray suit led them into one and closed the door behind them. He handed his bag to Sergio and planted himself in front of the door's window, his hands clasped and his gaze straight into the corridor.

Batya felt the air thickening with tension. Any moment, before someone came to get her, Sergio would ask for the ledger, and she would have to tell him where to retrieve it in a few days when Rafael returned. If the silent man who was checking the traffic outside their cabin was one of Moskowitz's goons, he would break her bones for the deception.

Sergio took a few items of clothing from his bag and laid them on the seat next to Batya. "Change into these." He rose to turn his back to her.

She fingered the unfamiliar clothes. "What are they?"

"A gaucho's outfit."

Her anxiety was assuaged at the safety precautions. She quickly pulled on the dark trousers—the first pair she'd ever worn—and removed her skirt. Her white shirt fit under the short leather vest, though it failed to hide the bulge of her breasts. She tied the red scarf around her neck, then glanced at the filth of the wide-brimmed brown felt hat. Gathering up her mane of hair, she tucked it into the hat's cavity.

When she sat down again, she saw that Sergio had tied a similar scarf around his neck, smeared a dark substance on his already tanned skin to make himself look dirty, and put on a similarly old hat.

Passengers passed in the corridor, and Batya could hear the thumping of valises in the cabins to the right and left. Porters called out, men gave orders, and women fussed over their broods and packages. Once in a while Sergio glanced through the glass at the goings-on or stepped into the corridor to check the platform, clearly alert to some danger.

"Sergio—" Batya began, but he raised his hand to hush her. She pressed her back to the seat. The last time she had been on a train, she was grieving the separation from her family, ashamed of her rape, and fearful of the unknown future. That old dread now felt like drinking milk that had gone sour. She was tired of being afraid.

The minutes stretched. Batya fidgeted in her seat. She would have liked to watch the platform to see for herself if someone was pursuing her, but her window faced away from it, onto other tracks and trains. She closed her eyes and willed her heartbeat to slow down.

The conductor passed through the corridor, calling out, "All aboard! All aboard!"

The tall man withdrew tickets from his pocket and fanned them out to count. Six, Batya noticed. He had bought the whole cabin, just as Moskowitz had once done. He handed them to Sergio, took the dress bag, nodded an acknowledgment to Batya, and closed the door behind him as he left.

A moment later the door reopened. Batya was shocked to see Ulmann. His hair was disheveled, he dragged his jacket by its loop, and perspiration damped his cotton shirt. Forgetting that she was dressed as a gaucho, she stood up, and recognized her mistake only when Ulmann's eyes widened. "I thought I saw you just as I got off my train from Montevideo. What are you doing?" His glance rested on Sergio and pain crinkled his brow. "You're running off with another man?"

Batya pasted a reassuring smile on her lips, hating what she had to do. "Oh, no! I'm only going to a dance competition. Remember?"

"Why are you dressed like this?" He shook his head. "And where is that competition supposed to be?"

"In Río Negro."

"You're on the wrong train."

A huge whistle tore the sky, and the train jerked. Sergio rose to his feet. He was taller and broader that Ulmann.

"She's mine." Ulmann began to weep. "Where are you taking her?"

"I must ask you to leave."

Forced to back away, Ulmann craned his neck to see Batya. "You told me not to give up. I've sold my merchandise. I have the money—"

Clammy fingers of fear traversed Batya's spine. If he believed that she wasn't running away, Ulmann might go directly to Moskowitz to negotiate. He'd report which train she was on. She stood, fighting her panic, hating to lie. "Please," she said. "Bernie, it's not what you think."

"You're coming back, then?" he cried as Sergio's chest pressed against him to edge him out of the cabin. "Don't leave me—"

She froze at his cry. Sergio might let her off at the next stop. Ulmann was handing her yet again her last chance at happiness. Batya reached out her hand, wanting to call out to him that she might be returning after all—

"Out!" Sergio, his back to her, commanded. When Ulmann stood his ground, Sergio pushed him.

"Please don't hurt him," Batya cried out. She collapsed on the seat, her hands over her ears to block the scuffling outside. "I'm so sorry, Ulmann," she whispered. "So sorry. You couldn't give me what I wanted most in the world."

The train began to move. Sergio returned alone.

"Is he hurt?" she asked, her tears welling up. "He's a dear man. A friend—"

"I should have considered we'd run into an admirer." Sergio shook his head. "I warned him that if he told Moskowitz you'd be killed."

Batya lowered her head. She had betrayed the one man who had ever given her his heart.

The car clanked as it hit another before settling into a rhythm and crawled out of the station. After the train gathered speed, Sergio rose, checked the corridor, then sat down.

"Sergio—" Batya began. "I don't have the ledger."

"I know."

The roots of her hair contracted as the blood drained from them. "What do you mean?"

"Are you sure you had it in the first place?"

"Of course I had it! I'd torn a page for you."

"It was found in the possession of some wretched man on the other side of town. Some villager brought it to the police."

"I—I hid it—"

Sergio held up his hand, stopping her. He leaned forward, his elbows on his knees. "Let me talk." His voice was just above a whisper.

Her cheeks burned. Poor Rafael. His brother must have found the ledger and handed it over to the authorities. That's why he had been angry with Rafael, as the pineapple vendor had reported.

"Are you listening?" Sergio asked. When Batya leaned forward, too, he continued. "There was a bombing this morning. In Joaquin Ramos's house. He was killed. His office burned down."

The meaning of Sergio's words sank in slowly, like dandelion seeds drifting into the grass. The prosecutor was dead. His investigation—his notes, the letters she had stolen, her written testimony—all had gone up in smoke. Batya dropped her face into her hands. There would be no revenge. No destroying Moskowitz, no taking down Zwi Migdal, no releasing of the thousands of sisters from bondage. She recalled the sight of the frantic charge of fire wagons. The blaze must have raged for hours after the bombing. It must have spread to nearby houses.

No! Please, God. The syncopated chugging of the train hammered in Batya's ears, noise filling her head. She heard the screams of people being burned alive. Her theft of the ledger had set off a deadly chain reaction. "It's me," she whispered. "I caused it. I hid the ledger in a sweets seller's cart—"

Sergio grabbed her hands. "No, you didn't. We know from our contact at the police that the ledger was delivered after the bombing. It couldn't have been the result of it. Do you understand? It could have resulted from no more than a suspicion based upon the many interviews Joaquin Ramos had conducted. He'd made his stance on the matter known." Sergio's voice softened. "We failed, but not because we didn't do the right thing." His hand rested on Batya's shoulder. The two of them were quiet for some time. She felt his hand tremble.

Although she'd never seen it unclothed, she knew his body so well. He was suffering, too.

"Tickets!" The conductor opened the door, breaking their contact. "Concepcion del Uruguay," he announced.

Uruguay? Ulmann was correct that she was on the wrong train. Batya waited until the conductor left before she asked, "Am I not going to Moïseville?"

"In light of the discovery, it's not safe for you to stay in Argentina. I'm taking you to Montevideo. There, you'll embark on a ship to Marseille, and from there, as soon as our agent finds a ship to Jaffa, you'll sail there."

She stared at him. "In the Holy Land?"

He smiled. "Is there another Jaffa?"

Jaffa, where Jonah had tried in biblical times to escape God's mission. Batya's brain worked slowly as she processed this new development. "What's in Jaffa?"

"Your father."

She sat up. "My father? My sisters, too?"

Sergio nodded. "He can't make the long ocean crossing to get here, but he can make the trip to the Holy Land. It is his wish, too."

"Is he well enough to travel?"

"The boat trip from Odessa to Jaffa takes several days, not weeks. They will all arrive there long before you do."

Batya smiled, a long-forgotten exhilaration rising in her. She would be reunited with her family! She would breathe her father's beard, meet Surale's husband, cry in Keyla's arms, meet all the children—and kiss Vida for the first time. Her mother's presence would envelop them all in its protective wings.

"What will we do in the Holy Land?"

"The same thing you'd planned to do in Argentina. The Baron has been supporting agricultural villages there."

She looked out the window. The Argentine landscape rolled by. She'd never ventured outside the city boundaries and now saw for the first time green fields stretching into the distance, their furrows like sheared corduroy. Soon, they were replaced by a farm with bales of hay stacked in an open barn. A few laborers, unshaven and wearing striped ponchos, sat around a fire. One of them poured from a kettle what must be yerba maté tea. Another turned a chunk of meat on a spit. It sizzled and smoked.

The train sped on, and Batya saw a farmer on a large cart, its bed piled high with green produce she couldn't identify. The cart was pulled by a pair of healthy bulls harnessed under a carved wooden yoke. The man wore a large straw hat, and his blue kerchief was tied low, over the center of his chest. From the upward tilt of his throat, she could tell he must be singing.

Next, Batya observed two women sitting on stools outside a stone farmhouse. Their legs were apart, their aprons sagging with the weight of the vegetables they were peeling. Moments later, a lake reflected the blue sky, and two fishermen cast their poles at its edge.

This was the Argentina she would never get to know, even if she knew its men too intimately. At last, she was departing, never to return. She was saying goodbye to the exotic fruits and vegetables she had grown to love and to the bustling city of Buenos Aires she had grown to enjoy. She would also be saying goodbye to tango and the passions it evoked—and, more so, to Sergio, this man who, by refusing to view her as *tme'ah,* had given her a new sense of herself.

Her carpetbag rested on the seat next to her. Batya opened

it, took out a pouch, then rose and slid open the window. She held it against the rush of air, loosened her grip, and let the wind snatch it out of her hand.

"What was that?" Sergio asked.

"My face paints." Batya broke into a laugh. It heaved and turned into a sob. The full sense of freedom she had so anticipated finally flooded her.

Esperanza was no more.

Epilogue

The Galilee, 1897

*B*atya adjusted the wide-brimmed hat that protected her face from the harsh sun. She straightened her back, wiped her brow, and gazed around her at the field. In both directions stretched furrows of soil she and the others had dug and turned, breaking the stubborn packed, reddish earth into soft clods eager to accept the next seeding. The field was cut into the slope and was enclosed by a low stone fence constructed of the thousands of rocks that had previously made the field impossible to plough. It had been liberating to smash each stone into smaller pieces so she could lift and carry them.

She had imagined each rock as Moskowitz's head.

There would be more opportunities for her silent revenge when she cleared the rocks out of the next section of the field—her own land, which hadn't been cultivated since biblical times. God must have sent her here to do His work.

In the distance she saw her neighbors, a husband-and-wife team, laboring together. Like the rest of the local farmers, all Yiddish-speaking, these were hardworking men and women who had arrived several years before Batya and welcomed every willing pair of Jewish hands. The settlers on this land had very little; every Turkish piastre and lira had to be saved for seeds and farm tools. But they gave their neighbors their hearts—and whatever energy was left in their arms and backs after toiling on their plots to eke out sustenance.

They had escaped pogroms. They had come broken yet revived by a Zionist zeal to reclaim the land of their ancestors. Each had a story—slaughtered siblings, mothers raped in front of their children, fathers' beards yanked out with the skin. None spoke of their private horrors; no one asked for anyone's story beyond "Where did you come from?" The name of the place told them all they needed to know.

Batya had said that she was from Komarinoe, where, she knew, no Jew had been left. No one could verify or dispute her story. Yes, she admitted to her sisters, she was the widow of a rich Argentine Jew, but after her sister-in-law's betrayal, she had erased that part of her life.

"It would add to your status," Surale had claimed.

"I didn't come to the Holy Land to brag about my good fortunes. I've learned how fleeting they are. In my heart, I never left Komarinoe—or you." When Surale persisted, Batya recruited Keyla, now living the dream she and Fishke had never brought to fruition.

"We're building an equal, just social order," Keyla explained to Surale. "Here no one is better than anyone else."

Batya had buried her five and a half years of captivity. If she had been robbed of her youth—of her innocence—she was still only twenty-two years old.

She would never speak Spanish again. Instead, she was learning Hebrew. The children in the family picked it up fast in school, and she tried to decipher words as she listened to them playing. Some of her male neighbors had learned to read it in their yeshivas or synagogues, but they, too, stumbled on the spoken version of the language that had only recently been revived from its biblical roots. It was pronounced differently, in the Sephardi style, that of Ovad's people. The revived Hebrew coined new words that hadn't existed in the Bible in order to fit these modern times, words that ranged from "brush" and "cream" to "wheelbarrow."

Batya smiled and raised her hoe again, striking the ground in short chops. Exerting her muscles felt good; it gave her a sense of her power. No one here had escaped their past unscathed—they had all suffered—but who had time to indulge in idle thoughts? They were creating a new Jewish identity in the Holy Land, each Jew both a soldier and a farmer. She looked forward to tonight, when they would dance the newly invented dance, so different from tango. Tango was the intertwining of man and woman— the masculinity and resolution of men against the softness and acquiescence of women. Their embrace excluded the outside world. The new dance, a Romanian hora, was about togetherness among a group of equals. With everyone's arms around one another's shoulders to create a circle, the slow gait quickly led into a faster beat that could go on for hours. Jumping and kicking in unity, the dancers would bond as they sang at the top of their lungs. Their new songs celebrated their vigor and commitment to rebuilding the land of their ancestors. Batya found it curious that Russian songs that had never been a part of their Jewish heritage had also been nostalgically translated into Hebrew, just like *tangele* had merged Yiddish culture with Argentine music. Jews adapted in so many ways, assimilating into the societies in which they lived while still maintaining their core beliefs.

Afterward, under the canopy of a night lit by a million stars, they would light a campfire and boil strong coffee. Exhausted from dance but not from the fervor of new ideas, they would speak about socialism and the combined power of laborers, swearing never to be exploited by capitalists. In their just community of the highest values, they would all share in the common good. What were scorpions lurking under rocks or the threat of malaria from attacking mosquitoes when Jews had such a glorious mission to build a fair and moral society? Even in Vienna, a journalist by the name of Theodor Herzl—who, like Batya, had been deeply touched by the Dreyfus affair—had begun a movement to settle the Holy Land and wrote about creating a Jewish state.

From a distance, Batya saw Surale stepping over the low wall of a neighbor's field terrace, three young children running alongside her and a baby propped on her right hip. As Surale crossed the furrowed lot, Batya waved, and the sight of the baby caused her breasts to wet with milk.

She planted her hoe in the soil to mark the spot where she should return and walked to the edge of her field, where an old sycamore tree cast a welcoming shadow. Surale met her there and handed her a tin canteen, and Batya drank the blessed water from a spring that fed the Jordan River.

The baby on Surale's side reached his arms to Batya. She took him, hugging him to her chest while feeling Vida's arms wrap around her thighs.

"*Ima,* Mommy," the little girl said. The new name—her new identity, Vida's mother—never failed to warm Batya's heart.

Surale spread a blanket on the ground, and Batya sat down, pressing Vida to her and kissing the girl's fair-haired head, like her own. The baby was pawing at her chest, and Batya lifted her shirt to let him suckle.

Her pregnancy had been the greatest surprise after the month-long voyage from Uruguay. One more miracle to add to the list of improbable events that had happened at the time of her escape. God had blessed her with her own son, who wouldn't be scraped out of her womb by the brothel's doctor. The sense of wonder hadn't lost its newness in the eleven months since his birth. It didn't matter who his father was—though she hoped that he inherited Ulmann's sensitivity. Her baby was all hers to love.

She had sold her jewelry, and the Jewish Colonization Association office in Jaffa had cashed her savings booklet. Combined with a subsidy from the Baron de Hirsch's coffers—he now worked with another Jewish baron, the French Edmond Rothschild, for the latter's colonization program in the Holy Land—she was able to acquire her own lot, hire masons, and build a small stone home for herself and her sisters' families. Surale's husband, Duvid, fashioned the furniture, and had since been earning money in the neighboring villages doing carpentry work. A new, proud Jew in the Holy Land, Duvid rode on the back of his mare, a gun strapped on his right side, his tool belt on his left, and his saw mounted behind him. He was a fine young man, and every time Batya witnessed the tenderness with which he treated his wife, she thanked the strength she had mustered to stave off her parents' pleas to bring Surale to Argentina. Her mother in heaven must have since forgiven her.

Batya switched the baby to her other breast, and he sucked hungrily as if he hadn't just emptied its twin. Her finger stroked the soft spot on his skull that reminded her of his vulnerability. Her baby. Yaakov, her father's real name, not its diminutive Koppel, because here her son would grow up to stand tall and proud, like his namesake ancestor, Jacob, who walked this land, promised to his grandfather Abraham.

In another miracle, her father had lived through his illness in Odessa and made his dream of seeing the Holy Land come true. He had been able to make the voyage from the Black Sea into the Mediterranean, and, upon disembarking the rowboat that had transferred him from the ship to the dock in the port of Jaffa, fell on the ground and kissed it. However, too sick to continue the three-day trip to reach the Galilee by a diligence, the stagecoach passenger service, he was checked into the missionaries' hospital. There, he wavered between life and death, waiting for Batya's arrival.

He was lucid the day she stood by his bed, holding his hand, both of them weeping. She bent and buried her face in his beard, breathing in the never-forgotten dairy scent, now mixed with the odor of the looming Angel of Death.

"I'm sorry you lost your fine husband," her father murmured, his eyes closed.

This was the moment to erase the lies that her father would otherwise take with him to the next world. Her mother, who was surely waiting for him to continue their decades of bantering, would reveal to him Batya's secrets. The obedient daughter must be cleansed from the lies.

"Moskowitz wasn't the man we all hoped for," she said, unsure whether her father had heard her, and she added for good measure, "He was a very bad man."

His hand gave a light squeeze, and a wave of relief washed over Batya. He'd heard her and she'd rid herself of the falsehood. Her mother would tell her father the rest. Batya brought her father's hand to her lips the same moment that he took his last breath.

She had managed to get her family out of Russia and at least give three of her four sisters a better future. Was it worth the suffering? The longer Batya lived, the more it became evident that God's plans were beyond her human comprehension.

Batya finished nursing Yaakov and bounced him on her knee. He squirmed, eager to slip from her hold and crawl on the ground. His hazel eyes took in the world around him with awe. Nothing escaped his scrutiny, and he seemed to want to touch and taste everything.

"In a month or two he'll be walking." Surale laughed. "He'll be a handful."

Batya smiled. "What did you bring me to eat?" she asked. Besides caring for the youngest children while the older ones were in school, Surale raised chickens, baked the family bread, and tended to the kitchen garden. Keyla alternated between toiling with Batya in the family's field and hiring herself out to care for farmers' cows. Batya hoped that in a year or two they'd be able to buy their own cow. They would name her Aggie.

Surale didn't answer but remained sitting on her haunches, grinning into Batya's face.

"What is it?" Batya asked.

"You got a letter. The mailman said it's from Argentina."

From Argentina? Dread and curiosity mixed in Batya's heart. No one from her old life knew where she'd gone. She had never mailed Ulmann her apology, concerned that, misguided or revengeful, he might reveal her whereabouts to Moskowitz.

"Maybe it's about money for Yaakov from your late husband's family?" Surale ventured. "You should sue her, for your son's sake, so he receives his just inheritance—"

"So she comes here to claim my baby? The law there says he belongs to the father's family." Batya knew of no such law, and she hated the lies that would never end. Luckily, Surale's illiteracy and the many months it took any letter to travel blurred the few months' lapse between Reb Moskowitz's supposed passing and Batya's pregnancy. Batya went on. "Freda should never know where I am. Another reason for you never to mention Argentina to anyone."

For the girls in the brothel, she had disappeared forever in the Pampas. They must have surmised that she had been murdered by Zwi Migdal. Batya missed her friends, especially Rochel. She still found it hard to reconcile the benevolent, gentle friend she had adored with the merciless pimp she suspected Rochel had become. These days, Rochel might be visiting auctions, probing a frightened naked girl's private parts, assessing the value of the merchandise.

Stop it, Batya told herself, watching her son crawl on the blanket, babbling. His baby sounds were music to her ears. She must shut off that world, just as once she had shut the real Batya away to allow Esperanza to take over.

She turned the envelope in her hands. It was stained, corners fraying, the ink of the return address smeared, testifying that it had made a long journey through oceans and mountains and too many hands. In spite of this, the chipped red wax seal was unbroken. She slipped a fingernail beneath it with care, so as not to damage the envelope any further.

The letter began with *Dear Batya*. She turned it over to see the signature. It was signed *Sergio Rosenberg*.

Sergio. Her heart skipped a beat. With a smile, she began reading.

Dear Batya,

I hope that this letter finds you in good health and spirits. Our office in Jaffa has reported that you purchased your own land and built a house on it. This is wonderful. I also know that you are reunited with your family, although I am sorry about your father's passing, may his soul live in the heart of your new baby.

After your departure I, too, left Buenos Aires. I have been learning agriculture in Moïseville, just as you have been doing in the Holy Land. However, your family's story has inspired me to follow in your footsteps to the land of our ancestors, and I plan to travel there as soon as the winter ocean winds calm down to make the long voyage less taxing.

I have been thinking about you a great deal these

past many months. I cherished our tango dancing.
Had life been written by a different divinity, we would
be performing together now, maybe winning more com-
petitions. It is my greatest regret that we failed in our
mission. Señor Joaquin Ramos's unfortunate fate will
discourage another brave prosecutor, district attorney,
or judge for years to come.

Batya stopped and placed her hand over her heart. How many
more thousands of girls would be lured and snatched to South
America? Could the Baron de Hirsch be this powerless against
Zwi Migdal?

You'll be glad to hear, though, that by an interesting
twist of events we recovered that critical lost document
I cannot name here. God willing, may it one day be
used for the purpose you and I had intended.

She heard her own gasp. The ledger was back in the possession of those who could help the sisters! Probably it had been
bought from a policeman on a night shift at the station.
"What is it?" Surale asked. "Bad news?"
"No. A letter from an old friend. Everything is well." She
read on.

On a more personal note, I would like to be brazen and
tell you that during our collaboration—both on the
dance floor and the investigation—I developed a great
admiration for your bravery and valor. In spite of all

that had befallen you, I saw neither bitterness nor the harsh cynicism that can chip away pieces of the soul until there's nothing left of humanity. At a time that you could have saved yourself, you thought not only of your family but also of all your suffering sisters.

You also taught me to look into myself and recognize my own prejudices even when I had meant well. I ask your forgiveness for any cruel remark I thoughtlessly uttered. Your values and morals should have been beacons of character to anyone who ever met you.

You have inspired me to do in the Holy Land what I am doing in Moïseville: be a gaucho. I wish to come live in your village, where, no doubt, a strong laborer will be able to raise a herd of milk-producing cows.

I recall how confident you sounded when you insisted that you could learn agriculture and help establish a women-only village for your lost sisters. If this is still your dream, once I am settled, I can liaise with the Baron's office in Buenos Aires to help establish such a village for formerly subjugated women who wish to immigrate and, like you, start a new life in the Holy Land.

Respectfully yours,
Sergio Rosenberg

Batya hugged the letter to her chest. There would be no tango in their future, but together they could choreograph their own dance. "Yes," she whispered. "Yes."

Acknowledgments

First, I would like to thank the anonymous librarian in Buenos Aires with whom I chatted in 2007. When I asked her about "the Jewish prostitutes and pimps," she forgot her English. That was my first clue to the depth of the dark secret of this shameful, long chapter not only in the history of Argentine Jews but in the history of all my people.

In researching *The Third Daughter*, I was greatly helped by Ana (Anita) Weinstein, director of the Documentation and Information Center on Argentine Jewry in AMIA, Buenos Aires, who also read the final manuscript for accuracy. My Spanish-language, Argentina-based assistants, Henry Osman and Mónica Correa, translated material and helped me study architecture, food, dress, urban development, and customs in Buenos Aires of the late 1800s.

The medical information research began with Dr. MaryAnn Millar, followed by Dr. Wendy Macias-Konstantopoulos, director, Human Trafficking Initiative, Massachusetts General Hospital, Boston. The latter's appreciation and interest in helping me make this complex subject public reconfirmed the importance of my telling the story of one such young victim.

My knowledge of tango dancing was enhanced by lessons from Jean Maurasse, Scott Edholm, and Craig Gordon and the comments of tango experts Sherry Palencia and Camille Cusomano.

I could not have written this novel without the steady constructive feedback of my writing group, Two Bridges, led by Walter Cummins. The thoughtful editing by Linda Davies and Susan O'Neill helped reshape the manuscript.

In the fall of 2015, I asked my friend Emily White (Klores) to walk with me in Central Park in New York City, where I mulled aloud my ideas for a new novel dealing with trafficking. Emily's free associations clicked synapses in my brain, and although the story that emerged once I sat down in front of my computer was not the one we had discussed, she had fueled my creative process and later commented on an advanced draft.

I found an abundance of English-language research material about Zwi Migdal on the internet and at university libraries. Among the many sources, I would like to single out Isabel Vincent's excellent book *Bodies and Souls: The Tragic Plight of Three Jewish Women Forced into Prostitution in the Americas* (William Morrow, 2005) and Mir Hayim Yarfitz's Ph.D. dissertation, "Polacos, White Slaves, and Stille Chuppahs: Organized Prostitution and the Jews of Buenos Aires, 1890–1939" (UCLA, 2012). Also worth mentioning are Donna J. Guy's *Sex and Danger in Buenos Aires: Prostitution, Family, and Nation in Argentina* (University of Nebraska Press, 1990) and Nora Glickman's *The*

Jewish White Slave Trade and the Untold Story of Raquel Liberman (Garland, 2000).

No birthing of a novel can take place without the dedicated midwifing of a team, starting with my wonderful agent, Annelise Robey from Jane Rotrosen Literary Agency. To my delight, my editor at William Morrow, the extraordinary Katherine Nintzel, had thought the topic "stupendous" when I first introduced it to her and loved the final product. Birthing *The Third Daughter* from its manuscript form, she has brought it to its final destination—the hands of my readers.

I could not have hoped for a better marketing team at HarperCollins—Jen Hart, Molly Waxman, Amelia Wood, Bianca Flores, and Vedika Khanna. I have been impressed by their professionalism and encouraged by their enthusiasm about the novel. Their dedication to making *The Third Daughter* a success has been reinforced by my own events coordinator, Lisa Bernard, who has galloped out of the gate to fill my calendar with dozens of speaking engagements.

And as always, there is Ron, whose love, devotion, and support are forever the wind in my wings that lifts me to new heights.

Glossary (Yiddish or Hebrew, unless listed otherwise):

a bissele—A little.

abacus—(Latin) A calculating tool constructed on a wooden frame with beads sliding on wires.

abrazo—(Spanish) Embrace, a tango position.

adornos—(Spanish) Embellishments of tango moves to demonstrate skill.

aliyah—Being called to face the congregation and read aloud a Torah portion.

alte-zachen—Old things. Refers to the ragman who sells them.

aperitivo—(Spanish) Appetite-stimulating alcoholic drink.

bandoneón—(Spanish) Early version of accordion played at *milongas*.

bella—(Spanish) Beautiful (feminine).

caballero—(Spanish) Knight, cavalier, gentleman, or horseman.

cachaça—(Spanish) Distilled spirit made from fermented sugarcane juice.

caftan—(Spanish) Pimp. Derived from *cafetão,* the long coat worn by religious Eastern European Jews.

casa chorizo—(Spanish) A long and skinny row of attached dwellings.

casita—(Spanish) Small house or a guest villa.

challah—Braided bread used for Shabbat and Jewish holidays.

charoset—Traditional Passover food of chopped apples, dates, raisins, nuts, and honey.

chazzan—Cantor.

chimichurri—(Spanish) Sauce made of herbs.

compadritos—(Spanish) Rural gauchos who appeared in Argentine cities as a result of urbanization.

conventillos—(Spanish) Little convents. An ironic name for Jewish tenements in Buenos Aires.

davening—Reciting the prescribed Jewish liturgical prayers.

diligence—(French) A horse-drawn stagecoach/passenger conveyance service.

dreck—Rubbish.

dulce de leche—(Spanish) Sweet condensed milk.

dybbuk—A malicious possessing spirit that enters the soul.

farshlepte plog—Chronic plague.

farshteyst—Do you understand?

ganef—Thief.

gehenom—Hell.

get—Jewish divorce.

goy—Non-Jew (plural goyim).

Haggadah—The Passover text recited at the Seder dinner, describing the Jews' exodus from Egypt over three thousand years ago.

halacha—Jewish law and jurisprudence, based on the Talmud.

Hashem—God (literally "the name").

ima—Mommy, mother.

kaddish—A prayer for the dead, recited in Aramaic.

kashrut—The overall rules determining what's kosher.

klezmer—Musician.

kneidlach—Matzo balls (for soup).

knish—Dough filled with either ground meat, mashed potatoes, kasha, or onions.

kosher—Food that adheres to Jewish dietary restrictions.

kreplach—Dumplings stuffed with meat, potatoes, or cheese.

kurve—A vulgar word for a prostitute.

lechayim—To life. A salutation upon drinking alcohol.

maven—An expert.

mazel—Luck, fortune.

mendeveshkes—(Russian) Pubic lice.

meshuge—Crazy, insane.

metziah—Great find, a bargain.

mezuzah—Piece of Torah-inscribed parchment in a tiny decorative case that is hung on the side of a door.

mikveh—Jewish communal ritual bath.

milonga—(Spanish) Dance hall for tango.

minyan—Quorum of ten men required by Jewish law for a public prayer.

mitzvah—(1) Good deed; (2) Decreed religious rule.

muzhik—(Russian) Peasant.

nigunim—Wordless Jewish religious melodies, joyous or mournful.

ocho—(Spanish) Eight. In tango, marking the figure eight on the floor.

Once—(Spanish) A district in Buenos Aires, so named because of the no. 11 train station. Pronounced "OWN-say."

palanca—(Spanish) In tango, levering a woman to help her jump.

peyes—Coiled sidelocks Orthodox Jewish men grow.

piastre—(Turkish) An Ottoman coin, one hundredth of a lira.

pikuach nefesh—The principle that the preservation of human life takes precedence over all the other commandments in Judaism.

pisherke—A nobody, an insignificant person (literally a boy who pees in his pants).

pitzik—Diminutive to describe a very small thing or person.

polaca(s)—(Polish) A derogatory name for prostitutes born in Eastern European countries.

pulke—Chicken drumstick, thigh.

punchkes—Jelly donuts (a Chanukah delicacy).

puta—(Spanish) A vulgar name for a prostitute.

quebrada—(Spanish) In tango, a sudden body twist.

reb—Mister. An honorific title, not a rabbinic one.

sarafan—(Russian) A long, trapezoidal traditional Russian jumper dress; a pinafore.

shaygetz—Non-Jewish man. (Also derogatory for any brute or scoundrel.)

Shema—A liturgical twice-daily prayer that expresses the Jewish faith in God.

sheyn meydele—Pretty girl.

shiksa—Non-Jewish female.

shiva—Seven days of mourning.

shtiebel—Makeshift prayer and meeting room.

shtille chuppah—"Silent" wedding, with only one witness, no rabbi.

shver—Father-in-law.

sofer—Scribe of religious documents.

tahara—Religious purification of the body in preparation for burial.

talis—Fringed prayer shawl worn by Orthodox Jewish men.

tangele—Yiddish tango in Argentina.

tchotchkes—Trinkets, knickknacks.

tijera—(Spanish) In tango, feet or legs scissoring.

tkhines—Women's prayers in Yiddish.

tme'ah—Contaminated; feminine (masculine plural *tme'yim;* feminine plural *tme'ot*).

tranvias—(Spanish) tram lines.

tsures—Problems, troubles.

tzaddik—A righteous man, a man of the highest virtues (plural *tsaddikim*).

verst—(Russian) A distance measure—about two-thirds of a mile.

yahrzeit—Anniversary of a death.

yapa—(Spanish) A bonus item for a purchase.

yerba maté, maté—(Spanish) A tea-like beverage drunk with a straw out of a hollowed gourd. Pronounced "MAH-teh."

yichus—Lineage, social status.

About the author

About the book

Insights,
Interviews
& More . . .

Meet Talia Carner

Steve Lars

TALIA CARNER is the former publisher of *Savvy Woman* magazine and a consultant to Fortune 500 companies. She is a board member of the Hadassah-Brandeis Institute, the Jewish women's research center at Brandeis University, as well as an honorary board member of several anti–domestic violence and child abuse intervention organizations. Her previous novels—*Hotel Moscow, Jerusalem Maiden, China Doll,* and *Puppet Child*—have been hailed for exposing society's ills. Dozens of Carner's award-winning essays, articles, and short stories have appeared in anthologies, literary reviews, and leading websites. She is a committed supporter of global human rights, having spearheaded projects centered on the subjects of female plight and participated as a panelist or delivered more than three hundred keynotes addresses at civic and cultural organizations. ∾

Buenos Aires, 1996

Ronald Carner

Following the 1994 bombing of the Asociación Mutual Israelita Argentina (AMIA) building, which housed all Jewish organizations in Buenos Aires—a bombing that left eighty-five dead and hundreds injured—author Talia Carner participated in a demonstration in front of the Argentine Department of Justice, which had been assigned the task of investigating those responsible for the attack.

For twenty-three years, all investigations met a brick wall, culminating in the murder of the key prosecutor, Alberto Nisman, in 2015, hours before he was to present his findings to the Argentine National Congress. Finally, in December 2017, a federal judge indicted former president Cristina Fernández de Kirchner for colluding with Iran in the cover-up of Tehran's role in the bombing.

With the destruction of the AMIA building, a huge archive of Jewish history in Argentina was destroyed. However, police and court records regarding Zwi Migdal can be found in other venues, such as the 1925–1926 files of Zacarias Zytnitzky, then president of Zwi Migdal, which had been stored in a private home.

Talia Carner thanks the authors and researchers who had viewed these Spanish- and Yiddish-language documents for distilling the information and thus helping her study this most shameful chapter in Jewish history. ∾

The Historical Background of *The Third Daughter*

This novel is set in Buenos Aires during a time when prostitution was legal in Argentina and the Varsovia (Warsaw) Society, which later changed its name to Zwi Migdal, operated as a mutual-aid union of Jewish pimps. The organization had a hierarchical structure and a strong internal code of ethics, and it spread throughout South America, with tentacles reaching India, China, South Africa, Germany, Poland, Turkey, and even New York City's Lower East Side. It operated with impunity from the early 1870s until 1939, when Jews could no longer travel to Central and Eastern Europe.

Zwi Migdal's method of kidnapping women for prostitution was as described in this novel: well-dressed men, speaking Yiddish and flaunting their success, would return to their native Eastern European countries on recruitment expeditions subsidized by the union. They offered marriages and jobs in the New World.

Four hundred years of the persecution of Jews in Europe through official anti-Semitic policies had severely restricted Jewish work occupations, land ownership, and permitted places of residence. Furthermore, these policies were coupled with repeated bloody pogroms in Russia, Belarus, Ukraine, and Poland. (In 1918–1919 alone more than 1,200 pogroms took place in Ukraine, and a pogrom was even reported in 1904 in Ireland.) The unrelenting savagery and slaughter to which the Jews were subjected made them vulnerable to the charm of the traffickers and their promises.

The victims, girls and women ranging in age from their early teens to early thirties, were repeatedly raped and beaten, caged, starved, and physically tortured. By the time their ocean voyage ended three to four weeks later, they were broken. There are no records of the suicide rate during this early stage of the "training." But in Inhaúma cemetery in Rio de Janeiro, Brazil, established by the local Jewish prostitutes, a large, separate section for suicide victims—as ordained by Jewish burial customs—tells the tragic story of many of these women once they were put to work. In the rest of the cemetery, the disproportionate number of tombstones of prostitutes who died in their twenties and thirties reveals the fate of the rest of them.

Zwi Migdal members regarded their "merchandise" in much the same way owners of black slaves in North America and the Caribbean did: they were less than human, with only economic value. However, unlike the enslavement of blacks by Caucasians, this was a Jew-on-Jew crime, with family members often preying on their own kin: not only were offers of a better life "in America" extended to nieces and sisters-in-law back home, but family men who had left their wives behind in Eastern Europe sometimes brought them to Argentina or Brazil in order to force them into prostitution. These men may have left Eastern Europe believing in the myth of incredible riches, but they were unskilled and did not speak the language and would inevitably fail to find jobs. The Warsaw Society embraced these men and convinced them to adopt the new entrepreneurial spirit in which the pimps viewed themselves as businessmen.

Pimping in Argentina was so culturally associated with Jews that the name for a pimp in Spanish, *caftan*, was borrowed from the word for the long black coat worn by Orthodox Jewish men. Similarly, *polaca*, the word for a prostitute, was adopted from the Yiddish name for Polish women.

Records of Jewish ownership of brothels from as early as the 1895 census in Buenos Aires show in one city block alone a concentration of twenty brothels housing two hundred women. Concurrently, an 1899 city registry of prostitutes in Buenos Aires reveals that 30 percent of them were Jewish. A record from 1913 shows more than 3,000 brothels in Buenos Aires (and 430 in Rio de Janeiro), with Jewish ownership disproportionally large—data corroborated by records of the Varsovia Society from that year, ▶

listing four hundred members (a roster that soon grew to more than five hundred). By the 1920s, Jewish brothels employed thirty thousand women, each generating on average 3,000 pesos a month in a country where the average monthly salary was under 100 pesos. At the turn of the twentieth century, Zwi Migdal's profits were reported at $50 million a year.

The union's activities comprised not only trafficking but also gaming houses and smuggling operations. Members pooled their resources to bribe government officials, policemen, and legislators, keeping many of them on a monthly payroll. When pimps were arrested, the mutual-aid society bribed judges and prosecutors or hired shrewd lawyers; either the charges were dropped or the cases won. The bribing at all levels included not only cash, entertainment, and expensive gifts, but also apartments and cars. Before long, Jews were seen as the source of the systemic corruption in Argentina, Brazil, and Uruguay.

WHO IN EUROPE knew what was going on? Victor Hugo wrote a letter in 1870 condemning "white slavery" from Europe to South America (although he didn't single out Jews). Sholem Aleichem, the popular Yiddish storyteller whose character Tevye the Dairyman appears in his collection *Railroad Stories,* wrote "The Man from Buenos Aires" in 1909. From a Polish newspaper report in 1891 to a Polish novel in 1930—and numerous articles about local arrests of traffickers during the in-between years—the published information was unlikely to reach the Yiddish-speaking Jewish population in Poland. They were not only illiterate in the language of the country where they lived but also too dispersed in the countryside to have access to news. In 1919, the Treaty of Versailles denounced trafficking as a crime, and in 1921, the League of Nations (the precursor to the United Nations) held an International Conference on White Slave Traffic. Two years later, the French journalist Albert Londres, who had ingratiated himself into the pimps' networks in South America, published in France a lengthy exposé that detailed the horrific conditions in which the women lived, with those in La Boca serving up to seventy men a day. The exposé was translated into Spanish and English in 1928 and was reviewed in the *New York Times.* None of these languages were spoken by the Eastern European victims or their families. Several plays about pimps and prostitutes were produced in Spanish and Yiddish in South America earlier in the century—dramas depicting current events—but they were too late for the women already enslaved there.

Though the reports—and even the occasional letter that sneaked past the pimps' vigilance—failed to reach families before they entrusted their daughters to the care of strangers or to alarm desperate widows seeking ways to feed their children, they finally spurred into action some benevolent organizations in the Jewish communities of Great Britain, Austria, and Germany. Women activists of Ezrat Nashim, the League of Jewish Women, and the Jewish Association for the Protection of Girls and Women roamed European train stations and seaports, on the lookout for naive girls traveling either alone or in the company of well-heeled men. These activists distributed flyers and attempted to offer advice and warnings before the would-be victims sailed away. Unfortunately, rarely was the advice heeded or even believed. The lure of the chance for a better life far from the starvation and hellish anti-Semitism of Europe was too strong.

ALARMED BY THESE developments and fearing a reprise of the horrendous anti-Semitism from which they'd fled, upstanding Jews in South America opposed this immorality that tainted them all. They shunned the pimps and prostitutes, blocked their access to synagogues, and refused to bury these *tme'yim* (sullied, impure) in their cemeteries. Local Jewish benevolent and charity organizations not only refused to extend services to prostitutes and their children, but also forbade any discussion of their cases at their meetings. However, the Jewish communities' efforts to discredit the pimps, refuse their generous donations to the synagogues and Yiddish theaters, and engage with the authorities to limit Zwi Migdal's influence were futile in Argentina, where a 1908 law allowed unlimited recruitment of prostitutes to brothels, further legalizing ownership of "white slaves." At times, in both Buenos Aires and Rio de Janeiro, the conflict between the two Jewish factions escalated into violent confrontations.

While ownership of prostitutes was legal, it was subject to restrictions such as thrice-weekly medical checkups, providing the women with clean living conditions, allowing them freedom of movement, and giving them the right to collect and keep their earnings—none which was met by the pimps. Therefore in some cases, subjugated women managed to lodge an official complaint. ▶

In 1896, eighteen-year-old Sophia Chamys, after five years of beatings and betrayals by her husband, Isaac Boorosky, spoke to a policeman in the Fourth Precinct in Rio de Janeiro. She had tried to complain once before, when her husband trafficked her in Buenos Aires, but got no traction with the police there. This time, the policeman wrote down her lengthy story. Boorosky was arrested— then promptly released. In 1910, in Buenos Aires, Rosa Schwartz, a.k.a. Lili of the Jewels, threatened to expose Zwi Migdal and was murdered. Ester K., Irena A., and Reise K. (full last names not recorded) were turned away from the police station when each independently attempted to file a complaint. In retaliation, their pimps sold them to brothels in the interior of the country. In Brazil, Klara Adam denounced her pimp, Sigmond Richter, with documents. Her testimony "evaporated" and, just like what happens to a woman in this novel, a "professor" penned a condemning letter to her family in Poland, shutting down her escape route back home.

WHAT FINALLY BROUGHT Zwi Migdal to its knees?

Early on, Argentina's government condoned prostitution. It let it thrive in the rapidly expanding colonial settings, not only because of the massive amounts of money the state received from the brothels in the form of taxes (in 1920, 25 percent of the state's money was generated by brothels), but also because, as a Catholic state, it believed that this necessary evil "protects good women, families and gender order."[*] However, Zwi Migdal's crimes and corruption motivated Julio Alsogaray, a federal police commissioner in Buenos Aires, to act. He had been working for a decade on his mission "to clean up the pollution of Argentina"[†] and had forged an alliance with Jews who condemned the pimps when, on New Year's Eve 1929, into his office walked Raquel Liberman. The twenty-nine-year-old prostitute, the widowed mother of two boys, had arrived from Poland seven years before. She had tried to get out of prostitution by investing her savings in an antique shop. Time and again, Zwi

---

[*] "First Wave Sexual Politics: Purity and Prostitution," UCLA History M187A, April 9, 2009.

[†] Mir Hayim Yarfitz, "Polacos, White Slaves, and Stille Chuppahs: Organized Prostitution and the Jews of Buenos Aires, 1890–1939," Ph.D. diss., University of California at Los Angeles, 2012.

Migdal sent goons to ransack her shop, forcing her back into a brothel.

Liberman's cooperation was what Alsogaray had been waiting for. In May 1930, after seventy years of Zwi Migdal operating with impunity, a ten-day police raid, accompanied by photographers and newspapermen, arrested three hundred pimps. Unsurprisingly, the union had been tipped off, and hundreds of Zwi Migdal members had fled the country—temporarily. Of the men arrested, only 112 went to trial, and of those, only 3 were sentenced to prison. The others were exiled, but they returned within three to five years. Unrelated to these events, in September 1930, a coup d'état brought a nationalist, fascist, and puritanical government to power in Argentina and the constitution was replaced, outlawing brothels and abolishing regulated prostitution (though allowing private exchanges of sex for pay).

Earlier, in 1913, the government of Brazil declared that it would not be a clearinghouse for the white slave trade. It deported 120 pimps, who transferred the running of their brothels to madams until they could return, which they did shortly afterward. However, in 1930, as in Argentina, a military coup d'état put the dictator Getúlio Vargas in power, and he aligned Brazil with Fascist Italy and Nazi Germany. He soon singled out the Jews as responsible for the country's economic woes. Jews were barred from entering the country, and pimps and prostitutes were sent back to their now Nazi-occupied countries of origin, where they most likely perished.

Zwi Migdal was weakened but did not cease its operation throughout South America. It continued until 1939, when Hitler invaded Poland and traveling there was no longer possible.

DESPITE ALL THE available documentation about this trafficking syndicate, researchers have been reluctant to pinpoint the number of girls and women kidnapped or enslaved over seventy years. It is estimated, based upon the known figures of the peak numbers of brothels, the number of workers, and the recorded earnings generated, that between 140,000 and 220,000 women fell victim to the scheme, not counting the thousands who committed suicide before they began working and therefore did not contribute to the confirmed profits.

This novel is their story. ∽

Ezrat Nashim Poster

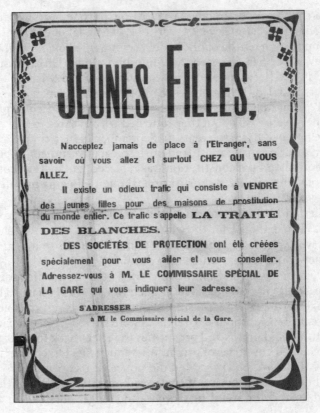

Young Girls,

Never accept a place abroad without knowing where you're going and especially WITH WHOM YOU'RE STAYING.

There is loathsome trafficking that consists of SELLING young girls to houses of prostitution in the entire world. This trafficking is called WHITE TRADE.

THE SOCIETIES OF PROTECTION were created especially in order to help you and counsel you. Approach the SPECIAL COMMISSION OF THE STATION, which will give you their address. ∾

Reading Group Guide

1. In her hours of despair, Batya thinks about and eventually attempts suicide. What prevents her or pulls her back? At what points in the story do you think she would say the life she is living is worth the trauma she has suffered? At what points would she not?

2. Some "sisters" at the brothel enjoy what this way of life gives them. They prefer it to the alternative of laboring in a sweatshop or a field, or living in the squalor of the shtetl. Discuss the options open to women at the time—and today.

3. While fleeing a pogrom, fourteen-year-old Batya feels responsible for her parents' well-being. Discuss her life decisions in light of her older sisters' choices. Is her love for her parents a burden or a gift?

4. Discuss the role faith plays in the book for each group of people: Batya and her "sisters"; Batya's family in Russia; the pimps and patrons of Zwi Migdal; the Jewish population of Buenos Aires. To what practices does each group adhere? What are the limitations and/or hypocrisies of each group?

5. Batya's mother is constantly on Batya's mind. How does Batya's perception of her mother change as she grows older? How does it change after her mother's death? How did her mother's presence influence Batya's decisions?

6. Both Nettie and Rochel, two of Batya's closest friends, undergo dramatic yet very different transformations. Discuss each one's background, character, and options. Why did each make the choices she made?

7. Batya tries to save money in order to bring her family to Argentina from Russia. Discuss the economic structure of the brothel: What are the financial incentives offered to Batya, and in what ways do those incentives ultimately keep her in bondage?

8. Toward the end of the book, Batya finds herself having to choose between Ulmann and Sergio. What are the risks and rewards of each? Whom did you think Batya should choose? Did you find yourself changing your mind at different points in the story?

9. How complicit was the Argentine government in the trafficking of women? How did Zwi Migdal exploit cultural and legal practices to grow its business? And how was it able to hold on to power, even against a rising backlash?

10. The methods and practices used by Moskowitz and other pimps in the book are still being used today. How and why are they so effective?